EISE

XENOS

More Warhammer 40,000 action

WAR OF THE FANG
Chris Wraight
Contains the novel 'Battle of the Fang' and the novella
'The Hunt for Magnus', featuring the Space Wolves

DAMOCLES
Ben Counter, Guy Haley, Phil Kelly & Josh Reynolds
Contains the novellas 'Blood Oath', 'Broken Sword',
'Black Leviathan' and 'Hunter's Snare',
featuring the White Scars, Raven Guard and Ultramarines

THE WORLD ENGINE
Ben Counter
A novel featuring the Astral Knights

SPEAR OF MACRAGGE
Nick Kyme
A novella featuring the Ultramarines

• **ADEPTUS MECHANICUS** •

SKITARIUS
TECH-PRIEST
Rob Sanders
A duology of novels featuring the Adeptus Mechanicus

PRIESTS OF MARS
LORDS OF MARS
GODS OF MARS
Graham McNeill
A trilogy of novels featuring the Adeptus Mechanicus

• **ASTRA MILITARUM** •

YARRICK: PYRES OF ARMAGEDDON
David Annandale
A novel featuring Commissar Yarrick

FIRST AND ONLY
GHOSTMAKER
NECROPOLIS
Dan Abnett
A series of novels featuring Gaunt's Ghosts

WARHAMMER
40,000

EISENHORN

XENOS

DAN ABNETT

BLACK LIBRARY

A BLACK LIBRARY PUBLICATION

First published in 2001.
This edition published in Great Britain in 2019 by
Black Library,
Games Workshop Ltd.,
Willow Road,
Nottingham, NG7 2WS, UK.

10 9 8 7

Produced by Games Workshop in Nottingham.
Cover illustration by Alexander Ovchinnikov.

A CIP record for this book is available from the British Library.

ISBN 13: 978 1 84970 872 2

See Black Library on the internet at

blacklibrary.com

Find out more about Games Workshop
and the world of Warhammer 40,000 at

games-workshop.com

Printed and bound by CPI Group (UK) Ltd, Croydon, CR0 4YY

For John Parsons, bonemagos.

It is the 41st millennium. For more than a hundred centuries the Emperor has sat immobile on the Golden Throne of Earth. He is the Master of Mankind by the will of the gods, and master of a million worlds by the might of His inexhaustible armies. He is a rotting carcass writhing invisibly with power from the Dark Age of Technology. He is the Carrion Lord of the Imperium for whom a thousand souls are sacrificed every day, so that He may never truly die.

Yet even in His deathless state, the Emperor continues His eternal vigilance. Mighty battlefleets cross the daemon-infested miasma of the warp, the only route between distant stars, their way lit by the Astronomican, the psychic manifestation of the Emperor's will. Vast armies give battle in His name on uncounted worlds. Greatest amongst His soldiers are the Adeptus Astartes, the Space Marines, bioengineered super-warriors. Their comrades in arms are legion: the Astra Militarum and countless planetary defence forces, the ever-vigilant Inquisition and the tech-priests of the Adeptus Mechanicus to name only a few. But for all their multitudes, they are barely enough to hold off the ever-present threat from aliens, heretics, mutants – and worse.

To be a man in such times is to be one amongst untold billions. It is to live in the cruellest and most bloody regime imaginable. These are the tales of those times. Forget the power of technology and science, for so much has been forgotten, never to be re-learned. Forget the promise of progress and understanding, for in the grim dark future there is only war. There is no peace amongst the stars, only an eternity of carnage and slaughter, and the laughter of thirsting gods.

**BY ORDER OF HIS MOST HOLY MAJESTY
THE GOD-EMPEROR OF TERRA**

**SEQUESTERED INQUISITORIAL DOSSIERS
AUTHORISED PERSONS ONLY**

CASE FILE 112:67B:AA6:Xad

Please enter your authority code > `● ● ● ● ● ● ● ● ● ● ● ● ● ●`

Validating...

Thank you, Inquisitor.

You may proceed.

VERBAL TRANSCRIPT
OF PICT-RECORDED DOCUMENT

LOCATION: MAGINOR
DATE: 239. M41

RECOVERED FROM SERVITOR RECORDING MODULE

TRANSCRIBED BY SAVANT ELEDIX,
ORDO HERETICUS INQUISITORIAL DATA-LIBRARY
FACULTY, FIBOS SECUNDUS, 240. M41

[Pict-record white noise segues to] Darkness. Sounds of distant human pain. A flash of light [poss. las-fire?]. Sounds of running.

Pict-source moves, tracking, vibrating. Some stone walls, in close focus. Another flash, brighter, closer. Squeal of pain [source unknown]. An extremely bright flash [loss of picture].

[Image indistinct for 2 minutes 38 seconds; some background noise.]

A man [subject (i)] in long robes, calls out as he strides past close to the pict-source [speech unrecoverable]. Surroundings, dark stone [poss. tunnel? tomb?]. (i)'s identity unknown [partial face view only]. Pict-source moves in close behind (i), observing as (i) draws a force hammer from a thigh loop under his robe. Close up on (i)'s hands as he grips haft. Inquisitorial signet ring in plain view. (i) turns [face obscured by shadow]. (i) speaks.

VOICE (i):   *Move in! Move in, in the name of all that's holy! Come on and* [words obliterated by sound-flash] *bastard monster to death!*

Further flashes of light, now clearly close las-impacts. Pict-source filters fail to block glare [white out].

[Image white out for 0 minutes 14 seconds; resolution slowly returning.]

Passing in through the high stone entrance of some considerable chamber. Grey stone, rough hewn. Pict-source pans. Bodies in doorway, and also slumped down interior steps. Massive injuries, mangled. Stones wet with blood.

VOICE OFF [(i)?]:   *Where are you? Where are you? Show yourself!*

Pict-source moves in. Two human shapes move past it to left, blurred [image-stall reveals one [subject (ii)] to be male, approx 40 years, heavy-set, wearing Imperial Guard-issue body plate [no insignia or idents], significant facial scarring [old], wielding belt-fed heavy stubber; other [subject (iii)] is female, approx 25 years, svelte, skin dyed blue, tattoos and body-glove armour of a Morituri Death Cultist initiate, wielding force blade [approx 45cm length].

Blurred shapes (ii) and (iii) move beyond pict-source. Pict-source pans round, establishing sidelong view of (ii) and (iii) engaged in rapid hand-to-hand warfare with adversaries on lower steps. Adversaries are heterogeneous mix: six humans with surgical/bionic implants, two mutants, three offensive servitors [see attached file record for stall-frame details]. (ii) fires heavy stubber [sound track distorts].

Two human adversaries pulped [backwash smoke haze renders image partially indistinct]. (iii) severs head of mutant, vaults backwards [transcriptional assumption – pict-source too slow to follow] and impales human adversary. Pict-source moves down [image jerky].

VOICE OFF: *Maneesha! To the left! To the l–*

Pict-source makes partial capture as (iii) is hit repeatedly by energy fire. (iii) convulses, explodes. Pict-source hit by blood mist [image fogs]. [Image wiped clear.] (ii) is yelling, moving ahead out of view, firing heavy stubber. Sudden crossfire laser effect [las-flare blinds pict-source optics].

[Various noise sources, indistinct voices, some screaming.]

[Image returns.] (i) is just ahead of pict-source, charging into wide, flat chamber lit by green chemical lamps [face illuminated by light for 0.3 seconds]. Subject (i) positively identified as Inquisitor Hetris Lugenbrau.

LUGENBRAU:*Quixos! Quixos! I put it all to the sword and the cleansing flame! Now you, monster! Now you, bastard!*

VOICE [unidentified]:   *I am here, Lugenbrau. Kharnagar awaits.*

Lugenbrau (i) moves off-image. Pict-source pans. Image jerky. Body parts scattered on chamber floor [composite identifies subject (ii) as one of nine corpses]. Major detonation(s) nearby. Image shakes, pict-source falls sidelong.

[Image blank for 1 minute 7 seconds. Significant background noise.]

[Image returns.] Lugenbrau partly visible off frame left, engaged in combat. Afterglow-residue of force hammer blows remain burned on image for several seconds [image indistinct].

Pict-source turns to focus on Lugenbrau. Lugenbrau engaged in hand-to-hand combat with unknown foe. Movements too fast for pict-source to capture. Blur. Human figures [identity unknown, poss. adversary troops] move in from right frame. Heads of human figures explode. Figures topple.

[White out. Pict-source blanked. Duration unknown.]

[Image returns, imperfect.] Jerky shots of ground and wall. Refocus blurring. Pict-source reacquires Lugenbrau and adversary in combat [smoke fumes haze view]. Combat as before too rapid for pict-source to capture. Extensive background noise. Glowing line [believed to be blade weapon]

impales Lugenbrau. Image shakes [some picture loss]. Lugenbrau immolates [image burns out].

[Pause/pict-blank of unknown duration.]

[Image returns.] Close up of face looking into pict-source.
Identity unknown [subject (iv)]. (iv) is handsome, sculptural,
smiling, eyes blank.

VOICE (iv):   *Hello, little thing. I am Cherubael.*

Light flash.

Scream [believed to originate from pict-source].

[Image out. Recording ends.]

ONE

A cold coming
Death in the dormant vaults
Some puritanical reflections

Hunting the recidivist Murdin Eyclone, I came to Hubris in the Dormant of 240.M41, as the Imperial sidereal calendar has it.

Dormant lasted eleven months of Hubris's twenty-nine month lunar year, and the only signs of life were the custodians with their lighted poles and heat-gowns, patrolling the precincts of the hibernation tombs.

Within those sulking basalt and ceramite vaults, the grandees of Hubris slept, dreaming in crypts of aching ice, awaiting Thaw, the middle season between Dormant and Vital.

Even the air was frigid. Frost encrusted the tombs, and a thick cake of ice covered the featureless land. Above, star patterns twinkled in the curious, permanent night. One of them was Hubris's sun, so far away now. Come Thaw, Hubris would spin into the warm embrace of its star again.

Then it would become a blazing globe. Now it was just a fuzz of light.

As my gun-cutter set down on the landing cross at Tomb Point, I had pulled on an internally heated bodyskin and swathes of sturdy, insulated foul weather gear, but still the perilous cold cut through me now. My eyes watered, and the tears froze on my lashes and cheeks. I remembered the details of the cultural brief my savant had prepared, and quickly lowered my frost visor, trembling as warm air began to circulate under the plastic mask.

Custodians, alerted to my arrival by astropathic hails, stood waiting for me at the base of the landing cross. Their lighted poles dipped in obeisance in the frozen night and the air steamed with the heat that bled from their cloaks. I nodded to them, showing their leader my badge of office. An ice-car awaited: a rust-coloured arrowhead twenty metres long, mounted on ski-blade runners and spiked tracks.

It carried me away from the landing cross and I left the winking signal lights and the serrated dagger-shape of my gun-cutter behind in the perpetual winter night.

The spiked tracks kicked up blizzards of rime behind us. Ahead, despite the lamps, the landscape was black and impenetrable. I rode with Lores Vibben and three custodians in a cabin lit only by the amber glow of the craft's control panel. Heating vents recessed in the leather seats breathed out warm, stale air.

A custodian handed back a data-slate to Vibben. She looked at it cursorily and passed it on to me. I realised my frost visor was still down. I raised it and began to search my pockets for my eye glasses.

With a smile, Vibben produced them from within her own swaddled, insulated garb. I nodded thanks, put them on my nose and began to read.

I was just calling up the last plates of text when the ice-car halted.

'Processional Two-Twelve,' announced one of the custodians.

We dismounted, sliding our visors down into place.

Jewels of frost-flakes fluttered in the blackness about us, sparkling as they crossed through the ice-car's lamp beams. I've heard of bitter cold. Emperor grace me I never feel it again. Biting, crippling, actually bitter to taste on the tongue. Every joint in my frame protested and creaked.

My hands and my mind were numb.

That was not good.

Processional Two-Twelve was a hibernation tomb at the west end of the great Imperial Avenue. It housed twelve thousand, one hundred and forty-two members of the Hubris ruling elite.

We approached the great monument, crunching up the black, frost-coated steps.

I halted. 'Where are the tomb's custodians?'

'Making their rounds,' I was told.

I glanced at Vibben and shook my head. She slid her hand into her fur-edged robes.

'Knowing we approach?' I urged, addressing the custodian again. 'Knowing we expect to meet them?'

'I will check,' said the custodian, the one who had circulated the slate. He pushed on up the steps, the phosphor light on his pole bobbing.

The other two seemed ill at ease.

I beckoned to Vibben, so she would follow me up after the leader.

We found him on a lower terrace, gazing at the strewn bodies of four custodians, their light poles fizzling out around them.

'H-how?' he stammered.

'Stay back,' Vibben told him and drew her weapon. Its tiny amber Armed rune glowed in the darkness.

I took out my blade, igniting it. It hummed.

The south entry of the tombs was open. Shafts of golden light shone out. All my fears were rapidly being confirmed.

We entered, Vibben sweeping the place from side to side with her handgun. The hall was narrow and high, lit by chemical glow-globes. Intruding frost was beginning to mark the polished basalt walls.

A few metres inside, another custodian lay dead in a stiffening mirror of blood. We stepped over him. To each side, hallways opened up, admitting us to the hibernation stacks. In every direction, rows and rows of ice-berths ranged down the smoothed basalt chambers.

It was like walking into the Imperium's grandest morgue.

Vibben swept soundlessly to the right and I went left.

I admit I was excited by now, eager to close and conclude a business that had lasted six years. Eyclone had evaded me for six whole years! I studied his methods every day and dreamed of him every night.

Now I could smell him.

I raised my visor.

Water was pattering from the roof. Thaw water. It was growing warmer in here. In their ice-berths, some of the dim figures were stirring.

Too early! Far too early!

Eyclone's first man came at me from the west as I crossed a trunk-junction corridor. I spun, the power sword in my hand, and cut through his neck before his ice-axe could land.

The second came from the south, the third from the east. And then more. More.

A blur.

As I fought, I heard furious shooting from the vaults away to my right. Vibben was in trouble.

I could hear her over the vox-link in our hoods: 'Eisenhorn! Eisenhorn!'

I wheeled and cut. My opponents were all dressed in heat-gowns, and carried ice-tools that made proficient weapons. Their eyes were dark and unforthcoming. Though they were fast, there was something in them that suggested they were doing this mindlessly, by order.

The power sword, an antique and graceful weapon, blessed by the Provost of Inx himself, spun in my hand. With five abrupt moves I made corpses out of them and left their blood vapour drifting in the air.

'Eisenhorn!'

I turned and ran. I splashed heavily down a corridor sluiced with melt water. More shots from ahead. A sucking cry.

I found Vibben face down across a freezer tube, frozen blood gluing her to the sub-zero plastic. Eight of Eyclone's servants lay sprawled around her. Her weapon lay just out of reach of her clawing hand, the spent cell ejected from the grip.

I am forty-two standard years old, in my prime by Imperial standards, young by those of the Inquisition. All my life, I have had a reputation for being cold, unfeeling. Some have called me heartless, ruthless, even cruel. I am not. I am not beyond emotional response or compassion. But I possess – and my masters count this as perhaps my paramount virtue – a singular force of will. Throughout my career it has served me well to draw on this facility and steel myself, unflinching, at all that this wretched galaxy can throw at me. To feel pain or fear or grief is to allow myself a luxury I cannot afford.

Lores Vibben had served with me for five and a half years.

In that period she had saved my life twice. She saw herself as my aide and my bodyguard, yet in truth she was more a companion and a fellow warrior. When I recruited her from the clan-slums of Tornish, it was for her combat skills and brutal vigour. But I came to value her just as much for her sharp mind, soft wit and clear head.

I stared down at her body for a moment. I believe I may have uttered her name.

I extinguished my power sword and, sliding it into its scabbard, moved back into the shadows on the far side of the hibernation gallery. I could hear nothing except the increasingly persistent thaw-drip. Freeing my sidearm from its leather rig under my left armpit, I checked its load and opened a vox link. Eyclone was undoubtedly monitoring all traffic in and out of Processional Two-Twelve, so I used Glossia, an informal verbal cipher known only to myself and my immediate colleagues. Most inquisitors develop their own private languages for confidential communication, some more sophisticated than others. Glossia, the basics of which I had designed ten years before, was reasonably complex and had evolved, organically, with use.

'Thorn wishes aegis, rapturous beasts below.'

'Aegis, arising, the colours of space,' Betancore responded immediately and correctly.

'Rose thorn, abundant, by flame light crescent.'

A pause. 'By flame light crescent? Confirm.'

'Confirm.'

'Razor delphus pathway! Pattern ivory!'

'Pattern denied. Pattern crucible.'

'Aegis, arising.'

The link broke. He was on his way. He had taken the news of

Vibben's death as hard as I expected. I trusted that would not affect his performance. Midas Betancore was a hot-blooded, impetuous man, which was partly why I liked him. And used him.

I moved out of the shadows again, my sidearm raised. A Scipio-pattern naval pistol, finished in dull chrome with inlaid ivory grips, it felt reassuringly heavy in my gloved hand. Ten rounds, every one a fat, blunt man-stopper, were spring-loaded into the slide inside the grip. I had four more armed slides just like it in my hip pocket.

I forget where I acquired the Scipio. It had been mine for a few years. One night, three years before, Vibben had prised off the ceramite grip plates with their touch-worn, machined-stamped engravings of the Imperial aquila and the Navy motto, and replaced them with ivory grips she had etched herself. A common practice on Tornish, she informed me, handing the weapon back the next day. The new grips were like crude scrimshaw, showing on each side a poorly executed human skull through which a thorny rose entwined, emerging through an eye socket, shedding cartoon droplets of blood. She'd inlaid carmine gems into the droplets to emphasise their nature. Below the skull, my name was scratched in a clumsy scroll.

I had laughed. There had been times when I'd almost been too embarrassed to draw the gang-marked weapon in a fight.

Now, now she was dead, I realise what an honour had been paid to me through that devoted work.

I made a promise to myself: I would kill Eyclone with this gun.

As a devoted member of his high majesty the God-Emperor's Inquisition, I find my philosophy bends towards that of the

Amalathians. To the outside galaxy, members of our orders appear much alike: an inquisitor is an inquisitor, a being of fear and persecution. It surprises many that internally, we are riven with clashing ideologies.

I know it surprised Vibben. I spent one long afternoon trying to explain the differences. I failed.

To express it in simple terms, some inquisitors are puritans and some are radicals. Puritans believe in and enforce the traditional station of the Inquisition, working to purge our galactic community of any criminal or malevolent element: the triumvirate of evil – alien, mutant and daemon. Anything that clashes with the pure rule of mankind, the preachings of the Ministorum and the letter of Imperial Law is subject to a puritan inquisitor's attention. Hard-line, traditional, merciless... that is the puritan way.

Radicals believe that any methods are allowable if they accomplish the Inquisitorial task. Some, as I understand it, actually embrace and use forbidden resources, such as the Warp itself, as weapons against the enemies of mankind.

I have heard the arguments often enough. They appal me. Radical belief is heretical.

I am a puritan by calling and an Amalathian by choice. The ferociously strict ways of the monodominant philosophy oft-times entices me, but there is precious little subtlety in their ways and thus it is not for me.

Amalathians take our name from the conclave at Mount Amalath. Our endeavour is to maintain the status quo of the Imperium, and we work to identify and destroy any persons or agencies that might destabilise the power of the Imperium from without or within. We believe in strength through unity. Change is the greatest enemy. We believe the God-Emperor has a divine plan, and we work to sustain the Imperium in stability until that plan is made known. We deplore factions and in-fighting... Indeed, it is sometimes a painful irony that our beliefs mark us as a faction within the political helix of the Inquisition.

We are the steadfast spine of the Imperium, its antibodies, fighting disease, insanity, injury, invasion.

I can think of no better way to serve, no better way to be an inquisitor.

So you have me then, pictured. Gregor Eisenhorn, inquisitor, puritan, Amalathian, forty-two years old standard, an inquisitor for the past eighteen years. I am tall and broad at the shoulders, strong, resolute. I have already told you of my force of will, and you will have noted my prowess with a blade.

What else is there? Am I clean-shaven? Yes! My eyes are dark, my hair darker and thick. These things matter little.

Come and let me show you how I killed Eyclone.

TWO

The dead awake
Betancore's temper
Elucidations by Aemos

I clung to the shadows, moving through the great tomb as silently as I knew how. A terrible sound rolled through the thawing vaults of Processional Two-Twelve. Fists and palms beating at coffin hoods. Wailing. Gurgling.

The sleepers were waking, their frigid bodies, sore with hibernation sickness, trapped in their caskets. No honour guard of trained cryogeneers waited to unlock them, to sluice their organs with warming bio-fluids or inject stimulants or massage paralysed extremities.

Thanks to Eyclone's efforts, twelve thousand one hundred and forty-two members of the planet's ruling class were being roused early into the bitter season of Dormant, and roused without the necessary medical supervision.

I had no doubt that they would all suffocate in minutes.

My mind scrolled back through the details my savant had prepared for me. There was a central control room, where I could disengage the ice-berth locks and at least free them all. But to what good? Without the resuscitation teams, they would fail and perish.

And if I hunted out the control room, Eyclone would have time to escape.

In Glossia code, I communicated this quandary to Betancore, and told him to alert the custodians. He informed me, after a pause, that crash-teams and relief crews were on their way.

But why? The question was still there. Why was Eyclone doing this?

A massed killing was nothing unusual for a follower of Chaos. But there had to be a point, above and beyond the deaths themselves.

I was pondering this as I crossed a hallway deep in the west wing of the Processional. Frantic beating sounds came from the berths all around, and a pungent mix of ice-water and bio-fluid spurted from the drain-taps and cascaded over the floor.

A shot rang out. A las-shot. It missed me by less than a hand's breadth and exploded through the headboard of an ice berth behind me. Immediately, the frantic hammering in that berth stopped, and the waters running out of its ducts were stained pink.

I fired the Scipio down the vault, startled by the noise it made.

Two more las-shots flicked down at me.

Taking cover behind a stone bulkhead, I emptied a clip down the length of the gallery, the spent shell cases smoking in the air as the pumping slide ejected them. A hot vapour of cordite blew back at me.

I swung back into cover, exchanging clips.

A few more spits of laser drizzled past me, then a voice.

'Eisenhorn? Gregor, is that you?'

Eyclone. I knew his thin voice at once. I didn't answer.

'You're dead, you know, Gregor. Dead like they all are. Dead, dead, dead. Step out and make it quick.'

He was good, I'll give him that. My legs actually twitched, actually started to walk me clear of cover into the open. Eyclone was infamous across a dozen settled systems for his mind powers and mesmeric tone. How else had he managed to get these dark-eyed fools to do his bidding?

But I have similar skills. And I have honed them well.

There is a time to use mind or voice tricks gently to draw out your target. And there are times to use them like a stub-gun at point-blank range.

It was time for the latter.

I pitched my voice, balanced my mind and yelled: 'Show yourself first!'

Eyclone didn't succumb. I didn't expect him to. Like me, he had years of resilience training. But his two gunmen were easy meat.

The first strode directly out into the middle of the gallery hallway, dropping his lasgun with a clatter. The Scipio made a hole in the middle of his forehead and blew his brains out behind him in a grotesque pink mist. The other stumbled out on his heels, realised his mistake, and began firing.

One of his las-bolts scorched the sleeve of my jacket. I squeezed the pistol's trigger and the Scipio bucked and snarled in my tight grip.

The round penetrated his head under his nose, splintered on his upper teeth and blew the sides of his skull out. He staggered and fell, dead fingers firing his lasrifle again and again, blowing the fascias out of the hibernation stalls around him.

Putrid water, bio-fluid and plastic fragments poured out, and some screams became louder.

I could hear footsteps above the screams. Eyclone was running.

I ran too, across the vaults, passing gallery after gallery.

The screaming, the pounding... God-Emperor help me I will never forget that. Thousands of frantic souls waking up to face an agonising death.

Damn Eyclone. Damn him to hell and back.

Crossing the third gallery, I saw him, running parallel to me. He saw me too. He wheeled, and fired.

I ducked back as the blasts of his laspistol shrieked past.

A glimpse was all I'd had: a short, wiry man, dressed in brown heat-robes, his goatee neatly trimmed, his eyes twinkling with malice.

I fired back, but he was running again.

I ran on, glimpsed him down the next gallery and fired again.

At the next gallery, nothing. I waited, and pulled off my outer robe. It was getting hot and damp in Processional Two-Twelve.

When another minute passed and there was still no sign, I began to edge down the gallery towards his last position, gun raised. I'd got ten paces when he swung out of hiding and blazed away at me.

I would have died right there, had not the joker-gods of fate and chance played their hand.

At the moment Eyclone fired, several cryo-tubes finally gave way and yowling, naked, blistered humans staggered out into the corridor, clawing with ice-webbed hands, mewling, vomiting, blind and ice-burned. Eyclone's shots tore three of them apart and hideously wounded a fourth. Had it not been for them, those las-shots would have finished me.

Footsteps, hurried. He was running again.

I pushed on down the gallery, stepping over the blasted ruins of the sleepers who had inadvertently spared me. The wounded one, a middle-aged female, compromised and naked as she lay in the melt-water, clutched at my leg, begging for salvation. Eyclone's gunfire had all but disembowelled her.

I hesitated. A merciful headshot now would spare her everything. But I could not. Once they were awake, the hierarchy of Hubris would not understand a mercy killing. I would be trapped here for years, fighting my case through every court in their legislature.

I shook off her desperate grip and moved on.

Do you think me weak, flawed? Do you hate me for setting my Inquisitorial role above the needs of one agonised being?

If you do, I commend you. I think of that woman still, and hate the fact I left her to die slowly. But if you hate me, I know this about you... you are no inquisitor. You don't have the moral strength.

I could have finished her, and my soul might have been relieved. But that would have been an end to my work. And I always think of the thousands... millions perhaps... who would die worse deaths but for my actions.

Is that arrogance?

Perhaps... and perhaps arrogance is therefore a virtue of the Inquisition. I would gladly ignore one life in agony if I could save a hundred, a thousand, more...

Mankind must suffer so that mankind can survive. It's that simple. Ask Aemos. He knows.

Still, I dream of her and her bloody anguish. Pity me for that, at least.

* * *

I pressed on through the tomb-vaults, and after another gallery or two, progress became slow. Hundreds of sleepers had now freed themselves, the hallways were jostling with their frantic, blind pain. I skirted those I could, staying out of the way of grasping hands, stepping over some who lay twitching and helpless on the floor. The collective sounds of their braying and whimpering were almost intolerable. There was a hot, fetid stench of decay and bio-waste. Several times I had to break free of hands that seized me.

Grotesquely, the horror made it easier to track Eyclone. Every few paces, another sleeper lay dead or dying, callously gunned down by murderers in desperate flight.

I found a service door forced open at the end of the next file, and entered a deep stairwell that wound up through the edifice. Chemical globes suspended in wall brackets lit the way. From far above, I heard shots, and I ascended, my pistol raised and braced, covering each turn of the staircase as Vibben had taught me.

I came up to what a wall-plaque told me was level eight. I could hear machine noise, industrial and heavy. Through another forced service door lay the walkways to the next galleries and a side access hatch of brushed grey adamite, which stencilled runes identified as the entrance to the main cryogenic generators. Smoke coughed and noise rolled from the hatch.

The cryogenerator chamber was vast, its roof reaching up into the pyramidal summit of Processional Two-Twelve. The rumbling equipment it contained was ancient and vast. The data-slate given to me in the ice-car had said that the cryogenerators that ran the hibernation tombs of Hubris had originally been constructed to equip the ark-fleet that carried the first colonists to the world. They had been cut and salvaged from the giant arks on arrival, and the stone tombs raised around them. A technomagos brotherhood, descended from the ark-fleet engineers, had kept the cryogenerators operating for thousands of years.

This cryogenerator was sixty metres tall and constructed from cast-iron and copper painted in matt-red lead paint. As it rose, it sprouted branches in the form of conduits and heat-exchangers that intertwined with the roof-vents. The hot air of the room vibrated with the noise of its operation. Smoke and steam wreathed the atmosphere and sweat broke out on my brow and back the moment I stepped through the hatchway.

I looked around and quickly noted where several inspection hatches had been levered away. The red paint was scored and scraped along each frame where a crowbar had been forced in, and hundreds of years of sacred unguents and lex-mechanical sigil-seals applied and tended by the technomagi had been broken.

I peered in through the open covers and saw rows of copper-wound cells, vibrating rack-frames wet with black lubricant, sooty ganglions of insulated electrical routing and dripping, lagged iron pipes. Sprung-jawed clips with biting metal teeth had been attached to some of the cells, and wiring from these clips trailed back to a small and obviously new ceramite module box taped inside the hatch frame. A digital runic display on the module flashed amber.

This was where Eyclone's men had artificially triggered the revival process. That meant he had either turned and recruited local technomagi or brought in experts from off-world. Either way, this signified considerable resources.

I moved on, and clambered up a ladder frame onto a raised platform of metal grille. There was something else here, a rectangular casket measuring about a metre and a half along its longest edge. It rested on four claw-like feet and had carrying handles built into its sides. The lid was open, and dozens of cables and leads snaked out, linking it to the cryogenerator's electromechanical guts, exposed by another prised-off hatch.

I looked into the casket, but could make little sense of what I saw there: circuit boards and complex mechanical elements linked by sheaves of cable. And there was a space, a padded recess in the heart of the casket's innards, clearly waiting to receive something the size of a clenched fist. Loose cable ends and plugs were taped in place, ready to be connected. But a key component of this mysterious device was evidently missing.

My vox-link chimed in my ear. It was Betancore. I could barely hear him over the noise of the cryogenerator as he made a quick report in Glossia.

'Aegis, heavens uplift, thrice-sevenfold, a crown with stars. Infamous angel without title, to Thorn by eight. Pattern?'

I considered. I was in no mood to take any more chances. 'Thorn, pattern hawk.'

'Pattern hawk acknowledged,' he said with relish.

I saw movement from the corner of my eye about a half-second after I broke the link with Betancore: another of Eyclone's black-eyed men, running in through the main hatch with an old-model laspistol raised in his hand.

His first shot, a twinkling ball of pink light, snapped the metal handrail of the platform I stood on with an explosive ping. His second and third passed over me as I dived down, and ricocheted off the cast-iron side of the cryogenerator with scorching crackles.

I returned fire, prone, but the angle was bad. Two more las-shots came my way, one cutting sideways into the edge of the platform deck and cutting a gouge through the grille. The gunman was nearly at the foot of the ladder-frame.

Now a second gunman entered the chamber, calling out after the first, a powerful autorifle in his hands. He saw me, and began to raise the weapon, but I had a cleaner angle on him, and dropped him quickly with two rounds through the upper torso.

The other was almost below me now, and fired a shot that punched clean through the grille just next to my right foot.

I didn't hesitate. I went up and over the rail and directly down onto him. We crashed onto the chamber floor, the powerful impact throwing the Scipio out of my grasp despite my efforts to hold onto it. The man was jabbering some insane nonsense into my face and had a good grip on the front of my tunic. I had him by the throat and by the wrist of his gun-hand, forcing the laspistol away. He fired it twice into the ceiling space above.

'Enough!' I commanded, modulating my tone to emphasise my will as I drove it into his mind. 'Drop it!'

He did, meekly, as if surprised. Psyker tricks of will often baffle those who find themselves compelled by them. As he faltered, I threw a punch that connected well and left him unconscious on the floor.

As I bent to recover the Scipio, Betancore voxed me again. 'Aegis, pattern hawk, infamous angel cast down.'

'Thorn acknowledged. Resume pattern crucible.'

I pushed on after my quarry.

Eyclone made it into the upper vaults and out onto a landing platform built into the sloping side of Processional

Two-Twelve. The wind was fierce. Eyclone had eight of his cult with him and they were expecting an orbital pinnace that would carry them away to safety.

They had no way of knowing that, thanks to Betancore, their means of escape was now burning in a deep impact gouge in the permafrost about eight kilometres north.

What rose above the landing platform out of the blizzard night, its down thrusters wailing, was my gun-cutter. Four hundred and fifty tonnes of armoured alloy, eighty metres from barbed nose to raked stern, landing gear still lowered like spider-legs, it rose on the blue-hot downwash of angled jets. Banks of floodlights under its beak-nose cut on and bathed the deck and the cultists in fierce white light.

Panicking, some of them fired up at it.

That was all the cue Betancore needed. His temper was hot, his mind void of anything except the fact that Vibben was dead.

The gun-turrets in the ends of the stubby wings rotated and washed the platform with withering heavy fire. Stone splintered. Bodies were reduced to sprays of liquid.

Eyclone, more intelligent than his men, had sprinted off the platform to the hatch as the gun-cutter rose into view.

And that's where he ran into me.

He opened his mouth in shock and I pushed the muzzle of Vibben's gun into it. I'm sure he wanted to say something important. I didn't care what it was.

I punched the gun so hard into his mouth the trigger guard broke his lower teeth. He tried to reach for something on his belt.

I fired.

Having emptied his brain-case and shattered it into the bargain, the round still had so much force it crossed the deck and pinked off the armoured nose of the hovering gun-cutter, just below the cockpit window.

'Sorry,' I said.

'Don't worry about it,' Betancore crackled back over the vox-link.

'Most perturbatory,' said Aemos. It was his most frequent expression. He was hunched over, peering down into the casket on the cryogenerator chamber platform. Occasionally, he reached in to tinker with something, or leaned down for a closer look. Gestures such as these made the heavy augmetic eye glasses clamped to his hooked nose make a soft dialling click as they auto-focused.

I stood at his shoulder, waiting, looking down at the back of his old, bald head. The skin was liver-spotted and thin, and a narrow crescent of white hair edged the back of his skull.

Uber Aemos was my savant, and my longest serving companion. He had come into my service in the first month of my career in the Inquisition, bequeathed to me by Inquisitor Hapshant, who was by then dying of cerebral worms. Aemos was two hundred and seventy-eight standard years old, and had provided his services as a savant to three inquisitors before me. He was alive only thanks to significant bionic augmentation to his digestive tract, liver, urinary system, hips and left leg.

In Hapshant's service he had been injured by a stub-round. Tending him, surgeons had found a chronically advanced and previously undiagnosed cancer rampant in his abdomen. Had he not been shot, he would have died within weeks. Thanks to the wound, the disease was found, excised and his body repaired with plastic, ceramite and steel prosthetics.

Aemos referred to the whole ordeal as his 'lucky suffering' and still wore the twisted plug of the stub round that had almost taken and certainly saved his life on a chain around his stringy neck.

'Aemos?'

He rose stiffly with a whine of bionics and turned to face me, shaking out the floor length green folds of his embroidered robe. His augmetic eye-wear dominated his ancient face. He sometimes reminded me of a curious insect with bulbous eyes and narrow, pinched mouth parts.

'A codifier of unique design. A series processor, similar in layout to the mind-impulse units used by the hallowed Adeptus Mechanicus to govern the linkage between human brain and god-machine.'

'You've seen such things?' I asked, a little taken aback.

'Once, in my travels. In passing. I do not pretend to have more than a cursory knowledge. I am certain, however, that the Adeptus Mechanicus would be interested in this device. It may be illicit technology or something derived from apparatus stolen from them. Either way, they would impound it.'

'Either way, they're not going to know about it. This is inquisitional evidence.'

'Quite so,' he agreed.

There were distracting noises from below us. Tomb custodians and technomagi from the cryogenerator brotherhood milled about in the chamber, supervising the mammoth and, in my opinion, futile operation to save the sleepers of Processional Two-Twelve. The whole tomb seethed with activity, and the awful screams had not yet died down.

I saw how Aemos watched the work with keen interest, making notes to himself on a data-slate strapped to his wrist. At the age of forty-two, he had contracted a meme-virus that altered his brain function for ever, driving him to collect information – any sort of information – whenever he got the chance. He was pathologically compelled to acquire knowledge, a data-addict. That made him an aggravating, easily sidetracked companion, and a perfect savant, as four inquisitors had discovered.

'Cold-bolted steel cylinders,' he mused, looking up at the heat exchangers. 'Is that to provide stress-durability in temperature change, or was it fabrication expedient? Also, what is the range of temperature change, given–'

'Aemos, please.'

'Hmm?' He looked back at me, remembering I was there.

'The casket?'

'Indeed. My apologies. A series processor... did I say that?'

'Yes. Processing what? Data?'

'I thought that at first, then I considered some mental or mental-transference process. But I doubt either now I've studied it.'

I pointed down into the casket. 'What's missing?'

'Oh, you noticed that too? This is most perturbatory. I'm still not certain, of course, but it's something angular, non-standard in shape and with its own power source.'

'You're sure?'

'There are no power inlets designed to couple to it, only power outlets. And there's something curious about the plugs. Non-standard mating. It's all non-standard.'

'Xenos?'

'No... human, just non-standard, custom made.'

'Yeah, but what for?' asked Betancore, climbing up the ladder frame to join us. He looked sour, his unruly black curls framing a dark-skinned, slender face that was usually alive with genial mischief.

'I need to make further evaluations, Midas,' said Aemos, hunching back over the casket.

Betancore stared my way. He was as tall as me, but lighter in build. His boots, breeches and tunic were made of soft black leather with red piping, the old uniform of a Glavian pilot-hunter, and over that he wore, as always, a short jacket of cerise silk with iridescent embroidery panels.

His hands were gloved in light bllek-hide, and seemed to wait ominously near the curved grips of the needle pistols holstered on his hips.

'You took a long time getting here,' I began.

'They made me take the cutter back to the landing cross at Tomb Point. Said they need the platform here for emergency flights. I had to walk back. Then I saw to Lores.'

'She died well, Betancore.'

'Maybe. Is that possible?' he added.

I made no reply. I knew how deep his foul moods could be. I knew he had been in love with Lores Vibben, or at least had decided he was in love with her. I knew things would get difficult with Betancore before they got better.

'Where is this off-worlder? This Eisenhorn?'

The demanding voice rolled up from the chamber below us. I looked down. A man had entered the cryogenerator chamber escorted by four custodians in heat-gowns, carrying light-poles aloft. He was tall, with pallid skin and greying hair, though his haughty bearing spoke of self-possession and arrogance. He wore a decorative ceremonial heat-gown of bold yellow. I didn't know who he was, but he looked like trouble to me.

Aemos and Betancore were watching him too.

'Any ideas as to who this is?' I asked Aemos.

'Well, you see, the yellow robes, like the light poles carried by the custodians, symbolises the return of the sun and thus heat and light. It denotes a high-ranking official of the Dormant Custodial Committee.'

'I got that much myself,' I muttered.

'Oh, well his name is Nissemay Carpel, and he's high custodian, so you should address him as such. He was born here,
on Vital 235, fifty standard years ago, the son of a–'

'Enough! I knew we'd get there eventually.'

I walked to the rail and looked down. 'I am Eisenhorn.'

He stared up at me, barely contained wrath bulging the
veins in his neck.

'Place him under arrest,' he told his men.

THREE

Nissemay Carpel
A light in endless darkness
The Pontius

I shot one, meaningful glance at Betancore to stay his hand, then calmly walked past him, slid down the ladder frame and approached Carpel. The custodians closed in around me, but at a distance.

'High custodian,' I nodded.

He fixed me with a steady but wary gaze and licked spittle off his thin lips. 'You will be detained until–'

'No,' I replied. 'I am an inquisitor of the God-Emperor of Mankind, Ordo Xenos. I will co-operate in any investigation you bring to bear here, fully and completely, but you will not and cannot detain me. Do you understand?'

'An... inquisitor?'

'Do you understand?' I repeated. I wasn't using my will at all, not yet. I would if I had to. But I trusted that he would have the sense to listen to me first. He could make things awkward for me, but I could make things intolerable for him.

He seemed to soften a little. As I had judged, part of his rage came from shock at this incident, shock that so many planetary nobles in his care had suffered. He was looking for somewhere to pin the blame. Now he had to temper that with the idea that he was dealing with a member of the most feared institution in the Imperium.

'Thousands are dead,' he began, a tremor in his voice. 'This desecration... the high born of Hubris, violated by a... by a–'

'A murderer, a follower of darkness, a man who, thanks to me, lies dead now under a plastic sheet on the upper landing platform. I mourn the great loss Hubris has suffered tonight, high custodian, and I wish I had been able to prevent it. But if I had not been here at all to raise the alarm... well, imagine the tragedy you would be dealing with then.'

I let that sink in.

'Not just this processional, but all the hibernation tombs... who knows what Eyclone might have wrought? Who knows what his overall ambition was?'

'Eyclone, the recidivist?'

'He did this, high custodian.'

'You will brief me on this entire event.'

'Let me prepare a report and bring it to you. You may have answers for me too. I will signal you in a few hours for an appointment to meet. I think you have plenty to deal with right now.'

We made our way out. Betancore presented the junior custodians with a formal register of evidence to be stored for my inspection. The list included the casket and the bodies of Eyclone and his men. None would be tampered with or even searched until I had looked at them. The gunman I had subdued in the cryogenerator chamber, the only one left alive, would be incarcerated pending my interrogation. Betancore made these requirements abundantly clear.

We took Vibben with us. Aemos was too frail, so Betancore and I handled the plastic-shrouded form on the gurney.

We left Processional Two-Twelve by the main vault doors into the biting cold of the constant night and carried Vibben down towards a waiting ice-car, taking her through the hundreds of rows of corpses the Custodians were laying out on the frozen ground.

My band and I had deployed onto Hubris the moment we arrived, such was the urgency of our chase. Now it looked like we would remain here for at least a week, longer if Carpel proved difficult. As we rode the ice-car back to the landing cross, I had Aemos make arrangements for our stay.

During Dormant on Hubris, while ninety-nine per cent of the planetary population hibernates, one location remains active. The custodians and the technomagi weather out the long, bitter darkness in a place called the Sun-dome.

Fifty kilometres from the vast expanse of the Dormant Plains where the hibernation tombs stand in rows, the Sun-dome sits like a dark grey blister in the ongoing winter night. It is home to fifty-nine thousand people, just a town compared with the great empty cities that slumber below the horizon line waiting for Thaw to bring their populations back.

I stared out at the Sun-dome as the gun-cutter swept us in towards it through wind-blown storms of ice. Small red marker lights winked on the surfaces of the dome and from the masts jutting from the apex.

Betancore flew, silent, concentrating. He had removed his tight-fitting gloves so that the intricate Glavian circuitry set

like silver inlay into his palms and finger tips could engage
with the cutter's system directly via the control stick.

Aemos sat in a rear cabin, poring over manuscripts and
data-slates. Two independent multitask servitors waited for
commands in the crew-bay. The ship had five in all. Two
were limb-less combat units slaved directly to the gun-pods
and the other, the chief servitor, a high-spec model we called
Uclid, never left his duties in the engine room.

Lowink, my astropath, slumbered in his chamber, linked
to the vox and pict systems, awaiting a summons.

Vibben lay shrouded on the cot in her room.

Betancore swung the cutter down towards the dome. After
an exchange of telemetry, a wide blast shutter opened in the
side of the dome. The light that shone out was almost unbear-
ably bright. Betancore engaged the cockpit glare shields and
flew us into the landing bay.

The inside surface of the vast dome was mirrored. A
plasma-effect sun-globe burned high in the roof of the dome,
bathing the town below in fierce white light. The town itself,
spread out beneath us, seemed to be made of glass.

We set down on the wide bay, a twenty-hectare metal platform that overlooked the town. The surface of the platform
gleamed almost white in the reflected glare. Heavy monotask servitors trundled out and towed us into a landing silo
off the main pad, where pit-servitors moved in to attach fuel
lines and begin fundamental servicing. Betancore didn't want
anybody or anything touching the gun-cutter, so he ordered
Modo and Nilquit, our two independent servitors, to take
over the tasks and send the locals away. I could hear them
moving around the hull, servos whirring, hydraulics hissing, exchanging machine code data bursts with each other
or with Uclid in the drive chamber.

Aemos offered to find accommodation for us in the town itself, but I decided a landing berth was all we needed. The gun-cutter was large enough to provide ample facilities for our stay. We often spent weeks, or months living aboard it.

I went to Lowink's small cabin under the cockpit deck and roused him. He hadn't been with me long: my previous astropath had been killed trying to translate a warp-cipher six weeks before.

Lowink was a young man, with a fleshy, unhealthy bulk hanging from a thin skeletal frame, his body already deteriorating from the demands of a psyker's life. Greasy implant plugs dotted his shaved skull, and lined his forearms like short spines. As he came to the door, some of these plugs trailed wires, each marked with parchment labels, which led back to the communications mainbox above his cradle. Thousands of cables spilled or dangled around his tiny cabin, but he instinctively knew what each one did and could set and adjust plug-ins at a moment's notice. The room reeked of sweat and incense.

'Master,' he said. His mouth was a wet pink slit and he had one lazy, half-hooded eye that gave him a superior air quite belying his actual timidity.

'Please send a message for me, Lowink. To the Regal Akwitane.' The Regal was a rogue trader we had employed to convey the gun-cutter and ourselves to Hubris. His vessel awaited us in orbit now, ready to provide further warp-passage.

'Give Trade Master Golkwin my respects and tell him we are staying for now. He can be on his way, there is no point in him waiting. We could be here for a week or more. The usual form, polite. Tell him I thank him for his service and hope we may meet again.'

Lowink nodded. 'I will do it at once.'

'Then I'd like you to perform some other tasks. Contact the main Astropathicus Enclave here on Hubris and request a full transcript of off-world traffic for the past six weeks. Also any record of unlicensed traffic, individuals using their own astropaths. Whatever they can make available. And a little threat that it is an inquisitor requiring this data wouldn't hurt. They don't want to find themselves caught up in a major inquisition for withholding information.'

He nodded again. 'Will you be requiring an auto-seance?'

'Not yet, but I will eventually. I will give you time to prepare.'

'Will that be all, Master?'

I turned to go. 'Yes, Lowink.'

'Master...' he paused. 'Is it true that the female Vibben is dead?'

'Yes, Lowink.'

'Ah. I thought it was quiet.' He closed the door.

The comment wasn't as callous as it sounded. I knew what he meant, though my own psychic abilities were nascent and undeveloped next to his. Lores Vibben was a latent psyker, and while she had been with us, there had been a constant background sound, almost subliminal, broadcast unconsciously by her young, eager mind.

I found Betancore outside, standing under the shadow of one of the gun-cutter's stubby wings. He was gazing at the ground, smoking a lho-leaf tube. I didn't approve of narcotics, but I let it go. He'd cleaned himself up these past few years. When I'd first met him, he had been an obscura user.

'Damned bright place,' he muttered, wincing out at the abominable glare.

'A typical over reaction. They have eleven months of pitch

dark, so they light their habitat to an excessive degree.'

'Do they have a night cycle?'

'I don't believe so.'

'No wonder they're so messed up. Extreme light, extreme dark, extreme mindsets. Their body clocks and natural rhythms must be all over the place.'

I nodded. Outside, I had begun to be disarmed by the notion that the night was never going to end. Now I had the same feelings about this constant noon. In his brief, Aemos had said the world was called Hubris because after spending seventy standard years getting here aboard their ark-fleet, the original colonists had found the surveys had been incorrect. Instead of enjoying a regular orbit, the world they had selected pursued this extreme pattern of darkness and light. They'd settled anyway, co-opting the cryogenerational methods that had got them here as part of their culture. A mistake, in my view.

But I wasn't here to offer a cultural critique.

'Notice anything?' I asked Betancore.

He made a casual gesture around the landing platform. 'They don't get many visitors in this season. Trade's all but dead, the world's on tick-over.'

'Which is why Eyclone thought it vulnerable.'

'Yes. Most of the ships here are local, trans-atmospheric. Some are for the custodians' use, the others are simply berthed-up over Dormant. I make three non-locals, aside from us. Two trader launches and a private cutter.'

'Ask around. See if you can find out who they belong to and what their business is.'

'Sure thing.'

'Eyclone's pinnace, the one you shot down. Did it come from here?'

He took a suck on his narc-tube and shook his head. 'Either came from orbit, or up from some private location. Lowink picked up its transmissions to Eyclone.'

'I'll ask to see those. But it could have come from orbit? Eyclone may have a starship up there?'

'Don't worry, I already thought to look. If there was one there, it's gone, and it made no signals.'

'I'd like to know how that bastard got here, and how he was intending to leave again.'

'I'll find that out,' said Betancore, crushing the tube stub under his heel. He meant it.

'What about Vibben?' he asked.

'Do you know what her wishes were? She never mentioned anything to me. Did she want her remains sent back to Tornish for burial?'

'You'd do that?'

'If that was what she wanted. Is it?'

'I don't know, Eisenhorn. She never told me either.'

'Take a look through her effects, see if she left any testament or instructions. Can you do that?'

'I'd like to do that,' he said.

I was tired by then. I spent another hour with Aemos in his cramped, data-slate-filled room, preparing a report for Carpel. I set out the basic details, reserving anything I felt he didn't need to know. I accounted for my actions. I made Aemos check them against local law, to prepare myself in case Carpel raised a prosecution. I wasn't unduly worried about him, and in truth I was bulletproof against local legislation, but I wanted to check anyway. An Amalathian prides himself on working with the structures of Imperial society, not above or beyond them. Or through them, as a monodominant might.

I wanted Carpel and the senior officials of Hubris on my side, helping my investigation.

When my report was complete, I retired to my room. I paused by Vibben's door, went in, and gently placed the Scipio naval pistol between her hands on her chest, folding the shroud back afterwards. It was hers, it had done its work. It deserved to be laid to rest with her.

For the first time in six years, I did not dream about Eyclone. I dreamed of a blinding darkness, then a light that refused to go away. There was something dark about the light. Nonsense, I know, but that was how it felt. Like a revelation that actually carried some grimmer, more profound truth. There were flashes, like lightning, around the edges of my dream's horizon. I saw a handsome, blank-eyed male, not blank-eyed like one of Eyclone's drones, but vacant like an immense, star-less distance. He smiled at me.

At that time in my life, I had no idea who he was.

I went to see Carpel at noon the next day. It was always noon in the Sun-dome, but this was real noon by the clock. By then, Lowink, Aemos and Betancore had all dredged up new information for me.

I shaved, and dressed in black linen with high boots and a formal jacket of scaled brown hide. I wore my Inquisitorial rosette at my throat. I intended to show Carpel I meant business.

Aemos and I descended from the landing platform superstructure by caged elevator and found yellow-robed custodians waiting to escort us. Despite the rancid white light all around, they still held ignited light poles. We made short, hard shadows on the dry rockcrete of the concourse as we crossed to an open limousine. It was a massive chrome-grilled beast with pennants bearing the Hubris crest fluttering on its cowling. There were four rows of overstuffed leather benches behind the centre-set driver's cockpit.

We hummed through the streets on eight fat wheels. The boulevards were wide and, needless to say, bright. To either hand, glass-fronted buildings rose towards the blazing plasma sun-globe high above, like flowers seeking the light. Every thirty metres along every street, chemical lamps on ornate posts strained to add their own light to the brilliance.

Traffic was sparse, and there were at most a few thousand pedestrians on the streets. I noticed most wore yellow silk sashes, and that garlands of yellow flowers decorated every lamp post.

'The flowers?' I asked.

'From the hydroponic farms on east-dome seven,' one of the custodians told me.

'Signifying?'

'Mourning.'

'Same as the sashes,' Aemos whispered in confidence. 'What happened last night is a major tragedy for this world. Yellow is their holy colour. I believe the local religion is a solar belief.'

'The sun as Emperor?'

'Common enough. Extreme here, for obvious reasons.'

The custodial hall was a glass spire close to the town centre, a solar disk overlaid with the double-headed eagle of the Imperium decorating its upper faces. Nearby was the local chapel of the Ecclesiarchy, and several buildings given over to the Imperial Administratum. It amused me to see they were all built of black stone and virtually windowless. Those Imperial servants stationed here obviously had as little truck as me with the constant light.

We drew in under a glass portico and were escorted into

the main hall. It was seething with people, most of them custodians in yellow robes, some local officials and technomagi,
some clerks and servitors. The hall itself was of the scale of
an Imperial chapel, but raised in yellow-stained glass on a
frame of black cast-iron. The air was full of golden light shaft-
ing down through the glass. The carpet was vast, black, with
a sun-disk woven into its centre.

'Inquisitor Eisenhorn!' declared one of my escorts through
a vox-hailer. The hall fell silent, and all turned to watch
us approach. High Custodian Carpel sat on a hovering
lifter-throne with gilt decorations. A burning chemical light
was mounted above the head of the floating chair. He swung
in through the parting crowd towards me.

'High custodian,' I said with a dutiful nod.

'They are all dead,' he informed me. 'All twelve thousand,
one hundred and forty-two. Processional Two-Twelve is dead.
None survived the trauma.'

'Hubris has my sincere sympathies, high custodian.'

The hall exploded in pandemonium, voices screeching and
shouting and clamouring.

'Your sympathies? Your damned sympathies?' Carpel
screamed above the roar. 'A great part of our ruling elite die
in one night, and we have your sympathies to console us?'

'That is all I can offer, high custodian.' I could feel Aemos
shivering at my side, making aimless notes on his wrist slate
about custom and clothing and language forms... anything
to take his mind from the confrontation.

'That's hardly good enough!' spat a young man nearby. He
was a local noble, young and firm enough, but his skin had
a dreadful, sweaty pallor and custodians supported him as
he stumbled forward.

'Who are you?' I asked.

'Vernal Maypell, heir-lord of the Dallowen Cantons!' If he expected me to fall to my knees in supplication, he was in for a disappointment.

'Because of the gravity of this event, we have roused some of our high-born early from their dormancy,' Carpel said. 'Liege Maypell's brother and two of his wives died in Processional Two-Twelve.'

So the pallor was revival sickness. I noticed that fifty or more of the congregation present were similarly wasted and ill.

I turned to Maypell.

'Liege. I repeat, you have my condolences.'

Maypell exploded with rage. 'Your arrogance astounds me, off-worlder! You bring this monster to our world, battle with him through our most sacred sanctums, a private war that slaughters our best and you–'

'Wait!' I used my will. I didn't care. Maypell stopped as if stunned and the vast hall rang silent. 'I came here to save you and deny Eyclone's plans. But for the efforts of myself and my companions, he might have destroyed more than one of your hibernation tombs. I broke none of your laws. I was careful to preserve your codes in pursuit of my work. What do you mean, I brought this monster here?'

'We have made enquiries,' answered an elderly noblewoman nearby. Like Maypell, she was ailing with revival sickness, and sat hunched on a litter carried by slaved servitors.

'What enquiries, madam?'

'This long feud with the murderer Eyclone. Five years, is it now?'

'Six, lady.'

'Six, then. You have hounded him here. Driven him. Brought him, as Liege Maypell said.'

'How?'

'We registered no off-world ship these past twenty days except yours, Eisenhorn,' Carpel said, reviewing a data-slate. 'The Regal Akwitane. That ship must have brought him as it brought you, to finish your war here and damn our lives. Did you choose Hubris because it was quiet, out of the way, a place where you might finish your feud undisturbed, in the long dark?'

I was angry by now. I concentrated to control my rage. 'Aemos?'

Beside me, he was muttering '...and what silicate dyes do they use in their stained glass manufacture? Is the structure armoured? The supports are early Imperial Gothic in style, but–'

'Aemos! The report!'

He started and handed me a data-slate from his leather case.

'Read this, Carpel. Read it thoroughly.' I pushed it at him – then snatched it away as he reached for it. 'Or should I read it aloud to all here assembled? Should I explain how I came here at the last minute when I learned Eyclone was moving to Hubris? That I learned that only by astropathic decryption of a cipher message sent by Eyclone two months ago? A cipher that killed my astropath in his efforts to translate it?'

'Inquisitor, I–' Carpel began.

I held up the data-slate report for them all, thumbing the stud that scrolled the words across the screen. 'And what about this? The evidence that Eyclone has been planning a move against your world for almost a year? And this, gathered this last night – that an unregistered starship moved in and out of your orbit to deliver Eyclone three days ago, unnoticed by your planetary overwatch and the custodian

"Guardians"? Or the itemised stream of astropathic communication that your local enclave noticed but didn't bother to
source or translate?'

I tossed the slate into Carpel's lap. Hundreds of eyes stared
at me in shocked silence.

'You were wide open. He exploited you. Don't blame me
for anything except being too late to stop him. As I said, you
have my sincere condolences.'

'And next time you choose to confront an Imperial inquisitor,' I added, 'you may want to be more respectful. I'm
excusing a lot because I recognise the trauma and loss you
have suffered. But my patience isn't limitless... unlike my
authority.'

I turned to Carpel. 'Now, high custodian, can we talk? In
private, as I think I requested.'

We followed Carpel's floating throne into a side annexe leaving a hall full of murmuring shocked voices behind us. Only
one of his men accompanied us, a tall, blond fellow in a dark
brown uniform I didn't recognise. A bodyguard, I presumed.
Carpel set his throne down on the carpet and raised a remote
wand that tinted the glass plates of the room at a touch.

Reasonable light levels at last. From that alone, I knew Carpel was taking me seriously.

He waved me to a seat opposite. Aemos lurked in the shadows behind me. The man in brown stood by the windows,
watching.

'What happens now?' Carpel asked.

'I expect your full co-operation as I extend my investigation.'

'But the matter is over,' said the man in brown.

I kept my gaze on Carpel. 'I want your consent for me to
continue as well as your full co-operation. Eyclone may be

dead, but he was just the blade-point of a long and still dangerous weapon.'

'What are you talking about?' the man in brown snapped.

Still I did not look at him. Staring at Carpel, I said, 'If he speaks again without me knowing who he is, I will throw him out of the window. And I won't open it first.'

'This is Chastener Fischig, of the Adeptus Arbites. I wanted him present.'

Now I looked at the man in brown. He was a heavy-set brute with a loop of shiny pink scar tissue under one milky eye. I'd taken him to be a young man with his clean skin and blond hair, but now I studied him, I saw he was at least my age.

'Chastener,' I nodded.

'Inquisitor,' he returned. 'My question stands.'

I sat back in my chair. 'Murdin Eyclone was a facilitator. A brilliant, devious man, one of the most dangerous I have ever hunted. Sometimes to hunt down your prey is to finish his evil. I'm sure you have experience of that.'

'You called him a "facilitator".'

'That was where his danger lay. He believed he could serve his obscene masters best by offering his considerable skills to cults and sects that needed them. He had no true allegiances. He worked to facilitate the grand schemes of others. What he was doing here on Hubris was to advance and develop someone else's plans. Now he is dead, and his scheme thwarted. We may be thankful. But my task is not done. I must work back from Eyclone, his men, from any clue he left and dig my way into whatever greater, secret darkness was employing him.'

'And for this you want the co-operation of the people of Hubris?' asked Carpel.

'The people, the authorities, you... everyone. This is the Emperor's work. Will you shrink from it?'

'No sir, I will not!' snapped Carpel.

'Excellent.'

Carpel tossed a gold solar-form badge to me. It was heavy and old, mounted on a pad of black leather.

'This will give you authority. My authority. Conduct your work thoroughly and quickly. I ask two things in return.'

'And they are?'

'You report all findings to me. And you allow the chastener to accompany you.'

'I work my own way–'

'Fischig can open doors and voiceboxes here in the Sun-dome that even that badge may not. Consider him a local guide.'

And your ears and eyes, I thought. But I knew he was under immense pressure from the nobility to produce results, so I said: 'I will be grateful for his assistance.'

'Where first?' Fischig asked, down to business at once, a hungry look on his face. They want blood, I realised. They want someone to punish for the deaths, someone they can say they caught, or at least helped to catch. They want to share in whatever successes I have so that they can look good when the rest of their population wakes up to this disaster in a few months' time.

I couldn't blame them.

'First,' I said, 'the mortuary.'

Eyclone looked as if he was asleep. His head had been wrapped in an almost comical plastic bonnet to contain the wound I had dealt him. Framed in the plastic, his face was tranquil, with just a slight bruising around the lips.

He lay on a stone plinth in the chill of the morgue below Arbites Mortuary One. His brethren lay on numbered plinths around him, those that had been recovered more or less intact. There were labelled bins of mostly liquescent material against the back wall, the remains of those that Betancore had slaughtered with the cutter's cannons.

The air in the underground vault was lit cold blue, and frost covered circulators pumped in sub-zero air directly from the ice-desert outside the Sun-dome. Fischig had provided us all with heat gowns for the visit.

I was impressed by what I saw: both the dutiful care and attention that had been used to sequester and store the bodies and by the fact that no one had touched them, according to my instructions. It seems a simple command to give, but I have lost count of the times that over-eager death-priests or surgeons have begun autopsies before I arrived.

The mortician superintendent was a haggard woman in her sixties called Tutrone. She attended us in red plastic scrubs worn over an old and threadbare heat-gown. Mortress Tutrone had a bionic implant in one eye socket, and blades and bonesaw manipulators of gleaming surgical steel built into her right hand.

'I have done as you instructed,' she told me as she led us down the spiral steps into the cold vault. 'But it is irregular. Rules state I must begin examinations, prelim examinations at least, as soon as possible.'

'I thank you for your diligence, mortress. I will be done quickly. Then you can follow protocol.'

Pulling on surgical gloves, I moved through the lines of dead – there were nearly twenty of them – dictating observations of Aemos. There was virtually nothing to be learned from the men. Some I gauged from build and coloration to be off-worlders, but they had no documents, no surgical identifiers, no clue whatsoever about their origins or identities. Even their clothing was blank... manufacturing tags and labels had been torn or burned off. I could begin a forensic investigation to identify the source of the clothing, but that would be a massive waste of resources.

On two of them, I found fresh scars that suggested subcutaneous ident markers had been surgically removed. Ident marking was not a local practice, so that at least suggested off-world. But where? Hundreds of Imperial planets routinely used such devices, and their placing and use was pretty standard. I had carried one myself for a few years, as a child, before the Black Ships selected me and it was dug out.

One of the corpses had a curious scarring on the forearms, not deep but thorough, searing the epidermis.

'Someone has used a melta-torch to remove gang tattoos,' Aemos said.

He was right. Again, it was tantalisingly incomplete.

I looked to Eyclone, where I thought my best bet lay. With the Mortress's help, I cut away his clothes, all of which were as anonymous as his followers' garb. We turned his naked corpse, looking for... well, anything.

'There!' Fischig said, leaning in. A brand mark above the left buttock.

'The Seraph of Laoacus. An old Chaos mark. Eyclone had it done to honour his then-masters twenty years ago. A previous cult, a previous employer. Nothing to do with this.'

Fischig looked at me curiously. 'You know the details of his naked flesh?'

'I have sources,' I replied. I didn't want to have to tell the tale. Eemanda, one of my first companions, brilliant, beautiful and bold. She had found that detail out for me. She had been in an asylum now for five years. The last report I had received said she had eaten away her own fingers.

'But he marks himself?' Fischig added. 'With each new cult he involves himself in, he carries their mark to show his allegiance?'

The man had a point, damn him. We looked. At least six laser scars on his body seemed likely to have been previous cult marks, burned off after he left those associations.

Behind his left ear, a skin inlay of silver was worked in the form of the Buboe Chaotica.

'This?' asked Tutrone, shaving the hair aside with her finger blades to reveal it.

'Old, as before.'

I stepped back from the body and thought hard. When I'd killed him, he had been reaching for something on his belt, or so it had seemed to me.

'His effects?'

They were laid out on a metal tray nearby. His laspistol, a compact vox-device, a pearl-inlaid box containing six obscura tubes and an igniter, a credit tile, spare cells for the gun, a plastic key. And the belt; with four buttoned pouches.

I opened them one by one: some local coins; a miniature las-knife; three bars of high-calorie rations; a steel tooth-pick; more obscura, this time in an injector vial; a small data-slate.

At the moment of death, which of these things had he been reaching for? The knife? Too slow and small to counter a man who has a naval pistol wedged into your mouth. Then again, he was desperate.

And then again, he hadn't reached for his holstered lasgun.

The data-slate, perhaps? I picked it up and activated it, but it needed a cipher to gain access. All manner of secrets might be locked inside... but why would a man reach for a data-slate in the face of certain death?

'Track marks, along the forearm,' Tutrone stated, continuing her exam.

Hardly surprising, given the narco-ware we'd recovered from him.

'No rings? No bracelets? Earrings? Piercing studs?'

'None.'

I pulled a plastic pouch from a dispenser on the surgical cart and put all his effects into it.

'You will sign for those, won't you?' Tutrone asked, looking up.

'Of course.'

'You hated him, didn't you?' Fischig said suddenly.

'What?'

He leaned back against a plinth, crossing his arms. 'You had him at your mercy, and you knew his head was full of secrets, but you emptied it with your gun. I have no compunction when it comes to killing, but I know when I'm wasting a lead. Was it rage?'

'I'm an inquisitor. I do not get angry.'

'Then what?'

I had just about enough of his snide tone. 'You don't know how dangerous this man is. I wasn't taking chances.'

'He looks safe enough to me,' Fischig smirked, looking down at the body.

'Here's something!' Tutrone called out. We all moved in.

She was working on his left hand, delicately, with her finest gauge scalpels and probes, her augmented fingers darting like a seamstress.

'The index finger of the left hand. There's unusual lividity and swelling.' She played a small scanner across it.

'The nail's ceramite. Artificial. An implant.'

'What's inside?'

'Unknown. A ghost reading. There's maybe... ah, there it is... a catch under the quick. You'd need something small to trigger it.'

She adjusted her bionic finger settings and slid out a very thin metal probe, thin like...

...a tooth pick.

'Back! Back now!' I yelled.

It was too late. Tutrone had undone the catch. The false nail sprang back and something flew out of the cavity in the finger tip. A silver worm, like a thread of necklace chain, flashed through the air.

'Where did it go?'

'I don't know, I said, pushing Tutrone and Aemos behind me. 'Did you see it?' I asked Fischig.

'Over there,' he said, pulling a short-nosed gloss-black autopistol out from his robes.

I reached for my own gun, then remembered I'd given it back to Vibben.

I snatched up a bone knife from the trolley.

The worm slithered back into the light. It was a metre long and several centimetres thick now. What foul sorcery had caused that expansion, I did not want to know. It was made of segmented metal, and the head was an eyeless cone split by a hissing mouth full of razor teeth.

Tutrone cried out as it flew at us. I pushed her down and the thing whipped across over us, hitting a corpse on a nearby plinth. There was a dreadful sucking, gnawing sound and the worm disappeared into the corpse's torso through a jagged hole.

The corpse vibrated and ruptured, filling the air with a foul mist of vapour. The worm swished up out of it and disappeared across the floor. By then, Fischig had opened fire and blasted the shattered corpse off its plinth. The worm was long since gone.

'Touch-activated mechanism,' Aemos was murmuring to himself, 'very discreet, probably of Xenos manufacture, a guard weapon, with some mass-altering system that expands it on contact with air and/or release, hunting by sound...'

'So shut up!' I told him. I bundled him and Tutrone against the far wall. Fischig and I moved in parallel courses down through the plinth rows, weapons ready.

It reappeared. By the time I saw it, it was almost on me, thrashing forward through the air on its metallic tail. In a split second, I reflected that this was how Eyclone had wanted me to die. This was what he had intended to unleash against me on the landing platform at Processional Two-Twelve.

Rage made me deny him. I stabbed out and my extended blade jabbed directly between the gaping teeth and down the gullet. The impact knocked me back. I found I had the whole, heavy, two-metre thing thrashing on the end of my knife like a lash.

Shots banged past me. Fischig was trying to hit it.

'You'll kill me, you idiot!'

'Hold it still!'

With a metallic rasping, it was chewing down the blade and the handle towards my hand.

Tutrone came in from behind me and together we wrestled the powerful, coiling thing onto a plinth. She activated a bone-saw on her augmetic hand and sliced down through its neck with a shrill scream of spinning blades.

The body continued to thrash. She grabbed it and dropped it into an acid trough usually reserved for bio-waste. The hissing head and the knife it was still chewing away at quickly followed it.

The four of us gazed down at the thrashing remains as they disintegrated.

I looked round at Mortress Tutrone and Fischig.

'I know which one of you I'd rather have around in a fight,' I muttered.

Tutrone laughed. Fischig didn't.

'What was it?' Aemos asked me as we raced in Fischig's landspeeder through the streets to the Arbites' headquarters.

'You guessed more than I know,' I replied. 'A gift from his masters, certainly.'

'What manner of masters make a thing like that?'

'Powerful ones, Aemos. The worst kind.'

Our meeting at the Arbites' grim chambers was brief. At my request, Fischig had summoned Magus Palastemes, the head of the cryogenerator technomagi.

He took one look at the casket in the evidence room and said, 'I have no idea what it is.'

'Thank you. That will be all,' I told him. I turned to Fischig. 'Have this sent immediately to my vessel.'

'It is state's evidence—' he began.

'Who do you work for, Fischig?'

'The Emperor.'

'Then pretend I'm him and you won't be far wrong. Do it.'

Hadam Bonz was waiting for us in the interrogation room. He had been stripped naked, but Fischig assured me nothing of import had been found in his clothes.

Bonz was the gunman I had laid out in the cryogenerator

chamber, the only one of Eyclone's men to have survived the night. His mouth was swollen from my blow. He had admitted nothing except his name.

Fischig, Aemos and I entered the room, a dull stone box. Bonz was shackled to a metal chair and looked terrified.

So should he, I thought.

'Tell me about Murdin Eyclone,' I said.

'Who?' The darkness had gone from his eyes now, Eyclone's spell broken. He was bewildered and confused.

'Then tell me the last thing you remember.'

'I was on Thracian Primaris. That was my home. I was a stevedore in the docks. I remember going to a bar with a friend. That is all.'

'The friend?'

'A dock master called Wyn Eddon. We got drunk, I think.'

'Did Eddon mention an Eyclone?'

'No. Look, where am I? These bastards won't say. What I am supposed to have done?'

I smiled. 'You tried to kill me for a start.'

'You?'

'I'm an Imperial inquisitor.'

At that, terror made him lose control of his body functions. He began pleading, begging, telling us all sorts of misdemeanours, none of which mattered.

I knew from the first moments that he was useless. Just a mesmerised slave, chosen for his muscle, knowing nothing. But we spent two hours with him anyway. Fischig slowly turned a wall dial near the door that vented in increasing measures of the sub-zero air outside the Sun-dome. In our heat gowns, we asked questions over and again.

When Bonz's flesh began to adhere to the metal chair, we knew there was nothing more.

'Warm him up and feed him well,' Fischig told his men as we left the cell. 'We execute him at dawn.'

I didn't ask if that meant some arbitrary time in the next cycle or real dawn, six months away, at the start of Thaw.

I didn't much care.

Fischig left us to our own devices for a while, and I ate lunch with Aemos at a public bistro almost directly under the Sun-dome. The food was sour, rehashed from freeze-dried consumables, but at least it was hot. Fountain banks projected walls of water around the edges of the bistro so that the sun-globe light made rainbows that criss-crossed the tables and aisles. On this sombre day of mourning, there were no other diners present.

Aemos was in good spirits. He chatted away, making connections I hadn't begun to see. For all his faults, he possessed a superb mind. Every hour I spent with him, I learned more techniques.

He was forking up fish and rice and reviewing his data-slate.

'Let's look at the transmission lag that Lowink detected in the messages Eyclone sent and received while on the planet.'

'They're all in cipher. Lowink hasn't unlocked them yet.'

'Yes, yes, but look at the lag. This one... eight seconds... that's from a ship in orbit... and the timeframe matches that period in which we know Eyclone's mysterious starship was here. But this... during your struggle with him last night. A lag of twelve and a half minutes. That's from another system.'

I stopped trying to macerate a lump of meat that resembled a slug and peered over. I'd never much considered the blurry side-bar that edged all astropathic message forms before.

'Twelve and a half? You're sure?'

'I had Lowink check.'

'So that gives us a reference frame?'

He smiled, pleased I was pleased. 'Three worlds in the picture. All between eleven and fifteen minutes' lag of here. Thracian Primaris, Kobalt II and Gudrun.'

Thracian Primaris was no surprise. That had been our last port of call, our last sighting of Eyclone. And, as far as we knew from the wretched Bonz, the place where he had recruited some or all of his servants.

'Kobalt's a nothing. I checked. Just an Imperial watch station. But Gudrun–'

'A primary trade world. Old culture, old families–'

'Old poisons,' he finished with a laugh, completing the proverb.

I dabbed my mouth with a napkin. 'Can we be more certain?'

'Lowink's researching for me. Once we break the cipher... I don't mean the message cipher itself, I mean the coded headers to the actual text, we'll know.'

'Gudrun...' I pondered.

My vox-link chimed in my ear. It was Betancore.

'Ever hear of a thing called the Pontius?'

'No. Why?'

'I haven't either, but Lowink's cracking some of the old transcripts. In the weeks before Eyclone arrived, someone was sending messages off the approved links to a location in the Sun-dome. They talk about the delivery of "The Pontius". It's all rather vague and indirect.'

'Do you have a location?'

'Why else do you employ us? Thaw-view 12011, on the west side of the dome, the high-rent quarter. Aristo turf.'

'Any names?'

'No, they're very exclusive and coy about such things.'

'We're on it.'

Aemos and I rose from the table. We turned to find Fischig standing there. He was wearing the full flak armour, carapace and visored helm of an Arbites now. I have to admit the effect was impressive.

'Going somewhere without me, inquisitor?'

'Going to find you, actually. Take us to Thaw-view.'

FOUR

The Sun-dome toured at speed
Thaw-view 12011
Questioning Saemon Crotes

The wealthiest Hubrites kept winter palaces on the west perimeter of the Sun-dome. According to Chastener Fischig, they 'enjoyed both light and dark' as if that was something indulgent. They looked inwards to the lit dome and had shutters that could be opened to view the dark landscape of the winter desert. It was a spiritual thing, Aemos suggested.

Fischig shut down his terrain-following guidance as we sliced through the streets, and his heavy speeder rose up above the traffic and buildings. We hooked hard turns between glass spires and roared west.

I think he was showing off.

In the rear seating, under the roll-bars, Aemos clung on and closed his eyes with a soft groan. I rode up front with the armoured Fischig, seeing a predatory grin on his face under the visor of his Arbites helmet.

The speeder was a standard Imperial model, painted

matt-brown and sporting the badges of the solar symbol and the chevrons and tail number of the local Arbites. Armoured, it turned heavily, the anti-grav straining to keep us aloft. There was a heavy bolter pintle-mounted forward of my seat. I glanced around and saw a locked rack of combat shotguns behind the rear seats.

'Give me one of those!' I yelled above the slipstream and the choppy thrum of the turbo-fans.

'What?'

'I need a weapon!'

Fischig nodded and keyed a security code into a pad built into his bulky control stick. The cage on the gun-rack popped.

'Take one!'

Aemos handed one over to me, and I began loading shells.

Thaw-view rose before us, a terrace of luxurious crystal-glass and ferrocrete dwellings built into the curve of the dome itself. We whipped low over stepped gardens, making ferns and palms shudder in our downwash.

Then Fischig keyed the fans to idle and we settled on a wide veranda deck, eight storeys up.

He leapt out, racking his shotgun.

I followed him.

'Stay here,' I told Aemos. He needed no further encouragement.

'Which one?' Fischig asked.

'12011.'

We edged along the wide, curving deck, clambering over dividing rails and trellises of climbing flowers.

12011 was glass-fronted, with wide sliding doors of mirrored window-plate.

Fischig swept up a warning hand, and took a coin from his

pocket. He flipped it onto the terrace and it was atomised by nine separate las-beams.

He keyed his vox. 'Chastener Fischig to Arbites control, copy?'

'Copy, chastener.'

'Access dome central and shut down auto-defences on Thaw-view 12011. Immediate.'

A pause.

'Shut down authorised.'

He made to step forward. I halted him and tossed a coin of my own.

It bounced twice on the basalt terrace and rolled to a halt.

'I like to be sure,' I said.

We came up either side of the main picture window. Fischig tried the slider but it was locked.

He stepped back, apparently preparing to shoot the window in.

'It's arma-plex,' I told him, rapping my knuckles off the material. 'Don't be stupid.'

I pulled the plastic bag containing Eyclone's effects from my jacket and searched for the compact las-knife. Before I found it, I found the plastic key.

Slim chances but what the crud, as Inquisitor Hapshant used to say.

I slid the key into the frame lock and the window slid aside on motorised rails.

We both waited. Perfumed air and light orchestral music wafted out past us.

'Adeptus Arbites! Make yourselves known!' Fischig bellowed, his voice amplified by his helmet speaker.

They did.

Rapid gunfire, heavy calibre, blew away the terrace rail,

decapitated potted shrubs and dwarf trees, cropped flower beds, and chopped down the deck's aerial mast.

'Have it your way!' bellowed Fischig and rolled in, pumping his shotgun. The blasts were deafening.

I clambered up a drain-spout onto the second level balcony, my shotgun dangling around my shoulders on its strap. Furious exchanges of fire rumbled below me.

I went in through a gauze-draped opening into the main bedrooms.

The room was over-warm and dark, dressed in red velvet with soothing, ambient music welling from hidden vox-speakers. The bed was in disarray. In one corner, on a gilt credenza, sat a portable vox-set. I padded forward and studied the responder log. Fischig's chaos down below rumbled through the floor like a distant storm.

The girl came out of a side room, a bathroom I imagine, and shrieked when she saw me. She was naked, and dived under the bedclothes for cover.

The muzzle of my shotgun tracked her.

'Who's here?'

She whimpered and shook her head.

'Inquisition,' I hissed. 'Who's here?'

She began to sob and shook her head again.

'Stay down. Get under the bed if you can.'

In the adjoining room, I heard whistling. A voice called out a name.

'Don't answer,' I told the weeping girl.

I moved slowly round to the side room door. Light shone out. There was a hint of steam and a smell of bath-oils. The whistling had stopped.

He was wary, I'll give him that. He didn't bluster out, gun blasting.

I tipped open the door with the snout of my weapon and five high velocity rounds shredded holes in the wood panel.

I fell to my belly on the floor and fired three shots in through the door gap.

'Inquisition! Throw down your weapon!'

Two more shots punched through the door.

I crawled backwards from the doorway and stood up, the gun resting in my hands.

'Come out.' I said, using my will.

A large, tattooed, naked male blundered out of the bathroom, half his face shaved and half covered with sudsy foam. A Tronsvasse Hi-Power autopistol was still in one hand.

'Put it down,' I commanded.

He hesitated, as if my will had no force. A conditioned mind, I supposed. Take no chances.

The autopistol was just pulling up to find me when I blew off his half-shaved face with the shotgun and sent his body splintering back through the half-open door.

The girl was still crouched, naked, at the end of the bed, shivering. I was surprised she hadn't bolted out of cover at my command too.

I spun to face her.

'What's your name?'

'Lise B.'

'Full name!' I snapped. I wasn't concentrating on her especially, but there was something about her. An air. A *tone*.

'Alizebeth Bequin! Pleasure girl! I worked the Sun-dome these past four Dormants!'

'You're here why?'

'They paid up front! Wanted a party! Oh lords...'

Her voice trailed away and she collapsed on the bed.

'Get dressed. Stay here. I will want to talk to you.'

I moved to the door of the chamber and looked out into the unlit hall. Below, down the stairwell, gunflashes and shouts echoed up.

Seeing my shape in the doorway, a man ran towards me.

'Wylk! Wylk! They've found us! They've–'

A moment before he realised I was not Wylk, I decked him with the butt of my weapon. He fell hard.

Two solid shots raked the doorframe next to me.

I ducked back in, sliding back the grip of the shotgun.

Shots punched through the wall above the bed-head. Bequin screamed and rolled off the bed.

I blasted back, punching two more large holes in the door.

Two men slammed into the room, wild-eyed and desperate. Both were dressed in light interior clothes. One had a laspistol, the other an autorifle.

I dropped the lasgunner with one direct shot that hurled his body against the wall. The man with the autorifle opened fire, his shots chewing through one of the bed-posts.

I dived for cover as the automatic fire ripped up tufts of carpet, shattered mirrors and demolished furnishings.

Rolling, I frantically sought cover.

My would-be killer dropped face-down onto the bed. The girl pulled a long retractable knife out of the back of his neck.

'I saved your life,' she told me. 'That'll make it better for me, right?'

I told the girl to stay put in the bedroom, and from her nod I was pretty sure she would.

I stepped out into the gloomy hall. The level below had fallen silent.

'Fischig?' I voxed.

'Come down,' his reply crackled back.

A spiral stairway led down into a large, split-level lounge area. The air was thick with smoke, which coiled out of the terrace window-doors we had opened. The hard daylight of the Sun-dome streamed in, making ladder-bars of light in the drifting haze. The opposite wall of the room was a wide segmented shutter. If opened, it would reveal a view over the freezing wastes beyond the dome.

A storm of gunfire had ruined the expensive furniture and decorative fittings. Five corpses lay twisted at various points on the floor. Fischig, his visor raised, was hauling a sixth man up into a high-backed chair. The man, wounded in the right shoulder, was wailing and crying. Fischig cuffed him into place.

'Upstairs?' Fischig asked me without looking round.

'Clear,' I reported.

I walked round the room, eyeing the dead and examining items left scattered on tabletops and bureaux.

'I know some of these men,' the chastener added, unsolicited. 'Those two by the window. Locals, low-grade labourers. Long list of petty convictions on both.'

'Hired muscle.'

'Seems to be your man's way. The others are off-worlders.'

'You've found papers?'

'No, it's just a hunch. None of them have got any ID or markers, and I haven't found a cache anywhere.'

'What about this one?' I walked over to join him by the prisoner he had cuffed to the chair. The man coughed and whined, rolling his eyes. Unless he possessed unnaturally boosted strength thanks to drugs or hidden augmetics, this man wasn't muscle. He was older, spare of frame, with grizzled salt and pepper growth on his chin.

'You didn't kill this one deliberately, did you?' I asked

Fischig. He smiled slightly, as if pleased that I had noticed.

'I– I have rights!' The man spat suddenly.

'You are in the custody of the Imperial Inquisition,' I told him frankly. 'You have no rights whatsoever.'

He fell silent.

'Off-worlder,' Fischig said. I raised an eyebrow. 'Accent,' Fischig explained.

I'd never have detected it myself. This was one of the reasons I used local help whenever I got the chance, even a potential troublemaker like the chastener. My work takes me from world to world, culture to culture. Slight differences in dialect or incongruities of slang regularly pass me by. But Fischig had heard it at once. And it made sense. If this was a leader rather than muscle, one of Eyclone's chosen lieutenants, then the odds were he was from off-world.

'Your name?' I asked.

'I will not answer.'

'Then I will not have that wound treated for a while.'

He shook his head. The wound was bad and he was obviously in considerable pain, but he resisted. I was even more certain he was a ringleader. He was no longer shaking or whining. He had switched in some mental conditioning, no doubt taught by Eyclone.

'Mind tricks won't help you,' I said. 'I'm much better at them than you are.'

'Go screw yourself.'

I glanced at Fischig out of courtesy. 'Brace yourself.' He stepped back.

'Tell me your name,' I said, using my will.

The man in the chair spasmed. 'Saemon Crotes!' he gasped.

'Godwyn Fischig,' spat the chastener involuntarily. He blushed and moved away, busying himself with a search.

'Very well, Saemon Crotes, where are you from?' I didn't employ any will now. In my experience, it took only one blow to loosen mental defences.

'Thracian Primaris.'

'What was your job there?'

'I was trade envoy for the Bonded Merchant Guild of Sinesias.'

I knew the name. Guild Sinesias was one of the largest mercantile companies in the sector. It had holdings on a hundred-plus planets and links to the Imperial nobility. It also, as Betancore had informed me just that morning, had a trade launch berthed at the Sun-dome landing stage.

'And what work brought you to Hubris?'

'That same work... as a trade-envoy.'

'In Dormant?'

'There is always trade to be had. Long-term contracts with the authorities on this world that require the personal touch.'

'And if I contact your guild, will it confirm this?'

'Of course.'

I walked around behind him. 'So what brought you here? To these private apartments?'

'I was a guest.'

'Of who?'

'Namber Wylk, a local trader. He invited me for a mid-Dormant feast.'

'This dwelling is registered to Namber Wylk,' Fischig put in. 'A trader, as he says, no priors. I don't know him.'

'What about Eyclone?' I asked Crotes, leaning down to stare into his eyes. There was a ripple of fear in them.

'Who?'

'Your real employer. Murdin Eyclone. Don't make me ask you again.'

'I don't know any Eyclone!' There was a ring of truth to his voice. He may well not have known Eyclone by that name.

I dragged up a chair and sat down facing him. 'There is an awful lot of your story that doesn't add up. You're found here consorting with recidivists who we can connect to a planetary conspiracy. There are charges of murder to be considered – a lot of them. We can continue this in far more intimate and comprehensive circumstances, or you can make me like you more by filling in some details now.'

'I... don't know what to tell you...'

'Whatever you know. About the Pontius, perhaps?'

A dark, stricken look crossed his face. His jaw worked for a moment, trying to form words. He quivered. Then there was a liquid pop and his head fell forward.

'Throne of Light!' Fischig cried.

'Damn it,' I growled, and bent down to lift Crotes's limp skull. He was dead. Eyclone had left failsafes in the conditioning that would trigger at certain subjects. The Pontius evidently was one of those.

'A stroke. Artificially induced.'

'So we know nothing?'

'We know a great deal? Weren't you listening? For a start we know the Pontius is the most precious secret they protect.'

'So tell me about it?'

I was about to, at least evasively, when the shutter barring the far wall to the climate extremes of the world outside the dome blew out. Hidden charges fired simultaneously. The metal sheet splayed outwards into the freezing dark. The blast-force threw both Fischig and myself to the ground.

A millisecond later, the shattered crystal in the portal blew back in at us, carried by the hurricane power of the Dormant winds outside – a blizzard of billions of razor-sharp slivers.

FIVE

Covered traces
The Glaws of Gudrun
Unwelcome companions

Deafened by the blast, I had wit enough left to grab Fischig and roll with him out through the terrace doors as the emergency shutter clanked down from its slit in the hardwood ceiling. We lay panting and half-blind on the terrace, the hard light and warmth of the Sun-dome thawing our cold-shocked bodies.

Alarms and warning bells sounded all along the Thaw-view residences. Arbites units were already on their way.

We got up. Our clothes and simple good fortune had protected us from the worst of the glass-storm, though I had a gash straight down my left cheek that would need closing, and Fischig had a long splinter of glass embedded in his thigh between armour joints. Apart from that, we had just superficial scratches.

'Bad timing?' he asked, though he knew it wasn't.

'The charges were set off by the same spasm that killed Crotes.'

He glanced away and rebuckled one of his gauntlets, giving himself time to think. His face was a dingy grey colour, mainly through shock. But I think he was now beginning to understand the resources and capabilities of the people we worked against. Their abominable crime at Processional Two-Twelve had demonstrated the scale of their malice, but he hadn't seen that first hand. Now he was witnessing the fanatical servants of a dark cause, men who would fight without hesitation to the death. And he had seen how brutally they would cover their traces, using mental-weapons and brain-wired booby traps that spoke of vast resources and frightening sophistication.

Arbites squads moved into the dwelling and secured it while local medicae servitors patched our wounds. The clearance squads brought out the shivering girl, Bequin. She was wrapped in blankets and her face was pinched blue with cold. Under my seal and instruction, they placed her in custody. She was too cold to voice a complaint.

Fischig and I re-entered wearing heat-gowns. It would be another two or three hours before engineer teams could replace the outer shutter. From the harsh light of the terrace, we passed through three hastily hung insulation curtains into the dim, blue twilight of the apartment. The far wall was gone and we looked directly into the clear, glassy night of Hubris, a glossy grey landscape of stark shadows and backscattered light stretching away from the edge of the Sun-dome. Once more I was exposed to the piercing cold of Dormant and my blood ached.

The main room where we had questioned Crotes was a gutted cavity, blackened by soot and jewelled with glass. Hard lacquers of frost caked furniture surfaces and twisted the faces of the dead. Blood spilt by the shredding storm of glass was crusted like rubies in the dark.

We played the smoky white beams of our lamps around. I doubted we would find much now. There was a good chance any valuable documents had been set to burn or delete on the same trigger signal that had blown the shutter and killed Crotes. And it also seemed likely these people carried all truly important information internally, as memory engrams, or meme-codes, the sort of techniques usually reserved for the higher echelons of diplomatic corps, the Administratum and elite trade delegations.

That turned my mind back to Crotes's employer, the Guild Sinesias.

'It's a common enough name in this sub-sector,' Aemos told me back in the comfortable half-light of the gun-cutter in its landing platform berth. He had been researching the name 'Pontius'. 'I've turned up over half a million citizens with that forename, another two hundred thousand with it as a middle name, plus another forty or fifty thousand spelling variants.'

He waved a data-slate at me. I brushed it aside, and used a hand mirror to study the line of metal butterfly sutures in the wound in my cheek.

'What about the definite article?'

'I have over nine thousand marks with that connection,' he sighed. He began to read them from his slate list. 'The Pontius Swellwin Youth Academy, The Pontius Praxitelles Translation Bureau, The Pontius Gyvant Ropus Investment Financiary, The Pontius Spiegel Microsurgical Hospi–'

'Enough.' I sat at the codifier, typing in name groups. Flickering runes hunted and darted across the view-plate. Text extracts drifted into focus. I searched through them by eye, my finger resting on the scroll bar.

'Pontius Glaw,' I said.

He blinked and looked at me. There was a half-smile of scholarly delight on his narrow face. 'Not on my lists.'

'Because he is dead?'

'Because he's dead.'

Aemos came over and looked across my shoulder at the screen. 'But it makes a sort of sense.'

It did. A kind of illogic that had the flavour of truth. The sort of spore an inquisitor gets a nose for after a few years.

The Glaw family was old blood, a thrusting noble dynasty that had been a main player in this sub-sector for almost a millennium. The primary familial holdings and estates were on Gudrun, a world that had already come to our attention. House Glaw was also a major shareholder and investor in the Regal Bonded Merchant Guild of Sinesias, so the codifier had just revealed to me.

'Pontius Glaw...' I murmured.

Pontius Glaw had been dead for more than two hundred years. The seventh son of Oberon Glaw, one of the great patriarchs of that line, he had suffered the fate of most junior siblings in that there had been precious little for him to inherit once his older brothers had taken their turn. His eldest brother, another Oberon, had become lord of the house; the second eldest had been gifted the control of the stock-holdings; the third had taken on the captaincy of the House Militia; the fourth and fifth had married politically and entered the Administratum at high level... and so it went.

From what I remembered of Pontius Glaw's biography, required reading as a trainee, Pontius had become a dilettante, wasting his life, his robust virility, charisma and finely educated intellect in all manner of worthless pursuits. He had gambled away a significant measure of his personal fortune, then rebuilt it on the revenues of slave-trading and pit-fighting. A ruthless sliver of brutality stained his record.

And then, in his forties, with his health ruined by years of abuse, he turned to a much darker path. It has always been suspected that this turn was triggered by some chance event: an artefact or document that fell into his hands, perhaps the strange beliefs of some of the more barbaric pit-fighters he enslaved. Instinct told me the propensity had always been within him, and that he was looking for a chance to let it flourish. It is documented he was a life-long collector of rare and often prohibited books. At what point might his appetite for licentious and esoteric pornography have spilled over into the heretical and blasphemous?

Pontius Glaw became a disciple of Chaos, a devotee of the most abominable and obscene forces that haunt this galaxy. He drew a coven around him, and over a period of fifteen years committed unspeakable and increasingly brazen acts of evil.

He was slain eventually, his coven along with him, on Lamsarrote, by an Inquisitorial purge led by the great Absalom Angevin. House Glaw participated in this overthrow, desperate to be seen to distance themselves from his crimes. It is likely this alone prevented the entire family from being pulled down with him.

A monster, a notorious monster. And dead, as Aemos had been so quick to point out. Dead for more than two centuries.

But the name and the connection of facts seemed too obvious to ignore.

I wandered up to the cockpit and sat with Betancore. 'We'll need passage off-world, to Gudrun.'

'I'll arrange it. It may be a day or two.'

'As fast as you can.'

I sent word to High Custodian Carpel, informing him of some, though not all, of my findings and telling him I would shortly be leaving to continue my investigations on Gudrun. I was reading through the confidential case records of Inquisitor Angevin when two Arbites brought Bequin to my gun-cutter. I had sent orders for her to be delivered into my charge.

She stood in the crew-bay, frowning in the gloom, cuffed. She had dressed in a tawdry gown and a light cloak, but despite the cheapness of her garb and the discomfort she was in, her considerable beauty was plain to see. Good bones, a full mouth, fierce eyes and long dark hair. Yet, again, there was that air about her, that tone I had detected before. Despite her obvious physical attractions, there was some-thing almost repellent about her. It was curious, but I was convinced I knew what it was.

She glanced round as I entered the crew-bay, her expres-sion a mix of fear and indignation.

'I helped you!' she spat.

'You did. Though I neither asked for nor needed your help.'

She pouted. That air was stronger now, an unpleasant feel-ing that made me want to bundle her out of the cutter and have done with her then and there.

'The Arbites say they will charge me with murder and conspiracy.'

'The Arbites desperately want someone to pin the crimes on. You are unhappily involved in those matters, though I don't believe deliberately.'

'Damn right!' she snarled. 'This has ruined me, my life here! Just when I was getting things together...'

'Your life has been difficult?'

She fixed me with a sneer that questioned my intelligence. I'm a pleasure girl, an object, it seemed to say, lowest of the low... How difficult do you think my life has been?

I stepped forward and removed the Arbites' cuffs. She rubbed her wrists and looked at me in surprise.

'Sit down,' I told her. I was using the will.

She looked at me again, as if wondering what the funny tone was all about, and then calmly took a seat on a padded leather bench along the crew-bay's back wall.

'I can make sure the charges are dropped,' I told her. 'I have that authority. Indeed, my authority is the only reason you haven't been charged or interrogated so far.'

'Why would you do that?'

'I thought you believed I owed you?'

'Doesn't matter what I believe.' There was sullen cast to her face as she looked me up and down. I found myself intrigued. Objectively, I was looking at a girl whose looks and vivacious spirit made her undeniably desirable. Yet I... I almost wanted to shout at her, to drive her away, to get her out of my sight. I had an entirely unwarranted and instinctive loathing for her.

'Even if you clear me, I can't carry on here. They'll hound me out. I'll be marked as trouble. That'll be the end of my work. I'll have to move on again.' She stared down at the floor and muttered a curse. 'Just when I was getting it together!'

'Move on? You're not from Hubris?'

'This miserable shit-pit?'

'Where then?'

'I came here from Thracian Primaris four years ago.'

'You were born on Thracian?'

She shook her head. 'Bonaventure.'

That was half a sector away. 'How did you get from Bon-aventure to Thracian?'

'By way of this and that. Here and there. I've travelled a lot. Never stayed put very long.'

'Because things get difficult?'

The sneer again. 'That's right. I'd stuck it out here longer than anywhere. Now that's all screwed up.'

'Stand up,' I snapped suddenly, using the will again.

She paused and shrugged at me. 'Make your mind up.' She got to her feet.

'I want to ask you some questions about the men who employed you at Thaw-view 12011.'

'I thought you might.'

'If you answer helpfully, I can cut you a deal.'

'What sort of deal?'

'I can take you to Gudrun. Give you a chance to make a new start. Or I can offer you employment, if you're interested.'

She smiled quizzically. It was the first positive expression I had seen on her. It made her more beautiful, but I didn't like her any better.

'Employment? You'd employ me? An inquisitor would employ me?'

'That's right. Certain services I think you can provide.'

She took two fluid steps over to me and placed her hands flat against my chest. 'I see,' she said. 'Even big bad inquisi-tors have needs, huh? That's fine.'

'You misunderstand,' I replied, pushing her back as politely as I could. Physical contact with her made the unnatural feeling of revulsion even stronger. 'The services I have in mind will be new to you. Not the sort of work you are accustomed to. Are you still interested?'

She set her head on one side and considered me. 'You're an odd one, all right. Are all inquisitors like you?'

'No.'

I ordered the servitor, Modo, to provide her with refreshment and left her in the crew-bay. Betancore was stood in the shadows outside the door, gazing in at her appreciatively.

'She's a fine sight,' he murmured to me as if I might not have noticed.

'You forget Vibben so quickly?'

He snapped round at me, stung. 'That was low, Eisenhorn. I was just commenting.'

'You'll like her less when you get to know her. She's an untouchable.'

'Seriously?'

'Seriously. A psychic blank. It's natural, and I haven't tested her limits. It's all I can do to be in the same room as her.'

'Such a looker too,' Betancore sighed, gazing back in at her.

'Useful to us. If she passes certain requirements, I'm going to employ her.'

He nodded. Untouchables were rare, and almost impossible to create artificially. They have a negative presence in the warp that renders them virtually immune to psychic powers, which in turn makes them potent anti-psyker weapons. The side-effect of their psychic blankness is the unpleasant disturbance that accompanies them, the waves of fear and revulsion they trigger in those they meet.

No wonder her life had been difficult and friendless.

'News?' I asked Betancore.

'Made contact with a sprint trader called the *Essene*. Master's one Tobius Maxilla. Deals in small units of luxury goods. Coming here in two days to deliver a consignment of vintage wines from Hesperus, then on to Gudrun. For a fee, he'll make room for the cutter in his hold.'

'Good work. So we'll be on Gudrun when?'

'Two weeks.'

I spent the next hour or so interviewing Bequin, but as I suspected she knew precious little about any of the men. We gave her accommodation in a small bunk-cell next to Betancore's quarters. It was scarcely more than a box, and Nilquit had to remove piles of stowed equipment to clear it, but she seemed pleased enough. When I asked her if she had any possessions she wished to collect from the Sun-dome, she simply shook her head.

I was reviewing yet more piles of data with Aemos when Fischig arrived. He was dressed in his brown serge uniform suit and carried two bulky holdalls over his shoulder, which he dropped to the deck with a declamatory thump as he stepped aboard.

'To what do I owe this visit, chastener?' I asked.

He showed me a slate bearing Carpel's official seal. 'The high custodian grants you permission to leave to pursue your inquiry. Dependent on this...'

I reviewed the slate and sighed.

'I'm coming with you,' he said.

SIX

Divination by auto-seance
A dream
Joining the *Essene*

I lodged a formal complaint with the high custodian's office, but it was simply for show. Carpel could manufacture serious problems for me if I tried to leave without his agent. I could do that, of course. I could do as I liked. But Carpel could delay me, and I didn't know how much co-operation from the elders and administrations of Hubris I'd need later if any part of this investigation led to trial.

Besides, Carpel knew I was going on to Gudrun, and he would plainly send Fischig there under an Arbites warrant to investigate anyway. On the whole, I decided I'd rather have Chastener Fischig where I could see him.

On the afternoon before our intended departure, I had Low-ink prepare for an auto-seance. I doubted whether anything further could be learned now, but I wanted to cover every avenue.

As usual, we used my quarters, with the cabin-door locked, and Betancore strictly instructed to prevent interruptions. I sat in a high-back armchair, and spent some quarter of an hour lowering my mind to a semi-trance state. This was an old technique, one of the first I had been taught when my abilities had originally been detected by the tutors of the Inquisition. On a cloth-covered table between us, Lowink laid out key evidence items: some of Eyclone's effects, some other pieces taken from Thaw-view 12011, and some from the processional. We also had the mysterious casket from the cryogenerator chamber.

Once he was satisfied I was ready, Lowink opened his mind to the warp, and filtered its raging influence through his highly trained mental architecture. This transitional moment was always a shock, and I shuddered. The temperature in the room dropped palpably, and a glass bowl on a side counter cracked spontaneously. Lowink was murmuring, his eyes rolled back, twitching and jerking slightly.

I closed my eyes, though I could still see my room. What I was seeing was a visualisation of our surroundings constructed by Lowink astropathically in the Empyrean itself. Everything shone with a pale blue light from within, and solids became translucent. The dimensions of the room shifted slightly, stretching and buckling as if they had difficulty retaining their coherence.

I took up the items on the table in turn, Lowink's projection enhancing their psychometric qualities, opening my mind's abilities to the signatures and resonances they carried in the warp.

Most were dull and blunt, with no trace of resonance. Some had wispy tendrils of auras around them, relics of passing contact with human hands and human minds. Eyclone's vox-device buzzed with the distant, unintelligible whinings of ghosts but gave up nothing.

Eyclone's pistol stung my hand like a scorpion when I touched it – and both I and Lowink gasped. I had a brief aftertaste of death. I decided not to touch it again.

His data-slate, which Aemos had yet been unable to open, was dripping with a sticky, almost gelatinous aura. The thickness of the psychic residue betokened the complex thought processes and data that had adhered to it. It gave up nothing, and I became frustrated. Lowink amplified my scrutiny and at last, as a whisper, I landed the word, or name, 'daesumnor'.

The final item for inspection was the casket. It resonated brightly with flickering bands of warp-traces. Our contact with it was necessarily brief because of the exhausting strength of its halo.

We probed, opening what seemed to be three levels of psychometric activity. One was sharp and hard, and tasted of metal. Lowink averred that this was a relic of the intellect or intellects that had crafted the casket. An undeniably brilliant but malevolent presence.

Beneath that, colder, smaller, denser, like a lightless collapsed star, lay a heavy, throbbing trace that seemed to be locked in the heart of the casket's machine core.

Around both, fluttering and swooping like birds, were the vestigial psychic agonies of the dead from Processional Two-Twelve. Their plaintive psychic noise rippled through our thoughts and sapped the emotional strength from us both. The dead souls of the processional had left their psychic fingerprints on this device that had been instrumental in their murder.

We were about to step back and end the seance when the second trace, the cold, distant, dense one, began to well up to the surface. I was intrigued at first, then stunned by its gathering force and speed. It filled my head with a nauseating, intolerable sense of hunger.

Hunger, thirst, appetite, craving...

It rose from the depths of the casket, wailing and yearning, a dark thing tearing up through the other trace energies. I glimpsed its malice and felt its consuming need.

Lowink broke the link. He slumped back in his seat, panting, his skin dotted with the stigmatic blood-spots of an astropathic augury taken far too far.

I felt it too. My mind seemed cold, colder even than the ministrations of Dormant. It seemed to take a very long time before my thoughts began to flow freely again, like water slowly thawing in an iced pipe.

I rose and poured myself a glass of amasec. I poured one for Lowink too as an afterthought. Neither of us ever came away from an auto-seance feeling good, but this was signally worse than usual.

'There was danger,' Lowink husked at last. 'Vile danger. From the casket.'

'I felt it.'

'But the whole seance was unseemly, master. As if distracted and spoiled by some... some factor...'

I sighed. I knew what he had felt. 'I can explain. The girl we have aboard is an untouchable.'

Lowink shuddered. 'Keep her away from me.'

I passed the word 'daesumnor' to Aemos in case it assisted his work on the data-slate and rested in my cabin to recover. Lowink had gone back to his tiny residence under the cockpit deck. I doubted he would be useful for much for a goodly while.

I gathered up the evidence items, re-bagged them and locked them in the cutter's strongbox, all except the casket, which was too big to fit. We kept it bagged and chained in a tarpaulin locker aft. As I hefted it up to return it to the locker, I felt the aftershock of its aura, as if we had woken something, some instinct. I considered this to be the imagination of my stung mind working overtime, but I completed the task only when I had buckled on a pair of work gloves.

Betancore joined me shortly afterwards. He had gone through Vibben's effects and found no will or instructions. Now we needed her cabin to house Fischig, so we placed her belongings and clothes in an underseat storebin in the crew-bay and together carried her wrapped body to the cot in the medical suite. I locked the door as we left.

'What will you do with her?' Betancore asked. 'There's no time to arrange a burial here now.'

'She once said she came with me to see what the stars were like. That's where we'll lay her to rest.'

Then I slept, turning fitfully despite my exhaustion. When sleep finally came, the dreams were cold and inhospitable. Murderously black, back-lit clouds rippled in fast motion across skies I didn't know, strobing with electrical flashes. Dark trees, and darker, higher walls, ranged around the edges of the dream. I felt the instinct, the hunger from the casket, lurking in some blind spot my eyes refused to find.

Carrion birds, a flock of them, swooped down from the upper reaches of the sky and took all the colour with them, staining the dream-world grey. All except for a spot of red that glittered in the colourless soil ahead of me.

With each step I took towards it, it receded. I began to run. It continued to display dream logic and moved away.

Finally, gasping for breath, I stopped running. The red spot had gone. I felt the hunger again, but now it was inside me, clawing at my belly, filling my throat with craving. The roiling clouds overhead froze suddenly, motionless, even the lightning flares stilled and captured in jagged, phosphorescent lines.

A voice spoke my name. I thought it was Vibben, but when I turned, there was nothing to see except the suggestion of a presence drifting away like smoke.

I woke. From the clock, I had been asleep only a couple of hours. My throat was raw and my mouth dry. I drained two glasses of water from the side cabinet and then fell back on the bed.

My head ached but my mind would not stop spinning. After that, no sleep came at all.

The vox-link chimed about four hours later. It was Betancore. 'The *Essene* has just made orbit,' he told me. 'We can leave whenever you like.'

The *Essene* lay slantwise above the inverted bowl of Hubris, silhouetted against the stars.

We had left the radiance of the Sun-dome into a blizzard squall. The air-frame of the cutter had vibrated wildly as Betancore lifted us out of the clutches of the ferocious, icy winds until we were riding clear over an ocean of frosty vapour.

The blizzard, a sculptural white continent, then dropped away below until we could see its tides and gusts and currents, the wide centrifugal patterns of its titanic force.

'There,' Betancore had said, with a nod to the raked front ports. Even at ninety kilometres, still rising through the thinning aeropause, he had made visual contact.

It had taken me a few more moments to find it. A bar of darkness distorting the pearly edge of the planesphere.

Another minute, and it had become a three-dimensional solid. A minute more, and I began to resolve the running lights glittering on its surface.

Yet another minute and it filled the ports. It resembled some colossal tower that had been ripped away from its earthly foundations and set adrift, tranquil, in the void.

'A beauty,' murmured Betancore, who appreciated such things. His inlaid hands flicked over the flight controls and we yawed to the correct approach vectors. The gun-cutter and the massive vessel exchanged automatic telemetry chatter. The flight deck pict-plates were alive with columns of rushing data.

'A bulk clipper, of the classic Isolde pattern, from the depot yards of Ur-Haven or Tancred. Majestic...' Aemos was muttering and annotating his idle observations into his wrist slate again.

The *Essene* was three kilometres long by my estimation, and fully seven hundred metres deep at its broadest part. Its nose was a long sleek cone like a cathedral spire made of overlapping gothic curves and barbed with bronze finials and spines. Behind that bladed front, the angular hull thickened into muscular buttresses of rusty-red plating, looped and riveted with ribs of dark steel. Crenellated tower stacks bulged from the dorsal hump. Hundred-metre masts stabbed forward from the hull like tusks and other, shorter masts projected from the flanks and underside, winking with guide lights. The rear portion of the juggernaut splayed into four heat-blackened cones, each of which was large enough to swallow a dozen gun-cutters at once.

Betancore turned us in and ran us along the flank heading

aft. To us, the great vessel seemed to wallow and roll as we joined its horizontal.

A lighted dot divorced itself from the *Essene* and ran out ahead of us, flashing ultra-bright patterns of red and green lamps: a pilot drone to lead us in.

Betancore gently chased the drone and swung to port as its lights instructed. We slid neatly between two mast arrays, crossed the ribbed belly, and finally braked to station-keeping under a rectangular belly-hatch edged with black and yellow chevrons. The hatch was one of a line of six down the hull's underside, but this was the only open one. A fiery orange glow washed down over us.

Exchanging a few terse comments with Uclid in the drive room, Betancore nudged the gun-cutter upwards through the yawning hatch. I watched the edges of the hatch-mouth, two metres thick and scratched in places to the bare metal, pass by alarmingly close.

There followed a series of gentle shudders, and mechanical thumps against the cutter's outer hull. Amber light bathed the cockpit. I looked up into the glow outside, but saw little except a suggestion of dark gantries and cargo-lifting derricks.

Another shudder. Betancore threw a row of switches and there was a whine as power-feeds and autosystems wound down. He pushed back from the control deck, and began pulling on his hide gloves.

He smiled at me. 'You needn't look so worried,' he mocked.

In truth, I am most disquieted by things I have no control over. Though I have rudimentary skills, and can manage an atmospheric craft, I am no pilot, certainly not one with Midas's Glavian pedigree. That's why I employ him and that's why he makes it look so easy. But sometimes my face betrays the alarm I feel in situations where I have no ability.

Besides, I was tired. But I knew sleep wouldn't come even if I tried, and there was business to attend to anyway.

Aemos, Bequin and Lowink would stay on the cutter for now. As soon as the hull door was closed and atmosphere recirculated into the *Essene's* hold, I opened the hatch and stepped out with Fischig and Betancore.

The hold where we were docked was vaulted and immense. I reminded myself it was just one of six accommodated by this vessel. The surfaces of the walls and decking were oily black, and sodium lighting arrays bolted to the ceiling filled the place with orange tinted luminescence. The spaces above us were busy with the skeletal shapes of cranes and monotask lifters, all shut down and lifeless. Packing materials littered the open floor. The gun-cutter was held over the sealed floor hatch in a greased crib of docking pistons and hydraulic clamps.

We crossed the hold, boots ringing on the metal deck-plates. It was cold, the chill of open space still lingering.

Betancore wore his usual Glavian pilot suit and garish jacket. He was cheerful and whistled tunelessly. Fischig was impassive, oozing command in his brown Arbites uniform. He had fixed his golden sun-disk of office to the breast of his jacket.

I wore a dark sober suit of grey wool, black boots and gloves and a long navy-blue leather coat with a high collar. I had taken a stub-pistol from the weapons locker and had it in a holster rig under my left arm. My Inquisitorial rosette was buttoned away inside a pocket. Unlike Fischig, I felt no need to make a statement of authority.

A hatch clanked open on servos, and light shone out from an internal companionway. A figure stepped out to meet us.

'Welcome to the *Essene*, inquisitor,' said Tobius Maxilla.

SEVEN

With the master of the *Essene*
A farewell
Scrutiny

Maxilla was a veteran trader who had run the *Essene* down
the lanes from Thracian Primaris to the Grand Banks for
fifty years. He told me he'd dealt in bulk consumables at the
start of his career, then begun to specialise in exotic goods
when the big bonded guilds began to dominate the whole-
sale market.

'The *Essene*'s got speed, a sprint trader. Pays me better to
carry luxury cargoes and deliver them express, even if I don't
run at capacity.'

'You run this route regularly?'

'For the past few decades. It's seasonal. Sameter, Hesperus, Thracian, Hubris, Gudrun, sometimes to Messina too.
When Dormant finishes on Hubris, there'll be a lot more
work there.'

We sat in the luxurious surroundings of his audience suite,
sipping vintage amasec from large crystal glasses. Maxilla

was showing off, but that was acceptable. He had a ship and a reputation to be proud of.

'So you know these routes well?' Fischig put in.

Maxilla smiled. He was a sinewy man of indeterminate age, dressed in a full-skirted coat of red velvet with wide button-back cuffs and an extravagant black lace cravat. His smile showed teeth that were inlaid with mother of pearl. Ostentation was common among ship's masters, it was part of showing off. Forget family lineage and noble blood, one had told me once, the lineage and pedigree of starships is where the new Imperial nobility is to be found. Ship's masters were the real Imperial aristocracy.

So Maxilla seemed to think, anyway. His face was powdered with white skin-dye, and he wore a sapphire as a beauty spot on his cheek. His imposing two-horned wig was spun from silver-thread. Heavy signet rings clinked against his balloon glass as he lifted it.

'Yes, chastener, I know them well.'

'I don't think we need to start interrogating Master Maxilla yet, Fischig,' I said plainly. Betancore snorted and Maxilla chuckled. Fischig glowered into his amasec.

A servitor, its torso and head casing wrought to resemble an antique ship's figurehead, a full-breasted damsel with gilt snakes in her hair, hummed across the expensive Selgioni rug and offered us trays of delicacies. I took one out of politeness. It was a sliver of perfect ketelfish, exquisitely sautéed and wrapped in a nearly transparent leaf of pastry. Betancore helped himself to several.

'You're a Glavian?' Maxilla asked Betancore. The two promptly fell to discussing the merits of the famous Glavian longprow. I lost interest and looked around the suite. Amid the finery were a series of priceless portraits from the

Sameter School, marble busts of planetary rulers, a Jokaero light-sculpture, antique weapons and mounted suits of ceremonial mirror armour from Vitria. Aemos would appreciate this, I thought. It was to be a journey of more than a week. I'd make sure he got a chance to see it.

'Do you know Gudrun?' Maxilla was asking me.

I shook my head. 'This will be my first visit. I have only been in this sub-sector a year or so.'

'A fine place, though you'll find it busy. There's a month-long festival under way to celebrate the founding of a new guard regiment. If you have the time, I recommend the Imperial Academy of Fine Arts, and the guild museums in Dorsay.'

'I may be a little occupied.'

He shrugged. 'I always make the time to do more than simply work, inquisitor. But I know your calling is rather more strenuous than mine.'

I tried to get the measure of him, but I was failing so far. He had agreed to give us passage, and for a modest fee considering what he might have demanded. I had already paid him with an Imperial bond. Most ship masters don't like to turn down a request from an inquisitor, even if they are charging. Was it just that Maxilla wanted to keep sweet with the Ordos? Or was he simply a generous man?

Or did he have something to hide?

I wondered. Truthfully, I didn't care. The other possibility was he might think this entitled him to some future favour.

If he did, he would be wrong.

The *Essene* left Hubris later that day, executed the translation to the Empyrean effortlessly, and made best speed for Gudrun. Maxilla provided quarters for us all in his state apartments, but we spent most of our time on the cutter, working. Betancore and the servitors ran an overhaul of the ship. Lowink slept. Fischig, Aemos and I worked through the paperwork on the evidence, and threw conjectures back and forth. I still held back what little I knew of the Pontius from Fischig, but it wouldn't be long before he started to make the connection himself.

Bequin kept herself to herself. She'd borrowed a set of fatigues from a work locker and I saw her about the ship, reading books she'd taken from my personal library. Poetry, mostly, and some historical and philosophical works. I didn't mind. It kept her out of my way.

On the third day of the voyage, I met Maxilla again, and we walked the upper promenade deck together. He seemed to enjoy telling me the histories and provenances of the ormolu-framed paintings displayed there. We saw the occasional servitor at work, but so far there had not been the slightest glimpse of any other living crewperson.

'Your friend, Fischig... he is an unsubtle man,' he remarked at length.

'He's no friend. And yes, he is unsubtle. Has he been asking you questions again?'

'I saw him briefly on the foredecks yesterday. He asked me if I knew a man called Eyclone. Even showed me a picture.'

'And what did you say?'

He flashed his pearly teeth at me. 'Now who's interrogating?'

'Forgive my imprudence.'

He waved a lace-cuffed hand. 'Oh, forget it! Ask anyway! Get your questions out into the open so we can clear the air!'

'Very well. What did you tell him?'

'That I did not.'

I nodded. 'Thank you for your candour.'

'But I was lying.'

I turned and looked at Maxilla sharply. He was still smiling. I had the sudden horrible notion that we had all walked into a trap and dearly wished I was carrying a weapon.

'Don't worry. I lied to him because he's an arrogant runt. But I'll give you the truth of it. I would never want to put myself in the path of an Imperial Inquisition.'

'A wise philosophy.'

Maxilla flopped down on a satin couch and smoothed the front of his coat. 'I was last on Thracian Primaris two months ago. There was talk of some cargo and I held some meetings. The usual. And that's when this Eyclone enters the frame. Didn't call himself that, of course. Bless me, I forget the name he used. But it was him. Had others with him, a sour, tight lot. One called Crotes, a trade envoy. He tried to have me believe your man was authorised by the Guild Sinesias, but that was rubbish, even though Crotes had the paperwork.'

'What did he want?'

'He was hiring to make a run, empty, to Gudrun, collect a cargo there, and bring it to Hubris.'

'The nature of the cargo?'

'We never got that far. I turned him down. It was preposterous. He was offering a decent fee, but I knew I'd make ten times that with my regular work.'

'You didn't get a contact name on Gudrun either?'

'My dear inquisitor, I'm just a shipman, not a detective.'

'Do you know who finally took his work?'

'I know who didn't.' He sat forward. 'I happen to keep up dialogues with other masters. Seems several of us turned it down, and most for the same reason.'

'Which was?'

'It felt like trouble.'

* * *

By the fifth day, my sleep patterns had begun to return to normal. Too normal, in fact, as Eyclone began to stalk my dreams again. In sleep, he came to me, taunting and threatening. I don't remember much detail, except the afterimage of his grinning face each time I woke.

In hindsight, though Eyclone was certainly in my dreams, I don't think it was his smiling face I was remembering.

The *Essene* translated back into real-space and entered the Gudrun system on the morning of the eighth day, ahead of schedule. Maxilla had boasted his ship was fast under optimum conditions and the boast hadn't been empty.

I had made arrangements with him to leave the Empyrean in the out-reach of the system, considerably short of the busy local trade lanes that most arrivals to Gudrun followed. He agreed without question. It would only be a short delay.

'Who was she?' Bequin asked me as we stood at an observation bay watching the pale shape of Vibben's shrouded body slowly turn end over end as it drifted away from the *Essene*.

'A friend. A comrade,' I replied.

'Is this how she wanted to go?' she asked.

'I don't think she wanted to go at all,' I said. Nearby, Aemos and Betancore gazed gravely out of the thick port. Aemos's expression was unreadable. Betancore's dark face was drawn and anguished.

Lowink hadn't joined us, and neither had Fischig. But as I turned, I saw Maxilla standing respectfully at the rear of the observation bay, wearing a long mourning coat of black silk and a short periwig with black ribbons. He moved forward as he saw me look.

'I hope I'm not intruding. My respects to your lost comrade.'

I nodded my thanks. He hadn't needed to make this effort,

but it seemed appropriate for the ship's master to be present during a void burial.

'I'm not sure how these things are formally conducted, Maxilla,' I said, 'though I think this is what she would have asked for. I have spoken the Imperial Creed, and the Oration of the Dead.'

'Then you have done her fine service. If it is appropriate...?'

He waved forward one of his gold-plated figurehead servitors, which carried a salver of glasses and a decanter.

'It is tradition to drink a toast to the departed.'

We all took a glass.

'Lores Vibben,' I said.

A minute or so's silence followed, then we slowly dispersed. I told Maxilla we could begin our approach run to Gudrun now, and he estimated it would take two hours to reach the inner system.

Returning to the cutter, I found myself walking with Bequin. She still wore the old work-suit she had liberated, though somehow it seemed to enhance her beauty rather than stifle it.

'We're almost there,' she said.

'Indeed.'

'What will my duties be?'

I had yet to explain to her what she was or why I had recruited her. There had been ample time en route, but I had been putting it off, I suppose. I'd found time to show Aemos the finery of Maxilla's state rooms, and play regicide with Betancore. I wished I could throw off my distaste at just simply being around her.

I walked with her to the promenade deck and began to explain.

I don't know how I expected her to take it. When she took it badly and became upset, my response was barely controlled irritation. I knew it was her nature that was making me react this way and fought to find the sympathy she deserved.

She sat weeping on a shot-silk chair beneath one of the massive paintings: a hunting scene of nobles riding thoroughbred ursadons in the chase. Every now and then, she would blurt out a curse or whine a regret.

It was clear she wasn't upset that I wanted to employ her. It was simply the fundamental knowledge that she was... abnormal. A friendless, loveless life of woes and hard knocks suddenly had an explanation and that explanation was her own nature. I believe that she had always, stoically, blamed the galaxy as a whole for her troubles. Now I'd as good as kicked that emotional crutch away.

I damned myself for not thinking the consequences through. I'd robbed her of self-esteem and what little confidence she could muster. I'd shown up her lifelong efforts to find comfort, love and respect as hollow, self-destructive, self-denying futility.

I tried to talk about the work she could do for me. She wasn't much interested. In the end, I pulled up another chair and sat next to her as she worked the painful truth through her mind.

I was still sitting there when I received a vox-signal. It was Maxilla.

'I wonder if you could join me on the bridge, inquisitor? I require your assistance.'

The bridge of the *Essene* was a wide domed chamber with floors and pillars of red-black marble. Silver servitors, immaculate and intricate as sculptures, were stationed at console positions sunk into the floor, their delicate geared arms working banks of controls set into polished mahogany fascias. The air was cool and still, and the only sound was the gentle hum and whirr of the working machines.

Maxilla, still dressed in his mourning robes, sat in a massive leather throne overlooking the room from a marble dais. Articulated limbs extending from the rear of the throne suspended pict-plates and consoles in his reach, but his attention was on the massive main observation port that dominated the front of the bridge.

I strode across the floor from the entrance. Each servitor wore a mask of chased gold, fashioned into a human face of classical perfection.

'Inquisitor,' Maxilla said, rising.

'Your crew are all servitors,' I remarked.

'Yes,' he said distractedly. 'They are more reliable than pure flesh.'

I made no other comment. Maxilla's relationship with the *Essene* seemed to me akin to the way the Adeptus Mechanicus worship their god-machines. Constant involvement with such ancient instruments had convinced them of the natural inferiority of the human species.

I followed his gaze and looked at the main port. The gleaming sphere of Gudrun lay ahead, a creamy swirl of clouds stained with the lime-green phantoms of great forests under the climate cover. Clusters of black shapes thickly dotted the space between us and the planet. These were huge groups of orbiting ships, I realised. Massive dreadnoughts at high anchor, trains of great merchant ships, convoys of trade freighters streaming in under tug supervision. I had seldom seen such a wealth of orbital activity.

'Is there a problem?' I asked him.

He looked over at me, something like anxiety in his eyes. 'I have performed legal manoeuvres and entered the trade lane approach. Gudrun control has allocated me a high-anchor buoy. All relevant data is in order and my tariffs are paid. But I have just been informed that we are to be boarded and inspected.'

'This is unusual?'

'It's been ten years since anyone even suggested such a thing of my ship.'

'Explanation?'

'They say security. I told you there was a founding festival under way. You can see considerable portions of Battlefleet Scarus on station. I think the military is being over-careful of its interests here just now.'

'You mentioned my assistance.'

'The inspection launch is on its way. I feel it would facilitate matters if they were met by a ship's master and an Imperial inquisitor.'

'I can't pull strings, Maxilla.'

He laughed humourlessly and looked me in the eye. 'Of course you can! But that's not what I'm asking. With an inquisitor present, they will treat the *Essene* with more respect. I'll not have them root through this vessel mindlessly.'

I thought for a moment. This smacked of the favour I had a feeling he might call in. Worse, it stank of impropriety on his part.

'I'll agree to be present for the sake of order, provided you can assure me you have nothing to hide.'

'Inquisitor Eisenhorn, I–'

'Save your indignation for the inspection, Maxilla. Your assurance is all I require. If I assist you only to find you have some dirty secret or illicit cargo, you will have a great deal more to worry about than the Imperial Navy.'

There was a look of great disappointment on his face. Either he was a superb actor, or I had truly wounded his feelings.

'I have nothing to hide,' he hissed. 'I fancied you and I had become... if not friends then decent acquaintances at least this voyage. I have shown you hospitality and freely given information into your confidence. I am hurt that you still suspect me.'

'Suspicion is my business, Maxilla. If I have wronged you, my apologies.'

'Nothing to hide!' he repeated, almost to himself, and led me off the bridge.

A Navy pinnace, matt-grey and deep hulled, drew alongside the massive *Essene* and clamped itself to the fore starboard airgate. Maxilla and I were there to meet it, along with Fischig and two of the ship's primary servitors, spectacular creations of gold and silver machine parts.

I'd summoned Fischig on the basis that if the sight of an inquisitor would help, then an Arbites chastener would do no harm either. Betancore was instructed to keep everyone else with the cutter.

The gate-locks cycled open and the hatch jaws gaped, exhaling torrents of steam. A dozen large figures emerged through the haze. They were all dressed in the grey and black body armour of naval security, with the crest and sector-symbol of Battlefleet Scarus displayed on their chests and gold braid edging their epaulettes. All were masked in form-moulded ceramite helmets with lowered visor plates and rebreathers. They were armed with compact, short-frame autoguns.

The leader stepped forward and his men grouped behind him. They didn't form a neat echelon. Messy, I thought, casual, lacking the usual drilled discipline of the infamous naval security arm. These men were bored and going through the motions. They wanted this formality over and done too.

'Tobius Maxilla?' barked the leader, his voice distorted by his mask and vox-amplified.

'I am Maxilla,' said the ship's master, stepping forward.

'You have been notified that an inspection of your vessel is due. Furnish me with crew lists and cargo manifests. Your full co-operation is expected.'

At a nod from Maxilla, one of the servitors moved forward on silent tracks and handed the security detail's leader a data-slate with the relevant material.

He didn't look at it. 'Do you have anything you wish to volunteer before the inspection begins? It will go easier for you if you make submissions of contraband.'

I watched the exchange. There were twelve troops, hardly enough to search a ship the size of the *Essene*. Where were their servitors, their scanning units, their crowbars, multi-keys and heat-detectors?

They had no way of knowing who I was from my appearance, but why had they not remarked on the presence of an Arbites?

My vox channel was set to the cutter's. I didn't speak, but I keyed it three times. A non-verbal part of Glossia Betancore would understand.

'You haven't yet identified yourself,' I said.

The lead security trooper turned to look at me. I saw only my reflection in his tint-coated visor.

'What?'

'You haven't identified yourself or shown your warrant of practice. It is a requirement of such inspections.'

'We're naval security–' he began angrily, stepping towards me. His men faltered.

'You could be anybody.' I pulled out my Inquisitorial rosette.

'I am Gregor Eisenhorn, Imperial inquisitor. We will do this correctly or not at all.'

'You're Eisenhorn?' he said.

There was no surprise in his voice at all. A tiny thing to notice but enough for me.

The warning was already rising in my throat as their guns came up.

EIGHT

A dozen killers
The procurator
Grain merchants from Hesperus

Maxilla uttered a yell of disbelief. The leader of the security detail and two of his men opened fire.

Their compact autoguns were designed for ship-board fighting and zero-gravity work: low velocity, low recoil weapons that fired blunt-nosed slugs which couldn't puncture a hull.

But they were more than capable of shredding a man.

I threw myself sideways as the first shots spanged off the deck or left ugly metal bruises on the wall. In seconds, it was utter chaos. All the security troopers were firing, some on semi-automatic. Smoke filled the air and the airgate chamber was shaking with muzzle flashes and gunfire.

One of Maxilla's servitors was decapitated and then punched into spare-part debris as it turned towards the attackers. The other tried to move to shield Maxilla, but more shots tore out its tracks and its torso.

Two shots ripped through my trailing coat, but I made it to the doorframe behind us. I yanked my stub-pistol from its holster.

Fischig had drawn his own sidearm and was blasting away as he backed towards the door. He dropped one of the troopers with a tight group of shots that sent the man flying in a puff of blood. Then Fischig was lifted off his feet by a hit to the stomach. Doubled over, he tumbled into the corner of the chamber and lay still.

Maxilla roared and raised his right hand. A beam of searing light spat from one of the ornate rings and the nearest trooper exploded, burned down to scorched bone and ragged armour in his midsection. As the smouldering ruin crashed to the deck plates, the man behind him caught Maxilla in a chasing arc of automatic fire and blasted him backwards through the glass doors of an evacsuit-bay.

The rest were charging my position. I braced and fired, placing a shot that shattered the visor of the first approaching security trooper. He fell on his face.

The stub-pistol, designed for concealment, had a four-shot clip and I had a spare magazine in my coat pocket. Seven shots remained and there were still nine of them.

At least the stubber had stopping power. The clips only held four shells because they were high-calibre solids, each the size of my thumb. The short, fat muzzle of my stubber barked again and another trooper spun sideways.

I backed down the corridor, hugging the wall. The access-way to the airgate was a wide, cable-lined passage, octagonal in cross-section and lit only by deck lights. The troopers' slow, buzzing shots hissed down the hallway at me. I fired back again, but missed my target. A salvo of rounds blew out a power relay on the wall nearby in a shower of sparks.

I ducked away into shadows, and found the latch-handle of a shutter in the small of my back.

I turned, pulled it free and threw myself through it as a blizzard of shots impacted along the access-way wall.

On the other side of the shutter, I found a narrow inspection tunnel for the airgate's main docking mechanisms. The floor was metal grille, and the tight walls were thick with networks of cables and plumper hydraulic hoses. At the end, a bare metal ladder dropped down through a floor-well or up into an inspection shaft.

There was no time to climb either way. The first trooper was pushing through the shutter and raising his weapon. I shot down the length of the tunnel and blew out his chest-plate, and then jumped off the grille into the ladder well.

Five metres down, I slammed into a cage-platform. There was only red auxiliary light down here. The troopers' visors had vision amplifiers.

I was down in the guts of the vast docking clamp now, crawling between huge greased pistons and hydraulic rams the size of mature bluewood firs. Gases vented and lubricant fluids drizzled amid dangling loops of chain. The throb of heavy-duty compressors and atmosphere regulators filled the air.

I got into cover. All four red tell-tale lights on the stubber's grip were showing. I ejected the disposable plastic clip and slid the fresh one into place. Four green lights lit up in place of the red ones.

There was noise from the ladder-well. Two bulky dark shapes were moving down, backlit by the light from above.

Their visors had heat-enhancement too. That was clear the moment they both started firing at my position. I buried myself behind a piston unit but a round ricocheted off the oily metal and slammed into my right shoulder, driving me forward against the deck. My face hit the grille, and it reopened the gash in my cheek, popping out several of the butterfly clips that were just beginning to get the torn flesh to knit back together.

More shots rattled off the scant metal cover. Another ricochet hit the toe of my boot, and another punched into my arm, smashing my hand back against the wall behind me.

The impact kicked the stubber from my grip. It bounced away across the floor, just out of reach, the four green lights taunting me.

There were at least three of them out there now, moving through the confined space between machinery, firing bursts my way. I crawled on hands and knees along behind a horizontal clamp piston, low-velocity rounds pinking off the wall behind and above me.

I thought about using the will, but I had no chance of getting line of sight to try any sophisticated mind trick.

At the back end of the massive clamp, I found cover by the arrestor baffles and giant kinetic dampers that soften the impact of another ship against the docking arms. Greenish light filtered from a small control panel mounted in the wall between the dampers. The panel had a toughened plastic hood over it like a public vox-booth, and a glance showed me it was a test-reset terminal for docking array maintenance. I tried punching several icons, but the small, oval plate displayed the message Terminal locked out. Automatic safety measures were in place because a ship – the naval security troopers' pinnace – was in the docking clamp, mated to the airgate on the deck above.

I could hear scrambling above the ambient noise. The first of the troopers was clambering down the side of the clamp, following my route back to the dampers.

I took out my Inquisitorial rosette. It is a badge of office and a great deal more besides. A press of my thumb deployed the micro multi-key from its recess, and I slid it into the terminal's socket. It engaged. The screen blanked. My rosette had up to magenta level Imperial clearance. I prayed Maxilla had not encoded his entire ship with personal encryptions.

The screen flashed again. I tapped a release order into the terminal.

'Dock array in active use,' it told me in blunt green letters.

I hit override.

With a tumultuous grinding, the docking clamp disengaged. Dampers roared. Steam vented explosively. Alarms started wailing.

There was an agonised scream as the trooper on my heels was gripped and then crushed from the waist down by ten tonnes of expanding piston-sleeve.

From the deck far above, there were explosive bangs and the shriek of shearing metal. I could barely hear them above the mechanical din in the clamp chamber.

When the sighing and hissing of the massive pistons died away and the venting gases reduced to a sporadic gasp, I clambered up from behind the dampers. The entire architecture of the chamber had altered as the massive docking engines had switched from active to disengaged. Two troopers had been crushed by the heavy gear, another lay dead under a steam vent, braised in his armour by a rush of superheated steam.

I took up a fallen naval-issue autogun and retraced my steps.

By my count, there were still four loose and active. I came back along the inspection tunnel and re-entered the access-way. Warning lights strobed all along the passage and muted alarms still sounded. A figure suddenly appeared to my left. I wheeled around. It was Betancore. He was looking straight past me, one of his elegant needle pistols aimed straight at me. He fired it twice.

A distinctive stinging buzz resounded loud in my ears – and a security trooper at the far end of the passage staggered out of cover. Another shot and the man slammed over, feet out from under him.

'Came as soon as you gave the signal,' said Betancore.

'What's your tally?'

'Four, so far.'

'Then we're probably done. But stay sharp.' I smiled at myself. Telling Midas Betancore to stay sharp was like telling a dog to stay hairy.

'You're a mess,' he told me. 'What the hell happened?'

Blood ran down the side of my face from the reopened gash, I was moving awkwardly from the glancing hits to my shoulder and arm, and I was thoroughly smirched in machine oil from the docking mechanism.

'This wasn't an inspection. They were looking for me.'

'Naval security?'

'I don't think so. They lacked precision and didn't know procedure.'

'But they had kit, weapons – a Navy pinnace, Emperor damn them!'

'That's what worries me.'

We went back to the airgate. An emergency shutter had come down to seal the breach when my makeshift undocking had torn the pinnace off the side of the *Essene*. Through side ports, I could see its grey hull skewed alongside us, still attached to the clamps by one of its own docking extensors, though that

was badly twisted. Its integral airgate had blown on discon-
nection and at least the passenger section was open to hard
vacuum. If the crew had survived, they would be in the fore-
section, though probably helpless. Glittering debris, scraps
of metal plating and sheared sections of extensor hung in
the void outside.

I checked Fischig. He was alive. His Arbites uniform was
heavily laced with armour, but the short-range impacts had
given him internal injuries; he was unconscious and leaking
blood from the mouth.

Betancore found Maxilla beyond the shattered glass doors
of the evacsuit-bay. He had crawled across the floor and
propped himself against a harness rack. From the chest down,
his rich clothes were shredded and his legs were gone.

But then, from the chest down, he wasn't human.

'So my... bare facts are revealed to you after all, inquisitor...' he said, managing a smile. I imagined he was in pain,
or shock at least. To control the sophisticated bionic lower
body he had to have intricate neural linkage.

'What can I do to help you, Tobius?'

He shook his head. 'I have summoned servitors to assist
me. I'll be back on my feet soon enough.'

There were many questions I wanted to ask him. Was his
reconstruction the result of old injury, disease, age? Or was
it, as I had a feeling, voluntary? I kept the questions to myself.
They were private and didn't concern my investigation.

'I need access to your astropathic link. I need to contact
battlefleet command and speed the closure of this matter.
These men weren't a naval security detail.'

'I'll instruct the bridge to provide you with the access you
need. You may care to extract the inspection requests from
my communication log.'

That would help. I didn't think the high commanders of Battlefleet Scarus would take this lying down.

I was half-right, but only half. Within half an hour I was on the bridge of the *Essene*, surrounded by attentive servitors, reporting the incident to battlefleet command by confidential astropathic link. Before long, I was in vox dialogue with aides from the staff office of Admiral Lorpal Spatian, who requested that I secure the *Essene* at its high-anchor buoy and await the arrival of a security detail and an envoy from the battlefleet procurator.

The idea of sitting tight and waiting for more troopers to arrive didn't especially appeal.

'Deserters, sir,' Procurator Olm Madorthene told me, two hours later. He was a grizzled, narrow man with cropped grey hair and an old augmetic implant down the side of his neck under his left ear. He wore the starched white, high collared jacket, red gloves, pressed black jodhpurs and high patent leather boots of the Battlefleet Disciplinary Detachment. Madorthene had been courteous from the moment he came aboard, saluting me and tucking his gold-braided white crowned cap under his arm respectfully. His detachment of troopers were dressed and equipped identically to the ones that had boarded the *Essene* to kill us, but from the moment of their arrival I noted their greater discipline and tight order.

'Deserters?'

Madorthene seemed uneasy. He clearly disliked entanglements with an inquisitor.

'From the Guard levies. You are aware a founding is presently under way on Gudrun. By order of the Lord Militant Commander, seven hundred and fifty thousand men are being inducted into the Imperial Guard to form the 50th Gudrunite Rifles. Such is the size of the founding, and the fact that this is notably the fiftieth regiment assembled from this illustrious world, that a planet-wide celebration and associated ceremonial military events are taking place.'

'And these men deserted?'

Madorthene delicately drew me to one side as his troopers carried the corpses of the insurgents from the vicinity of the airgate and bagged them. I had set Betancore to watch over them.

'We have had trouble,' he confided quietly. 'The muster was originally to have been half a million, but the Lord Militant Commander increased the figure a week prior to the founding – he is preparing for a crusade into the Ophidian sub-sector – and, well, many found themselves conscripted with little notice. Between you and me, the great festivities are partly an attempt to draw attention from the matter. There's been some rioting in barracks at the founding area, and desertion. It's been busy for us.'

'I can well imagine. You know for certain these men are deserters from the Guard?'

He nodded and handed me a data-slate. On it was a list of twelve names, linked to file biographies and blurry holo portraits.

'They absconded from Founding Barrack 74 outside Dorsay yesterday, took uniforms and weapons from the bursary at the orbital port and stole a pinnace. No one thought to challenge a squad of naval security troopers.'

'And no one questioned their lack of credentials and flight codes?'

'Regrettably, the pinnace had been pre-loaded with a course plan and transponder codes to take it into the fleet anchorage.

They would have been discovered long since had that not been the case. They were clearly looking for a non-military starship like this.'

'These are regular draftees? Infantrymen?'

'Yes.'

'Who could fly a pinnace?'

'The ringleader,' he referred back to the slate, 'one Jonno Lingaart, was a qualified orbital pilot. Worked on the ferries. As I said, a regrettable combination of events.'

I wasn't going to let this go. Madorthene wasn't lying, I was certain of that. But the information he was presenting me with was full of gaps and inconsistencies.

'What about the demand for the inspection?'

'That came from the pinnace itself. Entirely unofficial. They spotted your ship and improvised. We have sourced the inspection demand to the pinnace's vox-log.'

'No,' I said. He took a step backwards, alert to the anger that was growing in me.

'Sir?'

'I have checked the *Essene*'s communication log. It doesn't tell me the origin of the signals, but it shows the inspection demand came via astropathic link, not vox. The pinnace had no astropath.'

'That's–'

'This is the same astropathic link that allocated the *Essene* its high-anchor buoy. That's been shown as authentic enough. And these men were looking for me. Me, procurator. To kill me. They knew my name.'

He went pale and seemed unable to find a reply.

I turned away from him. 'I don't know who these men are – they may indeed have been guard draftees. But someone set them on this course to find me, someone who covered their movements, provided materials and transport, and authenticated their business with this ship. Someone either in the battlefleet or with an outrageous amount of access to its workings. No other explanation fits.'

'You're talking of... a conspiracy.'

'I am no stranger to underhand behaviour, Madorthene. Nor am I unduly perturbed by attempts on my life. I have enemies. I expect such things. This shows me my enemies are even more powerful than I suspected.'

'My lord, I-'

'What is your level of seniority, procurator?'

'I am grade one, magenta cleared, enjoying equivalency with the rank of fleet commodore. I answer directly to Lord Procurator Humbolt.' I knew this from his shoulder flashes, but I wanted to hear him tell me.

'Of course. Your superior wouldn't have trusted such a delicate matter to a junior officer. Nor did he want to show disrespect to me. I trust this matter is still held in the highest confidence?'

'Sir, yes sir! The lord procurator recognised its... delicacy. Besides, notices of any infractions are being suppressed by order of the Lord Militant Commander, so as not to foment further unrest. The details of this incident are known only to myself and my squad here, the lord procurator and his senior aides.'

'Then I'd like to keep it that way. I'd like my enemies to believe, for as long as possible, that this assassination attempt was successful. Can I rely on your co-operation, prosecutor?'

'Of course, inquisitor.'

'You will take an encrypted message back to your lord procurator from me. It will appraise him of the situation and my requirements. I will also supply you with a covert vox-link with which to contact me if any further information becomes available. Any further information, Madorthene, even if you don't believe I will find it relevant.'

He nodded keenly again. I didn't add the codicil that if I found this confidence broken I would come after him, the senior aides and the lord procurator himself like the wrath of Rogal Dorn. He could figure that out for himself.

After Madorthene and his crew had left the *Essene*, I turned to Betancore.

'What now?' he asked.

'How does it feel to be dead, Midas?'

We left the *Essene* at midnight aboard the gun-cutter. Fischig, conscious now, remained aboard Maxilla's ship, recovering from his punishing wounds in the *Essene*'s spectacularly equipped auto-infirmary.

Maxilla had agreed to keep the *Essene* at anchor for the time being. I had arranged to cover all revenues he stood to lose. I felt I might need a reliable ship at a moment's notice, and it also made sense that if the *Essene* suddenly departed, it would weaken the cover-story that we were all dead.

I talked it over with Maxilla in the bridge chamber. He sat in his great throne, sipping amasec while reconstruction servitors painstakingly restructured his lower limbs.

'I'm sorry you are now so involved, Tobius.'

'I'm not,' he said. 'This has been the most interesting run I've made in a long time.'

'You're prepared to stay until I give you word?'

'You're paying well, inquisitor!' he laughed at this. 'In truth, I am content to help you serve the Emperor. Besides, that oaf Fischig needs better care than your cutter's dingy medical suite can provide, and I can assure you I won't be running off anywhere until he's safely off my ship.'

I left the bridge, almost charmed by Maxilla's generous spirit. There could be many reasons why he assisted me so willingly – fear of the Inquisition being the chief one – but in truth, I was certain it was because he had rediscovered the pleasure of interaction with other humans. It was there in his eagerness to talk, to show off his art treasures, to help, to accommodate...

He had been alone in the company of machines for too long.

Betancore changed the transponder codes of the gun-cutter as we left the *Essene*'s hold. We kept a number of alternative craft identifiers in the codifier memory. For the past few months, and during the stop-over at Hubris, we had run as an official transport of the Inquisition, making no attempt to hide our nature.

Now we were a trade delegation from Sameter, specialising in gene-fixed cereal crops, hoping to interest Gudrun's noble estates in easy maintenance, pest-free crops now that the founding had drained their labour pool.

Betancore voxed Gudrun Control, identified us, and requested route and permission for landfall at Dorsay, the northern capital. They obliged us without hesitation. Another greedy trader in town for the festival.

We swept down through the vast elements of Battlefleet Scarus at high-anchor: rows of grotesque, swollen-bellied troop ships; massive destroyers with jutting prow-rams and proud aquila emblems; the vast battleships of the line, cold, grey orthogonal giants of space, blistered with weapon emplacements; barbed frigates, long and lean and cruel as wood-wasps; schools of fighter craft, running the picket.

Post-orbital space was seething with transports, scudding tugs, resupply launches, merchant cutters, bulky service lifters and skeletal loading platforms. Away to starboard, the mixed echelons of the merchant ships, the bulk freighters, the sleek sprint traders, the super-massive guild ships, the hybrid rogues. The *Essene* was out there somewhere.

Winking buoy lights, describing the stacks and levels of the anchor stations, filled the night, another constellation blocking out the real starfield.

Betancore nursed us down through the traffic, down into the crystal bright ionosphere, down into the opalescent ranges of the high clouds. We were heading across the crossover from night to day as the planet turned, making for Dorsay, where dawn was coming up on another day of the Festival of Founding.

NINE

At Dorsay
Market forces
In pursuit of Tanokbrey

Dorsay wasn't waking up. It had been awake all night. Vox-horns along the old streets, avenues and canals broadcast martial themes, and streamers and pennants flew from every available surface.

I had speed-read Aemos's summation of the planet: Gudrun, capital of the Helican sub-sector, Scarus Sector, Segmentum Obscurus. Boasting a human culture for three and a half thousand years, feudally governed by powerful noble houses, whose reach and power extended across three dozen other worlds in the Helican sub-sector. Thracian Primaris, that vast, bloated hub of industry and commerce, was the most populated and productive world in the region, but Gudrun was the cultural and administrative heart. And it was reckoned the combined wealth of the noble houses rivalled the commercial worth of the output of the Thracian hives.

Seen from our approach run, Dorsay gleamed white in the dawn. It lay on the coast, around the lip of a sea-fed lagoon, straddling the mighty river Drunner. From the cutter's ports as we turned in, we could see the white specks of sailboats out in the lagoon basin. Beyond the vast white spread of the city, I could see massive stockades and emplacements established in the rolling green hills and bluffs, temporary barracks for the founding regiment.

Betancore set us down at Giova Field, the municipal port serving Dorsay. It was built on a long, narrow island in the lagoon facing the city, and the space premium meant smaller ships like ours were lowered on monotasked heavy elevators and berthed in a honeycomb of compartments drilled into the porous lava-rock of the island's heart.

Lowink stayed with the cutter. Midas, Aemos, Bequin and myself prepared to go into Dorsay. We changed into simple, anonymous clothing: dark blue robes for Aemos, plain black suits of good cloth and long leather coats for Betancore and myself, and a long gown of porcelain blue crepe with a cream-lace shawl for Alizebeth Bequin. Betancore, with some reluctance, had reopened Vibben's possessions to find clothing suitable for Bequin.

She didn't seem to mind that their former owner was dead.

Under red awnings fluttering in the dawn breeze, the island jetties were thick with passengers waiting for transport to the mainland. We queued among groups of merchants, visiting dignitaries and fleet ratings on furlough. Busking musicians and pedlars plied the captive audience.

At length, we hired one of the grav-skiffs lining up at the jetty. It was a long, speartip-shaped airboat with a glossy violet hull. Open-topped, it provided seats for six, with the steersman perched high at the aft over the bulbous anti-grav generators. It slid us across the lagoon, keeping two metres above the choppy, dappled water.

Dorsay rose before us. Now on its level, we could appreciate how majestic, how towering the city was. Rising above the water on stilts formed of vast basalt stacks and pillars, the buildings were constructed from smoothly fitted, cyclopean stone blocks, their facades limewashed, their shallow roofs dressed with verdigrised copper tiles. Gargoyles yawned at gutter ends or curled around downpipes and drain sluices. Upper storeys had balconies with railings made of tarnished copper; many balconies also had canopies. Arched stone bridges and metal stair-walks linked neighbouring buildings, sometimes across the water-filled streets themselves. Along the canal sides, stone walkways formed a water-level street for pedestrians.

And there were many of those. The place was alive with movement, colour and noise. Once we got into the city proper, our passage down the canals was slowed by other grav-skiffs, water-buses, private yawls and motor-driven boats.

Above us, at high traffic levels, speeders and atmospheric fliers buzzed back and forth. Everywhere we looked were banners celebrating Battlefleet Scarus and the Gudrunite guard regiments, especially the 50th Rifles.

Aemos chattered to himself as usual, noting the elements of Dorsay into his wrist slate, his hunger for accumulating knowledge unstinted. I watched him for a while, his nervous moves, his boyish glee at new details, his obsessive-compulsive tapping at his slate.

The keypads of that battered old slate were worn smooth.

Midas Betancore was alert and sharp as always. He sat in the front of the grav-skiff, soaking up details like Aemos.

But the details he noticed would be far more pertinent and immediately useful than my old savant's.

Bequin simply sat back and smiled, the chop of the breeze fluttering her shawl. I doubted she could ever have come here under her own steam. Gudrun was the epicentre of the sub-sector culture, the big bright world she had always dreamed about and of which she yearned to be a part.

I let her have her fun. There would be hard work later.

We took a suite of rooms at the Dorsay Regency. I considered it expedient to have a base of operations on the mainland. Betancore drilled out the door frames with a hand tool and installed locator bolts with built-in flash deterrents. We also wired the internal doorways. The house servitors were given strict instructions not to enter when we were absent.

I stood on the heavy, limewashed balcony, under a faded awning of purple canvas, and listened to the March of the Adeptes as it played out, distorted, from the speaker horns that dressed the street.

The canal below was thick with traffic. I saw a skiff overladen with drunken Guardsmen, all wearing their newly issued red and gold kits. Men of the 50th Gudrunite Rifles, raising hell and risking death by drowning as they enjoyed their last hours on their homeworld. In a few days they would be packed into a troopship and bound for who knew what horror a sub-sector away.

One of them fell into the canal as they tried to stagger ashore. His comrades dredged him out, and baptised his head with the contents of a liquor bottle.

Aemos joined me, and showed me a data-slate map.

'The Regal Bonded Merchant Guild of Sinesias,' he said. 'Headquarters are five streets away.'

Guild Sinesias owned some of the most imposing premises in the commercial district of Dorsay. A spur of the Grand Canal actually fed in under the coloured glass portico of the main buildings, so that visiting traders could run their skiffs inside and disembark under cover in a tiled and carpeted reception dock.

Our grav-skiff carried us in, and we stepped out amid clusters of tall, thin, gowned traders from Messina, merchants from Sameter in ludicrously heavy hats and veils, and obese bankers from the Thracian hives.

I strode ashore and turned to offer Bequin my hand. She nodded courteously as she left the skiff. I hadn't briefed her much. The aristocratic airs and graces were her own spontaneous invention. Though I still loathed her, I admired her more with each passing moment. She was playing things perfectly.

'Your name and business here, sire, madam?' a Guild Sinesias chamberlain asked as he approached us. He was dripping in finery, gold brocaded gowns attiring every servant in the place. Augmetic implants blistered in place of his ears and he clutched a slate and stylus.

'My name is Farchaval, a merchant from Hesperus. This is Lady Farchaval. We come to tender grain contracts with the high houses of this world, and we are told Guild Sinesias will provide us the necessary brokerage.'

'Do you have a guild responser, sire?'

'Of course. My contact was Saemon Crotes.'

'Crotes?' the chamberlain paused.

'Oh, Gregor, I'm so bored,' Bequin suddenly announced. 'This is so, so very slow and dull. I want to cruise the canals again. Why can't we go back and deal with those spirited fellows at Guild Mensurae?'

'Later, my dearest,' I said, delighted and wrong-footed by her improvisation.

'You have already... visited another guild?' the chamberlain asked quickly.

'They were very nice. They brought me Solian tea,' Bequin purred.

'Let me escort you both,' the chamberlain said at once. 'Saemon Crotes is, of course, one of our most valued envoys. I will arrange an audience for you forthwith. In the meantime, please relax in this suite. I will have Solian tea sent up directly.'

'And nafar biscuits?' cooed Bequin.

'But of course, madam.'

He swept out and closed the double doors of the luxurious waiting room behind him. Bequin looked at me and giggled. I confess, I laughed out loud.

'What got into you?'

'You said we were monied merchants who expected the very best. I was just earning my salary.'

'Keep it up,' I said.

We looked around the room. Gauze-draped windows ten metres high looked out over the Grand Canal, but they were insulated to keep the noise out. Rich tapestries dressed the walls between Sameter School oils that Maxilla would have loved to own.

A burnished servitor brought in a tray of refreshments soon after that. It lowered it onto a marble-topped occasional table and trundled out.

'Solian tea!' Bequin squeaked, lifting the lid of a porcelain pot. 'And nafar biscuits!' she added with a smile, through the crumbs of the first one.

She poured me a cup and I stood by the fireplace, sipping it, striking an appropriately haughty pose.

The guild representative flew in through the doors a moment later. He was a small, spiky-haired man with flowing gowns and far too much jewellery. The Guild Sinesias brand mark was proudly displayed on his forehead.

He was, the brand indicated, property.

His name was Macheles.

'Sire Farchaval! Madam! Had I known you were visiting, I would have cancelled meets to be here. Forgive my tardiness!'

'I forgive it,' I said. 'But I'm afraid Lady Farchaval may be fast losing her patience.'

Bequin yawned on cue.

'Oh, that is not good! Not good at all!' Macheles clapped his hands and servitors trundled in.

'Provide the lady with whatever she requests!' Macheles told them.

'Ummm... vorder leaves?' she said.

'At once!' Macheles instructed.

'And a plate of birri truffles? Sautéed in wine?'

I winced.

'At once! At once!' Macheles yelped, shushing the servitors out of the room.

I stepped forward and put down my cup. 'I'll be straight with you, sir. I represent grain merchants on Hesperus, a significant cartel of grain merchants.'

I handed him my holo-dent. It was fake, of course. Betancore and Aemos had run it up, using Aemos's profound knowledge in general and his knowledge of Hesperus – gleaned from interviews with Maxilla – in particular.

Macheles seemed impressed enough by my identification.

'What sort of... size cartel are we talking about. sire?'

'The entire western continent.'

'And you offer?'

I produced a sample tube from my pocket. 'A gene-fixed strain of cereal that could be easily managed by many of your landowners now that their workforce is depleted. It is indeed a wonder.'

The servitors reappeared, delivering Bequin's delicacies.

As she munched the soft-fleshed birri, she said, 'The other guilds are bidding for this product, mister. I do hope Guild Sinesias won't miss out.'

Macheles shook the sample tube and looked at it.

'Is this,' he said, his voice dropping, 'xenos cultured?'

'Would that be a problem?' I asked.

'No, sire! Not officially. The Inquisition is of course very tight about such things. But that is precisely why we offer these discreet interviews. The entire guild buildings are buffered against trackers, intercept beams and vox-thieves.'

'I am pleased to hear it. So a xenos-cultured cereal strain would not be hard to market?'

'Naturally not. There are collective enterprises eager for assured crop yields. Especially those hot-housed by alien technology.'

'Good,' I lied. 'But I want the best return. Saemon told me that House Glaw should be the first to approach.'

'Saemon?'

'Saemon Crotes. The Guild Sinesias envoy I dealt with on Hesperus.'

'Quite so! You wish me to arrange a trade meeting with House Glaw?'

'I think that's what I said, didn't I?'

* * *

We left the Guild Sinesias dock twenty minutes later. Bequin was still licking her lips from the birri.

As soon as our skiff was clear of the building, the vox-ceiver woven into my cuff began to twitch.

'Eisenhorn.'

It was Lowink. 'I've just accepted a message from Tobius Maxilla. Do you want me to relive it?'

'Just a summary, Lowink.'

'He says the ship that took Eyclone's Gudrun-Hubris run is at anchor here. Says he's done some probing. The Rogue Trader Scaveleur. The master, one Effries Tanokbrey, is already planetside.'

'Signal Maxilla and thank him for his work, Lowink.' I said.

The identity of Eyclone's mysterious starship was now known to me.

We were taking lunch at a commercial tavern overlooking the Bridge of Carnodons when Macheles sent Sire Farchaval a private text message by vox-drone.

The drone, an oblate metal unit roughly the size of a small citrus fruit, came buzzing into the dining terrace like a pollen-insect, scudding from table to table at head-height on its tiny repeller motors until it found me. Then it hovered, chimed, and beamed its holographic cargo against the side of my crystal tumbler: the crest of Guild Sinesias, followed by a formal and obsequious text inviting Sire Farchaval and his entourage to a meeting at the Glaw estate the following afternoon. We were to meet Macheles at the guild building at four, where transport would be waiting.

The drone continued to project the message until I broke the beam with a wave of my hand and made a quick verbal assent, which it recorded. Dismissed, it bumbled away with its answer.

'How did it find us?' asked Bequin.

'A pheromonal trace,' Aemos replied. 'The guild building's master systems will have sampled you both during your visit and then it would have come searching until it matched the record in its sensors.'

Vox-drone messaging was common practice on higher tech Imperial worlds like this. It gave me an idea.

'You say the guild seemed comfortable dealing with xenos material?' Betancore was saying, raising his wine glass to sip.

I nodded. 'We'll concentrate on House Glaw for now. That's where our primary interest lies. But I'm not going to forget Sinesias. When we're done, the full weight of the Inquisition will come to bear on their dealings.'

Bequin was looking out at the fine ornamental bridge that arched over the Drunner below. 'What are those creatures?' she asked. The stone effigies of great quadruped predators decorated each span of the old crossing. The beasts were huge, with powerful, mastiff-like builds, brush tails and long snouts bristling with tusks.

'Carnodons,' Aemos said, once again delighted to be able to share his considerable knowledge. 'The heraldic animal of Gudrun. They feature in many crests and emblems here-abouts, symbolising the noble authority of the world. Rare now, of course. Hunted to near extinction. I believe only a few live wild now in the northern tundra.'

'We have a day at our disposal,' I told them, cutting through the idle talk. 'Let's use it well. Let's find this ship master, Tanokbrey.'

Betancore raised his eyebrows and was about to tell me how difficult that was going to be, until I explained my idea to him.

* * *

We used a clerical bureau on a water-street off the Ooskin Canal, and paid for a vox-drone message. I kept it simple, a brief enquiry to the master of the Rogue Trader Scaveleur concerning the possibility of off-planet passage. The cleric serving me took my text and payment without comment, and loaded the message into one of the three-dozen vox-drones that lay inert in a rack behind his seat. Then he accessed his data-files, retrieved the pheromone trace for Tanokbrey that the ship master had logged with the city administration at immigration, and installed that too.

The selected drone rose, buzzed, and floated away out of the office.

On the street outside, Betancore fired up the motor of the air-bike he had rented and made off after it.

Chances were it would lead us to our quarry. If it gave Betancore the slip, there was every reason to hope Tanokbrey would come to us. He was a commercial merchant looking for business after all.

Aemos, Bequin and I followed in a public grav-skiff, staying in vox-contact with Betancore. The canal traffic was thicker than ever, and local Arbites, as well as naval security details, were out in force. There was to be a major ceremonial caval-cade later that afternoon, and the route was being prepared. Already, crowds of spectators were gathering on the bridges and the walkways. Banners and well-wishing garlands were on display all around.

Betancore was waiting for us on a walkway in the Tersegold Quarter, a part of Dorsay famous for its taverns and clubs. I left Aemos and Bequin in the skiff.

'In there,' he said, indicating an old, bow-fronted estab-lishment. 'I followed it inside. It delivered to the fifth table from the left. Tanokbrey is the tall man in the rose-red jacket.

He has two men with him by my count.'

'Stay back and be ready,' I said.

The tavern was dark and crowded. Music and lights pulsed from the low roof, and the air was rank with the smells of sweat, smoke, hops and the unmistakable fumes of obscura.

My vox-drone was coming out through the door as I entered. It paused, delivered its message and then drifted away. A curt text informed me that the Scaveleur was not for hire.

Moving through the packed clientele, I located Tanokbrey. His rose-red jacket was of finest silk and his frizzy black hair was raked back into twists and tied with ribbons at the back of his head. He had a craggy, singularly unwelcoming face. His drinking companions were a pair of common crewmen in studded leather bodygloves.

'Master Tanokbrey?'

He looked round at me slowly and said nothing. His comrades fixed me with grim stares.

'Perhaps we could talk privately?' I suggested.

'Perhaps you could piss off.'

I sat down anyway. His men seemed astonished at my action, and stiffened. All Tanokbrey had to do was nod, I realised.

'Let me start with an easy question,' I began.

'Start by pissing off,' he replied. He was now fixing me with a caustic gaze. Without breaking eye contact, I noted that his left hand was inside his coat.

'You seem anxious. Why is that?'

No answer. His men stirred nervously.

'Something to hide?'

'I'm having a quiet drink. I don't want interruptions. Now sod off.'

'So unfriendly. Well, if these gentlemen aren't going to give us privacy, I'll press on regardless. I do hope I don't embarrass you.'

'Who the hell are you?'

Now I didn't reply. My eyes never left his. 'Your high-anchor fees are delinquent,' I said at last.

'That's a lie!'

It was, and so was what I said next. It didn't matter. The purpose was to undermine him. 'And your manifest papers are incomplete. Gudrun control may wish to impound your ship until the irregularities are cleared up.'

'Lying bastard–'

'It's an easy matter. You made a run to Hubris that is not logged, nor is any cargo list filed. How will they calculate import duties?'

His chair scraped back a centimetre or two.

'Why were you on Hubris?'

'I wasn't! Who says I was?'

'Take your pick. Saemon Crotes. Namber Wylk.'

'Don't know them. You've got the wrong man, you miserable bastard. Now frag off!'

'Murdin Eyclone, then. What about him? Didn't he hire you?'

That brought the nod at last. An imperceptible motion of his head.

The crewman beside me lunged out of his seat, a compact shock-flail snapping out of his sleeve and into his gloved hand.

'Drop it,' I willed, without even speaking.

The flail sparked as it bounced off the table top.

It was in my hand a second later. I whipped it back across its owner's face and smashed him sideways off his chair. Then I snapped it round, crushed the left ear of the other crewman and laid him full length on the floor at the foot of the table.

I sat back down, facing Tanokbrey, the flail in my hand. His face as grey and his eyes darted now with panic.

'Eyclone. Tell me about him.'

His left arm moved inside his jacket and I jabbed the flail into his shoulder. Unfortunately, I realised he was wearing armour under that silk.

He reeled from the impact, but his arm came up all the same, a short-snouted laspistol clutched in his fist.

I slammed the table into him and his shot went wild, punching through the back of a nearby ruffian. The victim toppled over, bringing another table smashing down.

Now the shot and the commotion had got the attention of the entire tavern. There was general shouting and confusion.

I didn't pay it any heed. Tanokbrey fired again through the overturned table and I dove aside, colliding with milling bodies.

The merchant was on his feet, kicking and punching his way through the mob to the exit. I could see Betancore, but the mass of bodies prevented him from blocking Tanokbrey.

'Aside!' I yelled, and the crowd parted like hatch shutters.

Tanokbrey was on the walkway outside, running for the quay at the end of the street. He turned and fired. Pedestrians screamed and ran. Someone was pushed into the canal.

Tanokbrey leapt into a grav-skiff, shot the protesting hire-driver, pushed the corpse off the steering perch, and gunned the craft away down the canal.

Betancore's air-bike was sat on its kickstand to my left. I cranked the power and swept off down the waterway in pursuit.

'Wait! Wait!' I heard Betancore yelling.

No time.

* * *

Tanokbrey's flight caused mayhem down the length of the busy canal. He drove his skiff into the jostling traffic, forcing craft to heave out of his way. Already the decorative golden filigree on the skiff's black hull was grazed and dented with a dozen glancing impacts. People on the banks and abroad on the water howled and yelled at him as he wrenched his way through. Where the street met a canal thoroughfare, he tried to extend his lead with a surge of speed. A fast-moving courier boat coming down the stream veered at the last moment, and struck the quayside with great force, sending the craft up over end, its hull shredding, its driver cartwheeling through the air.

I laced the air-bike through the disrupted traffic in Tanokbrey's wake. I wanted to gain height, and move to a level where I could coax more speed from the machine without fear of collision. But the vehicle's grav-plate had a governor unit that prevented anything more than three metres of climb. I had no time to figure out where the governor was or how to disable it. I aimed the bike between turning skiffs, water-buses heavy in the choppy canal, other darting air-bikes.

Ahead, I could hear the distant sounds of military bands.

Tanokbrey whipped out of a junction into the Grand Canal, and straight into the side of the afternoon's parade. A slow-moving river of skiffs, military barges and landspeeder escorts filled the entire width of the waterway. The craft were full of jubilant Imperial Guardsmen and officers, thundering regimental bands and battlefleet dignitaries. The air was glittering with streamers and banners, company standards, Imperial eagles and Gudrunite carnodons. One entire barge bore a massive golden carnodon sculpture to which whooping Guardsmen clung. Garlands fluttered from the barrels of a thousand brandished las-rifles. The walkways and bridges of the Grand Canal were choked with cheering civilians.

Tanokbrey's skiff smacked into the side of a troop-barge, and angry yells and jeers were loosed at him as he tried to turn. From the shore, the crowd pelted him with fruit, stones and other missiles.

Cursing back at the angry soldiers, he slammed his skiff round the rear of the barge, trying to force his way across the canal.

I was closing on him now, trying to avoid the displeasure of the mob. Hooters and sirens bayed at him from the parade boats as he jostled across their paths. A trooper from one barge leapt onto his skiff to waylay him, and Tanokbrey kicked him off into the water before he could get a good footing. That turned things even uglier. The noise of the booing and outrage was immense. The parade bunched up badly, and dozens of furious guardsmen pressed at the rails of their barges, trying to reach him.

He over-revved the skiff to get clear of them, and struck against a raft carrying a company band. Several instrument players toppled with the impact, and the proud Imperial anthem they had been playing dissolved in a cacophony of wrong notes and broken rhythms.

Enraged troopers in a smaller skiff drew alongside him, and rocked his craft dangerously as they tried to board. He pulled his handgun.

His last mistake. I pulled up short, and landed on the canal bank. There was no point in pressing the pursuit now.

Tanokbrey got off two shots into the mob. Then twenty or more freshly issued las-rifles on a neighbouring barge opened fire, smashing him and his stolen craft to pieces. The drive unit exploded, scattering hull fragments across the churning water. A curl of black smoke rose above the banners.

The young conscripts of the 50th Gudrunite Rifles had made the first kill of their military careers.

TEN

**A conflict of jurisdiction
The House of Glaw
Stalking secrets**

Long after midnight, I was attempting to sleep in my bed-chamber at the Dorsay Regency. Bequin and Aemos had both retired to their own rooms hours before. Reflected light from the canal outside played a series of silver ripples across the ceiling of my twilit chamber.

'Aegis, rose thorn!' Betancore's voxed whisper suddenly tapped at my ear.

'Rose thorn, reveal.'

'Spectres, invasive, spiral vine.'

I was already out of bed and into my breeches and boots, pulling my leather coat over my bare torso. I went out into the apartment lounge with my power sword in my hand.

The lights were off, but canal reflections played in here too, creating a fluttering half-light.

Betancore stood by the far wall, a needle pistol in each hand. He nodded at the main door.

They were good and they were very quiet, but we could both see slight movement against the cracks around the doors, backlit by the hall light.

A gentle vibration of the handle told me someone was springing the lock. Betancore and I dropped back against the walls either side of the doors. We closed our eyes and covered our ears. Any forcing of the door would trigger the deterrent charges, and we didn't want to wind up blind or deaf.

The door opened a crack. No flash charges roared. Our visitors had detected and neutralised the security counter-measures. They were even better than I first thought.

A slender telescopic rod extended smoothly in through the crack. An optical sensor on the end slowly began to pan around, searching the room. With a nod to Betancore, I moved forward, took hold of the rod and yanked hard. At the same moment, I ignited my power sword.

A body crashed into the doors, dragged forward by my hefty pull on the spy-stick, and came tumbling in. I leapt in to strad- dle the body, but despite his surprise, he writhed away with a curse, and threw a punch. I had a vague impression of a tall, thickly built man in form-fitting leather.

We flopped over together, wrestling, overturning a couch and knocking down a candle-stand. My opponent had a good grip on the wrist of my sword arm.

So I punched him in the throat with my left hand.

He collapsed, retching, onto the floor. I got up in time to hear a strong voice say, 'Put the weapons down now.'

A short, hunched figure stood in the open doorway. Betan- core had both pistols trained on it, but was slowly lowering them despite himself.

The figure had used the will. I brushed the tingle aside, but it was too much for Midas. The needle pistols thumped onto the carpet.

'Now you,' the figure said, turning its silhouette towards me. 'Disarm that power-blade.'

I seldom had an opportunity to feel the effect of psyker manipulation. The technique was different from the ones I employed, and the force of will was unmistakably potent. I braced myself for the hideous strain of outright telepathic combat.

'You resist?' said the figure. A blade of mental energy stabbed into my skull, rocking me backwards. I knew at once I was fundamentally outclassed. This was an old, powerful, practiced mind.

A second stab of pain, cutting into the first. The man I had left choking was now on his knees. Another psyker. More powerful than the first, it seemed, but with far less control or technique. His attack seared through my skull and made me bark out in pain, but I blocked him as I stumbled back and stung his eager mind away with a desperate, unfocused jab.

The boiling psychic waves were rattling the windows and vibrating the furniture. Glasses shattered and Betancore fell, whimpering. The hunched figure stepped forward again, and dropped me to my knees with renewed mental assaults. I felt blood spurt from my nose. My vision swam. My grip on the sword remained tight.

Abruptly, it stopped. Roused by the disturbance, both Aemos and Bequin had burst into the room. Bequin screamed. Her psychic blankness, abruptly intruding on the telepathic maelstrom, suddenly blew the energies out, like a vacuum snuffing the heart of a fire.

The hunched figure cried out and stumbled in surprise. I drove forward, grabbed him and hurled him bodily across the chamber. He seemed frail but surprisingly heavy for such a small mass.

Betancore recovered his weapons and lit the lamps.

The man I had pulled through the doors was little more than a youth, big built with a long, shaved skull and a slit of a mouth. He was crumpled by the windows, semi-conscious. He wore a black leather bodyglove adorned with equipment harnesses. Bequin relieved him of his holstered sidearm.

The other, the hunched figure, rose slowly and painfully, ancient limbs cracking and protesting. He wore long dark robes; his thin hands were clad in black satin gloves. A number of gaudy rings protruded from the folds of the gown. He pulled back his cowl.

He was very old, his weathered, lined face wizened like a fruit stone. His throat, exposed at the gown's neckline, betrayed traces of the augmetic work that undoubtedly encased his age-twisted body.

His eyes blazed at me from their deep sockets with cold fury.

'You have made a mistake,' he said, wheezing, 'a fatal one, I have no doubt.' He produced a chunky amulet and held it up. The sigil it bore was unmistakable. 'I am Inquisitor Commo-dus Voke.'

I smiled. 'Well met, brother,' I said.

Commodus Voke stared at my rosette for a few lingering seconds, then looked away. I could feel the psychic throbbing of his rage.

'We have a... conflict of jurisdiction,' he managed to say, straightening his robes. His assistant, now back on his feet, stood in the corner of the chamber and gazed sullenly at me.

'Then let us resolve it,' I offered. 'Explain to me why you invade my apartments in the dead of night.'

'My work brought me to Gudrun eight months ago. An ongoing investigation, a complex matter. A rogue trader had come to my attention, one Effries Tanokbrey. I had begun to close my net around him when he was scared into flight and got himself killed. Simple cross-checking revealed that a grain merchant called Farchaval had somehow been instrumental in that incident.'

'Farchaval is my cover here on Gudrun.'

'You see fit to play-act and hide your true nature?' he said scornfully.

'We each have our methods, inquisitor,' I replied.

I'd never met the great Commodus Voke before, but his reputation preceded him. An intractable puritan in his ethic, almost leaning to the hard-line of the monodominants but for the fact of his remarkable psychic abilities. I believe something of a Thorian doctrine suited his beliefs. He had served as a noviciate with the legendary Absalom Angevin three hundred years before and since then had played a key role in some of the most thorough and relentless purges in sector history. His methods were open and direct. Stealth, co-operation and subterfuge were distasteful concepts to him. He used the full force of his status, and the fear it generated, to go where he pleased and demand anything of anyone to achieve his goals.

In my experience, the heavy-handed, terror-inspiring approach closes as many doors as it smashes open. Frankly, it didn't surprise me to learn he had already been on this planet for a full eight months.

He looked at me as if I was something he had almost stepped in. 'I am discomforted when I see inquisitors holding to the soft, cunning ways of the radical. That way heresy lies, Eisenhorn.'

That made me start. I consider myself, as I have reported, very much of the puritanical outlook. Staunch, hard-line in my own way, though flexible enough to get the job done efficiently. Yet here was Voke gauging me as a radical! And at that moment, next to him, I felt I may as well be the most extreme, dangerous Horusian, the most artful and scheming recongregator.

I tried to push past that. 'We need to share more information, inquisitor. I'll take a guess and say your investigation somehow involves the Glaw family.'

Voke said nothing and showed no response, but I felt his assistant tense psychically behind me.

'Our work is indeed clashing,' I went on. 'I, too, am interested in House Glaw.' In short, simple terms I laid out the matter of Eyclone's activities on Hubris, and drew the connection to Glaw and Gudrun by way of the mysterious Pontius.

I had his interest now. 'Pontius is just a name, Eisenhorn. Pontius Glaw on the other hand, is long dead. I served with worthy Angevin in the purge that destroyed him. I saw his corpse.'

'Yet here you are, investigating the Glaws anyway.'

He exhaled slowly, as if making his mind up. 'After Pontius Glaw's eradication, the House of Glaw made great efforts to distance itself from his heresy. But Angevin, rest his immortal soul, always suspected that the taint ran deeper and that the family was not free of corruption. It is an ancient house, and powerful. It is difficult to probe its secrets. But from time to time, over the past two hundred years, I have turned my eye to them. Fifteen months ago, prosecuting a coven on Sader VII, I uncovered traces which suggested that particular coven, and several other minor groups, were collectively being run by an all but invisible parent cult – a cult of great scope and power, old and hidden, stretching across many worlds. Some traces led to Gudrun. That Gudrun is the Glaw's ancestral home was for me, too much of a coincidence.'

'Now we make progress,' I said, sitting down in a high-backed chair and pulling on a shirt Bequin brought to me from my chamber. Aemos poured six glasses of amasec from a decanter on the dresser. Taking one as it was offered, Voke sat down opposite me. He sipped, contemplatively.

His assistant refused the glass that Aemos offered and remained standing.

'Sit down, Heldane!' Voke said. 'We have things to learn here.'

The assistant took a glass and sat in the corner.

'I hunt out a cabal controlled by a notorious facilitator,' I continued, 'a cabal set on performing an abominable crime. The trail leads to Gudrun and the Glaws. You do the same with another heretical cell–'

'Three others, in fact,' he corrected.

'Three, then. And you see the shape of a far greater organisation. From the facts as they stand, we are both approaching the same evil from opposite sides.'

He licked his lips with a tiny, pallid tongue and nodded. 'Since coming to Gudrun I have rooted out and burned two heretical cells. I am reasonably sure of the activities of another nine, three here in Dorsay alone. I have allowed them to fester as I observe them. For months, they have seemed bent on preparation for some event. Abruptly, a matter of weeks ago, their behaviour changed. This would have been around the same time as your confrontation on Hubris.'

'Eyclone's undertaking was also great, with extensive preparatory work. Yet, at the eleventh hour, something either went wrong or plans were suddenly changed. Though I defeated and destroyed him, his plans were really thwarted by the fact that the Pontius didn't arrive. What has your work revealed of House Glaw?'

'I have visited them twice in three months. On both

occasions, they have made every effort to answer my questions, allowing me to search the estate and their records. I have found nothing.'

'I fear, perhaps, that is because they knew they were dealing with an inquisitor. Tomorrow, Sire Farchaval has a trade meeting with the Glaws at their estate.'

He mused on this. 'The Inquisition has a duty to stand together, firmly, against the arch-enemies of mankind. In the spirit of co-operation, I will wait and see what your dubious methods reveal. Precious little, I imagine.'

'In the spirit of co-operation, Voke, I will share all I learn with you.'

'You will do better than that. The Glaws know me, but not all of my students. Heldane will go with you.'

'I don't think so.'

'I insist. I will not have years of work ruined by another agency such as yourself running rough-shod through the matter. I require my own observer on the ground, or my co-operation will not be extended.'

He had me in a vice and he knew it. To refuse outright would simply confirm my radical, careless approach in his eyes. And I had no wish to draw battlelines against another of the Inquisition, especially a man as powerful and influential as Commodus Voke.

'Then he had better do exactly as I instruct him,' I said.

We left Dorsay for the Glaw estates the next afternoon at four. Dressed once more as wealthy but not ostentatious merchants, Bequin and I were accompanied by Aemos, Betancore and Heldane, Voke's man. Heldane, I was pleased to see, had made a reasonable job of adopting simple civilian dress. He and Betancore would pose as our bodyguard and escort, and Aemos was to take the part of a gene-biologist.

Macheles, and four other luxuriously robed envoys from the Regal Bonded Merchant Guild of Sinesias, were waiting for us at the guild headquarters. An atmospheric launch had been prepared.

The launch, a burnished dart bearing the guild crest, left the landing platform of the guild building's roof, and rose smoothly into the overcast sky. It was, Macheles informed us, to be a two-hour flight. A guild envoy circulated through the richly furnished cabin with trays of refreshment.

Macheles explained our itinerary: a formal dinner with the representatives of House Glaw that evening, an overnight stay, and then a tour of the estates the following morning. After that, negotiations if both parties were still interested.

We flew west, inland, leaving the inclement coastal weather behind and passing into a sunlit landscape of rolling pasture, low hills, and maintained forests. The snaking silver line of the Drunner winked below us. There were occasional small settlements, farmsteads, a compact market town with a tall Ecclesiarchy spire. Once in a while, we saw another air vehicle in the distance.

A dark range of hills began to fill the western skyline. Evening was beginning to discolour the clouds. The region approaching the hills rose in bluffs and headlands, a more majestic and wild landscape, thickly wooded on escarpments and deep vales.

Already, Macheles boasted, we were flying over Glaw property.

The estate itself loomed out of the dimming hills some minutes later: a three-storey main house built in the neo-gothic style, dominating a bluff and staring down across the deep valley from a hundred window eyes. The limewashed stone

glowed lambently in the twilight. Adjoining the main structure were substantial wings built at different times. One led
to stables and other considerable stone outbuildings along
the edge of the woodland, and I presumed this to be the
servants' block. The other wing edged the crown of the bluff,
and was dominated by a dome that shone gold in the sink-
ing sun. The place was huge, and no doubt labyrinthine.
The population of a modest town could have been accommodated within it.

The launch settled onto a wide stone yard behind the house.
At the edge of the yard, in what looked like converted coach
houses, three other launches were stationed in hangars with
well-equipped maintenance bays.

We disembarked into the yard. The air was cold and a night
breeze was bringing spots of rain with it. The wind sighed in
the stands of trees beyond the house. Heavy bars of cloud
laced the evening sky above the towering hills.

Servants in dark green liveries hurried out to us, taking up
our luggage and raising wide, long-handled parasols to shield
us from the drizzle. A number of uniformed guards from the
Glaws' house retinue flanked the yard. Haughty and confident
in their long emerald stormcoats and plumed silver helmets,
the guards seemed like experienced veterans to my eyes.

The servants escorted us and the guild envoys into an atrium
with a black and white tiled floor and a bright, silvery cast to
the light. Dozens of vast crystal chandeliers hung from the
high, arched roof. More guards flanked the doorways. The
Glaws' militia was clearly sizeable.

'Welcome to the House of Glaw,' a woman's voice said.

She approached us, a well-made woman of good, high
stock, her powdered face bearing the proud insouciance of
all nobility. She wore a regal black gown, floor length and

wide in the skirt and laced with a silver overstitching, and a great twin-cusped head-dress of black mesh and pearls that tied under her chin with a wide black ribbon.

Macheles and the envoys bowed ceremoniously and the five of us made more conservative nods.

'The Lady Fabrina Glaw,' announced Macheles. She approached, green-coated servants forming a human wake behind her.

'Lady,' I said.

'Sire Farchaval. I am so pleased to meet you.'

She gave us a brief tour of the main house. I have seldom seen such extravagance and riches outside of an Imperial court – or Tobius Maxilla's staterooms. Lean hunting dogs trotted with us. She pointed out a number of ancient paintings, mostly oil portraits, but some exquisite hololithic works, as well as vivid psyk-pict miniatures. Her illustrious family... uncles, grandfathers, cousins, matriarchs, warlords. Here was Vernal Glaw in the dress uniform of the house militia. Here was Orchese Glaw entertaining the royal house of Sameter. Over there, Lutine and Gyves Glaw, brothers at the hunt. There great Oberon himself, in the robes of an Imperial commander, one hand resting on an antique globe of Gudrun.

The envoys made appropriate noises of admiration. Fabrina herself seemed to just be going through the motions. She was acting the hostess. We were, after all, just grain merchants. This was a duty. An obligation.

I saw Aemos making surreptitious notes. I too made careful observations, especially of the house geography. In one long hallway, the stone floor was dressed by the rather worn pelts of three carnodons, skinned, spread-eagled, their massive tusked mouths and baleful eyes frozen in attitudes of

rage. Even in this sad state, the size and power of these creatures spoke for themselves.

'We hunted them, but there are few left now,' Fabrina Glaw
remarked, off-hand, seeing my interest. 'Old times, long
passed. Life was rather more feudal then. Today, House Glaw
looks entirely to the future.'

At dinner, in the massive banqueting hall, we were joined by
Urisel Glaw, the commander of the house militia, and his
eldest brother, Oberon, the current Lord Glaw. But the dinner was not solely in our honour. A cousin of the Glaw family
and his entourage were visiting from off-world, as were several other trade delegations and a wealthy ship master called
Gorgone Locke.

I was not surprised. Visiting grain traders, even ones accompanied by the prestigious Guild Sinesias, hardly merited a
formal banquet. It was appropriate we should be honoured
by our inclusion at a larger event. No doubt we were meant
to be impressed.

I attended with Bequin and Aemos. There was no place for
servants and bodyguards here, so Betancore and Heldane
had been escorted to our suite and food provided for them
there. That suited my approach fine.

There were five long tables in the hall, laden with roast
meat, fruit and countless delicacies. Attentive butlers and
serving staff moved everywhere, offering platters and topping
up glasses. Stern members of the house militia in green and
brocade dress uniforms and polished silver helmets stood at
every corner of the chamber.

We were on the third table, with a contingent of livestock
merchants from Gallinate, a city on Gudrun's southern continent. Our status afforded us the company of Lady Fabrina,

Captain Terronce from the household guard, and a talkative man named Kowitz, a House Glaw official responsible for buying produce.

Lord Oberon and his brother, Urisel, presided over the head table, with their visiting cousin, the ship master Locke and an elderly ecclesiarch called Dazzo. Kowitz was happy to tell me that Ecclesiarch Dazzo represented a missionary order from the sub-sector edgeworld Damask, which House Glaw was sponsoring.

In fact, it was difficult to shut Kowitz up. As the butlers refilled his cup, he rattled on, identifying the other parties of guests. House Glaw had interests on worlds throughout the sub-sector, and regular banquets such as this oiled the wheels and kept things moving.

Eventually, I managed to hand Kowitz off to Aemos, the only man I knew capable of out-talking him. The two fell to complex discussion of the sub-sector balance of trade.

I kept a close eye on the head table. Urisel Glaw, a bloated, thick-set man in bejewelled ceremonial battledress, was giving Gorgone Locke plenty of attention. I watched Urisel closely. There was something about the man, not the least that his wide, puffy face and slick, lacquered hair made his resemblance to portraits of his infamous ancestor Pontius uncanny. He drank unstintingly, and laughed a wet, loose laugh at the ship master's jokes. His fat, powerful fingers constantly pulled at the braided collar of his uniform jacket to ease his wide neck.

Lord Oberon was a taller, leaner man with generous, cliff-like cheekbones rising above a forked goatee. The familial characteristics of the Glaw line were plain in his physiognomy, but he was more regal and distinguished, and lacked the dissolute languor of his younger sibling. Lord Glaw spent the night chatting happily with his off-world cousin, a bumptious young cretin with a whooping laugh and flamboyant courtly manners. But his real interest seemed to lie with the quiet ecclesiarch, Dazzo.

I took note of the ship master too. Gorgone Locke was a raw-boned giant with hooded, sunken eyes. He had long red hair, tied back and beaded, and his jutting chin was peppered with silver stubble. I wondered about his ship, and his business. I would contact Maxilla and make enquiries.

The banquet lasted until past midnight. As soon as was polite, we retired to our rooms.

The Glaws had given us a suite of rooms in the west wing. Outside, the wind had got up, and was making plaintive sighs down the old chimney flues and open grates. Rain pattered against windows, and doors and shutters twitched and knocked in the drafts.

Heldane was alone in the suite's sitting room when we came back. He had several data-slates open for study on a table and looked up as we came in.

'Well?' I asked him.

He and Betancore had run sweeps of the immediate wing whilst we had been dining. He showed me the results. Most of the rooms were spy-wired with vox-thieves and a few pict-sensors, and there was a complex infrastructure of alarm systems. Heldane had set up a small jammer to blind the spy-ware in our suite.

'Comparisons,' he said, showing me an overlay of two charts on a data-slate. 'The green areas show the parts of the buildings my master gained access to during his visits.' Voke had been obliging enough to supply me with reports of his inspections.

'We can overlay in red the results of the sweeps your man and I have managed to make this evening.'

There were considerable discrepancies. Voke may have opened every door he could find, but this showed me ghost areas that he had not gained access to because he hadn't known they were there.

'These are cellars?' I asked.

'Underground rooms, certainly.' said Heldane. He had a soft, sickly voice that seemed to seep from his slit-like mouth. 'Adjoining the wine vaults.'

The drapes billowed in as an exterior window opened. Betancore, his hooded black bodyglove wet with rain, climbed inside. He pulled off his grip-gloves and boots, and unstrapped his equipment harness.

'What did you find?'

Dripping and cold, he took a glass of spirits Bequin brought him and showed me his scanner pad.

'The roof is lousy with alarms. I didn't dare probe too far, even with my jammers and sensors. There are rooms under the east wing that Inquisitor Voke didn't know about. A network of tunnels seems to link them to the west wing under the courtyard.'

I spent a few more minutes running through the details, and then went into my room to change.

I put on a heat-insulated bodyglove of matt-black plastic weave with a tight-fitting hood and supple gloves. Then I strapped a webbing harness around my torso and filled the integral pouches with a compact scope, a set of multi-keys, a folding knife, two spools of monofilament wire, a tubular torch, two jamming units and a scanner pad. I secured my vox-unit's earpiece under my hood, buckled an autopistol into the rig strapped across my chest, dropped two spare clips into a thigh pouch, and finally placed my inquisitorial rosette in my hip pocket.

This was an endeavour that risked discovery. The rosette would be my joker, to be played if it became necessary.

I went back into the sitting room and laced on the grip-gloves and grip-boots that Betancore had been using.

'If I'm not back in a hour, you can start to worry,' I told them.

Outside, blackness, rain and the assault of the wind.

The outside wall of the great house was soaked and old, the limewash crumbling in places. I had to test every move I made to make sure the overlapping teeth of the grip-pads on my hands and feet were secure.

I moved along the side of the house, feeling my way, until I was able to crouch on an outcrop of guttering. I'd taped Betancore's data-slate to my left forearm for easy reference. The tiny backlit screen showed a three-dimensional model of the building, and an inertial locator built into the slate moved the map and kept my current location centred.

Over the downpour, I heard feet crunching gravel two storeys below. I clung to the bricks and tapped off the slate so that the screen glow wouldn't give me away.

Two men from the house militia huddled in foul-weather capes passed below me, lit by the windows on the ground floor. They took shelter in a doorway porch and shortly after that I saw the flash of an igniter or match. Presently, the cloying odour of obscura drifted up to me.

They were almost directly below my perch and I didn't dare move until they were gone. I waited. My joints were going numb from the cold and from the hunched position I had been forced to adopt simply to stay on the gutter.

The rain grew still heavier and the wind swished the invisible trees of the steep woods behind the house. I could hear the men chatting. An occasional laugh.

This wouldn't do. I was losing time and the feeling in my legs.

I focused, drew in a calming breath and reached out with the will.

I found their minds, two warm traces in the cold below me. They were soft and blurred, their responses undoubtedly slowed by the opiate effects of the obscura. Difficult minds to plant strong suggestions in, but vulnerable to paranoia.

I drove in with the will, toying gently with their anxieties.

Within seconds, they started from the cover of the porch, hissing animatedly at each other, and headed off at a trot across the yard.

Relieved, I moved down the wall, bracing my weight against a jutting window ledge as I found footholds around a down-pipe bracket.

On the ground, I hugged the shadows of the west wing, and moved down the yard. Betancore's careful reconnaissance had shown up laser trips around the gatehouse, and others that extended from the edges of the border beds to the basin of a fountain in the yard. Though I could not see them, they were precisely marked on the slate, and I simply stepped over each in turn, all except the last, which ran at waist height and which I ducked under.

My goal was the launch hangars on the far side of the rear yard. The sweeps had shown up an access point to the cellar network there. Betancore had located others, but they were all in private areas of the house, or in staff sections such as the scullery, the cold store and the meat pantries.

The shutter doors of the launch hangars were closed, and the lights off within. I gripped my way up the outside stone, and up along the shallow tiled roof. At the summit of each hangar roof was a metal box-vent designed to expel exhaust fumes. With my folding knife, I prised a louvred metal panel away and slid into the duct, feet first.

The short metal funnel of the duct was open below me and I looked down at the top of a parked launch. A short drop and I was crouching on the back of the vehicle in the dim garage.

I got off the craft and went around behind it. A small wall-hatch led through into a servicing workshop, which then opened into a parts store. The ferrocrete floor was spotted with oil, and I had to move carefully in the dark to avoid knocking into obstructions such as lathes, tool-trolleys and dangling hoist chains.

I checked the slate. The access-way was at the rear of the parts store.

This door was taking itself much more seriously. A tamper-proof ceramite seal, a tumbler alarm and a keypad for entry-codes.

I sighed, though I hadn't expected this to be easy. I would need to tape a jammer to the latch to avoid tripping any alarm or access signal. Then it would be a job for the scanner to search and configure a usable code. Ten minutes' work if I was lucky. Hours if not.

I pulled off my grip gloves so I could more easily manipulate the tools, and paused. An idea struck me. My mentor, the mighty Hapshant, had lacked psychic skills of his own. A dyed in the wool monodominant, Emperor love him. But he had been a firm believer in gut-instinct. He told me a servant of the Emperor could do worse than trust a flash of instinct. In his opinion, the Emperor himself placed such feelings there.

I tapped the word 'daesumnor' into the pad. The lock cycled and the door opened.

* * *

A clean, warm, well-ventilated staircase, significantly newer than the main structures of the estate, took me down into the cellar system. There was a caged lamp every three metres down the wall. By the chart and my estimation, I was some ten metres underground, moving beneath the east wing. I removed my hood to hear better.

'Daesumnor' opened another hatch, and I entered a long hall with hatch-doors along one side. One stood open, and I could hear voices and smell smoke.

I edged along, and skirted the hatch so I could peer in.

'... secured with two weeks,' a voice was saying.

'Said that month ago!' another snorted. 'What's the matter, you trying to inflate your fee?'

The room was some kind of lounge or study. Books and slates were racked with archive-like precision in wooden stacks along the walls. Soft light glowed from pendant lamps, and also from a number of sealed, glass-topped caskets in front of the shelving. They reminded me of the protective, controlled environment units Imperial libraries used to display especially ancient and valuable texts.

The room was carpeted, and as I craned round, I could see four men sitting around a low table in throne-like armchairs. One had his back to me, but from the folds of his coat falling over the chair's arm, I was certain it was Urisel Glaw. Facing him, sitting back in his chair, was the ship master, Gorgone Locke. The other two I didn't know, but I had a feeling they'd both been at the dinner. They all had glasses of liquor and one of the unknown men was using a water-pipe to inhale obscura. Various objects lay on the table between them, some wrapped in velvet, others unwrapped and displayed. They looked like stone tablets, old relics of some sort.

'I'm just trying to explain the delay, Glaw,' Locke said.

'They're a difficult enough culture to deal with at the best of times.'

'That's why we pay you,' Glaw said with a scoffing laugh. He leaned forward and toyed with one of the tablets.

'But we won't stand much further delay. We've invested a great deal in this matter. Time, funds, resources. It's meant holding back or cancelling other enterprises, some of them very special to us.'

'You will not be disappointed, lord,' said the man with the narco-pipe. He was dressed simply in black, a slightly built, bald individual with watery blue eyes. 'The archaeoxenan provenance of these items speaks for itself. The saruthi are serious about their offer.'

Urisel started to reply and got to his feet. I ducked into cover and then moved away down the hall. Eyclone's code opened the door at the end and I crept through into a wide, circular vault. Two more hatches of regular pattern led off to either side. Ahead of me was a larger archway protected by a force screen instead of a door.

I backed into hiding alongside this opening as someone cancelled the force screen from inside. A figure stepped out, turning to raise the screen again. It was Kowitz.

I took him from behind, an arm locked around his throat to silence him, another hand pinning his right arm. He gurgled and struggled. I twisted him round and slammed his head against the doorframe.

Kowitz went limp. I dragged him in through the open force-portal. A control on the inner wall raised the screen again.

The chamber was long with a low ceiling. The climate-controlled air was dry. I realised it was a chapel of sorts, a stone-floored, rectangular nave leading to a shape that seemed to me an altar. The room was otherwise bare of features, even seats or pews. Light glowed from recessed lamps in the roof. Leaving Kowitz on the floor, I strode down the length of the chapel and took a closer look at the altar.

It was two metres high, black, fashioned from a single piece of obsidian. The glassy stone seemed to glow with an internal light. On top of it was a jewelled prayer box about thirty centimetres square. I lifted the lid carefully with the blade of my knife-tool. In a bed of velvet lay an intricate sphere. It looked like a jagged lump of quartz, the size of a clenched fist, inlaid with gold circuits and complex woven wires, like an oversized uncut gemstone in a bizarre, ornate setting.

I spun around at a sound from behind me.

Kowitz, blood dripping from his dented forehead, stood pointing a laspistol at me. His face was pale, angry, confused.

'Step away from the Pontius, scum,' he said.

ELEVEN

Revelations
The noble sport
Pacification 505

This was no place to be trapped. I dug into my reserves of concentration, and without any physical movement, struck him clean between the eyes.

A psychic goad like that, especially at close range and with a clear line of sight, should have felled him like a force hammer. Kowitz didn't even blink.

'Don't make me repeat myself,' he said, raising the weapon so it pointed at my head.

The room was psychically shielded, it had to be. Either that or something was leeching psychic energies out of the very air.

'There's been a misunderstanding, Kowitz,' I said. 'I went for a walk and must have taken a wrong turn.'

It was pretty lame, but I wanted to keep his responses engaged and his mind busy.

'I don't think so,' he hissed. He was groping behind himself with his free hand, trying to find the control panel for the entrance. There was an alarm stud on it.

I waited. At any second, he was going to glance round involuntarily to help his fumbling.

When the gesture came, I threw myself forward and down, pulling my autopistol.

He looked back with a cry and fired, but his aim was too high and the shot flared off the end wall.

From a prone stance, I punched two shots through his left collar bone, and threw him back against the force door, which crackled at the impact.

Kowitz collapsed face down on the floor and blood began to pool around him.

I reached the door control. An amber rune was flashing. The bastard had managed to press something. I hit the force door deactivator.

Nothing.

I punched 'daesumnor' into the key pad.

Nothing.

I realised I was in deep trouble.

I guessed that Kowitz had hit an alarm that locked everything out. That was what prevented me from opening the door.

Urisel Glaw and several of his house militia appeared outside the shimmering force door. I could see them peering in and shouting.

I backed from the doorway and snatched up Kowitz's laspistol. When the door opened, I would use both guns to take down anything that tried to get in.

Then something psychic, dark and monstrously powerful rushed into my mind from somewhere behind me and I blacked out.

* * *

A face was looking down at me as I came round. A handsome face with blank eyes. The face started to say something. Then it combusted and melted away, and I realised it was just a dream. And I awoke properly, into a world that was nothing but pain.

'Enough. Don't kill him,' said a voice. Another voice laughed, and a tremor of acute agony peeled through my forebrain, lungs and gut.

'Enough, I said! Locke!'

A mild, disappointed curse. The agony receded, and I was left with numbness and throbbing background pain.

I was spreadeagled, my wrists and ankles bitten by the manacles that locked me to a massive hardwood cross. They'd taken my equipment, harness, hood, earpiece, and everything else except the leggings of my bodyglove and my boots. What could only be dried blood caked my lips, mouth, chin and throat, and fresh blood still drooled from my nose.

I opened my eyes. A meaty fist was holding my Inquisitorial rosette in front of my face.

'Recognise this, Eisenhorn?'

I spat blood.

'Thought you'd wile your way in among us and then produce this crest and make us all cower in fear?'

Urisel Glaw took the rosette away and peered down into my face.

'Doesn't work that way with the House of Glaw. We're not afraid of your kind.'

'Then you... are very foolish indeed,' I said.

He slammed my head back into the cross with an open-palmed blow to my forehead.

'You think your friends are going to help you? We've

rounded them all up. They're just down the cell-block yonder.'

'I'm perfectly serious,' I said. 'Others know I'm here. And you really don't want to be messing with a servant of the Inquisition, no matter how much at your mercy you think he is.'

Glaw hunched down in front of me, his hands steepled. 'Don't worry. I don't underestimate the Inquisition. I'm just not afraid of it. Now, there are some questions I'd like answers to...'

He got up and moved back. I saw the filthy stone of the cell-chamber we were in, a double-locked hatch up in one corner at the head of a flight of stone steps. Lord Oberon Glaw and the obscura pipe-smoker from the library room stood at the foot of the steps, watching intently. The ship master, Gorgone Locke, sat astride a dirty wooden bench near by. He wore some strange apparatus on his right hand, a glove of segmented metal that ended each digit with a needle-like spike.

'You've got it wrong, Glaw. It's you who will provide the answers.'

Urisel Glaw nodded to Locke, who got up and moved towards me, flexing the needle glove.

'That is a strousine neural scourge. Our friend Mr Locke is quite an expert in its application. We were delighted when he volunteered to run this interrogation.'

Locke grabbed me by the throat with his bare hand, twisted my head up and his gloved fist disappeared out of my field of view below.

A second later, and cold lances of pain threaded my lungs and heart, and my windpipe went into spasm. I began to choke.

'Educated man like you knows all about pressure points,' Locke said, conversationally. 'So do the strousii. But they like to do more than tap them – they like to burn them out. I studied with one of their sacred torturers for a year or so. This grip, for example, the one that's choking you. It's also paralysing your respiratory system, and stopping your heart.'

I could barely hear him. Blood was drumming in my ears and explosive light and colour patterns were fogging my vision.

He withdrew his glove. The pain and choking stopped.

'Just like that, I can stop your heart. Burst your brain. Blind you. So play along.'

With all the strength I could muster, I smiled and told him his sister had particularly commended my love-making skills over his.

The glove gripped my face and needles lanced into my cheeks. I blacked out again for a moment.

'...haven't killed him!' I heard Locke hiss as consciousness swam back. Dull pain oozed through my face.

'Look at him! Look at him! Where's that cocksure smile now, you little bastard?'

I didn't answer.

Locke leaned close so his brow pressed against mine and his eyes were all I could see. 'Needlework,' he snarled, his foul, obscura-flavoured breath swamping my gasping mouth. 'I just lanced a few points in your face. You'll never smile again.'

I thought about telling him I didn't see a lot to smile about, but I didn't. Instead, I lunged forward and bit into his mouth.

His scream, transmitted by our contact, shook my jaws. Blood spurted. Fists struck repeatedly and desperately against my skull and neck. His long red hair came loose and the beaded ends whipped about my head. At last, he tore away, roaring. I retched out a mouthful of blood and a good fleshy lump of his lower lip.

His gloveless hand clamped around his torn mouth, Locke stumbled back, enraged, and then hurled himself at me. He kicked hard into my belly and hip, and punched me in the cheek so forcefully, it nearly snapped my spine apart.

Then I felt the needles stab in between my ribs on my left side, and breathless agony enfolded me.

Locke was screaming obscenities into my face. Once again, pain blacked me out.

I came back in a rush of excruciating discomfort and gasping breath as Urisel wrenched Locke off me and threw him across the cell.

'I want him alive!' Urisel bawled.

'Look what he did!' Locke complained incoherently through blood and torn lips.

'You should have been more careful,' said Oberon Glaw, stepping forward. He leaned down to study me, and I gazed back into his haughty, leonine face, bearded, powerful, commanding.

'He's halfway to death,' Oberon said with annoyance. 'I told you fools I wanted answers.'

'Ask me yourself,' I gasped.

Lord Oberon raised his eyebrows and stared at me. 'What brought you to my house, inquisitor?'

'The Pontius,' I replied. It was a gamble, and I wasn't hopeful, but there was always a chance that the very word might auto-slay them as it had done Saemon Crotes in the Sun-dome on Hubris. As I suspected, it didn't.

'You came from Hubris?'

'I stopped Eyclone's work there.'

'It was aborted anyway.' Lord Oberon stepped back from me.

'What is the Pontius?' I asked, trying and failing to focus my will. The pain in my body was overpowering.

'If you don't know, I'm hardly going to tell you,' said Oberon Glaw.

He looked round at Urisel, Locke and the pipe-smoker.

'I don't think he knows anything about the true matter. But I want to be certain. Can you be trusted to work efficiently, Locke?'

Locke nodded. He approached me again, flexing the needle glove, and slid a needle into my head behind my ear.

My skull went numb. It became almost impossible to concentrate.

'My index needle is lancing right into your parieto-occipital sulcus,' Locke crooned in my ear, 'directly influencing your truth centre. You cannot lie, no matter what. What do you know of the true matter?'

'Nothing...' I stammered.

He jiggled the needle and pain ignited inside my head.

'What is your name?'

'Gregor Eisenhorn.'

'Where were you born?'

'DeKere's World.'

'Your first sexual conquest?'

'I was sixteen, a maid in the scholam...'

'Your darkest fear?'

'The man with blank eyes!'

I blurted out the last. All were true, all involuntary, but that last one surprised even me.

Locke wasn't finished. He jiggled the needle, and pierced the back of my neck with others so that my body went into paralysis and ice flowed down my veins.

'What do you know of the true matter?'

'Nothing!'

Without wanting to, I began to weep with the pain.

Gorgone Locke continued to question me for four hours... four hours that I know about. Beyond those I recall nothing.

I woke again, and found myself lying on a cold rockcrete floor. Lingering pain and fatigue filled every atom of my being. I could barely move. At that time in my life, I had never felt such an extremity of pain and despair. I had never felt so close to death.

'Lie still, Gregor... you're with friends...' That voice. Aemos.

I opened my eyes. Uber Aemos, my trusted savant, looked down at me with a soulful expression even his augmetic eyes couldn't hide. He was bruised about the face and his good robe was torn.

'Lay still, old friend,' he urged.

'You know me, Aemos,' I said, and slowly sat up. It was quite a task. Various muscle groups refused to work, and I came close to vomiting.

I looked around blearily.

I was lying on the floor of a circular rockcrete cell. There was a hatch on one side, and a cage-gated exit opposite it. Aemos was crouched near me, and Alizebeth Bequin, her gown ripped and dirty, hunched behind him, staring over at me with genuine concern. Away across the cell stood Heldane, arms folded, and behind him cowered the guilder Macheles and the four other Guild Sinesias envoys who had escorted us. All of them looked pale and hollow eyed as if they had been weeping. There was no sign of Betancore.

Aemos saw my look and said, 'Aegis insubstantial, before the deluge' in perfect Glossia.

Which meant Betancore had somehow avoided the sweep that had incarcerated all my other companions. A tiny fragment of good news.

I got up, mainly thanks to my determination and the support of Aemos and Bequin. I was still stripped down to my leggings and boots, and my torso, neck, arms and head were washed in my own blood and stippled with bruised micro-puncture wounds. Gorgone Locke had been thorough.

Gorgone Locke would pay.

'What do you know?' I asked them as my breath returned.

'We're as good as dead,' Heldane said frankly. 'No wonder my master leaves this kind of work to you suicidal radicals. I just wish I hadn't agreed to join you.'

'Thank you for that, Heldane. Anyone else want to offer something less editorial?'

Aemos smiled. 'We're in a prison cell under the west wing, to the rear, almost under the woodlands. They burst into our quarters after you'd been gone three hours and seized us at gunpoint. I memorised a careful note of the route we were taking to this place, and have mentally compared it with Midas's map, so I'm fairly sure of our location.'

'What the hell did they do to you?' Bequin asked, dabbing at wounds on my chest with a strip of cloth torn from her gown.

Wincing, I realised that was why her gown was so shredded. She had been mopping my wounds while I was unconscious. A pile of torn and blood-soaked scads of material nearby stood testament to her devotion.

'They came here an hour ago and tossed you in with us. They didn't say anything,' Heldane added.

'Are you really an inquisitor, Sire Farchaval?' Macheles asked, stepping forward.

'Yes, I am. My name is Eisenhorn.'

Macheles began to sob and his fellow envoys did the same.

'We are dead. You have taken us to our deaths!'

I felt some pity for them. Guild Sinesias was rotten to the core, and these men were corrupt, but they were only in this predicament because I had duped them.

'Shut up!' Heldane told them.

He looked round at me, and slid a tiny something from the cuff of his body-glove. A small red capsule.

'What is it?'

'Admylladox, a ten gram dose. You look like you need it.'

'I don't use drugs,' I said.

He pushed it into my hand. 'Admylladox is a pain-killer and a mind clearer. I don't care if you do drugs or not, I want that in your system if that gate opens.'

I looked at the gate.

'Why?'

'Have you never been to a pit-fight?' he said.

The Glaws had got everything out of me they could. Now they wanted me dead. Me and my party.

And that meant sport.

The gate cranked open at what must have been dawn. Thin, grey light wafted in and was almost immediately replaced by hard, bright artificial luminescence.

House Glaw militiamen in body armour burst into our cell and drove us out through the gate with force shields and psyk-whips.

We were out in the open, blinking into the light, as the gate shut behind us.

I gazed around. A vast circular amphitheatre, enclosed by a dome high above, undoubtedly the golden dome we had seen on our approach. The floor of the pit was dank moss and earth, and lichen climbed the sheer sides of the ten-metre-high stone walls. Above the wall top, House Glaw and its guests sat in steep tiers, jeering down at us. I saw Urisel Glaw, Lord Oberon, Locke, Lady Fabrina, the ecclesiarch Dazzo, the pipe-smoking man. Terronce, the militia captain who had sat at our table during dinner, led an honour guard of nearly forty men of the retinue. All wore green armour, plumed silver helmets and all carried autoguns. More than two hundred baying members of the Glaw clan, house staff, militia and servants made up the rest of the crowd in the theatre. They'd been up all night, drinking and doing whatever other indulgence it took to turn them into hyperactive bloodthirsty hyenas by first light.

Ignoring the noise, I surveyed the compound. Breaks of trees sprouted at various places, and there were low outcrops of bare rock, giving the arena a sort of landscape.

Nearby stood a rack of rusty weapons. Macheles and his brethren had already rushed to it and taken blunt shortswords and toothless lances.

I went over and took a basket-hilted dagger and an oddly hooked scythe with a serrated inner blade.

I weighed them in my hands.

Heldane had taken a dagger and a long-hafted axe, Bequin a wicker shield and a stabbing knife. Aemos shrugged and took nothing.

The jeering and booing welled around us. Then it hushed and a chorus of gasps whispered from the auditorium.

The carnodon was six metres from nose to whipping tail. Nine hundred kilos of muscle, sinew, striped pelt and sawing tusks.

It came out from behind one of the clumps of trees, trailing a line of heavy chain behind it from its spiked collar, accelerated into a pounce and brought Macheles down.

Macheles, envoy of Guild Sinesias, screamed as he was destroyed. He screamed and shrieked far longer than seemed possible given the spurting body parts the carnodon was ripping away. It must have been my horrified imagination, but to me the screaming only stopped when he was a gnawed ribcage being shaken in the bloody moss by the vast predator.

The other envoys screamed and ran. One fainted.

'We're dead,' Heldane said again, raising his weapons.

I swallowed the capsule he had given me. It didn't make me feel much better.

Its huge bared mouth running with blood and its chain jingling, the carnodon turned on the other envoys.

Bequin shrieked.

A second carnodon sprang out of its trap towards us. It was slightly larger than the first, I noticed. It came right for me.

I stumbled and dived to my right and the feline dug its claws into the moss to arrest its pounce, overshooting and scrabbling round. Its trailing chain swished over my head. The creatures both made low, sub-sonic growls that shuddered in their cavernous throats and thumped the air.

The larger beast swung around and made for me again even as I regained my feet and leapt backwards. Heldane ran in from the side while its attention was on me, and hacked into its flank with the blade of his axe.

The carnodon issued a strangulated hiss and lashed around, hurling Voke's man across the arena, the clothing of his torso shredded by deep parallel claw marks. I jumped away and got a few of the twisted trees between it and myself.

The first carnodon had brought down another of the envoys. The shock of the impact and the crippling wounds simply silenced the man and he uttered no sound as his limp body was thrashed and worried.

The creatures were hungry, that much was evident from their prominent ribs. One factor in our favour then... when the carnodons brought down prey they were primarily interested in consuming it. The long chains secured them to ground spikes next to their traps, and allowed them free movement anywhere in the pit. Clearly the chains were measured carefully to prevent them leaping clear of the pit into the crowd.

Tail slashing back and forth, the larger predator circled the edge of the arena-bowl, its dark, deep-set eyes surveying the humans in range. Bequin had dug herself and Aemos into a corner, using her frail shield and a wall buttress as cover for them both, but the ruthless crowd were pelting them with coins and bottles and pieces of food to drive them out. They wanted sport. They wanted blood.

The circling carnodon, barking vapours of breath and spittle from its dripping snout, came round and began to accelerate towards Bequin and Aemos. Its pouncing mass alone would kill them, I was certain. I ran out from cover to intercept it side on, and the crowd whooped and stamped.

It faltered in its run up as it became aware of me rushing it from the flank, and started to turn as I cut in with the scythe. The old hook planed matted fur from its shoulder blade and left a long red scratch down its ribs. It turned hard to face me. A paw lashed out, jabbing. I jumped back, swung again, hoping to at least hit the huge paw, for its reach was far longer than mine. Then it threw itself forward, a throbbing roar welling from its throat.

I simply dropped on my back, stealing its chance to knock me down and shatter my bones. Then it was on me and over me, a paw crushing and slicing my chest, its head down, mouth open, reaching to bite off my face. Frantically, I thrust with my weapons, blind, and kicked up at its more vulnerable underside.

The weight was off me abruptly. The carnodon jerked away, making a terrible low moaning. My dagger was no longer in my hand.

The pommel was jutting down out of the beast's chin. The blade transfixed its mouth, pinning it closed. It pawed and tore at the weapon, trying to dislodge it, shaking its massive head like a horse bothered by a fly.

I got up. Blood ran from the fresh gashes on my chest. Heldane suddenly crossed my field of vision, his shredded tunic fluttering behind him. His axe came down square onto the great carnivore's back, cutting through the backbone with a loud crack. The carnodon went into spasms, thrashing and clawing, rolling in the dirt. Heldane brought the axe down again and stove in its skull.

The audience shook the pit with their howling. Missiles rained down on us. Heldane turned and looked at me with a murderous grin of triumph.

Then the huge weight of the other carnodon hit him from behind and flattened him face down into the arena floor.

It had finished with the other envoys, all except the one who had fainted, who still lay where he had fallen. It tore into the helpless Heldane, ripping his scalp, rending the flesh off his back.

With a guttural cry, I ran at it, caught it behind the ear with my scythe, and pulled. The curved blade hooked into the meat and I succeeded in yanking its head back for a second. Then a well-aimed bottle struck me on the side of the head and knocked me over. I lost my grip on the scythe.

The creature turned, leaving Heldane a mangled wreck, face down in the bloody soil. I scrambled back, kicking at it.

'Eisenhorn!' Bequin yelled, running forward on the other side. She threw her knife over the creature's back and I caught it neatly. Disturbed by her cry, the beast swung about and lashed at her, tearing the wicker shield into hanks of raffia and knocking her down.

I threw myself astride its back and thumped the dagger down repeatedly into its neck. The dagger barely seemed to bite into the thick hide.

It writhed, trying to throw me off. I saw the scythe dangling from its scalp behind the ear, grabbed it, and hooked the blade under its spiked collar.

The creature was frenzied now, pulling hard at its chain. I pushed the tooth of the dagger in through a link in the chain and down into its shoulder blade, then levered the weapon over with all the force I could muster.

The link twisted open. The chain parted.

The carnodon ran forward a few paces, bellowed, and lunged.

Effortlessly, it leapt up the side of the pit into the shrieking crowd. I was still attached to it by the scythe, the handle of which I clutched frantically. As we landed in the seating, I was thrown clear, and crashed down onto the frantic fleeing audience.

The beast was berserk. It tore into the crowd, hurling limp, mangled forms and gouts of blood into the air. The pandemonium shook the dome.

I got up, pushing away the individuals who fell and stumbled into me in their efforts to escape. Gunfire ripped out across the amphitheatre. In the higher stands, I could see the militia scrambling down, firing at the carnodon as Terronce and other men hustled towards the safety of a side exit. The militia's shots were hitting people in the crowd.

I jumped across the backs of several seats, and punched aside two servants who grabbed at me. On the steps of the seating tiers just above me, two household guards ran down, raising their autoguns to shoot at the creature loose in the crowd.

I felled one with a psychic lance powered by rage and adrenaline, and snatched his weapon from his hands. Before his companion could turn, I had blown him down the steps and over the rail into the pit with a short burst of gunfire.

I looked up at the seating where the Glaw nobles and their guests had been. Lord Glaw, Locke and the pipe-smoker had already disappeared and the guards were half-carrying Lady Fabrina and the ecclesiarch away. But Urisel Glaw was still there, bellowing at his men over the bloody tumult. He saw me.

'The Inquisition will show you no mercy,' I yelled at him, though I doubted he could hear.

Urisel stared down at me for a moment, then shouted some more oath-laden orders and turned his attention to the carnodon. It had ploughed beyond the common seating now and was disembowelling a member of the house militia. Multiple bloody gunshot wounds showed in its striped pelt.

Urisel snatched a hunting rifle that one of the men fetched for him. He took careful aim at the carnodon and fired.

The massive weapon roared and the huge bulk of the creature flipped over, its chest blasted open. Its falling bulk crushed the legs of a guard.

The crowd continued to flee, but the uproar decreased enough for me to notice that a series of bells had begun to ring. Metal bells, electrically triggered. From deeper in the vast mansion, other alarms sounded. Urisel lowered his rifle and gestured to some of his men to discover the meaning of the alarm. Those in the crowd not too far intoxicated or mindless with fear looked anxiously around.

There were distant, inexplicable sounds. I didn't wonder much about them. Urisel took aim again, at me this time.

I dived over and a section of wooden seats exploded.

I clambered up. Urisel was reloading the wide-bore hunting iron, and Terronce was heading down towards me, followed by other men.

Terronce fired. I aimed high and blew his head and his plumed silver helmet apart with another tight burst.

Urisel was about to fire again. He drew the hunting piece to his shoulder and found me in the crowd.

There was an abrupt, sizzling series of buzzing shots from somewhere behind me. Three of the militia guards at the pit rail juddered and fell, and Urisel Glaw was thrown backwards, his hunting rifle roaring as it fired wildly up into the dome. The crowd began to mob frantically again in a second, and the remaining soldiers swung their aim up, hunting for this new shooter.

I swept around and saw him at once. Midas Betancore, crouched up on the tiled slope of awning above the pit seating on the opposite side of the arena. His needle guns, one clutched in each hand, spat again, peppering the front stands with lethal shots. Members of the household and several more guards tumbled. One guard pitched over the rail and fell into the pit. Further along the front rail, the crowd's panic to get clear of the carnage turned into a stampede. The rail snapped and half a dozen pages and kitchen staff spilled down the side of the pit wall. One clung to a broken rail-end for a second before sliding off and dropping.

The remaining guards had found Midas now, and were firing up at the tiled awning with their autoguns. Tile chips exploded out in a haze of dust, but Midas was moving, sure-footed, along the terracotta shelf. Holstering his weapons, he slid down its length, grabbed the edge with both hands and executed a superb swing that carried him round and under the lip and into the emptying stands.

The guards tracked him, firing wildly, cutting down members of the screaming crowd.

I ran down to the rail. 'Cover! Cover!' I yelled down to Bequin and Aemos below. They were busy trying to drag Heldane's bloody form to the comparative safety of the pit wall. I ran to the nearby body of a guard and grabbed some more magazine clips from his harness.

A few shots whipped my way, but most were aimed across the pit at Midas. I took cover behind some seats and some of the carnodon's victims, and opened fire up at the stands, aiming short bursts at the militia. Return fire chopped my way and gobbets of wood and flesh sprayed up from my makeshift cover. Midas was moving again, his guns buzzing.

The alarms were still ringing, and now, behind them and the frenzy of the fleeing crowd, I could hear gunfire and the dull rumble of explosions.

Most of the arena had emptied now, except for the last handful of house guards trading gunfire across the pit with the stealthy Midas. The sounds of explosive fighting outside in the grounds and house were getting ever louder.

I reached the banks of seats where the masters of the house had sat. The Glaws and their honoured guests were now long gone. Urisel's hunting rifle lay on the ground, and blood flecked the seat. Midas had at least winged him with a needle round.

I pushed past the end of the seats and down into the stairwell, the autogun braced at my hip. The bodies of two staff members trampled in the press lay broken there.

Urisel Glaw had not gone far, bleeding badly from his shoulder wound. He heard me coming and staggered around, firing a small stub-pistol down the gloomy tunnel. Then he disappeared from view.

Gun-butt raised under my arm, I moved forward, searching the darkness of the dank stone tunnel. An opening to the left looked down into a stairwell that entered the cell bay below. To the right was a hatch that allowed access to the main house.

I pushed the hatch open with the barrel of the autogun.

Urisel came out of the cell-bay stairway, howling, and slammed into me from behind.

I hit the door frame face first, and the autogun fired off three shots as it twisted out of my grip.

Without even trying to turn, I doubled over and reached behind me, grabbing a fold of dress uniform cloth, and jerked Urisel Glaw around into the wall. He cried out.

I threw a left-handed punch that sent him reeling, then a right that smashed his teeth. He enveloped me in a bear hug and we stumbled back a few paces before I braced, kicked his legs out and jabbed a knuckle punch into his sternum.

The fight seemed to be out of him. I choked him with a clawing hand and cracked his skull back against the tunnel wall.

'There will be no redemption for you, sinner,' I spat into his bloody face, 'or your foul house! Use your last breaths wisely and unfold your truths to me, or the Inquisition will teach you pain that Gorgone Locke has yet to imagine!'

'You–' he gurgled through blood and spittle and flecks of shattered teeth, 'you cannot even begin to imagine the Imperial misery House Glaw will wreak. Our power is too great. We will pitch the bastard Emperor from his golden throne and make him grovel and feed upon excrement. The worlds of the Imperium will blister and burn before Oberon and Pontius. Exalted will be the Great Darkness of Slaanesh–'

I cared little for his heretical ramblings, but the mention of that daemon-blasphemy turned my stomach and chilled my heart. I knocked him down, and looked around for something with which to bind his wrists.

Beyond the tunnel, the House of Glaw shook as if caught in a war zone.

Midas Betancore appeared at the mouth of the tunnel, and saw me lashing Urisel Glaw to a heating pipe with lengths of awning cord. He holstered his needle pistols and walked down to join me. I heard him activate his vox-link and report his position. A curt response crackled back.

'What's going on?' I asked him.

'A Battlefleet Scarus naval action,' he replied smugly.

He'd been out in the dark when Glaw's men came to seize Aemos, Bequin and Heldane. I was, by then, two hours overdue, and he'd slipped away from our apartment to look for signs of me. The militia had fanned out through the estate searching for him, but Midas was the sort of man who wouldn't be found if he didn't want it to happen. He had avoided the hunting parties, broke into the house's communication annexe and sent a brief but comprehensive report in code directly to Commodus Voke in Dorsay.

Voke's response had been immediate and authoritarian. The Glaw family had forcibly detained a servant of the Imperial Inquisition and his associates. That was all the excuse Voke had needed.

His demands, which brooked no refusal, swept clean over the heads of Fleet Admiral Spatian and his officio, and went straight to the Lord Militant Commander himself. The Lord Militant had mobilised a detachment of naval security troopers into Voke's remit within half an hour.

As an inquisitor, I know I have the right and authority to demand such supportive responses myself, even from a Lord High Militant. And I have done, on a very few occasions. But I was still impressed by the respect and fear the old inquisitor conjured in men of such supreme rank.

A confident move like this was characteristic of Voke, characteristic of his crushing, heavy methods. He'd wanted the slightest reason to come down upon House Glaw with the proverbial wrath of Macharius, and I had given it to him.

My capture, at least. Part of me was certain this show of influence and authority was Commodus Voke's way of establishing himself as alpha male, inquisitorially speaking.

I didn't care. I was glad of it, in truth. The bloodshed in the arena might have broken us out, but without the assault, we'd have never made it out of the Glaw estate and the clutches of the militia alive.

The operation was coded 'Pacification 505', 505 being the topographical signifier for House Glaw. The troops had run in before dawn in four armoured dropships, hugging the rolling terrain of the inland bluffs to avoid the more than competent sensor system of House Glaw.

The ships held off behind the neighbouring hills as the sun rose, about the time we were languishing in the cell, to allow a forward team of naval security troopers to run ahead on foot and cut holes, electronically, in the perimeter defences of the great house. By then, they were in range of Betancore's personal vox set, and he had fed them logistic information and an insider's view of the militia's deployment.

At approximately the same moment when the first carnodon had lunged up out of its trap, the dropships had spurred forward from behind a long finger of copse and came powering up the vale towards the house. The Imperial Light

Intruder Frigate *Defence of Stalinvast*, retasked by Admiral Spatian on the Lord Militant's instruction to hold geosynchronous orbit above target/Glaw/505, had obliterated the launch hangars behind the yard with pinpoint strikes from its lance batteries.

Two dropships, rocketing smoke charges and antipersonnel grenades, had settled in front of the main house, blowing out all the windows. Forty black-armoured troopers from naval security had then made an assault landing and struck at the main facade. Bewildered, more than seventy men of the house militia had attempted to repel them.

The other two dropships circled behind the house and spilled their troops into a landing yard still lit by the blazing ruins of the launch block. Within three minutes a running gun battle was shuddering down the halls and corridors of House Glaw. The alarms were ringing soundly by then.

House Glaw owned close on four hundred fighting men in its retinue, not to mention another nine hundred staff, many of whom took up weapons. Glaw Militia were all trained men, veterans, well armoured in green ballistic cloth and silver helmets, well equipped with autoguns, heavy stubbers and grenades. An army, by most standards. I know more than one commander in the Imperial Guard who has taken cities, whole planets indeed, with such a number. And they had the advantage of home soil. They knew the layout, the strengths, the weaknesses, of the old estate.

Naval security took them apart. The elite of Battlefleet Scarus, armed with matt-black hell-guns and iron discipline, they conquered and purged the great house room by room.

Some pockets of resistance were heavy. The troopers lost three men in a virtually point-blank firefight around the kitchen area. A suicide run by two Glaw soldiers laden with tube charges vaporised another four and took twenty metres off the end of the east wing

Twenty-two minutes after the assault began, the militia had lost nearly three hundred men.

Numerous householders and low-ranking staff fled into the woods and valleys behind the house. A few made good their escape. Most were rounded up, and more than thirty killed by the tightening circle of Imperial Guard cordoning the estate. These men, two thousand of them, were recruits from the founding, Gudrunite riflemen roused from the barracks and shipped inland to experience a surprise taste of combat before ever leaving their birthworld.

The bloody resistance of the Glaw militia was mainly intended to give their nobles time to flee. The Glaws' off-world cousin and his retinue were cornered by the Gudrunite Rifles on the back path behind the house, arrested, and then massacred when they tried to fight their way out. Other traders and guests from the dinner surrendered to the enclosing forces.

Several orbital craft broke from the tree cover behind the main attack, launching from secret hangars in the woods behind the house. One was hammered out of the air by a trooper with a rocket launcher. Another two made it five kilometres down the valley before they were incinerated from above by the watchful *Defence of Stalinvast*.

Another, a fast and heavily armoured model, evaded the cover sweep and headed west. The *Defence of Stalinvast* launched a trio of fighters after it, and they eventually brought it down in the open sea after a lengthy chase. Only weeks of forensic recovery might reveal who had been aboard any of those craft, and there was no guarantee that an answer would be forthcoming even then. Smart money was on the likes of Lord Glaw, Lady Fabrina, Gorgone Locke, Dazzo the

Ecclesiarch and the nameless pipe-smoking man. Certainly, none of those persons were among the anguished scum rounded up by the Guard or by naval security.

Ninety minutes after it had begun, Pacification 505 was signalled as 'achieved' by Major Joam Joakells of naval security.

Only then did the launch carrying Commodus Voke move in.

TWELVE

In the ruins of the great house
Murmurings
Uprising

It was noon, but the night storm had persisted, and the fitful
rain washed the colour out of the sky and doused the burning
sections of House Glaw. A terrible, blackened ruin, it stood
on the hilltop, its windows burned out, its roofs ragged, tiled
lengths of beam, billowing grey and white smoke.

I sat in the yard, leaning back against the mudguard of an
Imperial Guard troop carrier, sipping occasionally from a
cut-glass decanter of amasec. My head was bowed. I needed
medical attention and painkillers, a psychic restorative, a
good meal, neural surgery to the hundreds of wounds Locke
had inflicted, a bath, clean clothes...

More than anything else, I needed a bed.

Troops marched past, crunching their boots in time on the
wet stone. Orders sang back and forth. Occasionally, a fighter
ship made a pass overhead and vibrated my diaphragm with
the throb of its afterburner.

My head swam. Fragments gathered and conflated in my unconscious and spilled over. Each time, I shook myself awake. The blank-eyed man was there, in the back of my head. I didn't want to think about him, and saw no place in this event for him, but his image lingered. Once, I was certain, he was standing across the yard from me, by the scullery door, smiling at me. I blinked him away.

I was still caked in blood, sweat and filth. Pain and fatigue clung to me like a shroud. A corporal from the naval security detail had recovered our confiscated possessions from Urisel Glaw's apartment, and I had pulled on a shirt and my button-sleeved leather coat. The trooper had handed me my Inquisitorial rosette, and I clutched it now, like a totem.

Eager men of the 50th Gudrunite Rifles jostled Glaw House staff through the yard. The prisoners had their hands behind their heads, and some were weeping.

Somebody slid down next to me on the cold flagstones and leaned back against the greasy track assembly of the carrier.

'Long night,' Midas said.

I passed the decanter to him, and he took a long swig.

'Where's Aemos? The girl?'

'Last I saw, the savant was bustling around somewhere, making notes. I haven't seen Alizebeth since we freed them from the pit.'

I nodded.

'You're half-dead, Gregor. Let me call up a launch and get you to Dorsay.'

'We're not done here,' I said.

Procurator Madorthene saluted me as he approached. He wasn't wearing his starchy white dress uniform now. In the coal-black armour of naval security, he looked bigger and more commanding.

'We've made a body exam,' he said.

'Oberon Glaw?'

'No trace.'

'Gorgone Locke? The churchman Dazzo?'

He shook his head.

I offered him the decanter with a sigh. To my surprise, he took it, sat down with us and drank a mouthful.

'They're all probably cinders in the craft that tried to escape,' he said. 'But I'll tell you this. Before it torched the two boats running the valley, the Defence of Stalinvast was sure it read no life signs.'

'Decoys,' said Betancore.

'The Glavian is right, for my money,' he said. Then he shrugged. 'But good armour can rob away signals. We may never know.'

'We'll know, Madorthene,' I promised him.

He took another tug on the decanter, handed it back to me and rose, brushing down his seamless armour.

'I'm glad naval security could serve you here, Inquisitor Eisenhorn. I hope it's restored your faith in the battlefleet.'

I looked up at him with a weak nod. 'I'm impressed you came to oversee yourself, procurator.'

'Are you kidding? After what happened on the *Essene*, the admiral would have had my head!'

He walked away. I liked him. An honest man doing his best amid the conflicting political interests of battlefleet command and the Inquisition. In later years, I would come to value Olm Madorthene's honesty and discretion immeasurably.

A fragile hunched figure clomped across the yard and stood over me.

'Now whose methods seem wise?' Commodus Voke asked, with a sneer.

'You tell me,' I replied, getting up.

* * *

Voke had brought a staff of nearly fifty with him, all clad in black robes, many with augmetic implants. They stripped the noble house of every shred of evidence they could find. Crates of papers, books, slates, artefacts and pict-tiles were carried out to waiting transports.

I was in no mood to argue. Pain and fatigue made my senses swim. Let Voke use his vast retinue and resources to do the painstaking work of recovery.

'Much has been deleted, dumped or burned,' a dour-faced savant called Klysis reported to Voke, as I walked with my fellow inquisitor into the shattered house. 'Much else is encrypted.'

We progressed into the basement system, and I led Voke to the force-shielded chamber where Glaw had trapped me. Kowitz's blood still marked the floor. The artefact from the altar plinth was gone.

'He referred to it as the Pontius,' I told Voke. The room no longer showed signs of being psychically shielded, so logic said the psyker-effects had been generated by the Pontius itself. As had the mental attack that had felled me, I was sure.

I leaned against the chamber wall and patiently told Voke the key points I had learned. 'Eyclone's mission to Hubris, involving the Pontius, was clearly important to them, but Oberon Glaw told me explicitly that said endeavour had been aborted... cancelled because something more vital had come into play. They referred to it as the true matter.'

'It would explain why your foe Eyclone was abandoned,' he mused. 'After all his preparations, the Glaws failed to deliver the Pontius as they had promised.'

'That fits. Dazzo and the shipmaster Locke were clearly deeply involved in this true matter. We need to establish more facts about them. I'm certain the work that concerned them touched on some archeoxenon material. They mentioned the "saruthi".

'A xenos breed, outlying the sub-sector,' said Voke's savant. 'Little is known of them and contact is forbidden. The Inquisition holds several investigations pending, but their space is uncharted, and while they keep themselves to themselves, more urgent matters have caused investigations to be postponed.'

'But a rogue like Locke may well have established lines of contact with them.'

Klysis and Voke both nodded. 'It will bear further research,' Voke said. 'Ordo Xenos must begin a survey of the saruthi. But for now, the matter is closed.'

'How do you reason that?' I asked with a contemptuous laugh.

Voke fixed me with his beady eyes. 'House Glaw is destroyed, its principal members and co-conspirators are slain. With them are lost the items precious to their cause. Whatever they were planning is finished.'

I didn't even begin to argue with the old man. Voke was sure of his facts. His main failing, in my opinion.

He was wrong, of course. The first hint came ten days later. I had returned to Dorsay with my colleagues, and had spent some time in the care of the Imperial Hospice on the Grand Canal where my many wounds and injuries were treated. Most of the cuts and gashes were superficial, and would heal in time. Locke's work on me had left deeper scars. Multiple neural injuries afflicted my system, many of which would never repair. Augmeticists from the battlefleet's Officio Medicalis conducted micro-surgery on shredded nerve transmitters in my spine, thorax, brainstem and throat. They implanted more than sixty sections of artificial nerve fibre and ganglions. I had lost a good deal of sensitivity in my palette and oesophagus, and the reflexes on the left side of my body were dulled. My face they could do nothing with. Neural systems there had been utterly scourged. Locke's promise had been lasting. I would never smile again, nor make much of any expression. My face, impassive, was now just a mask of flesh.

Aemos visited me every day, and brought more and more data-slates and old books to my private room in the Hospice. He had established a working relationship with Voke's savants (Klysis was but one of seventeen employed by Commodus Voke), and was sifting data as it was passed to him. We tried to source information concerning the Glaws' confederates, but there was damnably little, even with Voke's platoon of savants hard at work. Locke was a shadowy, almost mythical figure, his name and reputation well known throughout the Helican sub-sector, but nothing could be found about his origin, career, associates or even the name of his vessel. Dazzo also drew a blank.

The Ecclesiarchy had no record of a churchman of that name. But I remembered what Kowitz had told me during the banquet, that Dazzo had links to a missionary order sponsored by the Glaws on the edgeworld Damask. Damask was a real place, right enough, a harsh frontier planet at the very limit of the Helican sub-sector territory, one of a hundred worthless, seldom-visited places. Astrogeographically, it lay just a few months passage spinward of the uncharted regions of the mysterious saruthi.

Lowink accompanied Aemos on one of his visits as soon as I was strong enough, and extracted from my mind a likeness of the pipe-smoking man, which he realised psychometrically on an unexposed pict-plate. The image, a little blurred, was good enough, and it was copied and circulated through all branches of the investigating authorities. But no one could identify him.

Lowink recovered an image of the Pontius too, by the same means. This baffled all who viewed it, except Aemos who immediately confirmed that the strange artefact was precisely the correct size and dimensions to fit into the cavity in Eyclone's casket, the one recovered from Processional Two-Twelve. As we had conjectured, this was what Eyclone had been awaiting, what the mass-murder in the Hubris ice tomb had been for.

'Urisel Glaw referred to Pontius as if he was still alive,' I said to Aemos. 'Certainly something with great psychic force felled me in the chamber where the Pontius was secured. Could he be alive, in some sense, some part of him, perhaps some psychic essence, captured in that device?'

Aemos nodded. 'It is not beyond the highest Imperial technologies to maintain a sentience after great physical injury or even death. But for such technologies to be within the grasp of even a mighty family like the Glaws...'

'You told me it resembled something of the mysteries of the Adeptus Mechanicus.'

'I did,' he pondered. 'It is most perturbatory. Could the foul crime of Hubris have been some effort to siphon vulnerable life energies into this artefact? To give the Pontius a massive jolt of power?'

On the third morning, Fischig visited. His own injuries were healed, and he seemed annoyed to have missed the episode at Glaw House. He brought with him a priceless antique slate, a collection of inspirational verse composed by Juris Sathascine, curate-confessor of one of Macharius's generals. It was a gift from Maxilla, from his private collection.

Delayed by the excitement of the Glaw incident, the founding resumed. The new Imperial guardsmen were shipped to troop transports in the orbiting fleet and the final ceremonies were carried out. The Lord Militant Commander was now anxious to begin his expedition into the troubled Ophidian sub-sector, and felt enough time and manpower had been spent on this little local matter.

On the tenth day, it didn't look so much like a local matter any more. Via astropathic link, news came of incidents throughout the sub-sector: a rash of bombings on Thracian Primaris; the seizure and destruction of a passenger vessel bound for Hesperus; a hive decimated by a viral toxin on Messina.

That evening, a brief, bright star suddenly ignited in the sky over Dorsay. The *Ultima Victrix*, a four hundred thousand tonne ironclad, had exploded at anchor. The blast had crippled four ships nearby.

An hour later, it became clear the incident had grown signally worse. Exactly how was not clear, even to battlefleet intelligence, but the explosion had been identified in error as a sign of an enemy attack by several components of the fleet. A frigate wing commanded by a captain called Estrum had moved to engage, and several destroyers from the advance phalanx had mistaken them for fleet intruders and opened fire. For twenty-seven hideous minutes, Battlefleet Scarus waged war against itself through the anchor lines of Navy vessels and troop ships. Six ships were lost. Eventually, apparently heedless of countermands, Estrum broke off and, with a mobile group of fifteen vessels, went to warp to outrun 'the enemy'. Admiral Spatian gave chase with a flotilla of eight heavy cruisers. The remaining fleet elements struggled to regain control and handle the wanton destruction.

The Lord High Militant, I learned, had a fit of rage so extreme he had to be sedated by his private physician.

'That doesn't just *happen*,' Betancore said. We sat in my private room, by the tall windows, looking out across the city. Ghost-flares of energy and explosion, one trailing down in the sky like a falling star, marked the night.

'Imperial battlefleets are among the most ordered and disciplined organisations in space. Confusion like that doesn't just happen.'

'Like deserters don't just get a hold of a ship and uniforms and know the name of the man whose ship they chance to board, you mean? Our unseen foe is making his influence felt. Voke talked about a parent cult, overseeing many small cells and cabals. He reckoned the Glaws were the masters of this conspiracy. I'm not so sure. There could be a yet higher authority at work.'

Urisel Glaw was held in the Imperial Basilica. He had undergone hours of intense interrogation and torture since his capture. And he had given up nothing.

I went to him that night. Voke and his interrogators were still at work, now with a sense of urgency.

They held him in what could only be described as a dungeon, ninety metres below the massive grey stone fortress. All the other prisoners taken during the raid on House Glaw were sequestered here too. In order to contain and interrogate them all, Voke had co-opted local Arbites, soldiers of the Gudrun standing army, and officials of the Ministorum. They worked in concert with his own extensive staff.

Arriving by air launch, I was met by a tall, grey-haired man in a long maroon coat attended by two armed servitors. I knew him at once. Inquisitor Titus Endor and I were of similar ages and had both studied under Hapshant.

'You are recovered, Gregor?' he asked, shaking my hand.

'Well enough to continue my work. I didn't expect to see you here, Titus.'

'Voke's reports on the Glaw case have concerned our order's sub-sector officio. Lord Inquisitor Rorken has declared the need for a full disclosure. Voke's inability to get anything out of Urisel Glaw has annoyed him. I've been diverted to assist. And not just me. Schongard is here too, and Molitor is on his way.'

I sighed. Endor, a fellow Amalathian, I could work with, though there is a proverb about too many inquisitors. Schongard was a rabid monodominant, and a liability in my view, and Konrad Molitor was the sort of radical I felt had no place in the order at all.

'This is unusual,' I said.

'It's all down to connections,' Endor remarked. 'What has come to light through your work here, and Voke's, is a massive puzzle that itself connects dozens of separate cases and investigations. I burned a heretic on Mariam two weeks ago, and in his effects found documents linking him to the Glaws. Schongard is pursuing blasphemous texts that he is certain first came into the sub-sector in the cargoes of Guild Sinesias traders. Molitor... well, who knows what he's doing, but it no doubt connects.'

'Sometimes,' I told him, 'I think we work against each other. This comes out and, look! We all hold pieces to the same mystery. How might we have taken this enemy and his structure apart a month ago, two months, if we had exchanged information?'

Endor laughed. 'Are you questioning the working practices

of the most lauded Inquisition, Gregor? Working practices laid
down centuries ago? Are you questioning the motives of fellow members of our convocation?'

I knew he was joking, but my manner remained serious.
'I'm decrying a system where we don't even trust each other.'

We descended, under escort, into the depths of the prison
block.

'What of Glaw?'

'Gives up nothing,' said Endor. 'What he's endured so far
would have broken and cracked most men, or at least had
them begging for death or trying to kill themselves. He per-
sists, almost in good humour, almost arrogant, as if he expects
to live.'

'He's right. We'll never sign his death notice while he has
secrets.'

Voke's men were at work on Glaw in a foul-smelling,
red-painted cell. Glaw was a ruin, kept alive by expertise that
matched the skill used to torture him.

To unlock an answer from the mind of the heretic is the
greatest duty of an inquisitor, and I will not shrink from any
means, but this way was futile. Left to me, the physical torture would have stopped days before. One look showed that
Urisel Glaw was resolved not to talk.

I would have left him alone, for weeks perhaps. Despite his
agonies, our constant attention betrayed our desperation, and
that gave him all the strength he needed to endure. Silence
and isolation would have broken him.

Inquisitor Schongard stepped back from the table where
Glaw was strapped and pulled off soiled surgical gloves. He
was a broad man with thin brown hair and a chilling mask
of black metal surgically fixed to his face. No one knew if
this mask covered some grievous injury or was simply an

affectation. Dark, unhealthy, bloodshot eyes regarded Endor and myself through the oblong slits in the metal.

'Brothers,' he whispered. His phlegmy voice never wavered from that low, hushed level. 'His resistance is quite the dough-tiest I have seen. Voke and I agree that some monumental work has been done to his mind, allowing him to block out the manipulations. Psychic probes have been tried, but found wanting.'

'Perhaps we should have the Astropathicus provide us with one of their primary class adepts,' said Voke from behind me.

'I don't think there's a mind block there at all,' I said. 'You would see traces of the conditioning. He'd most likely be screaming for us to stop now because he knows he cannot tell us the answer.'

'Nonsense,' whispered Schongard. 'No raw mind could with-stand this.'

'I sometimes doubt whether my fellows know anything about human nature at all,' I said, mildly. 'This man is a fiend. This man is nobility. He has seen into the darkness we so fear, and he knows what power feels like. The promise of what lies at stake for him and his collaborators is enough to steel him.'

I crossed to the table and looked down into Glaw's lidless eyes. Blood bubbled at his flayed lips as he smiled at me.

'He promised the overthrow of worlds, the annihilation of billions. He boasted of it. What the Glaws are after is so great, that none of this matters. Isn't that right, Urisel?'

He gurgled.

'This is just a hardship,' I said, turning away from the heretic in disdain. 'He keeps going because he knows that what awaits him will make this all worthwhile.'

Voke snorted. 'What could be so?'

'Eisenhorn sounds convincing to me,' said Endor. 'Glaw will

protect his secrets no matter what we do, for those secrets will repay him a thousand fold.'

Schongard's masked face shook dubiously. 'I am with brother Voke. What reward could be worth the prolonged ministrations of the Inquisition's finest fleshsmiths?'

I didn't answer. I didn't know the answer, in truth, but I had some notion of the scale.

And the thought of it froze my soul.

If I had harboured any doubts that the Glaws' authority had survived, they were dispelled in the course of the next week. Campaigns of explosive, toxic and psychic sabotage plagued the worlds of the sub-sector, as if all the secret, dark cells of evil hidden away within Imperial society were revealing themselves, risking discovery as they turned on their local populations, as if orchestrated by some ruling power. The likes of Lord Glaw and his accomplices had either escaped destruction or they were but part of an invisible ruling elite that now mobilised all the hidden offspring cabals on a double-dozen worlds into revolt.

'There is another explanation,' Titus Endor said to me as we attended mass in the Imperial Cathedral of Dorsay. 'For all their power and influence, the Glaws were not the summit of their conspiratorial pyramid. There were yet others above them.'

It was possible, but I had seen the Glaws' arrogance first hand. They were not ones to bow to another master. Not a human master, anyway.

The unrest had broken out on Gudrun too by then. A bombing campaign had stricken one town in the south, and an agricultural settlement in the west had been exterminated by a neural toxin released into its water supply. Battlefleet

Scarus was still struggling to recover from the self-inflicted blow against it, and Admiral Spatian had returned from his mission to reassemble the panicked fleet units empty handed. Captain Estrum's mobile group had simply vanished. I had exchanged messages with Madorthene, who told me that no one in battlefleet command now doubted that the destruction of the Ultima Victrix and the subsequent mayhem had been anything other than sabotage. Our enemy's reach extended into the battlefleet itself.

Then two massive hives of Thracian Primaris rose in open revolt. Thousands of workers, tainted by the corrupt touch of Chaos, took to the streets, burning, looting and executing. They displayed the obscene badges of Chaos openly.

The Lord Militant's plans for a crusade into the Ophidian sub-sector were now indefinitely postponed. Battlefleet Scarus left anchor and made best speed to suppress the Thracian uprising.

But that was only the first. Open revolt exploded through the suburbs of Sameter's capital city and, a day later, a civil war erupted on Hesperus. In both cases, the stain of Chaos was there.

This miserable, shocking period is referred to in Imperial histories as the Helican Schism. It lasted eight months, and millions died in open warfare across those three worlds, not to mention hundreds of lesser incidents on other planets, including Gudrun. The Lord Militant got his holy crusade, though I am sure he hardly expected to be waging it against the population of his own sub-sector.

The authorities, and even my worthy fellow inquisitors, seemed stunned to the point of inactivity by this unprecedented outbreak. The archenemy of mankind often acted openly and brutally, but this seemed to defy logic. Why, after what may have been centuries of careful, secret establishment, had the hidden cults risen as one, exposing themselves to the wrath of the Imperial military?

I believed the answer was the 'true matter'. Urisel Glaw's almost gleeful resistance to our methods convinced me. The archenemy was embarked upon something so momentous that it was prepared to sacrifice all of its secret forces throughout the sub-sector to keep the Imperium occupied.

I believed, with all conviction, that it would be better for planets to burn than for that 'true matter' to be accomplished.

Which is why I went to Damask.

THIRTEEN

Damask
North Qualm
Sanctum

Under a leaden, rusty sky, the ball-tree forests followed the wind.

They looked like thick herds of bulbous livestock, surging across the rolling sweeps of scree, and the jostling, clattering noise they made sounded like hooves.

But they were trees: pustular, fronded globes of cellulose swelled by lighter-than-air gases generated from decomposition processes deep inside them. They drifted in the wind and dragged heavy, trailing root systems behind them. Occasionally, the pressure of one ball-tree against another caused a gas-globe to vent with a moaning squeal forced out through fibrous sphincters. Plumes of gas wafted above the tree herd.

I climbed to the top of a low plateau, where the bluish flint and gravel were caked in yellowish lichens. A couple of solitary ball-trees, small juveniles, scudded across the hill's flat summit. In the centre of the plateau's top stood a rockcrete pylon marker, commemorating the original landing place of the first settlers who had come to Damask. The elements had all but worn away the inscription. Standing by the marker, I slowly turned and took in the landscape. Black flint hills to the west, thick ball-tree forests in the wide river valley to the north, leagues of thorn-woods to the east, near to where we had set down, and grumbling, fire-topped volcanoes to the south, far away, sooting the sky with threads of sulphurous brown smoke. Clouds of small air-grazers circled over the forests, preparing to roost for the night. A surly, scarred moon was rising, distorted by the thick amber atmosphere.

'Eisenhorn,' Midas called over the vox.

I walked back down the plateau slope, buttoning my leather coat against the evening breeze. Midas and Fischig waited by the landspeeder that they had spent the past two hours unstowing and reassembling from the gun-cutter's hold. It was an old, unarmed model and it hadn't been used for three years. Midas was closing an engine cowling.

'You've got it working, then,' I said.

Midas shrugged. 'It's a piece of crap. I had to get Uclid to strip in new relays. All manner of cabling had perished.'

Fischig looked particularly unimpressed with the vehicle.

I seldom had a use for it. On most worlds, local transport was available. I hadn't expected Damask to be so... unpopulated.

Records said there were at least five colony settlements, but there had been no sign of any from orbit, and no response to vox or astropathical messages. Had the human population of Damask withered and died in the past five years since records were filed?

We'd left Aemos, Bequin and Lowink with the cutter, which had put down on the shores of a wide river basin. We'd carefully disguised it with camouflage netting. Midas had chosen a landing site within speeder range of some of the colony locations, yet far enough out to avoid being seen by anybody at those locations as we made descent. Tobius Maxilla awaited our pleasure aboard the *Essene* in high orbit above.

Midas fired up the speeder's misfiring engines and we moved off overland from the hidden cutter towards the last recorded position of the closest human settlement.

Tumble-brush scudded around the speeder, and we rode through scarpland where root-anchored trees spread aloft branches blistering with gas-sacks so that the whole plant seemed to strain against the soil and gravity in the wind. Grazers, little bat-like mammals with membranous wings, fluttered around. Larger gliders, immense headless creatures that were all flat wingspan and fluked tail, turned silently on the thermals high above us. The landscape was jagged, broken and had the bluish cast of flint. The air was dark and noxious, and we used rebreather masks from time to time.

We followed the frothy, brackish river waters for twenty kilometres and then left the wide flood banks and juddered up through rocky scarps, sculptural deserts formed by elementally shattered flint outcrops, brakes of dusty yellow fern, and seas of lichen trembling in the gusting wind. The ugly moon rose higher, though there was still daylight left.

Midas had to slew the speeder to a halt at one place where a group of much larger grazers broke across the trail, panicked by the sound of the engines. They were dove-grey giants with steep, humped backs, trunk-like snouts and long attenuated legs ending in massive pads. Their legs seemed too slender and long to support such bulks, but like the local plant life, I suspected the swollen torsos of these animals contained supporting bladders of gas.

They snorted and clattered away into the fern thickets. The

speeder had stalled. Midas got out and cussed at the rotors of the turbo-fan for a few minutes until the mechanism chuckled back into life. As we waited, Fischig and I stretched our legs. He climbed up onto an igneous boulder and fiddled with the straps of his rebreather as he watched the hot blue streaks of a meteor storm slice the gloomy sky on the western horizon.

I gazed across the fern thickets. Air-grazers chirruped and darted in the hushing leaves. The wind had changed, and a forest-herd of ball-trees scudded in through the edges of the ferns, squeaking and rasping as the wind drove their globes and root-systems through the grounded plants.

We pushed on another ten kilometres, coming down into a rift valley where the ground became thick, sedimentary soil, black and wet. The vegetation here was richer and more rubbery: bulb snakelocks and bright, spiky marsh lilies, clubmoss, horsetail, tousled maidenhair, lofty cycads festooned with epiphytic bromeliads and skeins of ground-draping gnetophytes. Clouds of tiny insects billowed in the damper glades and along seeping watercourses, and large, hornet-like hunters with scintillating wings buzzed through the damp air like jewelled daggers.

'There,' said Fischig, his eyes sharp. We stopped and dismounted. A muddy expanse near the track had once been a cultivated field, and the rusty carcasses of two tilling machines lay half-buried in the sucking soil.

A little further on, we passed a marker stone struck from flint. 'Gillan's Acre' it read in Low Gothic.

We'd passed the township itself before we realised, and turned back. It was nothing but the stumps of a few walls covered with wispy weed-growth and rampant gnetophytes. Until at least five years before, this had been a community of eight hundred. A scan showed metal fragments and portions of broken machinery buried under the soil.

Fischig found the marker screened by sticky cycads at the north end of the town plot. It had been fashioned from local fibre-wood, a carved symbol that was unmistakably one of the filthy and unnerving glyphs of Chaos.

'A statement? A warning?' Fischig wondered aloud.

'Burn it immediately,' I told him.

The vox-link warbled. It was Maxilla, from orbit.

'I've been sectioning the landscape as you requested, inquisitor,' he reported. 'The atmosphere is hindering my scans, but I'm getting there. I just ran a sweep of the volcanic region south of you. It's hard to tell because it's active, but I think there are signs of structures and operating machines.'

He pin-pointed the site to the speeder's navigation system. Another seventy kilometres, roughly the location of another possible settlement listed on our maps.

'That's quite a distance, and the light is failing,' Midas said.

'Let's get back to the cutter. We'll head south at dawn.'

In the night, as we slept, something approached the shrouded cutter and set off the motion alarms. We went out, armed, to look for intruders, but there was no sign. And no sign of drifting ball-trees either.

At dawn, we headed south. The volcanic region, its smouldering peaks rising before us, was thickly forested with fern and thorn-scrub. It was hot too, as stinking, heated gas leaked into the glades from the volcanic vents that laced the rocky earth. A half-hour into the sulphurous forests we were sweating heavily and using our rebreathers almost constantly.

Below the peak of one of the largest cones, the landspeeder's rudimentary scanners detected signs of activity as we rode up a long slope of tumbled, desiccated rock. Fischig, Midas and I dismounted from the speeder and clambered up a flinty outcrop to get a better view with our scopes.

In the shadow of the cone was a large settlement... old stone and wood-built structures, mostly ruined, as well as newer, modular habitats made of ceramite. There was machinery down there, generators and other heavy systems at work under tarpaulin canopies. Tall, angled screens of reinforced flak-board had been erected on scaffolding rigs to shield the place from ash-fall. Three speeders and two heavy eight-wheelers were drawn up outside the main habitat units. A few figures moved around the place, too distant to resolve clearly.

'The last survey showed no signs of active vulcanism in this region,' Midas reminded me, echoing an observation Aemos had made on our arrival.

'See there,' I said, indicating a portion of the settlement that ran into the slope of the largest cone. 'Those old buildings are partially buried in solidified ash. The original settlement predates the activity.'

Midas pulled a map-slate from his pocket and whirred through the index. 'North Qualm,' he said. 'One of the settler habitats, a mining town.'

We watched for fifteen or twenty minutes, long enough to feel the ground shudder and see a gout of white hot liquid fire spit from one of the cones. Alarms sounded in the settlement below, but were quickly stifled. A rain of wet ash and glowing embers fluttered down across the township and settled like black snow on the flak-board screens.

'Why would they persist in working this site with the constant threat of eruption?' Fischig growled.

'Let's take a closer look,' I suggested.

Covering the speeder with foliage, we set off down the forested valley. The ground between the feathery ferns and hard, dry thorn-trees was thick with fungal growth, some of it brightly covered and glossy. Though we worked carefully, we couldn't help kicking up puffs of spores and soredia.

I was wearing my button-sleeve black coat, Fischig his brown body armour, his helmet hooked on his belt, and Midas wore his regular outfit, though he had replaced his cerise jacket with a short, dark-blue work coat. All of us melted into the forest shadows.

I still wasn't sure why Fischig had come along. After Gudrun, the remit given him by Lord Custodian Carpel seemed done with, but he had refused to return to Hubris. It seemed he trusted my instinct that the matter was far from done with.

We crossed a low stream bed, steaming with hot, pungent water that bubbled up from the vents, and came silently up along the north edge of the settlement. Now the judder of generators could be made out, the distant growl of rock-drills. Guards in khaki drill fatigues worn under spiked and blackened segments of metal body armour wandered the length of an earthwork wall that had been banked up at the edge of the trees, running great bull-cygnids on long chains. The canines were meaty brutes with lolling tongues and beards of spittle. The guards that pulled on their chains carried newly stamped, short-form lasguns on shoulder slings. Their faces were masked behind heavy black rebreathers. Workgangs, some stripped to their leggings in the heat, toiled to sluice the smouldering ash from the flak-board screens with hoses and bucket chains.

Midas pointed out where the edges of the settlement had been ringed with motion detectors and antipersonnel mines.

All had been deactivated. The constant tremors had rendered both useless as defences. But there was no mistaking the aura I had felt since we had first begun to approach. A psychic veil utterly enclosed North Qualm.

I took out my scope and played it around the settlement. More guards, many more, and dozens of filth-caked workers, lounging by the entrance to one particularly large modular shed. Several supervisors moved back and forth among the resting work gangs, holding brief conversations and making notations on data-slates. Eight workers emerged from the shed carrying long, stretcher-like trays with high sides covered with clear-plastic wraps. I zoomed the magnification of the scope to get a closer look at the faces of the supervisors. I didn't recognise any of them. They were all dour, scholarly men in grey rainproof overalls.

Something vast suddenly crossed my field of vision. By the time I had reacted and adjusted the magnification, it had passed out of sight into the works shed. I had a brief memory of bright, almost gaudy metal and a shimmering, flowing robe.

'What the hell was that?' I hissed.

Midas looked at me, lowering his scope, actual fear on his face. Fischig also looked disturbed.

'A giant, a horned giant in jewelled metal,' Midas said. 'He came striding out of the modular hab to the left and went straight into the shed. God-Emperor, but it was huge!'

Fischig agreed with a nod. 'A monster,' he said.

The cones above roared again, and a rain of withering ash fluttered down across the settlement. We shrank back into the thorn-trees. Guard activity seemed to increase.

'Rosethorn,' my vox piped.

'Now is not a good time,' I hissed.

It was Maxilla. He sent one final word and cut off. 'Sanctum.'

'Sanctum' was a Glossia codeword that I had given Maxilla before we had left the *Essene*. I wanted him in close orbit, providing us with extraction cover and overhead sensor advantages, but knew that he would have to melt away the moment any other traffic entered the system. 'Sanctum' meant that he had detected a ship or ships emerging from the immaterium into realspace, and was withdrawing to a concealment orbit behind the local star.

Which meant that all of us on the planet were on our own.

Midas caught my sleeve and pointed down at the settlement. The giant had reappeared and stood in plain view at the mouth of the shed. He was well over two metres tall, wrapped in a cloak that seemed to be made of smoke and silk, and his ornately decorated armour and horned helmet were a shocking mixture of chased gold, acidic yellow, glossy purple, and the red of fresh, oxygenated blood. In his ancient armour, the monster looked like he had stood immobile in that spot for a thousand years. Just a glance at him inspired terror and revulsion, involuntary feelings of dread that I could barely repress.

A Space Marine, from the corrupted and damned Adeptus Astartes. A Chaos Marine.

FOURTEEN

A tale of repression
Rogue
Return to the flame hills

'We've not been idle,' Bequin told me with a smirk when we returned to the gun-cutter. It was noon, and river basin was filling with bumping clusters of ball-trees driven off the flint plains by the wind. They drifted over the shingle and splashed trailing roots into the water.

Bequin was dressed in work fatigues, a rebreather slung around her neck, and she carried an autopistol. As Midas and Fischig stowed the speeder under the netting, she led me into the crew-bay and waved the weapon in the direction of a thin, filthy man chained to a cargo-loop with cuff restraints. His hair was matted and his clothes, an assemblage of patched rags, were stiff with caked mud. He looked at me with fierce eyes through a shaggy fringe of wet hair.

'There were three of them, maybe more,' Bequin told me. 'Came to take a look at us using the ball-trees as moving cover. The others fled, but I brought him down.'

'How?' I asked.

She gave me that look which told me not to keep under-estimating her.

'Our intruders from last night?' I wondered aloud. Bequin shrugged.

I walked over to face the captive. 'What's your name?'

'He doesn't say much,' Bequin advised. I told her to move away.

'Name?' I asked again.

Nothing. I paused, collected my mind and then sent a gentle probe into the shady recesses of his skull.

'Tymas Rhizor,' he stammered.

Good. Another gentle push at his slowly yielding mind. The levels of fear and caution were palpable.

'Of Gillan His Acre, Goddes land.'

I switched to speech, without the psychic urge now. 'Gillan's Acre? You mean Gillan's Acre?'

'Seythee Gillan His Acre?'

'Gillan's Acre?'

He nodded. 'Theesey truth.'

'Proto-Gothic, with generational nuance shift,' Aemos said, coming near. 'Damask was colonised something over five hundred years ago, and was isolated for a lengthy period. The population may not have flourished, but the language has perpetuated vestiges of older linguaforms.'

'So this man is likely to be a native, a settler?'

Aemos nodded. I saw our captive was looking from my face to Aemos's, trying to follow our conversation.

'You were born here, on Damask?'

He frowned.

'Born here?'

'Ayeam of Gillan His Acre. Yitt be Goddes land afoor the working.'

I looked round at Aemos. This would take forever. 'I can manage,' Aemos said. 'Ask away.'

'Ask him what happened to Gillan's Acre.'

'Preyathee, howcame bye lossen Gillan His Acre?'

His story was painfully simple, and shaped by the ignorance of a man whose kind had worked the poor soil of a lonely edgeworld for generations. The families, as he called them, presumably the clan groups of the original settlers, had worked the land for as long as his memory and the memory of his elders went. There were five farming communities, and two quarries or mines, which provided building materials and fossil fuel in exchange for a share of the crops. They were devout people, dedicated to the nurture of 'Goddes land...' God's land, though there was no doubt that by 'God' they meant the God-Emperor. As little as four years ago, after the time of the last survey from which records we worked, there had been upwards of nine thousand settlers living in the communities of Damask.

Then the mission came. Rhizor reckoned this to have been three years before. A ship brought a small order of ecclesiarchs here from Messina. They intended to establish a retreat and spiritually educate the neglected settlers. There had been thirty priests. He recognised the name Dazzo. 'Archprieste Dazzo,' he called him. Other off-worlders came too, not priests like Dazzo and his brethren, but men who worked with them. From the way he described them, they sounded like geological surveyors or mining engineers. They concentrated their attentions on the quarries at North Qualm. After about a year, the activity increased. More ships came and went. Settlers, mostly strong males, were recruited from the farm communities to work the mines, often brutally. The ecclesiarchs didn't seem to mind. As their populations drained, the farming settlements began to fail and die off. No help was given to sustain them. A disease, probably an off-world import, killed many. Then the volcanic activity began, suddenly, without warning. Everyone in the farmsteads was rounded up and pressed into service at the pits as if some great urgency was now driving the task. Rhizor and many like him toiled until they dropped, and later managed to escape, living like animals in the thorn forests.

So Dazzo and his mission had come to Damask, enslaved the population into a workforce, and were now hell-bent on mining out something from the territory around North Qualm. It seemed likely to me that the vulcanism had been triggered by incautious mining work.

I reached into his mind again... he trembled in fear as he felt the psychic touch... and showed him an image of Dazzo. Eagerly, he confirmed his identity. Then Locke, another face he knew and regarded with ill-concealed hatred. Locke had been chief among the men who had pressed the farmers into service. His cruelty had left a lasting mark. I showed him the faces of Urisel and Oberon Glaw, neither of which were known to him. At last, I visualised an image of the pipe-smoking man.

'Malahite,' he announced, recognising him at once. According to Rhizor, the obscura addict with the watery blue eyes was Girolamo Malahite, chief of the surveyors and engineers.

Fischig, who had joined us during the conversation, asked about the fibre-wood marker we had found at Gillan's Acre. Rhizor wrinkled his face with grief. That had marked the mass grave where the off-worlders had buried all those who had resisted.

Midas called me to the cockpit. I told Aemos to feed Rhizor and question him further.

* * *

Midas sat in the leather pilot's throne, his lap draped with spools of scroll paper stamped out of the electric press.

'No wonder Maxilla hid,' he said by way of an opening. 'Look here.'

The scrolls were a transcription log of the astropathic and vox traffic Midas had been able to monitor from the ships in orbit. He slid a gloved finger down the jumbled columns of figures and text.

'I make out at least twelve vessels up there, maybe more. It's difficult to say an accurate figure. These here, for example, may be two ships in dialog or the same ship repeating itself.'

'Coding?'

'That's the interesting bit. It's all standard Imperial, the Navy code called Textcept.'

'That's common enough.'

He nodded. 'And look here, the question and answer pattern indicates a capital ship checking that its fleet components have all arrived in realspace. It's a typical Imperial structure. Military... one of ours.'

'A friendly fleet.'

'Not friendly, perhaps. Look at the command identifier here... that name translates as Estrum.'

'The missing captain.'

'The missing captain... perhaps not that missing after all. Perhaps... rogue. The whole incident at Gudrun anchorage, the mistaken recognition, the "panic"... could have been an excuse to withdraw ships loyal to him.'

'But he's still broadcasting in standard Imperial code-form.'

'If his officers alone are party to the deceit, he won't want to alert the crews.'

* * *

An hour later, a large launch with fighter escort broke from the fleet and swung down to the surface of Damask. The transport set down at North Qualm, and the fighters circled the area twice before returning to their base ship. From the cutter, we could hear the booming roar of their thrusters rolling around the plateaux and valleys. Midas quickly switched the cutter's systems to minimum operation so they wouldn't make a chance detection of our instrumentation.

Aemos talked with Rhizor for most of the afternoon, and he seemed calmer and more willing to help once food had been given to him. As the light began to fail and evening approached, Aemos came to find me.

'If you want a way back in, that man might be able to help you.'

'Go on.'

'He knows the mines and the excavations. He worked there for a goodly while. I've spoken to him at length, and he seems certain he could show you to a cave network that links with the mining structure.'

We set out after dark in the speeder. Fischig drove, using the terrain scanner to see rather than the lamps. That made progress slower but more discreet. I sat next to him, and Bequin rode in the back with Rhizor. There had been some debate about which of us should go, but I had made the final selection. The speeder could hold four, and though Midas was the most able combatant in my group, more able than even the chastener in my view, I wanted him at the helm of the cutter, ready to respond. Besides, Bequin had uses of her own that I considered vital to our endeavour.

It took a long time to make the trek back to the North Qualm region, and we didn't arrive until well into the second half of the night. Clouds had masked the sky, hiding the moon and stars, and the only light was the flare of the volcanic hills, underlighting the low clouds with a fluctuating red haze. The air was thick with sulphurous smoke.

We left the speeder concealed in a hollow, its position flagged by a marker tag, and headed west around the out-reaches of the area, the 'flame hills' as Rhizor called them.

Nocturnal creatures chattered and fluted in the darkness. Something larger and more distant howled. Pressing through the thorn-scrub, we became aware of the harsh artificial light-ing bathing the entire settlement. The volcanoes rumbled.

It took Rhizor a little time to find what he was looking for: a series of small, shallow pools, half-filled with geothermally heated water. The syrupy surfaces of the pools seethed and bubbled, and the site was plagued with insects drawn by the heat. Rhizor splashed cautiously into the largest pool, and worked his way around a massive boulder that was swathed in bright orange lichen. Behind it, masked by thorn and cycad, was a narrow cavity. This, he said, as best as I could under-stand him, was the route by which he had escaped from the slave-gangs.

We checked weapons and equipment and prepared to enter. I had opened the weapons locker on the cutter and provided us with as much efficient firepower as we could comfort-ably manage. I had my powersword, an autopistol in a rig under my coat, and a las-carbine with a lamp pack taped under the muzzle. Other items of equipment filled the pack on my back. Bequin had kept her autopistol, and taken a flat-bladed knife, and she too had a lamp. I'd given Fischig an old but well-maintained heavy stubber, which seemed to please him enormously. He had his Arbites pistol, and a satchel full of spare ammo drums for the stubber. Rhizor had refused a weapon. I was certain he would leave us once we were safely en route anyway.

The cavity allowed us to enter single file. I led the way, with Rhizor behind me, then Bequin, and Fischig brought up the rear. It was damnably hot in the narrow rock passage, and the sulphurous gases forced us to wear our rebreathers. Rhizor had no breather, but tied a swathe of cloth around his nose and mouth. This was the practice the slaves had used when working the mines.

The passage wound back and forth, and climbed for a while as it coiled into the hill. In places, it was so steep we had to climb up the ragged floor of the burrow. Twice we had to remove our equipment packs to ease through constricted sections.

After an hour, I began to feel the oppressive throb of the psychic veil shrouding North Qualm. As we penetrated it, I listened out for the sound of alarms or activity, but none came. Though she didn't know it, Bequin was already doing her job by creating a dead spot that allowed us to press on invisibly. I made sure none of us strayed too far from her aura of influence.

The lava flues were crawling with lifeforms adjusted to existence in the hot, chemical-rich environment: blind, toad-like hunters, transparent beetles, albino molluscs and spiders that looked like they were fashioned from white gold. A fat, pallid centipede as long as my arm spurred its way over the baked rock at one junction.

Every few minutes the earth trembled. Loose rock and dust showered down from the roof, and warm, reeking gases blew back along the winding rock halls.

The passage widened, and showed signs of excavation.

Thorn-wood props supported the ceiling, and marker boards with numbers chalked on them were nailed to every sixth post. Rhizor tried to explain where we were. He did his best, and I was able to ascertain we were in a section of mine that had been worked and then abandoned. He said other things too, but the meaning was beyond me. He led us to the end of one working, a low, propped tunnel, and I shone my light into a cavity that had been dug out of the loose shale and grit. Bequin knelt and brushed grit off the floor with her hand. She exposed old tiles, made of a dull, metallic substance I couldn't identify. The tiles were perfectly fitted, despite the fact that they were irregular octagons. They were strangely unsymmetrical, with some edges overlong. Yet they all fitted almost seamlessly. We could not begin to account for it, and the pattern they made was intensely uncomfortable.

At the rear of the cavity, ancient stonework had been exposed. I was no expert, but the stone, a hard pale material glittering with flecks of mica, didn't look local. There was evidence that parts of it had been cut away with rock drills and cutting beams.

'This is old,' said Fischig. He ran his hand across the riven stone facing, 'but the damage is new.'

'The wheel-graves,' Alizebeth Bequin said suddenly. I looked over at her. 'On Bonaventure,' she explained, remembering her homeworld. 'There were famous old sites in the western hills, made by races before man. They were arranged in radiating circles, like wheels. I used to go there, when I was a child. They had been decorated once, I suppose, but the surfaces had been cut away. Ransacked by later hands. It reminds me of this.'

'There are many who make a trade in archaeological plunder,' said Fischig. 'And if it's xenos artefacts, the penalty is high.'

I'd overheard Glaw and his allies mention archeoxenon materials. If this was such a site, connected in some way to the as yet mysterious saruthi, it accounted for the way they persisted in working it despite the volcano.

What had they taken from here? What was it worth to them? What was it worth to the saruthi?

We retraced our steps back to the main seam, passing three more abandoned cavities. Each one had shown signs of the old stonework, and each had been robbed like the first.

We came to the end of the seam, and a metal ladder rose up through scaffolding to an opening in the rock ten metres up.

We climbed up into another tunnel, and at once heard the rattle of rock drills. The atmosphere was clearer here, and we were able to remove our rebreathers. Cold air, from the surface, I guessed, breezed down the tunnel. With extreme caution, we passed along, crossing the mouth of a gigantic cavern that had probably been a magmatic reservoir. The walls were polished and fused by heat. Crouching low, we looked in, and saw work gangs of men and women, undoubtedly Rhizor's kinfolk, forming basket chains to clear rock debris from the workface. There were at least a dozen of the bestial guards in their black, spiked armour. One walked the work-line and administered encouragement with an electro-lash.

I peered in more intently, and tried to make sense of the main working. Two Damaskite slaves worked with rock drills, cutting back the crust of wall, exposing a wide stretch of the old stone facing. Other slaves, most of them women, laboured closely on the exposed section with small picks, awls and brushes, revealing carvings of intricate design.

A relay of shouts ran down the guard line, and we hid ourselves in the tunnel shadows. From up ahead, lamps bobbed and wove, and a party of men came down the tunnel from the surface into the cavern. Three were guards, two grey-shrouded supervisors with data-slates. The others were Gorgone Locke and the pipe-smoker Girolamo Malahite.

As I suspected, members of the Glaw cabal had escaped House Glaw alive. Estrum's rogue fleet had no doubt played a part in that salvation.

Locke was dressed in a leather robe with armoured panels woven into it. His mouth still showed the wound I had inflicted there. His mood was sullen.

Malahite was dressed in black as I had seen him before. He stood, studying data-slates, conferring with the dig supervisors and the leader of the guard team before moving to look at the exposed stretch of achaeoxenon material. The slave workers shrank back out of his way.

He exchanged a few words with the men around him, and the guard leader hurried off, returning with a bulky rocksaw. The tool trailed cables and tubes behind it, back to a socket junction at the mouth of the cavern, where it linked to a system of power and water supply lines running back up the tunnel to the generators and pumps at the surface.

The saw whined into life, pumping a sheen of water over its blade to keep it clean and cool. The guard leader carefully sliced the blade into the rock, the saw keening as it bit. In a few seconds, he had cut a slice of the carvings free. As far as I could tell, the carvings were made on individual stone blocks, and he was slicing the sculpted faces off the stones. He cut two more, and they were passed with reverence to Malahite, who studied them and then handed them on to be wrapped in plastic and placed in wooden carriers. The slices looked very much like the old stone tablets I had seen in that private study under House Glaw.

There was a loud crack. The guard leader had cut another

tablet away, but it had broken into fragments. He dropped the saw and began to collect up the fragments frantically as those around him cursed and shouted. Locke moved in.

He kicked the man hard and dropped him to the ground, then kicked him repeatedly as he lay there, trying to shield his face, begging for mercy. Malahite gathered up the fragments.

'You were told to be careful, you useless bastard!' Locke was growling.

'It can be repaired,' Malahite told the ship master. 'I can fuse it together.'

Locke wasn't listening. He kicked the man again, then dragged him up and threw him against the wall. He cursed at him some more and the man whimpered, pleading apologies.

Locke turned away from the battered wretch. Then he picked up the revving saw, swung back, and dismembered the guard leader.

It was inhuman. The agonised screams filled the chamber. All the slaves wailed and moaned, and even the guards looked away in distaste. Locke laid in with murderous glee, covering himself in blood.

Then he tossed the smoking saw onto the ground at his feet, and turned to another of the guards. He pointed to the saw.

'Make sure you do a better job,' he snarled.

With huge reluctance, the guard picked up the saw and set to work.

Locke, Malahite and their party left after another ten minutes, followed by a work gang carrying the wooden crates full of cut tablets. We waited a few minutes, then followed them up the tunnel.

There was daylight ahead, scarce and thin. The tunnel came up into what I guessed was the large modular shed I had seen from my reconnaissance. Workers milled around on rest breaks, and guards and the grey-robed overseers wandered back and forth. Dig equipment and tools were piled up in the poorly lit shed. Fischig found a door at the back of the shed behind equipment boxes and broke the lock. The four of us were able to slip out of the shed from the rear into the settlement without having to pass through the main mine entrance and thus be seen.

We were now in a back lane of North Qualm, with the volcano slopes behind us. Rotting and abandoned buildings stood close all around, and flurries of ash and soot blew down over us. We kept close to the walls, holding back out of sight when anybody passed.

Behind the next jumble of ruins lay a cleared area partly masked by more flak-board screens, designed to keep the ash out. Two launches sat on the scorched ground: a large Imperial Navy transport and a smaller, older shuttle. A thicker layer of ash coated the older shuttle's hull.

Figures moved around the entry ramps of both ships. Guards and workers were moving the wooden stretchers of excavated artefacts up into the belly hold of the Navy launch. I could see Locke and Malahite standing nearby with several of the supervisors and three battlefleet officers in shipboard fatigues. One, a lean man with a receding chin and bulging eyes, wore the ribbons and insignia of a captain. Our rogue, Estrum. As I watched, the ecclesiarch Dazzo emerged from a nearby building and crossed to them, holding the hem of his rich gown up out of the ash.

Shouting suddenly boomed across the yard. An angry human voice followed by a deeper, more savage sound that set the hairs on my neck up.

Lord Oberon Glaw, dressed in a cloak and body armour,

slammed out of the building Dazzo had emerged from, striding across the landing yard. A second later, the huge, ghastly bulk of the Chaos Space Marine followed him, raging and cursing.

Glaw wheeled and faced the giant monster, resuming his argument at the top of his voice. For all his size, the lord of House Glaw was dwarfed by the vividly armoured blasphemy. The Traitor Marine had removed his helmet: his face was a white, powdered, lifeless mask of hate, with smears of gold dust and purple skin paint around the hollow eyes and a dry, lipless mouth full of pearl-inlaid teeth. His only vaguely human face seemed to have been sutured onto his skull, the exposed parts of which were machined gold. There was a terrible stink of cloying perfume and organic corruption. I could not imagine the courage – or insanity – that it took to face down a Chaos Space Marine in a furious argument.

The wind was against us, and all we could hear was the violent snarl of the voices instead of actual words. Dazzo and Malahite quickly crossed to Glaw's side, and most of the other guards and workers present cowered back.

The wind changed a little.

'...will not deny me any longer, you human filth!' The awful voice of the Traitor Marine could suddenly be heard.

'You will show me respect, Mandragore! Respect!' Glaw yelled back, his voice powerful but seemingly frail against the roar of the Chaos warrior.

The Marine bellowed something else that ended in '...slay you all and finish this work myself! My masters await, and they await the perfect completion of this task! They will not idle their time while you vermin dawdle and slacken!'

'You will abide by our pact! You will keep to our agreement!'

I realised I had almost become hypnotised. Staring at the

monstrous, raging figure, drawn to him by his power and sheer horror, my eyes had lingered too long on the obscene runic carvings that edged the joints of his armour, the insane sigils that decorated his chest plate. I was entranced, captivated by the golden chains that dressed his luridly painted armour, the gems and exquisite filigree covering his armour plate, the translucent silk of his cloak, and the words, the alien, abominable words, inscribed upon his form, twitching and seething with secrets older then time... secrets, promises, lies...

I forced myself not to look. Soul-destroying madness lay in the marks and brands of Chaos if one looked too long.

Mandragore shrieked in fury and raised a massive gloved fist, spiked with rusty blades, to smash Lord Glaw.

The blow didn't fall. I started, as if slapped, as a burst of psychic power rippled across the concourse.

Mandragore stepped back a pace. Dazzo moved towards him. Smaller than Glaw or Locke, Dazzo seemed even more insignificant next to the monster, but with each step he took, the Chaos Marine moved backwards.

He didn't speak, but I could hear his voice in my head. The presence and the words were so foul I barely managed not to vomit.

'Mandragore Carrion, son of Fulgrim, worthy of Slaanesh, champion of the Emperor's Children, killer of the living, defiler of the dead, keeper of secrets – your presence here honours us, and we celebrate our pact with your fellowship... but you will not seek to harm us. Never raise your hand to us again. Never.'

Dazzo was simply the most potent psyker I had ever encountered. With his mind alone, he had forced down one of the vilest of the traitors, a Space Marine sworn to the corrupt service of Chaos.

Mandragore turned away, and strode off across the compound. I saw now how Lord Glaw wilted from the confrontation, his bravado spent. Many of the workers present were weeping with the trauma of the exchange, and two of the guards were throwing up.

Shaking, I looked round at my companions. Fischig was ashen-faced and trembling, his eyes closed. Rhizor had curled up in a ball in the ashy mud, his back against the wall.

Bequin had vanished.

FIFTEEN

Exposed in the midst of the foe
An ill-matched war
Flight

I had a second to realise that wherever Bequin had gone, it had left us exposed, outside the veil of her untouchable aura. I heard a cry, a strangled warning from the old ecclesiarch that was immediately accompanied by the hoot of sirens.

In the landing yard, guards were racing towards us. Dazzo was pointing directly at the section of ruin that concealed us. Locke pulled a laspistol from his robe. Angry voices, the raucous bark of cygnids.

'Fischig!' I cried. 'Fischig! Move or we're dead!'

He blinked, still pale, as if he didn't recognise his own name.

I slapped him hard around the side of his head.

'Move, chastener!' I yelled.

The first of the guards had reached the ruins, and one was kicking his way in through a boarded-up door. I saw his staring face looking out of a dirty black visor. He raised his lasgun.

I swung the powerful carbine up and laced him and the doorway with a spray of laser shots. Stone and wood debris spat and flew from the multiple impacts.

Las-shots whined in through gaps in the stone work and exploded against the outside wall.

Fischig's heavy stubber chattered into life. He played the sweep of blazing tracer shots down the dark cavities of the ruin to our left, tearing apart two more guards who were forcing their way in.

More guards, to my right, fired their weapons. My las-carbine crackled on full auto, a blur of high-pitched whines, as I raked the narrow entrance and dropped another three.

Still firing, Fischig backed into the depths of the ruin.

'Come on!' he snarled. I backed with him, our weapons laying down a storm of explosive metal and piercing energy that rippled across the ruin walls, scattering debris, spraying ash dust and bursting bodies.

Rhizor, his mind utterly gone with terror, lay on the ground. I grabbed him by the scruff of his rags and dragged him after us. He fought at me, despairing.

A large figure came leaping in though the window space in the wall through which we had observed the dealings in the yard. It was Locke. He rolled as he landed, his laspistol retching shots.

One shot clipped my left shoulder. Another three slammed into Rhizor's back and he toppled into me, knocking me flat.

Fischig saw Locke, and swung round, his finger not lifting from the stubber's blunt trigger. The rapidly cycling mechanism of the heavy weapon made a high, grinding metallic noise overlaid with the frenetic blasts of the shots.

The scant cover around Locke disintegrated, and he cried out as he threw himself behind a section of wall. He fired as he moved, and Fischig grunted in pain as a las-shot punched into his side.

'Eisenhorn! You bastard!' Locke bellowed. I pulled myself out from under Rhizor's corpse, sad that that ragged slave had paid such a price for assisting an inquisitor. Another crime on the shoulders of Gorgone Locke.

Damning the ship master's name, I pulled a frag grenade from my pack, and tossed it in Locke's direction. Then Fischig and I moved as fast as we could out through the rear of the smoke-filled ruin.

The grenade blew out the back of the structure. I hoped to the Emperor it had torn Locke limb from limb.

Coughing and spitting, Fischig and I came out into a ditch that ran behind the ruined dwellings of North Qualm and the newer modular buildings. Angled over us were the large flak-board baffles of the ash-screens.

Las-shots chipped and whacked into the screens and wailed down the dim ditch. Guards tumbled into the ditch twenty metres away, rabidly howling cygnids pouring in with them.

Fischig made the ditch his killing field, and emptied his second drum of ammunition down the length, pulverising guard and canine alike. We hurried in the opposite direction as he struggled to clamp in a fresh drum.

Guards were shooting at us through the ruins, blowing chunks from the mouldering stonework. We ran on, chased by the furious salvos.

The ditch ran out into a small yard where an eight-wheeler truck was parked. We exchanged shots with three guards who rounded the corner into the yard and dropped them, but a fourth appeared, loosing a trio of cygnids from their leashes. Baying, they pounded across the yard. I killed one with my carbine, but the truck blocked any shots at the others. The big vehicle rocked as one leapt up into its frame. A moment later, it was leaping over onto us. I put a las-round through its skull as it came down, its muscled bulk just missing me. The other came out from under the truck, filthy with axle grease, and leapt at Fischig. It knocked him over, its huge jaws locked around his armoured forearm.

I drew my powersword and thrust the crackling blade through its body.

More shots, thumping into the truck.

'Get up!' I told Fischig as we rolled the canine's dead weight off him.

The entire compound closing around us, we sprinted to the rear of a modular shed and broke the door in.

It was an equipment store, stacked with spare blades for rock drills, spools of cable, lamp-cells, and all manner of other mining equipment. We moved low between the piles of equipment, hearing shouts and running footsteps outside.

I paused, changing cells in my carbine, and keyed my vox-link.

'Thorn wishes aegis, rapturous beasts below.'

'Aegis, arising, the colours of space,' came the response immediately.

'Razor delphus pathway,' I instructed. 'Pattern ivory!'

'Pattern confirm. In six. Aegis, arising.'

Guards burst into the back of the shed, and Fischig blew them back out through the prefab wall with a wild burst of shots.

I looked around, and saw a stack of black metal boxes raised on a pallet in the corner of the shed. The paper labels were old and faded, but I prised off the lid of one box and confirmed their contents.

'Get ready to move,' I said, arming my second grenade.

'Oh shit!' said Fischig, seeing what I was doing. He was already half out the door as I placed the grenade on the top of the boxes.

We came out firing, met by a dozen or more guards who were sectioning the street looking for us. Most were pit guards in their black, ugly armour, but three were naval security troops in black cloth fatigues, no doubt part of the traitor captain's contingent.

We fired as we ran. The grenade was on a ten-second fuse. The fact that we ran through the midst of them caught them unawares. None of them was able to get a clean shot off.

Fischig and I dived headlong over a crumbling section of wall that had once surrounded North Qualm's market yard.

The grenade went off. And so did the stack of mining explosives it had been sitting on.

The shockwave concussion flattened every wall for thirty metres. The upwards force of the blast, driving before it a blistering fireball, lifted the whole modular shed twenty metres into the air and sent the shredded remains of the structure crashing down onto neighbouring buildings.

Scraps of metal, cinders and shreds of burning flak-board rained down on Fischig and myself. There was a dazed silence broken only by the warble of alarms, cries of the injured and desperate shouting. The air was fogged by ash dust. Pulling on our rebreathers, we stumbled through the murk.

I felt a jab of pain in my head. Deep, insidious, burning. Dazzo was reaching out with his terrifyingly potent mind, looking for us.

We stumbled through the smoke down an aisle between modular sheds whose windows had been blown out in the detonation.

The pain grew more intense.

'Eisenhorn. You cannot hide. Show yourself.'

I gasped as the pain took deeper hold.

Suddenly, it eased.

'Fischig! In here!'

I pushed him into an old stone outbuilding. I guessed it had once been a wash-house in North Qualm's more rural heyday.

Bequin was cowering in a corner, filthy, tearful. The sight of the Child of the Emperor Mandragore had sent her fleeing in blind panic. Like me, she had made the mistake of looking at the runes and marks on his foul, dazzling armour. Unlike me, she hadn't had the sense to look away.

She couldn't speak. She barely registered us. But we were back inside her muzzling aura and out of Dazzo's clutches for the moment.

'What now?' asked Fischig. 'They'll regroup quickly enough.'

'Midas is coming. We have to get back to the landing yard. It's the only area big enough for him to set down in.'

Fischig looked at me as if I was mad. 'He's going to fly into this? He'll be killed! And even if he does pick us up, they'll launch interceptors from the fleet. They'll launch them the moment he powers up for take off!'

'It'll be tight,' I admitted.

We dragged Bequin with us and moved out of the derelict wash-house. Outside, the settlement was still swathed in ash lifted by the blast. Fierce fires glowed in the smoke. Voices screamed orders and cygnids bayed. There was a deeper, furious bellowing too. I had a nasty feeling it was the Chaos Marine.

'Thorn attending aegis, main yard area,' I voxed.

'Aegis, main yard in three, the heavens falling.' So, they were on to him. The fleet had launched ships after the cutter.

We ran now. The smoke was slowly clearing.

A guard gang moved past us and we were forced to double back around. More guards blocked the next street.

'Through the buildings!' said Fischig.

We were behind a modular building, one of the newest and largest that Dazzo's unholy mission had set up. There was no door, but we scrambled up onto the low roof, pulling Bequin with us, and entered through a skylight.

The room we dropped into was carpeted and well furnished, an office or private study for one of the senior supervisors. There were racks of data-slates, and piles of charts and storage tiles. Several large travel trunks had been piled in one corner, with a cloak and two overcoats draped over them. One of the new arrivals from the launch had left these things here and not yet unpacked them.

'Come on!' hissed Fischig, checking the door that led out of the office into the rest of the building.

'Wait!' I said. I cut the locks off the trunks with my power-sword and threw the lids back. In the first, clothes, slates, a boxed lasgun, ornate and inlaid with the name Oberon. Other miscellaneous effects.

'Come on!' Fischig repeated, frantic.

'Aegis, main yard in two,' crackled the vox.

'Eisenhorn? What are you playing at?' Fischig demanded.

'These are Glaw's things!' I said, searching

'So what? What are you looking for?'

'I don't know.' I turned to the second trunk. More clothes, some crude and unpleasant religious icons.

Fischig grabbed me by the shoulder. 'With respect, inquisitor, that would suggest this isn't the time to be doing it!'

'We have to get out of here, we have to get the hell out of here,' Bequin murmured, her eyes darting back and forth at every sound from outside.

'There'll be something... an edge, a clue... something we can use when we get out of here...'

'We'll be lucky to escape with our lives!'

'Yes!' I stared up at him. 'Yes, we will – and if we do, we'll want to continue our struggle against Glaw, won't we?'

He threw his hands up in despair.

'Please... please...' Bequin murmured.

'Aegis, main yard in one,' crackled the vox.

The third trunk. A wrapped set of stainless steel surgical tools whose purpose I didn't even want to imagine. A small dice and counter game in a hardwood box. Clothes, more damn clothes!

With something solid wrapped in them.

I took it out.

'Satisfied?' asked Fischig.

I would have smiled if Locke had left me able.

'Go!' I said.

Beyond the stateroom was an outer annexe. More luggage trunks stood on the grilled floor, as well as wooden boxes draped in plastic.

'Don't even think about it!' Fischig snapped, seeing me look at the trunks.

'Aegis, on site!' The vox-burst was partly drowned out by the vibrating roar of a powerful aircraft passing low and fast overhead. There was a chatter of small arms, the whip of las-rifles.

I led the way out of the annexe, through a hatchway that opened onto the landing yard. Figures milled around, mainly slave-guards and naval troopers, looking skywards and firing at the looming gun-cutter that banked overhead. On the far side of the yard, by the lowered ramp of the Navy launch, Malahite saw us and shouted out. The men swung around, firing. Shots crackled around us.

Then I saw Mandragore, over to the right of the yard, charging towards us with a baleful howl.

'Back inside! Inside!' I yelled and the three of us tumbled back in through the door.

The outer wall of the building didn't stop the Chaos-beast. Neither did the hatch. Ceramite and steel shod fists tore the lightweight metal apart, twisted adamite support beams, punctured plastic panels like paper. Mandragore's baying wail preceded him, shaking us to the core.

Bequin screamed.

The vilely misnamed Child of the Emperor exploded through the end wall of the annexe, white lips drawn back around pearl teeth as he hurled out noise from his augmented torso. The boltgun in his fist was enormous.

'Not a step closer!' I yelled. With one hand, I held the primed grenade up so he could see it.

He laughed, a deep, booming chuckle of contempt.

'I mean it,' I added and kicked the crate at my feet. It was laden with plastic wrapped tablets from the mine.

'One second fuse. Another step and all this will be gone.'

He faltered. Lord Glaw and several guards appeared through the shredded wall behind him.

'For pity's sake, do as he says!' Glaw barked.

With a growl, Mandragore lowered his boltgun.

'Back off, Glaw! Back right off and take them with you!'

'You can't hope to escape, inquisitor,' said Glaw.

'Back off!'

Glaw waved his men back and retreated. Mandragore backed out slowly, a growling hiss rising from his throat.

'Grab the crate!' I told Fischig. He slung his stubber over his shoulder and did as he was told.

We edged out into the smoky daylight. Fischig and I were

side by side, and I held the grenade over the crate he was carrying. Bequin cowered behind us.

In the yard, Glaw was ordering his men back. There were forty or more troops: guards, naval troopers, supervisors. I saw Dazzo, Malahite and the rogue captain Estrum among them. Mandragore did not back off as far as the others. He stayed to the right of us, his shimmering cloak drifting in the breeze, his armour gleaming. The growl continued to purr in his throat.

'Midas,' I said into my link, 'set down, hatch open.'

'Understood,' he replied. 'Be advised there are three Navy interceptors inbound. Arrival in three.'

The gun-cutter swung in over the yard, casting a wide shadow, its thrusters lifting clouds of ash. As it came in to rest on its bulky hydraulic landing skids, the cargo ramp under the cockpit whined and lowered.

Slowly, we moved around until the cutter and the ramp were behind us. The assembled enemy watched us intently, weapons raised.

'A stand-off, inquisitor,' said Glaw.

'Get your men to lower their weapons. Even the ones I can't see. Don't even consider dropping me. Midas... train the wing cannons on myself and the chastener. If anything happens to us, open fire.'

'Confirm.'

The powerful cannons in the wing mounts traversed to target us.

'Shoot us and the crate is vaporised.'

'Weapons down!' Glaw yelled, and the troops obeyed.

'Now call off those interceptors. Order them right back to their carrier.'

'I–'

'Now!'

Glaw looked round at Estrum, who started to speak into a vox link.

'The interceptors have aborted their run,' Midas told me. 'They're turning back.'

'Very good,' I told Glaw.

'What now?' he asked.

What now indeed? We had the upper hand for a moment: they didn't dare shoot or rush us, and Bequin was blocking Dazzo and any other psyker they had.

'An answer or two,' I suggested.

'Eisenhorn!' Fischig hissed.

'An answer?' laughed Glaw. Some of his men laughed too, and Mandragore rumbled a snigger. I noticed Dazzo and Malahite were both unamused.

'This material is archaeoxenon, from an old saruthi site,' I said, lifting one of the ancient, unsymmetrical tablets from the crate in Fischig's grasp with my free hand. 'It clearly has value to you, because it must have value to the saruthi. You're recovering it for them in return for what?'

'I'm not about to tell you anything,' Glaw said. 'I'm not even going to confirm your suppositions.'

I shrugged. 'It was worth trying.'

'My question remains,' said Glaw. 'What now?'

'We leave,' I told him. 'Unmolested.'

'So leave,' he said, with a mild, dismissive hand gesture. 'Put down the crate and leave.'

'This crate is the only thing that's stopping you from obliterating us. It comes with us, as insurance.'

'No!' Dazzo cried, pushing forward. 'Unacceptable! We would lose it forever!' He looked at Glaw. 'This man is our blood foe. We could never recover the artefacts. Even if we agreed to safe passage, he would not honour a deal and leave them for our recovery.'

'Of course not,' I said. 'Just as you would not honour any deal struck with me. It is a sad but true fact that no commitment or agreement of honour can be made between us. Which is why this crate comes with me. We have no other surety.'

'We're not here to offer you surety, flesh-blister,' Mandragore said sonorously. 'Only death. Or if you're unlucky, pain and death.'

'You should keep him out of the negotiations,' I told Glaw with a sideways nod at Mandragore. 'We are leaving with the crate, because you will destroy us otherwise.'

'No,' said Glaw. He stepped forward, pulling a lasgun from his coat. 'You are tripping on your own smooth logic, inquisitor. If we are to lose those artefacts for ever, I'd rather it was here, with your deaths as consolation. If you try to leave with the crate, we will fire anyway and damn the consequences. Set them down and I will give you ten heartbeats to leave.'

I could tell it was no bluff. They would go only so far to protect their trinkets. And they were not fools. They knew I would never return these items. Ten heartbeats. If we tried to board with the crate, they would fire at once. If we set it down... they would fire, but perhaps more hesitantly for fear of hitting the crate. And the cutter's guns were still a point in our favour.

'Back up to the ramp,' I whispered to Bequin and Fischig. 'Throw the crate down when I say.'

'Are you sure?'

'Do as I say. Midas?'

'Ready drive, ready cannons.'

'Now!'

The crate crashed over in the dust. The cutter's engines shrieked into power. They didn't wait ten heartbeats. The three of us were on the ramp, and the ramp was swinging shut under us, and the cutter was lifting around us. A fusillade of weapons fire hammered off the hull. The cutter's cannons roared.

The cutter swung hard about, and we tumbled as the deck pitched. Fischig cried out and fell on the ramp, spilling half out of the gently closing entryway. I grabbed him and hauled him inside before his dangling legs could be severed by the vicing ramp or shot by the enemy below.

We were away. I could tell by the angle of the deck and the vibration of the ship's frame that Midas was accelerating hard and keeping low, letting the landscape shield us from the ground fire. Alarm lights flashed in the crew-bay, indicating damage.

'Strap yourself in!' I yelled at Aemos, who was attempting to rise to assist us. 'Fischig, get Bequin in a harness! Yourself too!'

The chastener pulled the terrified girl across the deck and into a seat. I clambered forward, along the companionway, and up into the cockpit.

Midas was pulling on the controls, taking us higher. The blotchy landscape of Damask flickered past beneath us. I dropped into the seat beside him.

'How close?'

'The fighters have peeled back, on a direct intercept course. They have altitude in their favour.'

'How close?'

'Six minutes to intercept. Damn!'

'What?'

He pointed to the main tactical screen. Behind the smaller bright cursors, larger shapes were moving against the three-dimensional magnetic map of the planet's magnetosphere. 'Their fleet's moving too. The capital ships. And that's two more fighter wings launched.'

'They don't want us to get away, do they?' he added.

'With what we know?'

'They won't let us out of the system alive, will they?'

'Midas, I think I've told you the answer to that.'

He grinned, white teeth contrasting sharply with his dark skin in the cabin's half-light.

'We're going to have some fun, then,' he decided. His bare hands, sparkling with the inlay of Glavian bio-circuits, darted across the controls, adjusting our course.

'Ideas?' I asked.

'A few possibles. Let me massage the data.'

'What?'

'Trust me, Gregor, if we've even a shred of hope of getting out of the Damask system alive, it'll be through skill and sub-tlety. Shut up and let me compute their speeds and intercept vectors.'

'We took damage from the ground fire,' I persisted. That hopelessness was seeping into me again, the feeling of having no ability to influence the situation.

'Minor, just minor,' he said distractedly. 'The servitors have got it covered.'

He made a course change. From the screen, I saw this brought us around almost side on to the chasing fleet components, drastically reducing their time to intercept and firing range.

'What are you doing?'

'Playing the percentages. Playing safe.'

The bright globe of Damask was dropping away beneath us, and we were driving out into planetary space beyond the highest orbit points at full thrust.

'See?' he said. Another light had appeared on the tactical screen, moving around ahead of us.

'Standard Imperial battlefleet dispersal. There's always a picket ship positioned on the blind side of the subject world. If we'd kept straight on we'd have flown right into its fire-field.'

Lights flashed out in the void beyond the cockpit windows. The picket ship, a medium frigate, was firing anyway, running interference, driving us on.

'It's launched fighters,' Midas reported in a sing-song voice. 'Range in two. Chasers have range in four.'

So matter-of-fact.

I looked at the power levels. Every one of the cutter's powerful thrusters was red-lining.

'Midas...'

'Sit back. There it is.'

'What is?'

The small moon was suddenly filling our front ports as we veered around. It didn't look that small. It looked like we were about to smash into it.

I blurted out a curse.

'Relax, dammit!' he assured me, then added, 'Range in one.'

We dived towards the scarred, pocked lime-green rock that filled our vision at full thrust. Nose guns beginning to flash; six interceptors of the Battlefleet Scarus elite fighter school followed us in.

SIXTEEN

Void duel
Betancore's last stand
Traces

The moon was called Obol, the smallest and innermost of Damask's fourteen satellites. It was a dented, irregular nugget of nickel, zinc and selenium, six hundred kilometres across at its widest dimension. Lacking atmosphere and riddled with cavities and gorges, it shone with a lambent green glow in the light of the star, rugged terrain features and craters thrown into stark relief.

I was forcing my mind to calm, forcing my pulse rate down. The old mind skills Hapshant had trained me in.

I focused on the data-file for Obol that I had punched up on the screen – nickel, zinc, selenium, smallest of fourteen – not because I wanted to know but because the facts would act as psychopomps, little fetishes of detail to occupy my mind and steal it away from the hazard.

I looked up from the glowing text bar. A jagged crater, vast enough to swallow Dorsay city and its lagoon whole yawned up at us.

'Brace yourselves,' Midas told us all.

Just a kilometre above, he executed his move. By then, we were deeply committed to Obol's gravity and diving at full thrust. There was no question of performing a landing, or even a conventional turn.

But Midas had been flying ships since he was young, schooled in the pilot academies of Glavia. By way of his inlaid circuitry, he understood the nuances of flight, power and manoeuvre better than me, and better than most professional pilots in the Imperium. He had also tested the capabilities of the gun-cutter almost to destruction, and knew exactly what it could and couldn't do.

What worried me most was what he hoped it might do.

He cut the drive, fired all the landing thrusters, and pulled the nose around so that the cutter began to corkscrew. The view whirled before my eyes and I was flung around in my harness.

The spin seemed uncontrolled. But it was measured and perfect. With the landing jets driving us up away from the vertical, we fluttered, like a leaf, using the corkscrew motion to rob the vessel of downward momentum. Ninety metres from the dust of the crater floor, we flattened out, burning jets hard, white hot, and then arced around as Midas cut the main drive in again.

The ground leapt away under us, and we hugged across it, climbing in a savage jerk to skip over the crater lip.

From the tactical display, I saw all six fighters had dropped back to six minutes behind us. None wanted to try duplicating that move. They were diving in more conventional, slower arcs.

Midas hugged the moon, slicing us low around bluffs and buttes, down deep dry valleys hidden from the sun, across wide dust plains that had never seen a footprint. At one point, we flew between two massive cliffs of striated rock.

'They're breaking,' Midas said, leaning us to port.

They were. Four dropped into dogged pursuit, chasing us low over the landscape. The other two had broken and were heading anti-clockwise around the blindside of Obol.

'Contact?'

'We'll meet them head on in eight minutes,' said Midas. He was smiling.

He pulled a hard starboard turn down a rift valley the topographer screen had only just illuminated.

Then he slowed down to what seemed a painful, easy velocity, and banked the gun cutter around a butte that glistened green and yellow in the hard sunlight.

'What are you doing?'

'Wait... wait...'

The tactical screen showed that our four chasers had swept beyond the rift valley.

'This low to the terrain, it'll take them a moment to figure out we're no longer ahead of them.'

'What now?'

He gunned the engines and threw us out over a dust bowl after the pursuit ships.

'Mouse becomes cat,' he said.

Within seconds, a bright blob on the weapons array had been covered with red crosshairs.

Ahead of us, through a landscape of giant rocks and towering mesas that whipped by at a distressing speed, I saw the flare of afterburners.

'Scratch one,' said Midas, firing the wing cannons.

The engine flare far ahead flashed and then turned into an expanding ball of burning gases which swept past us in jagged streaks.

I was pulled back into my seat as we jinked painfully down another valley. There was another flash, of sunlight off metal, a kilometre ahead.

'And two,' said Midas.

The read-out on the autoloaders notched up red tags as drums expended. The flash blossomed with light, and then again more brightly as it spun and struck the valley wall.

Something blindingly brilliant went off to our right, and the cabin rocked, alarms squealing.

'Smart boy, too close,' said Midas, hauling on the stick to avoid an incoming cliff.

One of the fighters had gauged our feint and come around across us.

'Where's the other? Where's the other?' Midas murmured.

We had firepower on our side, firepower and Midas. The fighters were Lightnings, small, fast and dextrous, less than a quarter our size. For all intents and purposes, the gun-cutter was a transport, but its drive and weapon enhancements and its vertical thrust capability made it a formidable fighting ship when it came to a skirmish close down over terrain like this.

Something hit us hard, and we went over in a dizzying fall. Midas cursed and drew us back round in a tight turn. An Imperial fighter, just a blur of silver, crossed our field of vision.

Midas turned us again, and went after it. It ducked and turned down the deep gorges of the moon, flying by instruments alone in the cold shadows.

The gun-sensors picked up its heat trail. Midas fired on it.

He missed.

It tried to turn in a loop to come round at us. Midas fired again.

Another miss.

It came right at us. I could see the tracer jewels of its shots ripping at us.

Head to head. In a steep, deep gorge.

No room for manoeuvre. No room for error.

'Goodbye,' said Midas, thumbing the fire stud.

An explosion lit the deep gulf and we flew right through the flame wash.

'Had enough yet?' Midas asked me.

I didn't reply. I was too busy gripping my armrests.

'I have,' he said. 'Time for phase two. There's another hunter right around us, and the blindsiders will be coming up in ninety seconds. A little theatrics now. Uclid?'

The chief servitor warbled a response.

We went into a dive, hard. A display told me we were venting a trail of engine gases.

'Damage?' I asked.

'Play acting,' he told me.

The dark canyon floor rushed up to meet us.

'Jettison, Uclid,' Midas ordered.

There was a thump and a bang. The cutter rocked. Behind us, something flared.

'What was that?'

'Two tonnes of spares, trash and expendable supplies. Plus all the grenades from your weapons store.'

He banked us around hard, and we zoomed into a darker cavity, a wide, deep cave in the canyon base. The walls and roof seemed dangerously close.

Six hundred metres into the cave, Midas turned the cutter

to the left, cutting the thrust, floodlights piercing the gloom and reflecting off the jagged cavity.

Another hundred metres, and we settled into the dust on our landing struts. Midas cut power, cut the lights, cut everything except the most rudimentary life support.

'Nobody make a sound,' he said.

The wait, which lasted for sixty-six hours, was neither comfortable nor pleasant. We wore heat gowns and sat in the gloom as, above us, the heretic fleet scoured Obol and its immediate zone for traces of us. Eight times in the first ten hours our passive sensors registered vehicle movement and scanning in the gorge where we had faked our destruction. The deception was apparently convincing.

But we bided our time. There was no telling how persistent they would be, or how patient. Midas thought it likely they might be playing the same trick as us, lying up quiet and waiting until we betrayed ourselves by movement or signal.

After forty hours, Lowink was confident he had overheard astropathic traffic exchanges indicating a fleet departure, shortly followed by a tremor in the fabric of the fathomless immaterium. But still we waited. Waited for the one thing that I would take as convincing.

Just after the turn of the sixty-sixth hour, it came. An astropathic signal in Glossia: 'Nunc dimittis.'

We lofted from the darkness of Obol into the starlight. Everyone on the ship, myself included, I freely admit, was suddenly talking too loud and too much as we moved around, basking in the bright cabin lights and the restored heating systems. The silent, cold wait had been like a penance.

The *Essene*, slow and majestic, moved in to meet us. Once

the heretic fleet had left the system, Maxilla had emerged from hiding in the star's corona and sent his signal.

As soon as we were docked, I went straight to the bridge where Maxilla greeted me like a brother.

'Are we all alive?' he asked.

'In one piece, though it was close.'

'I'm sorry I had to desert you, but you saw the size of that battlegroup.'

I nodded. 'I'm hoping you can tell me where it went.'

'Naturally,' he replied. His astronavigators had not been idle. The chief of them emerged from their annexe at the side of the domed bridge and hummed across the red-black marble of the floor to join us. Like all of his crew, it was essentially mechanical. Its organic, human component – my guess was no more than a brain and some key organs – supported both physically and biologically in a polished silver servitor sculpted in the form of a griffin, its draconian neck swept back so its beaked visage stared down at us. It floated on anti-grav plates built into its eagle wings.

It paused before us, and projected a holographic chart from its open beak. The star map was complex, and incomprehensible to the unschooled eye, but I made out some detail.

'The Navigators have analysed the warp-wake of the departing fleet and made a number of algorithmic computations. The heretics are moving out of the Helican sub-sector, out of Imperial space itself, into the forbidden stellar territories of a breed I believe are known as the saruthi.'

'I had guessed as much. But that in itself is a considerable area, more than a dozen systems. We need specifics.'

'Here,' said Maxilla, indicating a point on the shimmering three dimensional chart with one gloved hand. 'The charts have it as KCX-1288. Under optimal conditions, it's thirty weeks away from here.'

'And what is the margin for error on this calculation?'

'No greater than point zero six. The warp-wake of the fleet was quite considerable. They may of course break the journey and re-route, but we will be watching for changes in their wake.'

'Of course,' he added, 'They will presume us to be following. Even if they think you're dead, they'll know you had to have had a starship that brought you here. One they couldn't find.'

The thought had crossed my mind too. Glaw and his conspirators must at least now be expecting pursuit, or expecting someone to inform on their whereabouts and destination. They would now be trusting on vigilance, their considerable massed firepower, and their headstart.

I already had Lowink busy preparing an emergency communiqué to send back to Gudrun and Inquisition command.

'What do you know of the saruthi and their territory?'

'Nothing,' he said. 'I've never travelled there.'

I thought this a curiously brief answer for a man so usually talkative.

'So,' he said at length, 'apart from our knowledge of where they're going, have we any other advantages?'

'We have.' I took from my coat pocket the item that had rested there ever since I had liberated it from Glaw's travelling trunk in North Qualm. Maxilla regarded it with frank perplexity.

'This,' I told him, 'is the Pontius.'

We used a large, empty hold in the depths of the *Essene*. Some of Maxilla's servitors arranged lighting and powerfeeds. My own servitors – Modo and Nilquit – carried the claw-footed casket in and set in on the cold steel floor.

I stood watching, my hands buried deep in my overcoat pockets against the cold of the chamber. Aemos hunched over the casket and, with Nilquit's aid, began to connect cables. I looked over at Bequin. She stood next to Fischig, and was bundled up in a heavy red gown with a grey shawl, and there was an expression of grim reluctance on her face. She'd found it all fun at first, a game, even in the face of danger at House Glaw. But Damask had changed things for her. The monster Mandragore. She knew it wasn't a game anymore. She'd seen things that many – perhaps even most – citizens of the Imperium never see. Most lives are spent on safe worlds far from the touch of war and horror, and the obscenities that lurk out there in the darkest parts of the void are myths or rumours... if that.

But now she knew. Perhaps it had changed her mind. Perhaps she didn't want to be here any more. Perhaps she was now regretting jumping so eagerly for the offer I'd made her.

I didn't ask her. She'd tell me if she had to. We were all too committed now.

'Eisenhorn?' Aemos reached out his hands and I placed the cool hard ball of the Pontius in them. With almost priestly care, he fitted it into place.

I ordered everyone back out of the hold, even the servitors, everyone except Bequin and Aemos. Fischig closed the hold door behind him.

Aemos looked at me and I nodded assent. He made the final connection and then backed away from the casket as hurriedly as his old and augmetised limbs could manage.

At first, nothing. Small tell-tale lights winked along the edge of the casket – Eyclone's casket – and the internal wiring glowed.

Then I felt a change in air-pressure. Bequin looked at me sharply, feeling it too.

The metal walls of the hold began to sweat. Beads of moisture popped and dribbled down the wall plating.

There was a faint crackling sound, like the gentle crisping of paper in flames. It spread, growing louder. Frost was forming on the casket, on the floor around it, spreading out across the hold's decking, up the walls, across the ceiling. A glittering thickness of diamond frost coated the interior of the hold in less than ten seconds. Our breath steamed in the air and we brushed jewels of ice-dust off our clothes and eyelashes.

'Pontius Glaw,' I said.

There was no answer, but after a moment or two, a series of animal grunts and barks mewled from the vox-speakers built into the casket.

'Glaw,' I repeated.

'What–' said an artificial voice.

Bequin stiffened.

'What have you woken me to?'

'What is the last thing you remember, Glaw?'

'Promises... promises...' the voice said, coming and going as if drifting away from the microphone and then back. 'Where is Urisel?'

'What promises were made to you, Glaw?'

'Life...' it murmured. 'Where is Urisel?' There was a tone now, an anger or an impatience. 'Where is he?'

I began to frame another question, but there was a sudden flash of activity, a crackle of electronic synapses firing across the crystal surface of the ball. It had lashed out with its mind, with its potent psychic powers. If Bequin had not been here, cancelling it out, no doubt Aemos and I would have been dead.

'Temper, temper...' I said. I took a step towards the casket. 'I am Eisenhorn, Imperial inquisitor. You are my prisoner and you only enjoy cognitive function because I allow it. You will answer my questions.'

'I... will... not.'

I shrugged. 'Aemos, disconnect this menace and prepare it for disintegration!'

'Wait! Wait!' the voice was pleading despite its colourless artificiality.

I knelt down in front of the casket. 'I know that your life and intellect were preserved in this device, Pontius Glaw. I know you have waited for two centuries, trapped in a bodiless state, desperate to be made whole again. That is what your family promised you, wasn't it?'

'Urisel promised... he said it be so... the methods were prepared...'

'To sacrifice the nobility of Hubris so that their life energies might be siphoned off into you through this casket. To give you the power to create a body for yourself.'

'He promised!' The stress fell on the second word, anguished and deep.

'Urisel and the others abandoned you, Pontius. They abandoned the Hubris project at the last minute in favour of something else. They are now all in the custody of the Inquisition.'

'Nooooo...' The word turned into a hiss that died away. 'They would not...'

'I'm sure they wouldn't... unless it was something so vital, so unmissable that they had no choice. You'd know what that would be, wouldn't you?'

Silence.

'What would be more important to them than you, Pontius Glaw?'

Silence.

'Pontius?'

'They are not caught.'

'What? Who are not?'

'My brethren. My kin... If you had them, you would not be asking these questions. They are free and you are desperate.'

'Not at all. You know how it is... so many lies, so many conflicting stories. Your pitiful family trying to sell each other out in exchange for freedom. I came to you for the truth.'

'No. Credible but no.'

'You know what it is, Pontius.'

'No.'

'You know what it is. They woke you from time to time to keep you informed, woke you from the oblivion that surrounds you in that globe. Beneath House Glaw, for example, in that chapel they built to contain you. I saw you there. You subdued me with your power.'

'I would do so again,' it said, traces of fire once more flickering along the golden filaments and woven circuits that encased the jagged, quartz-like lump.

'You know what it is. They told you.'

'No.'

I reached down and grasped a sheaf of wires. 'You're lying,' I said and yanked the wires out.

A brief moan rolled from the vox-speakers and faded. The lights on the casket went out. Air temperature and pressure began to climb again. The frost began to dissolve.

'Not much then,' said Bequin.

'We're just beginning,' I replied. 'We've got thirty weeks.'

SEVENTEEN

Discourses
Speculation on an unsymmetrical theme
Betrayal

I went to the hold each day with Bequin and Aemos and we repeated the procedure. For the next few days, he refused even to answer. After about a week, he began to goad us and abuse us with threats and obscenities. Every few days, he tried to lash out psychically, thwarted each time by Bequin's untouchable presence.

All the while, the *Essene* plunged through the immaterium towards the distant stargroup.

In the fourth week, I changed tactics, and entered into discussion with him on any subject that occurred to me. I didn't ask a single question concerning the 'true matter'. He refused to engage for the first few days, but I remained cordial and greeted him patiently each session. At last, discourses began: on astral navigation, high ecclesiarch music, architecture, stellar demographics, antique weapons, fine wines...

He could not help himself. The isolation of his condition made him crave such contacts with a real, vibrant world. He longed to taste and read and see and live again. Within two weeks he needed no encouragement to talk. I was no friend, and he was still wary, and keen to insult on any occasion, but he clearly welcomed our conversations. When, deliberately, I missed a day, he complained sullenly, as if wounded or let down.

For my part, I had the chance to realise how dangerous Glaw was. His mind was brilliant: charming, witty, incisive, and formidably knowledgeable. It was a pleasure to talk to him and learn from him. It was a salutary reminder of the quality of mind that Chaos can steal. The greatest of us, the brightest, the most urbane and learned, can fall prey.

One day in the tenth week, I entered the chamber with Bequin and Aemos as usual and we woke him. But an uncommon sensation troubled me.

'What is this?' I said. It seemed to me the casket was not quite in the same place as usual. 'Have you been in here, Aemos?' I asked. 'Even to make standard checks?'

'No,' he assured me. The hold was locked as a matter of course after each session.

'My imagination then,' I decided.

Our discourses continued, pleasantly, each morning for an hour or so. We often discussed Imperial policies and ethics, subjects on which he was astonishingly well-read. He never strayed, never allowed himself to profess a belief or concept that might be deemed counter to the strictures of the Imperium, as if he recognised that such an admission would perforce end our entente. On occasions, I gave him openings to do so, conversational gambits that would allow him space and opportunity to criticise or denounce the way of the God-Emperor and the rule of Terra. He resisted, though at times I felt he was desperate to voice his own, contrary beliefs. But his need for activity and contact was paramount. He would not risk losing our interaction.

He could quote, extensively, chapter and verse from Imperial texts, philosophies, poetry, ecclesiarchal lore. His scholarship rivalled Aemos's. But just as he refrained from condemning himself with heretical utterances, he also refrained from actually professing loyalty to the Golden Throne. He conducted our conversations in a subjective, uninvolved way. He did not attempt to dissemble and play the part of the loyal citizen. I appreciated that this represented his respect for me. He did not insult my intelligence by lying.

More often still than politics and ethics, we talked of history. Again, in this area, his learning was tremendous, but there was also, for the first time, an eagerness, a hunger. He never asked directly, but it was clear he longed to know in detail about the events that had taken place in the two hundred and twelve years since his death. His family had clearly told him little. He made leading remarks to draw answers out of me. I gave him some, and sometimes volunteered accounts of major events, political changes and Imperial gains. I had decided beforehand not to make any mention of Imperial defeats or losses, to avoid giving him anything he might relish. The picture that Pontius Glaw got from me was of an Imperium stronger and more healthy than ever before.

Even so, it delighted him. Precious glimpses of a galaxy he had long been divorced from.

The rest of that long transit time was spent in preparation and study, daily regimes of weapons practice and combat training.

Fischig ran hand-to-hand sessions each afternoon, and set himself to honing Bequin's natural dexterity and speed. I pressed weights in a makeshift gymnasium, and ran tens of kilometres each day around the empty halls and corridors of the *Essene*. Slowly, I brought myself back to peak fitness.

I worked my mind too. A disciplined regime of psychic exercises, some conducted with Lowink's help.

Aemos and I studied extensively. We worked through all the archive data we had to hand, researching the saruthi. It added little to our knowledge. The extent of their territories was known, but virtually nothing beyond that. There had only been a handful of officially recorded contacts in the past two thousand years. I wondered how much was known about them by the rogue traders who sailed beyond the Imperial veil, men like Gorgone Locke.

All we knew with any certainty was that the saruthi were an old xenos culture – insular, secretive, lying outside the bounds of the Imperium. They were technically resourceful, mature and well-established. We knew nothing of their culture-type, beliefs, language... not even their physical appearance.

'We can at least conjecture they have some religious beliefs or values,' Aemos told me. 'Or, at the very least, they hold certain relics of their past in high regard for some symbolic or sacred purpose. Our foes only excavated that material on Damask because they knew it had value to the saruthi.'

'Holy items? Icons?'

He shrugged. 'Or ancestor spirits – or simply a desire to recover and repatriate cultural materials from their past.'

'And we know their territory was once bigger. Extending as far as Damask, even if that was but a distant outpost,' said Lowink.

We sat around an inlaid table in one of Maxilla's staterooms, the polished table top smothered in open books, scrolls, data-slates and record tiles.

'And Bonaventure,' I said. 'The wheel-graves. Bequin remarked that the site at North Qualm reminded her of those on her birthworld.'

'Perhaps,' said Aemos. 'But I am no archaexenon expert. The wheel-graves of Bonaventure are classified as "of unknown xenos manufacture" in all the texts I can find. They are but one among hundreds of unidentified relic sites in the Helican sub-sector. All traces of a long-vanished, or at least long-shrunk, saruthi civilisation... or the remnants of many miscellaneous forerunner species that roamed this part of space before man ever came this way.'

I set down a data-slate and picked up the item that lay in the centre of the table, wrapped in felt. It was the single ancient tablet that had escaped Damask with us. I had taken it from the crate during the stand-off, and it had still been in my hand when we had thrown ourselves aboard the gun-cutter. Like the stonework dug-out in the flame hill mine, it was made of a hard pale material glittering with flecks of mica that we all agreed was not indigenous to Damask. And it was octagonal, but not regularly so, being peculiarly long on two edges. The back of it was burned and scored where it had been cut away. The reverse showed a bas-relief symbol, a five-pointed star sigil. But it, too, was irregular: the radiating spars of the star were of unmatched length and they protruded at a variety of angles.

'Most perturbatory,' said Aemos, looking at it for the umpteenth time. 'Symmetry – at least, basic symmetry – is a virtual constant in the galaxy. All species – even the most obscene xenos kinds like the tyranid – have some order of it.'

'There's something wrong with the angles,' agreed Lowink,

furrowing his unhealthy, socket-pocked brow. I knew what he meant. It was as if the angles in the star symbol made up more than three hundred and sixty degrees, though that of course was unthinkable.

'Who has been in here?' I asked at the start of my next session with Pontius. I glanced around the frost-caked chamber. Bequin shrugged, blowing on her hands. Aemos also looked puzzled.

'The casket has been moved again. Just slightly. Who has been in here?'

'No one,' Pontius remarked, his artificial voice colourless.

'I was not directing the question at you, Pontius. For I doubt you would tell me the truth.'

'You wound me, Gregor,' he answered softly.

'Are you sure it's not your imagination?' Aemos asked. 'You said before–'

'Perhaps.' I frowned. 'I just feel something is... changed.'

I dined with Maxilla most evenings during the long voyage, sometimes in company with the others, sometimes alone. One evening in the twenty-fifth week, only Maxilla and I sat at the stateroom table, as the gilt servitors brought in our meal.

'Tobius,' I said at length, 'tell me about the saruthi.'

He paused, and set his food-laden fork back down on his salver.

'What would you have me tell you?'

'Why you claimed to know nothing of them when I told you we were heading into their territory.'

'Because such places are forbidden. Because you are an inquisitor, and it does not do to admit transgressions to one such as you.'

I toyed with the lip of my half-empty glass. 'You have aided me eagerly and generously up to now, Tobius. I suspected your motives at first, a detail for which I have apologised. I see now you are as keen to serve the Emperor of Mankind as I. It troubles me that you would withhold information now.'

He bared his pearl-inlaid teeth and dabbed at his lips with the corner of his napkin. 'It does more than trouble me, Gregor. It has plagued me, a crisis of conscience.'

'It is time to speak then.' I refilled both of our glasses with vintage from the decanter. 'Imperial knowledge of the saruthi is scant, and as you say, forbidden. I am more than aware that rogue traders know a great deal more about the outside systems and their species than we do. You are no rogue, but you are of the merchant elite. I think it unlikely that you have never come across any information pertaining to this xenos breed.'

He sighed. 'As a young man, over ninety years ago, I travelled into saruthi space. I was a junior crewman aboard a rogue trader called the *Promethean*. The master was Vaden Awl, long dead I imagine. Now there was a true rogue. He was sure he could strike a trading deal with these unknowns, or at least rob them blind of treasures.'

'And did he?'

'No. Remember, I was junior crew. I never left the bowels of the ship, or went to the surface of any worlds. All I knew was the miserable duration of the voyage. The senior crewmembers were tight-lipped. It took them, as I understand it, a long time to find the saruthi at all, and then they were less than forthcoming. The third officer, a man I knew reasonably well, confided to me that the saruthi played tricks on Awl's trade envoys, hid from them, tormented them.

'Tormented how?'

'Their worlds were eerie, disarming, uncomfortable – something about the angles, the officer said.'

'The angles?'

He laughed sourly and shrugged. 'As if something ill and twisted had infected their dimensions. We came back empty-handed after a year. Many of the crew quit and left the *Promethean* on our return, especially when Awl, who was a sick and driven man by then, declared he was going back to try again. I quit then too, but only because I couldn't face another year below decks.'

'And Awl?'

'He went back. I presume so, anyway. A few years later I heard his ship had been taken in the Borealis Reach by eldar renegades. That's the sum of it. You can perhaps see why I was unwilling to tell you these things before... because there is nothing useful to tell. Except to incriminate myself by admitting I had gone beyond.'

I nodded. 'In future, do not hold information back from me.'

'I will not.'

'And if you "remember" anything else...'

'I will tell you at once.'

'Tobius,' I paused. 'You say the voyage of the *Promethean* was long and fruitless, and the crewmembers were tormented by the beings they eventually encountered. Do you not have misgivings about returning there?'

'Of course.' He smiled a thin smile. 'But I am bound to serve you as an agent of the Emperor, and I will do so without question. Besides, part of me is curious.'

'Curious?'

'I want to see these saruthi with my own eyes.'

I should mention the dreams.

They did not over-trouble me during the voyage, but still

they lingered, every few days or so. I seldom dreamed specifically of the blank-eyed, handsome man, but he lurked obliquely in other dreams, a bystander, looking on, observing, never speaking.

The lightning flashes escorted him, closer in each dream.

At ship-dawn of the third day of the twenty-ninth week, I rose silently and left my quarters, heading down towards the hold area where Pontius was secured. It was a good four hours until our daily conversation was due to start.

I climbed into a service duct adjoining the hold space, and crawled down until I reached a circulation grille that looking down into the hold itself.

There was frost on the grille.

Below, a figure crouched by the casket, huddled in robes, lit only by a hand-lamp. The overhead lights were not on.

Pontius was awake. The frost told me that much, and I could see the tiny flashes of firing synapses and hear the low hiss of his voice.

'Tell me of the Border Wars, the ones you mentioned last time. Imperial losses were great, you said?'

'I tell you much and you tell me little back,' replied the figure. 'That was not our agreement. I said I would secretly help you if you helped me. Power, Pontius, information. If you want me to act as your emissary, I need a show of trust. How can I communicate your will to your allies, if I know nothing of the "true matter"?'

A pause.

'What is this about?' the figure asked. 'What is at stake, what thing of great value?'

Another pause.

'You should go before they discover you. Eisenhorn is becoming suspicious.'

'Tell me, Pontius. We're nearly there, just a few days to go. Tell me so I can help you.'

'I... will tell you. The Necroteuch. That is what we are after, Alizebeth.'

EIGHTEEN

KCX-1288 by the light of the quill-star
Into the Wound
The wrongness

On the first day of the thirty-first week, just under a day out-side Maxilla's estimate, the *Essene* burst back into realspace deep inside the system designated KCX-1288. Almost at once we were in danger.

The local star was a vast, swollen fireball pulsing and retch-ing out its last few millions years of life. Distended and no longer spherical, it glowed with a malevolent pink fire beneath a cooling crust of black shreds and tatters that looked like rot infecting its granular skin. Firestorms swirled and blistered across its enlarged surface and vomited gouts of stellar mat-ter out into the system. An immense column of excreting gas and matter plumed away from the behemoth star, almost a light year long. It looked like a huge, luminous quill stabbed into the soft ball of that sun.

From the moment of our arrival at the translation point, sirens and alarms began shrilling on the bridge. External radiation levels were almost immeasurable, and we shuddered and rocked through waves of searing star debris. The entire system was lousy with drifting radioactive banks, ash clouds, flares and the splinters of matter they projected, and magnetic anomalies. Our shields were full on and already we were taking damage.

Maxilla said nothing, but furrowed his brow in concentration as he steered the juddering ship in through the treacherous course, negotiating the gravity pools and radioactive undertows.

'It's falling apart,' said Aemos, awed, gazing at the main projection screen and the furiously scrolling bars of data that flickered across it. 'The whole damn system is in a state of collapse.'

'Any sign of them?' I called to Maxilla.

'We must be right on their tail. They were half a day ahead of us, no more. Damn this interference. Wait–'

'What?'

He said something I couldn't hear over the cacophony.

'Say again!'

Maxilla cancelled the screaming sirens. The juddering and shaking continued, and now we could hear the groaning and creaking of the *Essene*'s hull under stress. He pointed to the pict-plate that overviewed the *Essene*'s sensor operations.

'I'm picking up their drive-wake and gravitational displacement, but in these conditions it's getting really hard to read them with accuracy. There–' He tapped a gloved finger on the plate. 'That's undoubtedly a drive-wake, but how do you explain it?'

I shook my head. I'm no mariner.

'They've split,' said Midas, looking over our shoulders. 'The main portion has fallen back, maybe out of the system itself to a safe distance, and a smaller, core group has continued on in. Maybe five ships, six at most.'

'That's how I read it too,' Maxilla agreed. 'A fleet division. I'd guess they didn't want to risk sending their biggest ships into this maelstrom.'

'I can see why,' murmured Bequin, gazing at the seething turmoil on the main display.

'Forget about the ones that have withdrawn. Follow the lead group in,' I said.

'I would advise-' Maxilla began.

'Do it!'

With the aid of his navigational servitors, he adjusted the *Essene*'s trajectory and set on after the drive-wake of the smaller group, driving in system.

'There! There, look!' Maxilla called out suddenly, adjusting a secondary display unit to magnify and enhance an image. It was distant, but we could see the burst-open hulk of an Imperial cruiser drifting in a halo of slowly dissipating energy.

'Definitely one of Estrum's ships. Holed by meteor storms. They ran into trouble the moment they pressed on.'

The *Essene* shook again.

'What about us?' I asked.

Maxilla conferred with Betancore. There was a particularly violent shudder and the main lights went out for a second.

'We need shelter,' Maxilla told me frankly.

As far as the *Essene*'s bewildered and over-taxed sensors could establish, there were fifteen planets in the system, as well as millions of planetoid fragments, mostly ragged embers of wasted rock and venting energy. Our quarry's drive wake led directly to the third largest, one of the inner worlds. It was a scabby, ruined, semi-shattered ball with lingering swathes of swirling bluish atmosphere. Craters covered its northern hemisphere; some impacts had been so large that they had torn open the mantle and exposed the livid red core beneath, like a skull cracked with devastating wounds. Even as we watched, we saw scatters of light dot and blossom across the surface as meteors struck and incinerated continents far below.

We tore in through the convulsing fabric of space, past moons of blood and striated mackerel clouds of dust. A vast sheet of stellar fire swept out at us, throwing the ship wildly off course and hurling silver lumps of rock and ice against our shields.

'Madness!' cried Fischig. 'They wouldn't have come here! It's death!'

Maxilla looked at me, as if hoping I'd agree with the chastener and call us off for the sake of the *Essene*. 'You are sure of their traces?'

Maxilla, his hands flexing on the controls, swallowed and nodded.

'Get us down there, into whatever shelter the planet's bulk can give us. At least let's confirm their corpses before we leave.'

Descent took twenty minutes, none of them smooth and none of them guaranteeing a sequel. I wanted to use the time to get Lowink or Maxilla's astropaths to check on the approach of the task force from Gudrun that had set out, on my instructions thirty weeks ago, to rendezvous with us here.

But it was impossible. The stellar distortion rendered astrotelepathy blind.

I cursed.

We went in steeply, down towards the dark side of the wounded planet. Blooms of fire consumed crater-pocked landmasses in the darkness below and ammoniacal storms raged in oceanic measures. Even here, with the planet between us and the convulsing sun, the ride was hard and rough. We saw, for a second as we passed, another ship ruin, another of Estrum's fleet splintered and destroyed. A death world; a death system.

'Our enemies must have made a mistake,' said Aemos, holding on to the edge of a console to steady himself. 'The saruthi can't be here. If they ever inhabited this system, they must have long since abandoned it.'

'Yet,' I countered, 'the heretic fleet's advance group presses on with great determination and purpose.'

The *Essene* continued to descend, closer than it would normally come to a planetary body. Only ribbons of atmosphere remained, and Maxilla clung to the ragged surface, passing barely ten kilometres above the bare rock. Drizzles of shooting stars rained past us.

'What's that?' I asked.

Maxilla adjusted his sensors and the resolution of the display. A huge wound in the planet's crust yawned before us, a thousand kilometres wide; a cliff-like lip of impact-raised rock with a vast cavity beneath.

'The sensors can't resolve it. Is that meteor damage?'

'Perhaps, from an angled strike,' said Aemos.

'Did they go past or in?' I asked.

'In?' barked Maxilla, incredulously.

'In! Did they go in?'

Aemos was leaning over the servitor at the sensor station. 'The drive wake ebbs and disappears here. Either they were vaporised en masse at this point or they indeed went inside.'

I looked at Maxilla. The *Essene* bucked again, thrown by a gravity pool, and the bridge lights went out briefly for a second time.

'This is a star-going ship,' he said softly, 'not built for sur-face landing.'

'I know that,' I replied. 'But neither were theirs. They have more information than we do... and they have gone inside.'

Shaking his head, Maxilla turned the *Essene* down towards the vast wound.

The rift cavity was dark, and limitless according to the sensors, though in my opinion, the sensors were no better than useless now. A dull red glow suffused the darkness far below us. The violent shaking had stopped, but still the hull creaked and protested at the gravitational stress.

We had the sudden impression of moving through some structure, then another, then a third. The display revealed the fourth before we passed under it: an angular hoop or arch eighty kilometres across. Beyond it, more in the series, towering around us as we progressed, as if we were passing down the middle of a giant rib-cage.

'They're octagonal,' said Aemos.

'And irregular,' I added.

No two of the rib-arches were the same, but they displayed the same form and lack of symmetry as their companions – the shape we now instantly associated with the saruthi.

'These can't be natural,' said Maxilla.

We continued in under the cyclopean spans, passing through a dozen, then a dozen more.

'Light sources ahead,' a servitor announced.

A dull, greenish glow fogged into being far away down the avenue of octagonal arches.

'Do we continue?' asked Maxilla.

I nodded. 'Send a marker drone back to the surface.'

A moment later, the rear display showed a small servitor

drone struggling back up the vast channel towards the surface, running lights winking.

We ran on past the last arch. There was another judder.

Then we were riding clear into light, smooth, pale, green light.

There seemed to be no roof or ceiling to whatever we were in, though inside the planetary cavity we undoubtedly were. Just hazy green light, and below, a carpet of wispy cloud.

All turbulence stopped. We were like a ship becalmed.

The atmosphere in this place – logic battled to make us remember we were inside the crust of a planet – was thin and inert, a vaguely ammoniacal vapour. None of us could explain the source of the pervasive luminescence or the fact that the *Essene* sat comfortably at grav anchor in the serene quiet. As Maxilla had pointed out, it was not a trans-atmospheric vessel and it should have been impossible to stabilise it this close to a planetary body without severe stress damage.

From its system registers, the *Essene* seemed happy enough, happy to have ridden out the vile stellar storms of KCX-1288 into this safe harbour.

Apart from minor impact damage, only two of the ship's systems were inoperative. The sensors were blind and giving back nothing but odd, dead echoes. And every chronometer on the ship had stopped, except two that were running backwards.

Betancore and Maxilla studied the imperfect returns of the sensor arrays and concluded land of some sort lay beneath us, under the cloudbank. We estimated that it was six kilometres straight down, though in this vague, hazy rift it was difficult to say.

If Glaw's heretics were here, they had left no trace. But with our sensors so badly occluded, their advance fleet could be anchored just on the other side of the clouds.

We dropped to the cloudbank from the *Essene* in the gun-cutter shortly afterwards. All of us had buckled on hard-armour vacuum suits from Maxilla's lockers. Lowink, Fischig, Aemos and I shambled about the crew bay, getting used to the heavy plate and bulky quilting of the suits.

Bequin was in the cockpit with Betancore, watching him take us down. The pair of them wore borrowed vacuum suits too, and she was pinning up her hair so it would not interfere with the helmet seal.

'Good hunting, inquisitor,' crackled Maxilla from the *Essene* above us.

'He'll be down there, won't he?' asked Bequin, and I knew she was referring to Mandragore.

'It's likely. Him... and whatever this is all about.'

'Well, you heard what Pontius said,' she replied.

How could I not have? The Necroteuch. One doesn't hear a word like that and forget it. It had taken her weeks to gain the confidence of our bodiless prisoner, to play the part of a disaffected traitor. I hadn't been sure she was up to it, but she had performed with patience and a finely gauged measure of play-acting. It had been a risk, letting her slip in to see Pontius alone. She had assured me she could do it and she had not been wrong.

The Necroteuch. If Pontius Glaw was telling the truth, our enterprise had even greater urgency now. I had wondered what could be so precious, so important as to galvanise our enemies so, make them risk so much. I had my answer. Legend said the last extant copy of that abominable work had been destroyed millennia before. Except that by some means, in antique ages past, a copy had come into the hands of the saruthi race. And now they were preparing to trade it back to Glaw's Imperial heretics.

We came down through the clouds and saw the land below, a wide, rolling expanse of dust sweeping down to what seemed to be a sea. Liquid frothed and broke along a curved shoreline a hundred kilometres long. Everything was a shade of pale green, bathed by the radiance that glowed through the wispy clouds. There was a misty softness to it all, a lack of sharp focus. It seemed endless, toneless, slow. There was a calm, ethereal feel that was at once soothing and unnerving. Even the lapping sea seemed languid. It reminded me of the seacoast at Tralito, on Caelun Two, where I had spent a summer recuperating from injuries years before. Endless leagues of mica dunes, the slow sea, the balmy, hazy air.

'How big?' I asked Midas.

'Is what?' he asked.

'This... place.'

He pointed to the instruments. 'Can't say. A hundred kilometres, two... three... a thousand.'

'You must have something!'

He looked round at me with a smile that had worry in it. 'Systems say it's endless. Which is, of course, impossible. So I think the instruments are out. I'm not trusting them, anyway.'

'Then what are you flying by?'

'My eye – or the seat of my pants. Whichever you find most reassuring.'

We followed the slow curve of the endless bay for about ten minutes. At last, details emerged to break up the uniform anonymity.

A row of arches, octagonal, jutting from the sand a few

hundred metres back from the waterline, ran parallel to the water. They were each about fifty metres broad, in everything but scale the twins of the arches Maxilla had guided the *Essene* through. They extended away as far as we could see in the green haze.

'Set us down.'

We sat the gun-cutter on the soft dusty-sand half a kilometre from the shore, clamped on our helmets and ventured out.

The radiance was greater than I had expected – the cutter's ports had been tinted – and we slid down brown-glass over-visors against the glare.

I hate vacuum suits. The sense of being muffled and constrained, the ponderous movement, the sound of my own breath in my ears, the sporadic click of the intercom. The suit shut out all sounds from outside, except the crunch of my feet on the fine, dry sand.

We shuffled down to the water's edge in a wide file. All of us except Aemos carried weapons.

It looked like a sea. Green water, showing white at the breakers.

'Liquid ammonia,' Aemos said, his voice a low crackle over the vox.

There was something strange about it.

'Do you see it?' he asked me.

'What?'

'The waves are moving out from the shore.'

I looked again. It was so obvious, I had missed it. The liquid wasn't rushing in and breaking, it was sucking away from the shore and rolling back into itself.

It was chilling. So simple. So wrong. My confidence withered. I wanted to strip off the claustrophobic suit and cry out.

And I would have, except for the stark red warning lights on the atmosphere reader built into my suit's bulky left cuff.

What was it Maxilla had said? The saruthi had tormented the men of the *Promethean*? I didn't know for a moment if the unnatural behaviour of the sea was their doing – how could it have been? But I understood how insidious, distressing torment might have played upon them.

Fischig and Betancore had approached the first of the arches. I looked across and saw them dwarfed by the unsymmetrical structure. The next in the line was three hundred metres away, and they seemed regularly spaced. Each one, as far as I could see, was irregular in a different way, though the size and proportions were identical.

Bequin was kneeling on the shoreline, brushing the sand aside gently with her gauntlet. She had found what was perhaps the most distressing detail so far.

Under the sand, a few centimetres down, the ground was tiled. Tessellated, irregular octagonal tiles, just like the ones she had found on the floor of the mine working at North Qualm. Once more, they fitted perfectly, impossibly, despite their shape.

The more of them she uncovered, the more she brushed the sand away.

'Stop it,' I said. 'For our sanity, I don't think it's worth trying to discover if they cover the entire beach.'

'Can all of this... be artificial?' she asked.

'It can't be,' said Aemos. 'Perhaps the tiles and the arches are part of some old structure, long abandoned, that has since been flooded and covered with the dust... due to... to...'

He didn't sound at all convincing.

I crossed to Fischig and Betancore and stood with them gazing up at the first arch. It was wrought from that odd, unknown metal we had seen on Damask.

'What do we do know?' Fischig asked.

'Well, I hate to state the obvious,' said Aemos from down the beach, 'but the last row of these we found formed a deliberate pathway that led the *Essene* in here. Should we assume this serves the same purpose?'

I stepped forward, through the broad, towering shape of the first arch. 'Come on,' I said.

We walked for what I estimated was perhaps twenty minutes. Estimated. All of our chronometers were dead. After the first few minutes we began to hear a distant, repetitive boom; a low, almost sub-sonic peal like thunder that rolled out from somewhere far away over the sea. Or seemed to. It came every half minute or so. There were long intervals of silence, and just when we'd thought we'd heard the last, another boom would come. Like the crunch of our own footsteps, we could hear it through the suits, even with our vox circuits switched off.

I voxed to Maxilla. 'Can you hear that?'

There was a crackle, and no immediate reply. Then a sudden burst of transmission. Maxilla's voice: '...as you instruct, Gregor, but it's not going to be easy. Say again... what did you say about Fischig?'

'Maxilla! Repeat!' I began, but his voice continued over the top, incoherent. It wasn't a reply. I was just picking up his voice. I felt my spine go cold.

More static.

'Tell Alizebeth, I agree with that! Ha!'

It went dead.

I looked back at the others. Their pale faces gazed out of the tinted brown faceplates like ghosts.

'What... was that?' I murmured.

'An echo?' Aemos whispered. 'Some kind of transmission anomaly caused by the atmosphere and the–'

'It's not a conversation I've ever had.'

Another boom of thunder rolled across the dry, softly lit shore.

After my estimated twenty minutes, we passed through what was suddenly the last arch. We all stopped. Ahead of us, the land rose more steeply, into hills and low ridges. The terrain there was darker, inhospitable. The overall radiance had dulled, and the sky was a deep green, oozing into blackness over the hills.

'There... there were more in the row!' Fischig exclaimed. 'More arches!'

He was right. The octagonal colonnade had disappeared as we passed through the last arch. I stepped back through, imagining perhaps that from the other side the arches might reappear. They didn't. The booming continued.

We set off towards the hills. Bursts of static hissed through our vox units.

'Transmissions,' said Lowink. He fiddled with his vox-channels. 'I can't tune them in, but they're chatter. Military. Back and forth.'

Our quarry, perhaps.

'Look!' said Betancore, pointing behind us. Beyond the shore and the retreating line of arches, three ominous dark shapes hung under the clouds, out over the sea. Two Imperial frigates and an old, non-standard merchantman, floating at grav-anchor.

'How did we not see them when we passed?'

'I don't know, Midas. I'm not sure of anything anymore.'

When I turned back to the rest of the group, I saw Aemos unclasping his helmet.

'Aemos!'

'Calm yourself,' he said, uncovering his wizened old head. With the wide locking collar of the suit around him, he looked like a tortoise, pushing its gnarled head from its shell. He raised his left arm and showed me the atmosphere reader. The lights were green.

'Human-perfect atmosphere,' he said. 'A little cold and sterile, but human-perfect.'

We all unclasped our helmets and pulled them off. The chilly air bit my face, but it was good to be free of the suits. There was no scent to the air, none at all. Not salt or ammonia or dust.

We helped each other fasten our helmets to our shoulder packs. The booming was duller and more distant now it didn't have our hollow helmets to resonate through. We could hear each other's footsteps, each other's breathing, the suck and lap of the ocean. I could suddenly smell Bequin's perfume. It was reassuring.

I led the group on, and we climbed slowly into the rising land. Now free of the helmet, I understood our ponderous progress was a result of more than our heavy suits. It was somehow difficult to gauge distance and depth. We stumbled every now and then. The whole place was profoundly wrong.

We came upon them very suddenly. The sudden resumption of the vox-traffic was our only warning. Our speakers burst into life simultaneously.

'Run! Move up! Segment two!'

'Where are you? Where are you?'

'Cover to the left! That's an order! Cover to the left!'

'They're behind me! They're behind me and I c–'

A fierce hiss of static.

Ahead, coming down the ridges and slopes of the dark rise, we saw soldiers. Imperial Guard, wearing red and gold combat armour. Gudrunite riflemen.

'Cover!' I ordered, and we dropped down into the shelter of the rising dunes, readying weapons.

There were sixty or more of them, hurrying down the upper slopes towards us in a wide straggle, running. There was no order to it. They were fleeing. An officer in their midst was waving his arms and shouting, but they were ignoring him. Many had lost helmets or rifles.

A second later, their pursuers came over the rise and fell upon them from behind. Three black, armoured speeders in the livery of Navy security, and a following line of thirty troopers in their distinctive black armour, ordered, disciplined, marching in a spaced line, firing their hell-guns into the backs of the fleeing conscripts. The landspeeders swept in low, drizzling the slopes with cannon fire. The shots threw up plumes of dust, and the mangled bodies of men. A second later and all three landspeeders passed over us at what seemed like head-height, overshooting across the ammonia sea and banking round to follow in on another pass.

Some of the Gudrunites were firing back, and I saw one trooper topple and fall. But there was no co-ordination, no control.

'What the hell! Do we stay hidden?' gasped Bequin.

'They'll see us soon enough,' said Fischig, sliding open the feed slit of his heavy stubber's box magazine.

The odds were terrible, and ever since the incident on the *Essene*, I'd had a morbid loathing of the black-clad troopers.

But still...

I pulled out my heavy autopistol and tossed it to Aemos, freeing my las-carbine from the fastener lugs on my pack.

Bequin drew her own weapons, a pair of laspistols. Lowink and Midas had their firearms – a las-carbine and a Glavian needle-rifle respectively – already braced in their hands.

'Look to the troops,' I told Fischig, Lowink and Bequin. 'Do what you can, Aemos. Midas – the fliers are down to us.'

We bellied forward through the dunes, and then came up firing. Fischig's big gun smashed into the lip of the high ridge, kicking up dust, before he found range and demolished three of the stalking troopers.

Lowink's carbine cracked out, and Aemos fired the auto-pistol hesitantly.

Bequin was amazing. She'd used her time well during the thirty-week passage, and Midas had clearly instructed her carefully. A laspistol in each hand, she whooped out a battle-cry of sorts and placed careful shots that dropped two more of the troopers.

The troopers balked in their ruthless advance, realising the situation had suddenly changed. The scattering Gudrunites also wavered, and some of them, the officer included, turned and began to confront the killers. I had been counting on this. We couldn't take them alone. I had trusted that our sudden intervention might galvanise the Guardsmen.

Still, many ran.

A fierce firefight erupted along the ridge between the halted troopers and those Gudrunites below who were turning to fight. Lowink. Fischig, Aemos and Bequin moved forward in support.

The landspeeders swept back, hammering the shore with shells.

Betancore dropped to one knee, raised his exotic weapon and fired. The long barrel pulsed and made a sound like a whispered shriek. Explosive splinters tore through the nearest speeder as it crossed down over us and it blew apart in the air.

Burning wreckage scattered across the sand.

I chased a second with my carbine. It was turning to present on us, and the turn made it slow. My shots missed or deflected from the armour. As its heavy cannon began to fire, pulverising the sand in a stitching row towards me, I shot the pilot through the face plate.

Still firing, it plunged suddenly and hit the beach fifty metres behind me. It bounced, shredding apart, struck again and crashed into the breakers in a spray of debris that threw up thousands of mis-matched splashes.

The third speeder turned in and made another pass, killing six more of the fleeing Gudrunites, who presented easy targets on the sand. Midas had his weapon trained on it and fired as it passed over, missing. He fired again, striking its rear end as it burned away.

It kept going. Over the beach. Out to sea. I have no idea what he hit – the crew, the control systems – but it just kept going, on and on, until it disappeared from sight.

We pressed up the slope, in among the Gudrunites now. They were dirty and dishevelled to a man, none older than twenty-five. Seeing us and the damage we had wrought, they cheered, perhaps imagining we were part of some greater rescue force.

On the upper ridge, the last few troopers were crumpling. Fischig charged them, his stubber wailing, and a dozen Gudrunites went with him, eager to turn on their tormentors.

The ridge fight lasted another two minutes. Fischig lost two of the Gudrunites with him, but made certain none of the troopers survived. Law enforcement, I remember thinking, had robbed the military of a fine soldier in Chastener Fischig.

I sought out the Gudrunite officer as his men collapsed, weary with exhaustion and relief. Some were weeping. All of them looked scared. Smoke from the battle drifted down the ridge in the windless air.

The officer, a sergeant, was no older than his men. He had attempted to grow a beard, but his facial hair wasn't really up to it. He saluted me even before I had shown him my badge of office. Then he fell on his knees.

'Get up.'

He did.

'Inquisitor Eisenhorn. And you are...?'

'Sergeant Enil Jeruss, second battalion, 50th Gudrunite Rifles. Sir, is the fleet here? Have they found us?'

I held up my hand to quieten him down.

'Appraise me, quickly and briefly.'

'We wanted no part of it. We were mustered to the frigate *Exalted*, waiting to ship out. When we ran from Gudrun high anchor, the captain told us all Gudrun had fallen and we were relocating.'

'The captain?'

'Captain Estrum, sir.'

'And then?'

'Thirty weeks in transit to get here. The moment we arrived, we knew something was wrong. We protested, demanded to know what was happening. They called it dereliction and sent dozens to the firing squads. We were given a chance to follow orders or die.'

'Not much of a chance.'

He shook his head. 'No, sir. That's why I tried to get the men out. We broke and ran, once we'd got in there, once they were busy. They came after us to hunt us down.'

'In where?'

He gestured back over the ridge. 'The darkness.'

'Tell me what you saw,' I said.

NINETEEN

Jeruss makes his report
At the plateau
The true matter

'I don't even know what world we're on,' Sergeant Jeruss said. 'They never told us. The ride in was rough, though.'

'It has no name, as far as I know. Go on.'

'They deployed us from the ships along this beach as an escort detail for the main party.'

'How many men?'

'Over a hundred naval security troopers, and three hundred or so of us guard.'

'Vehicles?'

'Speeders like you saw, and a pair of heavier personnel carriers for some crates of cargo and the main party.'

'What do you know of them?'

Jeruss shrugged. 'Of the cargo, nothing. In the main party was the captain, and Lord Glaw of Gudrun. He's a worthy nobleman from my homeworld.'

'I know him. Who else?'

'Some others too: a merchant, an ecclesiarch, and a great and terrible warrior that they tried to keep away from us regular troops.'

Mandragore, no doubt. And Dazzo and Locke. The core of Oberon Glaw's cabal.

'Then what?'

Jeruss pointed up the slopes in the dark, forbidding uplands. 'We advanced into that. It seemed to me they knew where they were going. Things changed as we went further in. It got darker and warmer. And it was hard to negotiate the way, as if–'

'As if what?'

'We couldn't judge distances. Sometimes it was like wading through hot wax, sometimes we could barely slow ourselves down. Some of the men panicked. We found polygons, like these on the beach.'

It was his word for the hoop-like arches.

'There were rows of them, aisles, marching away into the uplands. They were so irregular they disturbed the mind. They seemed to vary, to change.'

'What do you mean "irregular"?'

'I went to no officer school, sir, but I am educated. I understand simple geometry. The angles of the polygons did not add up, yet they were there.'

Chilled, I recalled Maxilla's mention of the 'unwholesome' angles, and thought too of the marking on the tile I had taken from Damask.

'We followed some of these rows, passing through polygons on occasions. The ecclesiarch and the merchant seemed to be leading us. And there was another man, a tech-priest type.'

'Slim build? Blue eyes?'

'Yes.'

'His name is Malahite. He played a part in choosing your path?'

'Yes, they deferred to him on several occasions. Finally, we came to a plateau. A great raised, wide space, overlooked by jagged peaks of rock. The plateau was artificial. Tiled with smooth stones that–'

He tried to make a shape with his index fingers and thumbs but shrugged and gave up.

'More impossible polygons?'

He laughed nervously. 'Yes. The plateau was vast. We waited there, the men grouped around the outside of the space, the main party and the vehicles in the centre.'

'And then?'

'We waited what seemed like hours, but it was impossible to tell because our chronometers had all stopped. Then there was some kind of dispute. Lord Glaw was arguing with some of the others. I saw this as a chance. I got the men ready. Nearly ninety of us, ready and eager to trust to chance and flee. All eyes were on the shouting match. The big warrior – God-Emperor save me! – he was shouting by then. I think the sound of his voice was what decided us. We slipped away in twos and threes, from the back of the ranks, down the sides of the plateau, and ran back the way we'd come.'

'And they discovered your escape?'

'Eventually. And came hunting for us. The rest you know.'

I waited a few moments for him to collect himself, and gathered the men around. There were about thirty riflemen left, all of them scared, and another three or four wounded. Aemos did what he could for them.

I rose and addressed them all. 'In defying your officers and leaders, you have served the Emperor. The men who brought you here are Imperial heretics, and their enterprise is criminal.

My purpose here is to stop them. I intend to press on at once on that mission. I cannot vouch for the safety of any who follow me, but I count it as a mark of honour to the Emperor himself that you will. He needs our service here, now. If you take seriously the oaths you made to the Imperium when you became Guardsmen, then you will not hesitate. There is no more vital battle in which you might give your lives.'

Wild, frightened faces stared back at me. There was a murmur of agreement, but these were young inexperienced men, some no more than boys, who had been thrown into the deep waters of madness.

'Steel yourselves, and know that the Emperor is with you and for you in this. I don't exaggerate when I say the future rests in our hands.'

More voluble assent now. These men weren't cowards. They just needed a purpose and a sense that they were fighting for a worthy cause.

I whispered briefly to Fischig and he immediately stepped up and raised his voice to the Imperial creed, and the song of allegiance, hymns that every child in the Imperium knew. The Gudrunites joined in lustily. It centred and focused their determination.

Still, the booming came along the shore.

With Betancore's help, I stripped arms and equipment from the fallen. There were enough weapons to make sure every man had a lasrifle or a hell-gun. We also managed to assemble three intact naval trooper uniforms, mixing and matching from the dead.

I stripped off my bulky vacuum suit and began to put on the polished black combat armour of a naval security trooper. Midas attempted to do the same, but his build was too slim for the heavy rig. The troopers were, to a man, large brutes.

We dressed Fischig in the armour instead, and then, so as not to waste the third set, chose a heavy-set Gudrunite from Jeruss's group, a corporal named Twane.

'What's the Gudrunite command channel?' I asked Jeruss as I adjusted the helmet vox set.

'Beta-phi-beta.'

'And of the men you left in there at the plateau, how many others might side with us?'

'All the Gudrunites, I would say. Sergeant Creddon's unit, certainly.'

'Your job will be to rally them to us when we get inside. I'll give the word.'

He nodded.

We left the wounded on the shore, as comfortable as we could make them, and advanced into the dark uplands.

As Jeruss had told me, it quickly became darker and warmer. The sleek black body armour I was now wearing had an integral cooling system, but it didn't seem to help. And the wrongness still afflicted us. It was difficult to walk without stumbling in places.

We came upon the first of the arches, and Jeruss led us through, though we would have been able to follow the course without difficulty. Footsteps and the tracks of heavy vehicles had left deep prints and ruts in the soft dusty soil.

We were advancing up a cluster of hills, dark and uninviting with a glowering sky above. There were many rows of arches, some overlapping. We became disoriented. It seemed on occasions that as we passed through one arch, we came out through another in a different row. The tracks never wavered or broke, but we seemed to blink between one aisle of hoops and another. And the angles of the

joints in the arches were – as Jeruss had said – geometri-
cally incorrect.

'I think,' Aemos said quietly to me as we walked onwards, 'the
lack of symmetry is in every particular and every dimension.'

'Meaning?'

'The three we can see and the fourth – time. Dimensions
have been stretched and warped. Perhaps accidentally. Perhaps to torment us. Perhaps for some other purpose. But I
think that is why things are so twisted and wrong.'

We came at last upon the place Jeruss had called the plateau. It was a flat-topped mound nearly a kilometre across,
smoothly tiled with octagonal tesserae that mocked logic. The
sides sloped down to the dusty soil and all around, the site
was ringed by ragged brown peaks and crags. Above, the sky
was dark and flecked with stars.

On our side of the plateau, a semi-circle of several hundred
men sat huddled around the rim, waiting. I could feel their
tension. More than half of them were Gudrunites; the others were troopers. Smaller groups of soldiers stood in ordered
ranks further towards the centre of the plateau, escorting two
Navy troop carriers in which figures sat, and a pair of empty
landspeeders. A pile of crates had been removed from the
carriers and piled on the tiled ground.

On the far side of the plateau, a row of arches led away into
the surrounding rocks.

We lay in cover and waited, watching.

After an interminable period, there was movement on the
far side and figures emerged from the arches. Even at a distance, I could tell they were Dazzo and Malahite, with four
naval troopers in escort. They came out briskly, signalling to

the main group at the vehicles. All the troops around the rim got to their feet.

Other shapes now appeared through the arches. They were impossible to define at first; grey, reflective shapes that had no human form or intelligible movement.

I took out my scope, and trained it on them, carefully resolving the magnification.

And I saw the saruthi for the first time.

There were nine of them, as far as I could tell. They made me think of arachnids, or crustaceans, but neither comparison was entirely accurate. From their flat, grey bodies extended five supporting limbs, jointed in such a way so that the main mid-limb joint was raised higher than the horizontal torso. There was no symmetry to the arrangement of limbs, or to the way in which they moved. Their scuttling pace was irregular and without repetition of order. It was disturbing merely to watch them walk. Each limb ended in a calliper of polished silver, a metal stilt clasped in the digits of each limb, lifting them a further metre or so off the ground. The metal spikes of the stilts made a clacking, tapping sound on the hard tiles that I could hear despite the distance. Their heads were oblate shapes rising on thick, boneless columns from the tops of their bodies. They had long skulls and lacked obvious mouths or eyes, though several flaring, nostril-like openings showed on their snouts. There was no symmetry to the arrangement of these openings either, nor to the shape of the skulls, and their necks sprouted off-centre from their backs.

They were loathsome, filthy things. Each creature was twice the mass of a man, with gleaming grey flesh.

Shouts and noises of alarm came from some of the waiting men. Several turned and fled from the plateau, scrabbling, wailing.

The nine saruthi clicked their way out into the open from the hoop, fanning out until they formed a semi-circular line facing Dazzo and Malahite. I saw Oberon Glaw, Gorgone Locke, Estrum and the monstrous form of Mandragore descend from the vehicles to join their comrades.

I confess that I was, by then, as afraid as those with me. I have seen horror, and horror itself does not terrify me. Nor indeed was there anything horrific about these beings. Alien, yes, and as a puritan that was alarming. But objectively, they were impressive, striking creatures; assured, almost majestic.

My fear stemmed from a deeper, gut instinct. As with this world we had entered, there was a wrongness to them, to their shape, their movement, their design. Each scuttling limb, each swaying head, betrayed an unholy nature. I could not have believed how reassuring symmetry could be, and how distressing might be its lack. They were warped things, warped from any civilised sense of grace, any human understanding of aesthetics. Their bodies and limbs were so irregular, they didn't even seem to make sense as if, like the tiles and the arches, their angles didn't add up correctly.

Fear, then, swayed me. I looked around at my companions, and saw fear on their gazing faces too; fear, revulsion, disbelief.

Aemos saved my life and sanity. He and he alone stared in wonder at the saruthi, a perplexed smile of intellectual delight on his ancient face.

'Most perturbatory,' I heard him murmur.

That simple detail made me laugh. My confidence returned, and with it, my resolve. I waved Fischig and the soldier, Twane, over to me, and then made certain that Bequin, Midas and Jeruss were sufficiently in control of their faculties to be left in charge. Jeruss and Twane needed some fierce cajoling.

Bequin was already prepared, her weapons drawn. The sight of Mandragore had fired her will.

'Wait for my signal,' I told Midas. To Fischig I said, 'Keep an eye on our friend here,' meaning Twane.

The three of us crept down from cover and approached the edge of the plateau. The men were all on their feet, murmuring, alarmed, looking at the meeting taking place at the centre of the platform. Naval security officers scolded the Gudrunites and kept them in line, but I could tell they were uneasy too.

We came up the slope and melted into the watching crowd. Gudrunites got out of our way – three more naval oppressors with blank visors and low-strapped hell-guns.

We came almost to the front of the crowd. A trooper near me growled, 'I didn't sign up for this!' as he stared at the saruthi two hundred metres away.

'Pull yourself together!' I snapped to him and he looked at me sharply.

'It isn't right!' he murmured.

'We'll see, won't we?' I said, patting my hell-gun. 'If Estrum and these others have led us into a nightmare, they'll see how Scarus Fleet's troopers account for themselves!'

He nodded and readied his own weapon.

Twane, Fischig and I moved forward again. No one paid us any heed. Indeed, many troopers were moving forward to flank the vehicles now.

I looked again at the meeting. Oberon Glaw, his long robes spilling down from upraised arms, was greeting the saruthi with words I couldn't hear. It went on a while.

Finally, he half turned and gestured towards the waiting crates. His voice reached me.

'And in good faith we have brought the properties as agreed.'

Locke moved back from the group. 'Attend me!' he ordered

to the naval troopers around him. I moved forward at once, and so did Fischig. In a second, we were part of a team of more than a dozen troopers carrying the first of the crates forward. I was right next to Locke, my black-gloved hands clutching the carrying handle next to his brawny fists.

We set the crates down in front of the saruthi and withdrew a few paces. Locke remained and opened a crate lid as one of the saruthi clattered forward.

I saw them now, close to. It was no better. Their grey skin was covered with whorled pores, and the nostrils on their snouts flared and clenched. I could see that each of their limbs ended in what looked abominably like a human hand, grey skinned, gripping the cross-bar of each silver stilt.

The saruthi that had moved forward set two of his stilts down on the tiles and reached into the open crate with flickering fingers. It searched by touch for a moment, and then withdrew its hands empty. Its eyeless skull swayed slightly on its neck. Then it raised those free hands high, clasped together, as a man might raise his hands over his head in victory.

The long, rubber-jointed fingers of each hand – and I cannot say for sure how many digits each hand had or even if they each had the same number – twisted and clenched around each other and formed a shape. A visage. A human face. Eyes, a nose, a wide mouth. Perfect, impossible, chilling.

The raised effigy of a face seemed to study us. Then the mouth moved.

'Your bond you have with truth made, being man.'

There was a hush of alarm in the crowd at my back. The voice was dull and tuneless, without inflection, but the finger-mouth puppeted the speech with awful precision.

'Then we may trade?' Glaw stammered.

The hands parted and the face vanished. The creature took

up its stilts again and scuttled backwards. Its kin also moved back, away from the arch.

More creatures emerged, more saruthi identical to those who had already appeared, flanking other things. There seemed to be four of them, with body structures similar to the aliens, but they were bloated and misshapen. Their rugose flesh was white and sickly and blotched with marks that seemed like disease. Instead of stilts, their limbs were fitted with heavy, metal hooves, linked all around by wires that acted like shackles. These pallid, wretched things – slaves of the saruthi I had no doubt – moaned as they moved, filling the air with a sickly whining. The waiting saruthi jabbed at them with the points of their stilts as they clattered past onto the plateau.

Between them, on their backs, the four slave-things carried a trapezoidal casket of black metal, covered with irregularly spaced wart-like protuberances. They came to a halt and sank down onto their bellies.

Dazzo and Malahite moved forward, approaching the casket bearers. A stilted saruthi scuttled around beside them, reached a long limb over to extend his silver calliper, and pressed the point against one of the protuberances.

The casket opened on invisible hinges, like the petals of a malformed flower. I think I had expected light to radiate out, or some other show of power.

There was none. Malahite stepped forward between the kneeling limbs of the slave-things and reached out, but Dazzo pushed him back with a curse and a slap of psychic power that sent him sprawling.

A ripple of response ran through the saruthi, making them scuttle on the spot.

Now Dazzo reached into the casket. He took out a tiny

oblong, no bigger than a boltgun's magazine, and held it in trembling hands, gazing at it.

A book. Ancient parchment encased in a sleeve of black saruthi metal, closed with a clasp.

'Well, ecclesiarch?' Glaw growled. 'We need confirmation.'

Dazzo unclasped the cover and turned the first antique page.

'The true matter is ours,' he stammered, and fell to his knees.

The Necroteuch. They had the Necroteuch.

It was now or never, I thought.

TWENTY

My ally, confusion
The wrath of Mandragore
Against Oberon

I bellowed, 'Look out! They're attacking!' and slammed myself hard into the two troopers by my side. As we went over in a clumsy, thrashing heap, I fired my hell-gun wildly for good measure.

Tension among the humans gathered around the plateau was intense. The saruthi, I firmly believe, had deliberately used their devices and environment to foment that tension, perhaps intending to weaken and cow the humans they found themselves dealing with. If so, they had done too good a job. Gudrunites and troopers alike were at snapping point, their minds and spirits rattled by their location and by what they had seen. A warning voice and a few shots was all it took to spill the tension over.

All around me, men yelled out and weapons crackled. Assuming an attack on their high-born leaders, the troopers still firmly loyal to Glaw and Estrum surged forward, firing on the saruthi with their assault guns. Others wavered in confusion and lashed out at those around them. The Gudrunites around the rim of the plateau turned their guns on their oppressors, or fired at the vehicles.

From the rim of the plateau, Midas and Bequin led our rearguard in a charge, weapons blazing.

In a second, the air was full of shouts and screams, gunfire and skittering las-bolts. Total confusion reigned.

I could hear Jeruss on the guard vox channel rallying his comrades, calling for them to turn on the Navy personnel. The naval security combat channel was riven with orders and countermands, squeals of rage and bellowed curses. I heard Oberon Glaw screaming for order, and the baying howl of Mandragore behind it all.

'Fischig! Twane! Sow confusion! Make for the target!'

Disguised like me, the pair moved forward. The mayhem was too dense and frenzied for there to be any sense of opposing sides. Guards fought naval troopers, or even each other, and indiscriminate fire whipped in all directions.

I shot down a trooper who ran past me, and another nearby who turned in dismay. Past them, I saw the tall, spare form of the rogue captain, Estrum, gazing at me through the smoke wash with incredulity. His eyes bulged more than ever. 'What the hell are you doing, trooper?' he managed to bark, his pronounced Adam's apple bobbing furiously.

'Performing the ministry of the sacred Inquisition,' I told him and shot him through the head.

The saruthi had been thrown into a state of great agitation. I have no way of knowing what emotions they were experiencing, if they experienced any at all. But they reacted as if horrified by the turn of events, distressed and appalled. Hell-gun fire from troopers who were convinced that the aliens were the aggressors blasted into two of them. One burst open and collapsed onto the tiles in a spreading pool of grey ichor and gristle. The other lost a limb and began to drag itself towards the arches with its remaining stilts.

Over the tumult of gunfire and human voices, the saruthi began to wail. Whether it was a threat, a warning, a call of distress, or an order to retreat I could not tell. They scuttled maniacally, their alien shriek shaking the air.

Two clattered forward suddenly, towards the bewildered trooper escort. Electric-blue discharges fizzled around the saruthi's swaying heads and then spat raking beams of ice-bright energy at their attackers. Two troopers were vaporised, their constituent matter boiling away in searing flashes of light.

I caught sight of Mandragore. The brute had already killed one trooper in an attempt to curtail the mindless wildfire, but now the saruthi had fired on them, the troopers clearly felt justified in their action and redoubled their efforts. An alien beam sliced into Mandragore's arm, and rage consumed him. He attacked the saruthi himself, wielding a massive chain-axe.

I hoped they'd kill him.

I pushed through a jumble of bodies and came out on the other side of the parked vehicles. Ahead I saw Dazzo, still kneeling by the ghastly white slave-beasts as if in a trance. The unholy prize was clenched in his hands.

I ran at him.

Fischig, his helmet missing, appeared alongside me. His borrowed black armour was awash with blood.

'Twane!' he bawled over his shoulder, and the disguised Gudrunite appeared, running after us, firing from the hip. Grenades were now exploding amid the mindless fighting.

Bodies and chips of octagonal tiling were hurled into the air. One of the troop carriers was on fire.

The three of us were closest by far to the accursed 'true matter'. A saruthi came ploughing forward, spurring the jostling, frenzied slave-things aside with its stilt-spikes as it made for Dazzo.

With a juddering blow from one stilt, it knocked the kneeling man over and sent the Necroteuch scattering from his hands.

Malahite, on his hands and knees by the slave-things, let out a cry and dived after it. The saruthi jittered around to stop him just as Fischig and Twane blew it apart with hell-gun shots. Stringy grey fluid splashed across the tessellated tiles.

Another saruthi, its skull crackling with electrical power, blasted its kin's murderers. Twane convulsed and exploded in a drizzle of matter. By his side, Fischig was thrown over by the blinding detonation, his armour ripped open.

There was no time to help him. Clutching the book, Malahite was running away across the plateau, away from the straggled, brutal warfare. I severed his left leg at the knee with a round from my hell-gun and he dropped onto his face. When I reached him, he was clawing forward, daubed in blood, reaching for the fallen book.

'Leave it!' I snapped, pulling off my helmet and pointing the hell-gun down at him one handed. He saw my face and cursed. I knelt and picked up the little volume. Even through my armoured gloves, I could feel its heat. For a second, a long hypnotised second, it was all I knew. I understood why Dazzo had remained kneeling there for so long after he first grasped it. The content of the book, that ancient lore, was alive somehow, fidgeting, rustling, calling to me.

Calling me by name.

It knew me. It beckoned to me, telling me to open it and

experience its wonders. I didn't even think to resist. What it was showing me was so wondrous, so sublime, so beautiful... the stars themselves, and behind the stars, the mechanisms of reality, the intricate and oh-so perfect workings of a transcendent natural force we misguidedly and dismissively called Chaos.

I undid the wire-like claps that kept the book shut...

Abruptly, a rough, foul psychic force burst into my mind, breaking the spell. I began to turn, to look away from the opening book. That half-turn was just enough to stop me dying.

I was felled by a monumental blow to the shoulder. As I dropped, the book spun helplessly from my yearning hand. The tiles underneath me were awash with blood.

My blood.

I rolled over as the next blow came. The screaming teeth of the chain axe missed me by a hair's breadth and shattered the bloody tiles.

Mandragore, bastard child of the Emperor.

I scrambled backwards in blind panic. The stinking Chaos warrior was right on me, his lurid armour flecked with human blood and alien ichor. My dazed half-turn at the last moment had spoiled his first blow, but still the back plate of my naval trooper combat armour was shredded; the left shoulder guard was completely ripped away. The glancing shoulder wound was savage and deep. Blood gouted through torn flesh and armour, cascading down my left arm. Writhing backwards, I found my hands slipping on the blood-washed octagons.

I lashed out with my mind. It was no match for his fearsome psychic capacity, but it was enough to put him off his swing. The shrieking chain-blade of the axe sawed through the air over my ducking head.

My fallen hell-gun was out of reach, and I doubted it would have made a dent in the monster anyway. His baying face, its sutured-on skin stretching around the gaping jaws of his skull, was all I could see.

My left arm was numb and useless. I threw myself to my feet, pulling my sword from my webbing.

The device is a fine weapon, of the old kind. It has no material blade like other, cruder models I have seen. It is a hilt, twenty centimetres long, inlaid and wound with silver thread, enclosing a fusion cell that generates a metre-long blade of coherent light. The Provost of Inx himself blessed it for me, charging it to 'protect our brother Eisenhorn always from the spawn of damnation.'

I prayed now that he hadn't been wasting his breath.

I ignited the blade and fended away the next axe swing. Sparks and metal shrapnel flew from the clash, and the beast's huge strength nearly struck it from my hand. I jumped back a pace or two from the next whistling bow. My head was swimming. Was it the loss of blood or the after-effects of that seductive book?

Mandragore was incandescent with fury now. I was proving to be annoyingly difficult to slay – for a mere mortal.

I had a dread feeling it wouldn't last.

He rushed me again, towering over me, and I managed to deflect the force of the chain-axe. But immediately he brought the butt of the weapon's long haft around and struck me in the chest, sending me flying. I actually left the ground and cleared several metres.

I landed hard on my injured shoulder. The pain rendered me insensible for a second. That was all he needed.

He crossed the blood-flecked tiles to me in two strides, the axe rising in the air as his growl rose in pitch. With a flailing motion, I kicked the Necroteuch towards him. It struck the toe of one great boot.

'Don't forget what you came for, abomination!' I rasped out.

Mandragore Carrion – son of Fulgrim, worthy of Slaanesh, champion of the Emperor's Children, killer of the living, defiler of the dead, keeper of secrets – paused. With a hacking laugh, his soulless eyes never leaving me, he stooped for the book.

'You counsel well, inquisitor, for... a...'

His fingers were around the Necroteuch, the metal-shod digits dwarfing it. His voice trailed away. Triumph faded from his hideous face; rage drained away; blood-lust dimmed. His mask of skin hung slack from its sutures. The light in his blood-rimmed eyes dulled.

The Necroteuch sang through every fibre and shred of corrupted being, stealing from him all sense of the outside world.

I stood, unsteadily, flexed my grip on the power sword, and sheared his head from his shoulders.

Before it had even struck the ground, the spinning skull combusted and blazed white hot, dripping liquid flame onto the tiles. The fireball bounced and rolled, rocked over, and consumed itself in a ferocious, dirty fire that swiftly left nothing behind but blackened shards of skull in a smouldering scorch mark.

The body remained standing, burning from within the torso, shooting long tongues of sickly green flame up out of the neck cavity. A column of filthy black smoke rose into the still air. The gaudy robes and cloak quickly caught, and thick flames enfolded the headless, metal ruin.

At the last moment, I struck off Mandragore's fist with the sword's bright blade, and the Necroteuch it clutched fell clear of the flames. I felt as though it was pleading with me to take it up again, to immerse myself again in the wonders it contained.

Such wonders. I bent down, torn by duty. The thing should be destroyed, but it held such secrets! Could not the Inquisition, and the Imperium as a whole, benefit from the infinite truths it contained? Had I even the right to destroy something so priceless?

The puritan part of me had no doubt. But another part abhorred the idea of wasting it. Knowledge is knowledge, surely? Evil stems from how knowledge is used. And such knowledge was here...

Perhaps if I read a page or two, I could make a better decision.

I shook my head to cast away the insidious thoughts. The noise of the battle came rushing back. I looked back across the plateau, beyond Mandragore's upright, burning corpse and the sprawled body of Malahite. The last few pockets of fighting were playing out, and the great tiled platform was littered with dead and debris. Both carrier vehicles were ablaze. The saruthi had gone, taking even their corpses with them. It seemed to me the Gudrunites had overwhelmed the troopers by sheer numbers. Few figures were still standing, and I could see none of my companions.

His regal cloak torn and his face bloodied, Oberon Glaw strode towards me, a laspistol clenched in his right hand.

'Throw that down, Glaw. It's over.'

'For you, yes.' He raised the weapon. A munitions canister on one of the burning carriers ignited and blew the armoured vehicle apart in a stunning conflagration. Flung out by the blast, broken armour plating and sections of track whizzed through the air like missiles. A chunk of trans-axle impaled Lord Glaw through the back of the head. He fell without a sound.

I grabbed a piece of smoking hull plate, and scooped the Necroteuch up on it. I would heed no more of its soft entice-ments. I let it slide off the makeshift scoop into Mandragore's upright corpse, so that it fell down through the open neck of the blazing armour into the furnace of the torso.

The flames turned red, then darker still. The blaze grew more intense. Something without a mouth screamed.

I limped away from the pyre. Malahite was alive and awake, calling out, 'Locke, please! Please!' in a hoarse voice.

Across the plateau, one of the naval speeders lifted into the air. Gorgone Locke was at the controls, with Dazzo slumped in the seat beside him. In moments, the racing speeder was disappearing over the ragged peaks, away from the plateau, towards the endless beach.

Midas, Bequin, Aemos and Lowink had survived the ordeal and the battle, though all had minor injuries. Two dozen Gudrunites were also still alive, including Jeruss.

Aemos wanted to see to my wound, but I had bound it tight to stanch the flow of blood and I wanted to waste no more time.

'I think it would be prudent to get out of here,' I told them.

Fischig lay on a makeshift stretcher. The saruthi weapon that had obliterated Twane had cost him an arm and half of his face. Mercifully, he was unconscious. Two Gudrunites bore him up.

'It pains me to say this, but we're taking him too,' I told Midas and Jeruss, indicating the collapsed Malahite.

'Are you sure?' Betancore asked.

'The Inquisition will want to plunder his brain.'

* * *

Our ragged, battered party left the dark uplands and retraced our steps to the hazy levels of the beach. The booming had increased in volume and frequency and the sky was growing dark.

'It is as if,' said Aemos ominously, 'this place is coming to an end.'

'We don't want to be here when that happens,' I said.

From the beach, we could see the two Imperial frigates and the merchantman had departed. A wind, thick with an afterburn of ammonia, was picking up. Their vacuum suits more or less intact, Midas and Lowink went ahead to recover the gun-cutter.

My vox link crackled. Maxilla's voice suddenly sang out.

'Eisenhorn? For pity's sake, are you there? Are you there? Three ships just left, moving right past me! Conditions are worsening. I cannot stay here much longer. Respond! Please respond!'

'Maxilla! This is Eisenhorn! Can you hear me? We need you to move in and pick us up. We have injuries... Fischig and several others. This whole environment may be collapsing. Repeat, I need you to move the *Essene* in to my location and pick us up!'

A moment or two of static. Then his answer.

'As you instruct, Gregor, but it's not going to be easy. Say again, what did you say about Fischig?'

'He's hurt, Maxilla! Come and get us!'

'Hurry!' Bequin shouted over my shoulder. 'We don't want to be here any more!'

More static. 'Tell Alizebeth, I agree with that! Ha!'

The echoes, delays and dislocations were catching up with themselves. The wrongness was righting itself and, I thought with irony, that made things no better for us.

TWENTY-ONE

**A gathering of peers
Lord Rorken contemplates
Malahite's secrets**

Two days later, aboard the *Essene* at anchor beyond the
treacherous reaches of system KCX-1288, we made our rendezvous with the Imperial taskforce outbound from Gudrun.

We'd made good our escape from the world of the plateau
in less than two hours. As Aemos had predicted, the place
seemed to unravel around us, as if that apparently timeless
realm of the sea, the beach and the uplands had been nothing
but an ingenious construct, a space engineered by the saruthi
to accommodate the meeting with their human 'guests'. As we
rode the gun-cutter back to the waiting *Essene*, the hazy radiance had begun to dim and atmospheric pressure dropped.
We were beset by turbulence, and natural gravity began to
reassert its influence. The impossible cavity had begun to
decompose. By the time Maxilla was running the *Essene* down
the dark corridor of arches as fast as he dared, the inner space
where we had confronted the aliens was nothing but a dark

maelstrom of ammonia and arsenical vapours. Our chronometers and horologiums had begun to run properly again.

We left the fractured planet behind, braving flares and gravity storms as we made a dash for the outer system. Forty minutes after leaving that place, rear-aligned sensors could find no trace of the 'wound', as if it had collapsed, or had never been there to begin with.

How the saruthi came and went I had no idea, and Aemos was little help. We had seen no sign of other vessels or other points of egress from the planet's crust.

'Do they live within the planet?' I asked Aemos as we stood at an observation platform, looking back at the retreating star through glare-dimmed ports.

'I fancy not. Their technologies are beyond my ken, but I feel that they might have arrived on the plateau through those archways from another world, into a place they had built for the meeting.'

Such a concept defied my imaginings. Aemos was suggesting interstellar teleportation.

Outside the system, there had been little trace of the heretical fleet. As far as Maxilla was able to tell from drive and warp wakes, the three ships, no doubt bearing Locke and Dazzo, had rejoined their attentive flotilla and moved away almost at once into the immaterium.

Other warp indicators informed us that the taskforce was approaching, no more than two days away. We dropped grav-anchor, saw to our wounds, and waited.

Thirty weeks before, as we departed Damask, I had sent my request for assistance to Gudrun via Lowink astropathically. I had outlined as much of the situation as possible, providing what detail and conjecture I could, and had hoped the Lord

Militant would send a military expedition to support me. I
did not demand, as the likes of Commodus Voke were wont
to do. I was sure the urgency and importance of my communiqué would speak for itself.

Eleven ships loomed out of the empyrean before us in battle
formation: six Imperial frigates running out in the van, fighter
wings riding out ahead of them in formation. Behind this
spearhead of warships came the battleships *Vulpecula* and
Saint Scythus, each three times the size of the frigates, each
a bristling ogre of a vessel. To the rear was an ominous trio
of cruisers, black ships of the Imperial Inquisition. This was
no military expedition. This was an Inquisitorial taskforce.

   We exchanged hails, identified ourselves and were escorted
into the fleet pack by an honour guard of Thunderhawks.
Shuttles transferred our wounded, including the still unconscious Fischig and the prisoner Malahite, to medicae faculties
aboard the Saint Scythus. An hour later, at the request of
Admiral Spatian, I also crossed by shuttle to the battleship.
They were awaiting my report.

My left arm bound and tightly slung in a surgical brace, I
wore a suit of black and my button-sleeved leather coat, my
rosette pinned at my throat. Aemos, in sober green robes,
accompanied me.

   In the echoing vault of the *Saint Scythus's* docking bay,
Procurator Olm Madorthene and a detail of Navy storm-
troopers waited to greet us. Madorthene wore the impressive
white dress uniform in which I had first seen him, and the
men's blue armour was rich with gold braid and ceremonial
decoration.

   Madorthene greeted me with a salute and we strode as a

group towards the elevators that would carry us up into the command levels of the ship.

'How goes the uprising?' I asked.

'Well enough, inquisitor. We understand the Lord Militant has declared the Helican Schism over and quashed, though pacification wars are still raging across Thracian.'

'Losses?'

'Considerable. Mainly to the population and materials of the world affected, though some fleet and guard units have taken a beating. Lord Glaw's treason has cost the Imperium dear.'

'Lord Glaw's treason has cost him his life. His body rots on a nameless world in the system behind us.'

He nodded. 'Your master will be pleased.'

'My master?'

Lord Inquisitor Phlebas Alessandro Rorken sat in a marble throne at the far end of a chapel-like audience hall two decks beneath the main bridge of the *Saint Scythus*. I had met him twice before, and felt no more confident now for those experiences. He wore simple robes of crimson over black clothing and gloves, and no other decoration except for a gold signet ring of office on one knuckle. The austere simplicity of his garb seemed to accentuate his authority. His noble skull was shaved except for a forked goatee. His eyes, deep set and wise, glittered with intelligence.

Around him was his entourage. Ten Inquisitorial novices of interrogator rank or below, upheld banners, sacred flamer weapons, caskets of scrolls and slates, gleaming tools of torture on red satin cushions, or open hymnals. Flanking them were four bodyguards in red cloaks with double-handed broadswords held stiffly upright before their faces. Their armour was ornate, and the full visors had been fashioned and painted into the likenesses of four apostolic saints: Olios, Jerido, Manezzer and Kadmon. The masks were flat-eyed and expressionless and almost naive, lifted exactly from representations on illuminated manuscripts of old. A huddle of dark-robed savants waited nearby, and a dozen cherub servitors in the form of podgy three-year-olds with golden locks and the spiteful faces of gargoyles circled around, scolding and mocking, on grav-assisted golden wings.

'Approach, Eisenhorn,' Lord Rorken said, his soft voice carrying down the chamber effortlessly. 'Approach all.'

At his words, other figures emerged from anterooms along the sides of the hall, and took their seats to either hand. One was Admiral Spatian, an ancient, skeletal giant in white dress uniform, attended by several of his senior staff. The others were inquisitors. Titus Endor, in his maroon coat, unescorted save for a hunched female savant. He cast me an encouraging nod as I passed by. Commodus Voke, wizened and shuffling, helped onto his seat by a tall man in black. The man's head was bald and hairless apart from a few sickly clumps. His scalp, neck and face were livid with scar-tissue from injuries and surgery. It was Heldane. His encounter with the carnodon had not improved his looks. Like Endor, Voke nodded to me, but there was no friendship in it.

Next to him, Inquisitor Schongard, stocky and squat, the black metal mask obscuring everything but his raddled eyes. He took his seat and was flanked by two lean, supple females, members of some death-cult by the look of them, both nearly naked save for extensive body art, barbed hoods and harnesses strung with blades.

Opposite Schongard sat Konrad Molitor, an ultra-radical member of the ordos I had little love or respect for. Molitor was a fit, athletic man dressed from head to toe in a tight

weave-armour bodyglove of yellow and black check with a
polished silver cuirass strapped around his torso. His black
hair was close-trimmed and tonsured and he affected the air
of a warrior monk from the First Crusade. Behind him stood
three robed and hooded acolytes, one carrying Molitor's
ornate powersword, another a silver chalice and paten, and
the third a reliquary box and a smoking censer. Molitor's
pupils were bright yellow and his gaze never wavered from me.

Last to take his seat, at Lord Rorken's right hand, was a giant
in black power armour, a Space Marine of the Deathwatch,
the dedicated unit of the Ordo Xenos. The Deathwatch was
one of the Chambers Militant, Chapters founded exclusively
for the Inquisition, obscure and secret even by the standards
of the blessed Adeptus Astartes. At my approach, the warrior
removed his helmet and set it on his armoured knee, revealing a slab-jawed, pale face and cropped grey hair. His thin
mouth was curled in a frown.

Servitors brought a seat for me, and I took my place facing
the Lord Inquisitor. Aemos stood at my side, silent for once.

'We have read your preliminary report, Brother Eisenhorn.
Quite a tale it is. Of great moment.' Lord Rorken savoured
the last word. 'You pursued Glaw's heretic fleet to this
Emperor-forsaken outer world, certain that they planned to
trade with a xenos breed. That trade, you stated, was for an
item whose very nature would threaten the safety and sanc-
tity of our society.'

'I reported correctly, lord brother.'

'We have known you always to be earnest and truthful,
brother. We did not doubt your words. After all, are we not
here in... unusual force?'

He gestured around and there was some laughter, most of
it forced, most of it from Voke and Molitor.

'And what was this item?'

'The aliens possessed a single copy of a profane and forbidden work we know as the Necroteuch.'

The reaction was immediate. Voices rose all around, in surprise, alarm or disbelief. I heard Voke, Molitor and Schongard all calling out questions and scorn. The assembled retainers, novices and acolytes around us whispered or gabbled furiously. The cherubs wailed and fluttered into hiding behind Lord Rorken's throne. Rorken himself studied me dubiously. I saw that even the grim Space Marine looked questioningly at the inquisitor.

Lord Rorken raised his hand and the hubbub died away.

'Is that confirmed, Brother Eisenhorn?'

'Lord, it is. I saw it with my own eyes and felt its evil. It was the Necroteuch. As far as I have learned, the xenos breed – known as the saruthi – came upon a lost copy thousands of years ago, and through recently established lines of communication with the Glaw cabal, agreed to exchange it for certain artefacts of their own culture.'

'Preposterous!' spat Commodus Voke. 'The Necroteuch is a myth, and a wretched one at that! These twisted alien filth have fabricated this as a lure for the gullible heretics!'

I looked over at Voke and repeated, 'I saw it with my own eyes and felt its evil. It was the Necroteuch.'

Admiral Spatian looked up at Lord Rorken. 'This thing, this book – is it so valuable that these heretics would throw the entire sub-sector into schism to cover their attempts to retrieve it?'

'It is priceless!' cut in Molitor from across the chamber. 'Beyond worth! If the legends of it are even fractionally true, it contains lore surpassing our understanding! They would not think twice of burning worlds to get it, or of sacrificing their entire resources to acquire the power it would bring them.'

'It has always been plain,' Endor said softly, 'that the stakes in this matter have been astonishingly high. Though I am shocked by Brother Gregor's news, I am not surprised. Only an icon as potent as the Necroteuch could have set this bloodshed in motion.'

'But the Necroteuch! Such a thing!' Schongard hissed.

'Were they successful, Inquisitor Eisenhorn?' the Space Marine asked suddenly, staring directly at me.

'No, brother-captain, they were not. The effort was desperate and close run, but my force was able to spoil their contact with the xenos saruthi. The aliens were driven off, and most of the heretics' advance guard, including Lord Glaw and a blasphemous child of the Emperor allied to his cause, were slain.'

'I read of this Mandragore in your report,' said the Space Marine. 'His presence was fundamental in the decision for my unit to accompany this force.'

'The Emperor's Children, Terra damn their souls, clearly wanted the book for themselves. They had sent Mandragore to assist Glaw in its recovery. That beings such as they took it seriously confirms the truth of my story, I believe.'

The noble Space Marine nodded. 'And Mandragore is dead, you say?'

'I killed him myself.'

The Deathwatch warrior sat back slightly, his brows rising gently in surprise.

'Some heretics escaped your purge?' Schongard asked.

'Two key conspirators, brother. The trader, Gorgone Locke, who I believe was instrumental in forging the original contact between the saruthi and Glaw's cabal. And an ecclesiarch named Dazzo, who I would see as the spiritual force behind their enterprise. They fled from the fight, rejoined the waiting elements of their fleet, and left this system.'

'Destination?' asked Spatian.

'It is still being plotted, admiral.'

'And how many ships? That bastard traitor Estrum ran with fifteen.'

'He lost at least two frigates in that star system. A non-standard merchant ship that I believe belongs to Locke is with them.'

'Have they taken to their heels and run defeated, or have they some further agenda?' Lord Rorken asked.

'I have further research to make before I can answer that, lord.'

Spatian stood and looked towards the Lord Inquisitor. 'Even if they're running, we can't permit them to escape. They must be hounded down and annihilated. Permission to retask the battle-pack and prepare to pursue.'

'Permission granted, admiral.'

Then Molitor spoke up. 'No one has asked the most important question of our heroic Brother Eisenhorn,' he said, stressing the word 'heroic' in a way that did not flatter. 'What happened to the Necroteuch?'

I turned to face him. 'I did what any of us would have done, Brother Molitor. I burned it.'

Uproar followed. Molitor was on his feet, accusing me of nothing short of heresy at the top of his reedy voice. Schongard raised his own serpentine tones in support of the accusations, while Endor and Voke shouted them down. The retinues howled and bickered across the floor. Both the Deathwatch captain and I remained seated and silent.

Lord Rorken rose. 'Enough!' He turned to the glowering

Molitor. 'State your objection, Brother Molitor, quickly and simply.'

Molitor nodded, and licked his lips, his yellow eyes darting around the room. 'Eisenhorn must suffer our sternest censure for this act of vandalism! The Necroteuch may be a foul and proscribed work, but we are the Inquisition, lord. By what right did he simply destroy it? Such a thing should have been sequestered and brought before our most learned savants for study! To obliterate it out of hand robs us of knowledge, of wisdom, of secrets unimaginable! The contents of the Necroteuch might have given us insight into the archenemy of mankind, incalculable insight! How might it have strengthened us and armed us for the ceaseless fight? Eisenhorn has disgraced the very heart of our sacred Inquisition!'

'Brother Schongard?'

'My lord, I agree. It was a desperate and rash action by Eisenhorn. Carefully handled, the Necroteuch would have provided us with all measure of advantageous knowledge. Its arcane secrets would have been weapons against the foe. I may applaud his rigorous efforts in thwarting Glaw and his conspirators, but this erasure of occult lore earns only my opprobrium.'

'Brother Voke? What s–' Lord Rorken began, but I cut him off.

'Is this a court, my lord? Am I on trial?'

'No, brother, you are not. But the magnitude of your actions must be analysed and considered. Brother Voke?'

Voke rose. 'Eisenhorn was right. The Necroteuch was an abomination. It would have been heresy to permit its continued existence!'

'Brother Endor?'

Titus did not rise. He turned in his seat and looked down the hall at Konrad Molitor. 'Gregor Eisenhorn has my full support. From your moaning, Molitor, I wonder what kind of man I am listening to. A radical, certainly. An inquisitor? I have my doubts.'

Molitor leapt up again, raging. 'You knave! You whoreson bastard knave! How dare you?'

'Very easily,' replied Endor, leaning back and folding his arms. 'And you, Schongard, you are no better. Shame on you! What secrets did you both think we could learn, except perhaps how to pollute our minds and boil away our sanity? The Necroteuch has been forbidden since before our foundation. We need not know what's in it to accept that prohibition! All we need is the precious knowledge that it should be destroyed, unread, on sight. Tell me, do you need to actually contract Uhlren's Pox yourself to know that it is fatal?'

Lord Rorken smiled at this. He glanced at the Space Marine. 'Brother-Captain Cynewolf?'

The captain made a modest shrug. 'I command kill-teams charged with the extermination of aliens, mutants and heretics, lord. The ethics of scholarship and book-learning I leave to the savants. For whatever it's worth, though, I would have burned it without a second thought.'

There was a long silence. Sometimes I was almost glad no one could tell when I was smiling.

Lord Rorken sat back. 'The objections of my brothers are noted. I myself commend Eisenhorn. Given the extremity of his situation, he made the best decision.'

'Thank you, my lord.'

'Let us retire now and consider this matter. I want to hear proposals for our next course of action in four hours.'

'What now?' Titus Endor asked as we sat in his private suite aboard the *Saint Scythus*. A female servitor brought us glasses of vintage amasec, matured in nalwood casks.

'The remnants must be purged,' I said. 'Dazzo and the rest of the heretic fleet. They may have been cheated of their prize, and they may be running now. Perhaps they'll run for years. But they have the resources of a battlegroup at their disposal, and the will to use it. I will recommend we hunt them down and finish this sorry matter once and for all.'

Aemos entered the chamber, made a respectful nod to Endor, and handed me a data-slate.

'The admiral's astronavigators have finished plotting the course of the heretic fleet. It matches the estimations Maxilla has just sent me.'

I scanned the data. 'Do you have a chart, Titus?'

He nodded and engaged the functions of a glass-topped cogitator unit. The surface glowed, and he entered the reference codes from the slate.

'So... they're not running back into Imperial space. No surprise. Nor out to the lawless distances of the Halo Stars.'

'Their course takes them here: 56-Izar. Ten weeks away.'

'In saruthi territory.'

'Right in the heart of saruthi territory.'

Lord Inquisitor Rorken nodded gravely. 'As you say, brother, this business may be less finished than we thought.'

'They cannot hope to count the saruthi as allies, or believe they would give them safe haven. The entente between Glaw's forces and the xenos breed was fragile and tenuous to say the least, and what peace existed between them was ruined by the violence. Dazzo must have some other reason to head there.'

Lord Rorken paced the floor of his state chamber, brooding, toying with the signet ring of office on his gloved finger.

His flock of cherubs roosted uneasily along the backs of arm-chairs and couches around the room. Twitching their gargoyle heads from one side to another, they watched me keenly as I stood waiting for a reply. 'My imagination runs wild, Eisen-horn,' he said at last.

'I intend to question the archeoxenologist, Malahite, directly. I am sure he can furnish us with additional intelligence. Just as I am sure he lacks the capacity to resist displayed by his aristo master Urisel.'

Rorken stopped pacing and clapped his gloved hands together with a decisive smack. Startled, the cherubs flew up into the air and began mobbing around the high ceiling. 'Course will be laid for 56-Izar at once,' said Lord Rorken, ignoring their lisping squawk. 'Bring me your findings with-out delay.'

Naval security had imprisoned Girolamo Malahite in the secure wing of the battleship's medicae facility. The injury I had given him had been treated, but no effort had been made to equip him with a prosthetic limb. I was looking forward to opening his secrets.

I passed through the coldly lit infirmary, and checked on Fischig. He was still unconscious, though a physician told me his condition was stable. The chastener lay on a plastic-tented cot, wired into wheezing life-supporting pumps and gurgling circulators, his damaged form masked by dressings, anoint-ing charms and metal bone-clamps.

From the infirmary, I passed down an unheated main com-panionway, showed my identification to the duty guards, and entered the forbidding secure wing. I was at a second check-point, at the entrance to the gloomy cell block itself, when I heard screaming ringing from a cell beyond.

I pushed past the guards and, with them at my heels, reached the greasy iron shutters of the cell.

'Open it!' I barked, and one of the guards fumbled with his ring of electronic keys. 'Quickly, man!'

The cell shutter whirred open and locked into its open setting. Konrad Molitor and his three hooded acolytes turned to face me, outraged at the interruption. Their surgically gloved hands were wet with pink froth.

Behind them, Girolamo Malahite lay whimpering on a horizontal metal cage strung on chains from the ceiling. He was naked, and almost every centimetre of skin had been peeled from his flesh.

'Fetch surgeons and physicians. And summon Lord Rorken. Now!' I told the cell guards. 'Would you care to explain what you are doing here?' I said to Molitor.

He would, I think, have preferred not to answer me, and his trio of retainers looked set to grapple with me and hurl me from the cell.

But the muzzle of my autopistol was pressed flat against Konrad Molitor's perspiring brow and none of them dared move.

'I am conducting an interview with the prisoner...' he began.

'Malahite is my prisoner.'

'He is in the custody of the Inquisition, Brother Eisenhorn...'

'He is my prisoner, Molitor! Inquisitorial protocol permits me the right to question him first!'

Molitor tried to back away, but I kept the pressure of the gun firm against his cranium. There was no mistaking the fury in his eyes at this treatment, but he contained it, realising provocation was the last thing I needed.

'I, I was concerned for your health, brother,' he began, trying to mollify, 'the injuries you have suffered, your fatigue. Malahite had to be interrogated with all speed, and thought I would ease your burden by commencing the–'

'Commencing? You've all but killed him! I don't believe your excuse for a moment, Molitor. If you'd truly intended to help me, you would have asked permission. You wanted his secrets for yourself.'

'A damn lie!' he spat.

I cocked the pistol with my thumb. In the confines of the iron cell, the click was loud and threatening. 'Indeed? Then share what you have learned so far.'

He hesitated. 'He proved resilient. We have learned little from him.'

Boots clattered down the cell bay outside and the guards returned with two green-robed fleet surgeons and a quartet of medicae orderlies.

'Throne of Terra!' one of the surgeons cried, seeing the ruined man on the rack.

'Do what you can, doctor. Stabilise him.'

The physicians hurried to work, calling for tools, apparatus and cold dressings. Malahite whimpered again.

'Threatening an Imperial inquisitor with deadly force is a capital crime,' said one of the hooded acolytes, edging forward.

'Lord Rorken will be displeased,' said another.

'Put away your weapon and our master will co-operate,' the third added.

'Tell your sycophants to be silent,' I told Molitor.

'Please, Inquisitor Eisenhorn.' The third acolyte spoke again, his soft voice issuing from the shadows of his cowl. 'This is an unfortunate mistake. We will make reparations. Put away your weapon.'

The voice was strangely confident, and in speaking for

Molitor, displayed surprising authority. But no more than
Aemos or Midas would have done for me should the situation have been reversed.

'Take your assistants and get out, Molitor. We will continue
this once I have spoken with Lord Rorken.'

The four of them left swiftly, and I holstered my weapon.

The chief physician came over to me, shaking his head. 'This
man is dead, sir.'

At Lord Rorken's request, the warship's senior ecclesiarch
provided a great chapel amidships for our use. I think the
shipboard curia was impressed by the Lord Inquisitor's fury.

We had little time to repair the damage done by the incident,
even though the medicae had placed Malahite's lamentable
corpse in a stasis field.

Lord Rorken wanted to conduct the matter himself, but
realised he was duty bound to offer me the opportunity first.
To have denied me would have compounded Molitor's insult,
even if Rorken was Lord Inquisitor.

I told Rorken I welcomed the task, adding that my working knowledge of the entire case made me the best candidate.

We assembled in the chapel. It was a long hall of fluted columns and mosaic flooring. Stained glass windows depicting
the triumphs of the Emperor were backlit by the empyrean
vortex outside the ship. The chamber rumbled with the
through-deck vibration of the *Saint Scythus*'s churning drive.

The facing ranks of pews and the raised stalls to either side
were filling with Inquisitorial staff and ecclesiarchs. All my
'brothers' were in attendance, even Molitor, who I knew would
not be able to stay away.

I walked with Lowink down the length of the nave to the

raised plinth where Malahite lay in stasis. Astropaths, nearly thirty of them, drawn from the ship's complement and the Inquisitorial delegation, had assembled behind it. Hooded, misshapen, some borne along on wheeled mechanical frames or carried on litters by dour servitors, they hissed and murmured among themselves. Lowink went to brief them. He seemed to relish this moment of superiority over astropaths who normally outranked him. Lowink had not the power to manage this rite alone; his resources were enough for only the simplest psychometric audits. But his knowledge of my abilities and practices made him vital in orchestrating their efforts.

I looked at Malahite, flayed and pathetic in the shimmering envelope of stasis. Grotesquely, he reminded me of the God-Emperor himself, resting for eternity in the great stasis field of the golden throne, preserved until the end of time from the death Horus had tried to bestow upon him.

Lowink nodded to me. The astropathic choir was ready.

I looked around and found Endor's face in the congregation. He had placed himself near Molitor and had promised to watch the bastard closely for me. Schongard sat near the back, disassociating himself from his fellow radical's transgression.

I saw Brother-Captain Cynewolf and two of his awe-inspiring fellow Space Marines take their place behind the altar screen. All of them were in full armour and carried storm bolters. They weren't here for the show. They were here as a safeguard.

'Proceed, brother,' Lord Rorken said from his raised seat.

The choir began to nurse the folds of the warp apart with their swelling adoration. Psychic cold swept through the vault, and some in the congregation moaned, either in fear or with involuntary empathic vibration.

Commodus Voke, helped from his seat by the baleful

Heldane, shuffled forward to join me. As a concession to Lord
Rorken for allowing me this honour, I had agreed that the veteran inquisitor could partake of the auto-seance at my side.
The risk was great, after all. Two minds were better than one,
and in truth, it would be good to have the old reptile's mental power at close hand.

'Lower the stasis field,' I said. The moaning of the astropaths grew louder. As the translucent field died away, Voke
and I reached out ungloved hands and touched the oozing,
skinless face.

The veil of the warp drew back. I looked as if down a pillar
of smoke, ghost white, which rushed up around me. In my
ears, the harrowing screams of infinity and the billion billion
souls castaway therein.

Blue light, streaked with storm-fires. A sound that mingled
seismic rumbling and the ethereal plainsong of long decayed
temples. A smell of woodsmoke, incense, saltwater, blood...

A cosmic emptiness so massive and ever-lasting, my mind
numbed as I raced across it. It was gone in a blink, just fast
enough to prevent the sheer scale taking my sanity with it.

Another blink. Flares of red. Colliding galaxies, catching
fire. Souls like comets furrowing the immaterium. Voices of
god-monsters calling from behind the flimsy backdrop of
space.

Blink. Oceanic blackness. Another snatch of plainsong.

Blink. Stellar nurseries, fulsome with embryonic suns.

Blink. Cold light, eons old.

Blink.

'Gregor?'

I looked around and saw Commodus Voke. I had not recognised his voice at first. It seemed to have been softened, as if the event had humbled him. We stood on a slope of green shale, under a pair of suns that radiated enormous heat. Desiccated mountains lined the horizon, looming like fortresses.

We moved across the clinking shale towards the sound of the excavator. An ancient monotask, its pistons slimy with oil, dug into the side of a rock face with shovel-bladed limbs. It gouted steam and smoke from its boiler stack and excreted rock waste down a rear conveyor belt into heaps of glittering spoil.

We moved past it, and past other excavations in the rock face where smaller servitors brushed and polished fragments from the exposed strata and laid them carefully on find-trays.

Malahite stood watching them work. He was younger here, youthful almost, tanned and fit by the suns and the work. He wore shorts and loose fatigues, his skin streaked with dust.

'I thought you'd come,' he said.

'Will you co-operate?' I asked him.

'I've little time to talk,' he said, bending down to examine items that a servitor had just placed on a tray. 'There's work to do. A great deal to uncover before the rains come in a week or so.'

He knew who we were, but still he could not quite divorce himself from the reality around him.

'There's plenty of time to talk.'

Malahite straightened up. 'I suppose you're right. Do you know where this is?'

'No.'

He paused. 'A fringe world. Now I come to think of it, I've forgotten its name myself. I am happiest here, I think. This is where it starts for me. My first great recovery, the dig that makes my name and reputation as an archaeoxenologist.'

'It is later events we wish to speak of,' said Voke.

Malahite nodded, untied his bandanna and wiped the sweat from his cheeks. 'But this is where it begins. I will be cele-brated for these finds, feted in high circles. Invited by the noble and famous House of Glaw to dine with them and enter their service as a prospector. Urisel Glaw himself will recruit me, and offer me a lucrative stipend to work for him.'

'And where will that lead?' I asked. 'Tell us about the saruthi.'

He bristled and turned away. 'Why? What can you offer me? Nothing! You have destroyed me!'

'We have means, Malahite. Things can be easier for you. The House of Glaw has doomed you to an unthinkable fate.'

He caught my eye, curious intent. 'You can save me? Even now?'

'Yes.'

He paused and then picked up one of the trays. It was sud-denly full of the chipped octagonal tiles from the Damask site. 'They had an empire, you know,' he said, sorting through the tiles, showing some to us. The pieces meant nothing. 'The his-tory is here, inscribed pictographically. Our eyes do not read it though. The saruthi have no optical or auditory functions. Smell and taste, the two combined in fact, are their primary senses. They can detect the flavours of reality, even those of dimensional space. The angles of time.'

'How?'

He shrugged. 'The Necroteuch. It warped them. Their empire was small, no more than forty worlds, and very old by the time the book came into their possession. Carried by humans, fleeing persecution on Terra in the very earliest days. Thanks to their taste-based sensory apparatus, they derived from the Necroteuch more than a simple human eye could read. From that first taste, the profound lore of the Necroteuch passed through their culture like wildfire, like a pathogen, transforming and twisting, investing them with great power. It led to war, civil war, which collapsed their empire, leaving worlds burned out or abandoned, contracting their territory to the far-flung fragment we know today.'

'They are corrupted – as a species, I mean?' asked Voke.

Malahite nodded. 'Oh, there's no saving them, inquisitor. They are precisely the sort of xenos filth you people teach us to fear and despise. I have encountered several alien races in my career, and found most to be utterly undeserving of the hatred that the Inquisition and the church reserves for any-thing that is not human. You are blinkered fools. You would kill everything because it is not like you. But in this case, you are right. The contagion of the Necroteuch has overwhelmed the saruthi. Never mind that they are xenos, they are a Chaos breed.'

He shivered, as if a chill wind was picking up but the suns continued to beat relentlessly.

'What are their resources, their military capability?'

'I have no idea,' he said, shivering again. 'They abandoned their spaceship technology centuries ago. They had no further need of it. As I said, the Necroteuch had warped their sen-sory abilities. They became able to undo the angles of space and time, to move through dimensions. From world to world. They mastered the art of constructing spaces in four dimen-sions, environments that existed only at specific time-points.'

'Like the one where the trade was meant to take place.'

'Yes. KCX-1288 was once part of their empire, ravaged in their civil war. They chose it for the meeting because it was remote from their main population centres. They built the tetrascape inside specifically for us.'

'Tetrascape?'

'Forgive me. I coined the term. I thought I might use it in a learned paper one day. A tailored, four-dimensional environment. In that particular case, engineered with a human climate. We were their guests, you see.'

'How was the deal arranged?'

'Locke, the rogue trader. He was on a retainer to the House of Glaw, had been for years. A mercenary roaming the stars at the behest of the Glaws. He ventured into saruthi territory, and eventually made contact. Then he discovered the existence of the Necroteuch, and knew what it would be worth to his masters.'

'And they agreed to trade?' I was becoming impatient. Time, surely, was running out.

He shuddered again. 'It's cold,' he said. 'Isn't it? Getting colder.'

'They agreed to trade? Come on, Malahite! We can't help you if you delay.'

'Yes... yes, they agreed. In exchange for the return of artefacts and treasures from worlds they had abandoned and no longer had access to.'

'Wasn't the Necroteuch precious to them?'

'It was in their souls, in their minds, woven into their genetic code by then. The book itself was incidental.'

'And you were employed to excavate the materials that the Glaws intended to trade?'

'Of course. I was promised such power, you know...'

His voice tailed off. Beyond the distant mountains, the sky

was growing dark. A strengthening breeze scattered loose shale around our feet.

'The rains?' he said. 'Surely not this early.'

'Concentrate, Malahite, or you'll slip away! The Necroteuch is destroyed, the trade prevented, and House Glaw is shattered and defeated! So why are Locke and Dazzo leading their fleet into saruthi territory?'

'What's that?' he asked sharply, holding up a hand for quiet. It was indeed colder now, and chasing clouds obscured the suns. A distant, plaintive threnody was just audible.

'What are they doing?' Voke spat.

He looked at us as if we were stupid. 'Repairing the damage you've done to their cause! The high and mighty masters of the Glaw cabal have masters of their own to please! Masters whose wrath defies thought! They must assuage them for the loss of the Necroteuch!'

I looked across at Voke. 'You mean the Children of the Emperor?' I asked Malahite.

'Of course I do! The Glaws couldn't do all this alone, even with their power and influence. They made a pact with that foul Chapter for support and security, in return promising to share the Necroteuch with them. And now that's gone, the Children of the Emperor will be most displeased.'

'And how do they hope to avoid this displeasure and make amends?' Voke asked. Like me, he was becoming alarmed by the stain in the sky and the sound in the wind.

'By obtaining another Necroteuch,' I said, realising, answering for Malahite.

The archeoxenologist clapped his hands and smiled. 'Brains, at last! Just when I was giving up hope for you. Well done!'

'There is another?' asked Voke with a stammer.

'The saruthi happily traded back their human copy because

they had their own,' I said, cursing myself for not seeing the obvious sense before.

'Well done again! Indeed they have, inquisitor.' Malahite was gleeful and smiling, though he was clearly shivering now, and desperate for warmth. 'It's a xenos transcription, of course, composed in their, I'd say language, but perhaps flavour is a better word. However, the arcane knowledge it contains is still the same. Dazzo and his masters will have the Necro-teuch, despite the set-backs you have caused.'

Lightning flashed, and the wind lifted walls of dust and storms of shale particles around us.

'Our time is up,' Voke cried to me.

'How true,' said Malahite. 'And now, your promise. I have answered you fully. Are you men of your word?'

'We can't save you from death, Malahite,' Voke told him. 'But the abominations you have chosen to align yourself with are coming to consume your soul. We can at least be merciful and extinguish your spirit now, before they arrive.'

Malahite grinned, flecks of shale clicking off his exposed teeth. 'Damn your offer, Commodus Voke. And damn you both.'

'Move, Voke!' I cried. Malahite had simply been keeping us talking, padding his story out. He knew damn well we had nothing much to offer him except a swift end. That didn't interest him. He wanted revenge. That was his price for speaking. He wanted to make sure we were still here, when the end came, to die with him.

The desert behind him ruptured upwards, throwing rock and dust into the cyclonic gale. A column of blood exploded out of the ground like a geyser, half a kilometre wide and a dozen high. It rose like a gigantic tree, swirling with pustular flesh, sinew, muscle, ragged tissue and a million staring eyes that coated it like glistening foam.

Branch-like tendrils of bone and tissue whipped out from the swirling, semi-fluid behemoth and tore Malahite apart.

It was the most complete, most devastating fate I have ever seen a man suffer. But he was still smiling, triumphantly, as it happened.

TWENTY-TWO

In the mouth of the warp
A mandate to purge
56-Izar

The psychically manifested memory of the fringe world and its excavation site blurred away, shattering like an image in a broken mirror. But the towering daemon-form remained, keening in the lethal darkness, driving the tempest of damnation down upon us.

I felt Voke lash out with his mind against the thing, but it was a futile gesture, like a man exhaling into the face of a hurricane.

'Back!' I yelled, my voice lost and distant even to me.

I saw him falling into the void at my side, reaching for me. I yelled his name again, holding out my hand. He cried out an answer I couldn't hear.

Instead, I heard shouting, screaming and the blast of gunfire.

I sprawled painfully onto the cold paved floor of the chapel, soaked with blood and plasmic-residue, gasping for air, my heart bursting. The noises now were all around me, deafening and clear.

I rolled.

Panic was emptying the chapel. Priests and novices alike, acolytes and retainers, all were fleeing, wailing, overturning pews. Lord Rorken was on his feet, his face pale, and his devoted bodyguard, with their saintly masks, were charging forward, their broadswords whirring as they described masterful figures of eight.

I saw Voke, unconscious, nearby. Like me, he was saturated with inhuman gore and the drooling liquor of the immaterium.

I couldn't find my balance, and there was a dullness in my head. I retched clots of blood. I knew I was damned. Damned by the warp, ruined and stained. I had strayed too close too long.

The astropaths were staggering backwards, frantic, shrieking. Some were already dead, and others were convulsing or haemorrhaging. As I looked up, two exploded simultaneously, like blood-filled blisters. Arcs of warp-energy flashed among them, frying minds, fusing bones and boiling body fluid.

Malahite's corpse had gone. In its place on the plinth, crouched a thrashing, screeching horror of smoke and rotting bone. The astropaths had broken the link, having staunchly sustained it long enough for Voke and I to escape. But something had come back with us.

It had no form, but suggested many, as a shadow on a wall or a cloud in the sky might flicker and resemble many things in a passing moment. Inside its fluttering robes of smoke, starlight shone and teeth flashed.

The first of Rorken's bodyguards was on it, slicing with his sword. The razor-keen blade, engraved with votive blessings and curial sacraments, passed harmlessly through wispy, ethereal fog.

In response, a long, attenuated claw of jointed bone, like a scythe with human teeth growing from the blade edge, lashed out and chopped through his torso and his holy blade, bisecting both.

I fumbled for a weapon, any damn weapon.

There was a cacophony of gunfire.

Storm bolters blasting, the three Deathwatch Marines advanced towards the horror. Their black armour was rimed with psychic frost. Over his vox-speaker, Cynewolf could be heard, admonishing the foe and barking tactical instructions to his comrades.

Their Chapter-wrought bolters continued to boom in unison until the unremitting fire had blasted the thing from the warp backwards in a scrambling, shrieking smear of blackness and bone limbs. It fell back off the plinth into the retreating astropaths, crushing dead and living alike.

Brother-Captain Cynewolf moved ahead of his companions, faster than seemed to me possible for such a heavily armoured form. Tossing aside his spent bolter, he drew his chainsword and hacked again and again into the writhing mass, driving it backwards into the adulatory stalls, which splintered like tinder wood.

Lord Rorken strode past me, wielding a ceremonial silver flamer he had snatched from one of his attendants. The acolyte ran behind, struggling to hold on to the gold-inlaid fuel tanks and keep pace with his master.

Rorken's voice sang out above the mayhem. 'Spirit of noxious immateria, be gone from hence, for as the Emperor of Mankind, manifold be his blessings, watches over me, so I will not fear the shadow of the warp...'

Holy fire spurted from the Lord Inquisitor's weapon and washed across the warp-spawned thing. Lord Rorken was chanting the rite of banishment at the top of his lungs.

Endor pulled me to my feet and we both lent our voices to the words.

There was a tremor that seemed to vibrate the entire ship.

Then nothing remained of the vile creature except a layer of ash and the devastation it had wrought.

As penance for the act of transgression that had led to this warp-invasion, Konrad Molitor was charged with rededicating and reconsecrating the violated chapel. The work, overseen by the arch-priests of the curia and the techno-adepts of the Glorious Omnissiah, took all of the first six weeks of our ten-week transit time to 56-Izar. Molitor took his duties seriously, dressed himself in a filthy sackcloth shirt of contrition, and had his retainers scourge him with withes and psychic awls between ceremonies.

I thought he got off lightly.

I spent a month recovering from the physiological trauma of the auto-seance in one of the battleship's state apartments. The psychological damage I suffered during that event lasted for years after. I still dream of that geyser of blood, clothed in myriad eyes, filling the sky. You don't forget a thing like that. They say memory softens with time, but that particular memory never has. Even today, I console myself that to have forgotten would have been worse. That would have been denial, and denial of such visions eventually opens the doors of insanity.

I lay upon the apartment's wide bed all month, propped up with bolsters and pillows. Physicians attended me regularly, as did members of Lord Rorken's staff, dressed in their finery. They tested my health, my mind, my recovering strength. I knew what they were looking for. A taint of the warp. There was none, I was sure, but they couldn't take my word for it, of course. We had come close, Voke and I, close to the precipice, close to the edge of irreconcilable damnation. Another few seconds...

Aemos stayed with me, bringing me books and slates to divert me. Sometimes he read aloud, from histories, sermons or stories. Sometimes he played music spools on the old, horn-speakered celiaphone, cranking the handle by hand. We listened to the light orchestral preludes of Daminias Bartelmew, the rousing symphonies of Hanz Solveig, the devotional chants of the Ongres Cloisterhood. He warbled along with operettas by Guinglas until I pleaded with him to stop, and mimed the conductor's role when the Macharius Requiem played, dancing around the room on his augmetic legs in such a preposterous, sprightly fashion it made me laugh aloud.

'It's good to hear that, Gregor,' he said, blowing dust off a new spool before fitting it into the celiaphone.

I was going to answer, but the strident war-hymns of the Mordian Regimental Choir cut me off.

Midas visited me, and spent time playing regicide or plucking his Glavian lyre. I took these recitals as a particular compliment. He'd been dragging the lyre around for years, ever since I had first met him, and had never played in my hearing, despite my requests.

He was a master, his circuit-inlaid fingers reading and playing the coded strings as expertly as they did flight controls.

On his third visit, after a trio of jaunty Glavian dances, he set his turtle-backed instrument down against the arm of his chair and said 'Lowink is dead.'

I closed my eyes and nodded. I had suspected as much.

'Aemos didn't want to tell you yet, given your condition, but I thought it was wrong to keep it from you.'

'Was it quick?'

'His body survived the seance invasion, but with no mind to speak of. He died a week later. Just faded away.'

'Thank you, Midas. It is best I know. Now play again, so I can lose myself in your tunes.'

Strangely, I came to enjoy Bequin's visits most. She would bustle in, tidying around me, tut-tutting at the state of my water jug or the collapse of my bolsters. Then she would read aloud, usually from books and slates Aemos had left, and often from works that he had already declaimed for my edification. She read them better, with more colour and phlegm. The voice she put on to do Sebastian Thor made me laugh so hard my ribs hurt. When she got to reading Kerloff's Narrative of the Horus War, her impersonation of the Emperor was almost heretical.

I taught her regicide. She lost the first few games, mesmerised by the pieces, the complex board and the still more complex moves and strategies. It was all too 'tactical' for her, she announced. There was no 'incentive'. So we started to play for coins. Then she got the gist and started to win. Every time.

When Midas visited me next, he said sourly, 'Have you been teaching that girl to play?'

Towards the end of my third week of recuperation, Bequin arrived in my apartment and declared, 'I have brought a visitor.'

The ruined side of Godwyn Fischig's face had been rebuilt with augmetic muscle and metal, and shrouded with a demi-visage mask of white ceramite. His lost arm had also been replaced, with a powerful metal prosthetic. He was clad in a simple, black jacket and breeches.

He sat at my bedside, and wished me a speedy recovery.

'Your courage has not been forgotten, Godwyn,' I said. 'When this undertaking is over, you may wish to return to your duties on Hubris, but I would welcome your presence on my staff, if you choose so.'

'Nissemay Carpel be damned,' he said. 'The high custodian of the Dormant Vaults may call for me, but I know where I want to be. This life has purpose. I would stay here in it.'

Fischig remained at my side for hours, long into the night, by ship-time. We talked, and joked occasionally, and then played regicide with Bequin looking on. At first, his problems in manipulating the pieces with his unfamiliar new limb afforded us plenty of amusement. Only when he had beaten me in three straight games did he admit that Bequin, in her infinite wisdom, had been coaching him for the past few weeks.

I had one last visitor, a day or two before I was finally able to walk and go about my business uninterrupted by periods of fatigue. Heldane wheeled him in on a wire-spoked carrier chair.

Voke was shrunken and ill. He could only speak by way of a vox-enhancer. I was sure he would be dead in a matter of months.

'You saved me, Eisenhorn,' he husked, haltingly, through the vox augmetic.

'The astropaths made it possible for us to live,' I corrected.

Voke shook his gnarled, sunken head. 'No... I was lost in a realm of damnation, and you pulled me back. Your voice.

I heard you call my name and it was enough. Without that, without that voice, I would have succumbed to the warp.'

I shrugged. What could I say?

'We are not alike, Gregor Eisenhorn,' he continued, tremulously. 'Our concept of inquisition is wildly at variance. But still I salute your bravery and your dedication. You have proven yourself in my eyes. Different ways, different means, is that not the true ethic of our order? I will die peacefully – and soon, I think – knowing men such as you maintain the fight.'

I was honoured. Whatever I thought of his modus operandi, I knew our purposes pointed in the same direction.

With a weak gesture he beckoned Heldane forward. The man's raw, damaged head was no prettier than when I had last seen it.

'I want you to trust Heldane. Of all my students, he is the best. I intend to recommend his elevation to the level of high interrogator, and from there, inquisitional rank beckons. If I die, look to him for my sake. I have no doubt the Inquisition will benefit from his presence.'

I promised Voke I would do so, and this seemed to please Heldane. I didn't like the man much, but he had been resilient and unfaltering in the face of savage death, and there was no doubting his ability or dedication.

Voke took my hand in his sweaty claw and rasped 'Thank you, brother.'

As it turned out, Commodus Voke lived on for another one hundred and three years. He proved nigh on impossible to kill. When Golesh Constantine Pheppos Heldane was finally elected to the rank of inquisitor, it was all Voke's doing.

The sins of the father, as they say.

* * *

Invasion training began three weeks off 56-Izar. Initially, Admiral Spatian's plan was for a fleet action, a simple annihilation of any targets from orbit. But Lord Rorken and the Deathwatch insisted that a physical invasion was required. The recovery and destruction of the xenos Necroteuch had to be authenticated, or we would never know for sure that it was truly gone. Only after that objective was achieved could extreme destructive sanction be unleashed on 56-Izar.

All that could be learned from my associates and the surviving Gudrunites concerning the saruthi tetrascapes – ironically, we were using Malahite's term by then – was collated during a scrupulously searching series of interviews conducted by naval tacticians and Brytnoth, the Deathwatch's revered librarian and strategist.

The collected information was profiled by the fleet's cogitators, and simulations created to acclimatise the ground forces. To my eyes, the simulations conveyed nothing of the wrongness we had experienced on the world of the plateau.

Brytnoth himself conducted my interviews, accompanied by Olm Madorthene. Shaven-headed, a giant of a man even without his armour, Brytnoth was nevertheless cordial and attentive, addressing me with respect and listening with genuine interest to my replies. I tried to do verbal justice to my memories of the experience, and additionally related the theories that Malahite had expounded during that fateful seance.

Eschewing the luxury of a servitor scribe or clerk, Brytnoth made his own notes as he listened. I found myself engrossed watching the warrior's paw working the dwarfed stylus almost delicately across the note-slate.

We sat in my apartments for the sessions, which often lasted hours. Bequin brought in regular trays of hot mead or leaf infusions, and Brytnoth actually extended his little finger as he lifted the porcelain cups by the handle. He was to me the embodiment of war in peacetime, a vast power bound into genteel behaviour, striving to prevent his awesome strength from breaking loose. He would lift the cup, small finger extended, consult his notes and ask another question before sipping.

The fact that small finger was the size and shape of an Arbites' truncheon was beside the point.

'What I'm trying to establish, brother inquisitor, is whether the environments of the saruthi xenos will hinder our forces or deprive them of optimum combat efficiency.'

'You can be sure of that, brother librarian.' I poured some more Olicet tea from the silver pot. 'My comrades were disoriented for the entire duration of the mission, and the Gudrunite riflemen had broken because of the place more than anything else. There is a wrongness that quite disarms the senses. It had been conjectured by some that this is a deliberate effect used by the saruthi to undermine sentients used to three physical dimensions, but the traitor Malahite made more sense in my opinion. The wrongness is a by-product of the saruthi's preferred environments. We can expect the effect to be the norm on any homeworld of theirs.'

Brytnoth nodded and noted again.

'I'm sure your Chapter's experience and specialised sensor equipment will be a match for it,' put in Madorthene. 'Myself, I'm worried about the Guard. They'll be the mainstay of this action.'

'They've all seen the preliminary briefing simulations,' Brytnoth murmured.

'With respect, I have too and they hardly do justice to the places we will find ourselves in.' I looked across the table into Brytnoth's face. His rugged features were sunken and colourless, the common trait of one who spends most of his life hidden within a combat helmet. His hooded eyes regarded me with interest. What wars, what victories, had those eyes witnessed, I wondered. What defeats?

'What do you suggest?' Brytnoth asked.

'Adverse cross-training,' I replied. I'd thought about it long and hard. 'Olm here knows I'm no military man, brother-librarian, but that's the way it seems to me. Make the troops practise overburden and off-balance. Blindfold them in some exercises, cuff them in others, alter gravity in the training vaults. Make the weighted packs they carry off centre and awkward. Switch light levels without warning. Crank the temperature and air pressure up and down. Simply make it hard for them. Train them to run, cover, shoot and reload in off-putting extremes. Make them learn all their essential combat procedures so well they can do them anywhere, under any circumstances. When they hit the ground at 56-Izar, let the fight be all they worry about. Everything else should be instinctive.'

Madorthene smiled confidently. 'The infantry forces at our disposal are primarily Navy troopers and Mirepoix light elite from the Imperial Guard, seasoned soldiers all, unlike the poor Gudrunite foundees you had to nursemaid, Gregor. We'll put them through the hoops and raise their game for the big push. They've got the combat hours and the balls to do it.'

'Don't stint,' I warned Madorthene. 'And those foundees you refer to – Sergeant Jeruss and his men. I want them with me when I go in.'

'Gregor! We can give you a crack squad of Mirepoix who–'

'I want the Gudrunite survivors.'

'Why?' asked Brytnoth.

'Because whatever their combat inexperience, they've seen a tetrascape. Those are the men I want at my side.'

Madorthene and Brytnoth exchanged glances, and the procurator shrugged. 'As you wish.'

'As for the others, like I said, don't stint on the training regime.'

'We won't!' he chuckled, mock-outraged at the idea. 'The drill masters will work the regiments so hard, they'll yearn for real battle.'

'I'm serious,' I said. 'Every man that deploys on to 56-Izar – the venerated Deathwatch included, Emperor bless them – should be ready to lose control of his senses, his judgment, his fortitude and even his basic mental faculties. They're going to be hit hard, but in an insidious way. I don't care if every man jack of them forgets his own mother's name and wets himself, they must still know how to hold a line, fire and reload, adore the Emperor and respond to orders.'

'Succinctly put,' Brytnoth said. 'I will, of course, temper your proposals before I put them to my battle brothers.'

'I don't care what you tell them,' I chuckled, 'as long as you don't let on who it came from.'

'Your anonymity is assured.' He smiled. A wonder, that. I consider myself one of the very few mortals to have made a Librarian of the Adeptus Astartes smile. To have seen a Librarian of the Adeptus Astartes smile even.

Brytnoth pushed his slate and stylus aside and looked over at me with curiosity. 'Mandragore,' he said.

'The bastard child of the Emperor? What of him?'

'I'm told you killed him yourself. In single combat. Quite a feat for one such as you – and I mean no disrespect.'

'No disrespect is taken.'

'How did you do it?' he asked frankly.

I told him. I kept it simple. Brytnoth made no reaction but Madorthene was quietly agog.

'Brother-Captain Cynewolf will be fascinated,' Brytnoth said. 'I promised him I'd find out the details. He was dying to ask you about it, but he didn't dare.'

Now that was funny.

We prepared ourselves for the approaching war. It was going to be arduous, and, unlike most campaigns, not divided into two sides. I observed training sessions, impressed by the efforts and the discipline. I even had the terrifying pleasure of watching Captain Cynewolf's kill-team conduct a target-decoy hunt through the hold levels.

We were ready. Ready as we'd ever be.

In the ninth week of transit, Lord Inquisitor Rorken and Admiral Spatian issued a joint declaration, officially enforced by will of the Ecclesiarchy. A Mandate To Purge 56-Izar, as the term and parameters are understood in the Imperial codes. That was the seal on the action. There was no turning back now. We were heading through the immaterium at high warp to invade and, if necessary, destroy the saruthi world.

Through my weeks of convalescence, I dreamed little. But on the last night before our arrival at 56-Izar, the blank-eyed, handsome man returned to stalk the landscape of my dreams.

He was talking to me, but I couldn't hear his words, nor understand his purpose. He led me through drafty halls in a ruined palace, and then departed silently into the dream wilds beyond, leaving me alone, naked, in a ruin that tottered and crumbled down onto me.

The saruthi were in my dreams too. They rose through the brick debris of the collapsed palace effortlessly, finding angles and pathways that I could not see. The multiple nostrils on

their swaying heads flared as they got the taste of me. Their
skulls coruscated with energy...

I woke, soaked with night-sweat, more out of my wide bed
than in it. Dislodged bolsters were scattered over the floor.

The vox-link on my night stand was beeping.

'Inquisitor Eisenhorn?'

'Sorry to wake you,' said Madorthene. 'But I thought you'd
want to know. The fleet exited the immaterium twenty-six
minutes ago. We are entering invasion orbit of 56-Izar.'

TWENTY-THREE

Invading the invasion
Bent angles
In the gardens of the saruthi

The war had already begun.

56-Izar hung like a pearl in space, milky white and gleaming. Vivid flashes and slower blossoms of destruction underlit its translucent skin of cloud. The heretic fleet had arrived two days ahead of us, and had begun its assault of the planet.

I kept thinking of it as Estrum's fleet, but it wasn't of course. I'd made certain of that. This was Locke's battle fleet now, I was sure.

The thirteen ships had blockaded 56-Izar in a non-standard but effective conquest pattern. Serial waves of their fighter-bombers, interceptors and dropships rained down on the planet and the orbiting heavies bombarded the surface with their entire batteries.

They detected our battle-pack the moment we came out of warp. Their picket ships, the heavy destroyers *Nebuchadnezzar* and *Fournier*, wheeled round to protect their hindquarters.

Admiral Spatian held our battle-pack off orbit and chased the frigates *Defence of Stalinvast, Emperor's Hammer* and *Will of Iron* straight in to clear the way.

On their heels, he sent out the massed fighter squadrons of the expeditionary force, and diverted the battleship *Vulpecula* to engage the enemy flagship, a heavy cruiser named the *Leoncour*.

The *Emperor's Hammer* and the *Will of Iron* pincered and torched the *Nebuchadnezzar* after a brief but fierce exchange. The explosion lit the void. The *Defence of Stalinvast* and the *Fournier* locked each other tightly in a longer, slower dance of warships, and eventually slammed together, squeezing boarding parties and naval security units into each other's hulls.

The locked ships tumbled away, in an embrace of death.

The *Vulpecula* raced forward and misjudged the *Leoncour's* evasion, suffering a trio of broadsides. Coming about, spilling debris into the gulf, the Imperial battleship raised its guns and hammered the *Leoncour* so hard and so furiously that the enemy flagship broke up and blew out like a dying sun.

Limping, the *Vulpecula* turned slowly and began its long-range harrying of the enemy ships closer to the target world's atmosphere. Spatian committed the rest of his group then, ranging them forward in a three-pronged division, of which the central and largest was headed by the majestic *Saint Scythus*.

Distances closed. The near-space of 56-Izar was awash with fire patterns and the streaking comets of missiles. Now the ferocious, high-velocity small ship phase began as waves of interceptors and light bombers from both fleets met and buzzed around each other like rival swarms of insects. The tiny lights whirled and danced in the void, faster and more numerous than the unaided eye could follow. Even the tactical displays overwhelmed the senses: pict-plates flickering with thousands of type markers and flashing cursors, spinning, overlaying, vanishing and reappearing.

The heretics had seeded a buffer zone behind their deployment with mines, and the *Emperor's Hammer*, spurring forward in a fleet intruder role, suffered heavy damage and was forced to break away. Heretic interceptors fell upon the stricken ship like carrion flies on a dying beast.

The *Will of Iron* moved past the *Emperor's Hammer* and began to sweep a path through the mine zone with its specialised clearing devices. Triggered by probing force cones, the floating weapons began to detonate in their thousands.

Spatian's intent was to cut a wedge into the enemy's wide formation and bring at least some of his ships within range of the planet's surface. Once that bridging objective was achieved he could begin to unleash the planetary assault, confident of providing the dropships with some covering fire.

The *Saint Scythus* was first to secure such a position. Its main guns mercilessly disposed of the heretic cruiser *Scutum* and forced the carrier frigate *Glory of Algol* into a desperate retreat.

Hundreds of dropships rushed like a blizzard out of the battleship and the two frigates and the Inquisitorial black ship that had moved in behind it.

Most of the dropships were the grey landing boats of the Imperial Guard, jets firing as they hammered down into the cloudy atmosphere of 56-Izar. But scattered among them were a handful of scarab-black landing craft and drop-pods of the Deathwatch.

The counter-invasion had begun.

* * *

Within the first hour of the war, we managed to land more than two-thirds of our one hundred and twenty thousand Mirepoix Light Elite Infantry on the surface of 56-Izar, almost half of the motorised armour brigades, and all sixty Adeptus Astartes warriors of the Deathwatch.

Sensor sweeps showed 56-Izar to be a bland, unremarkable world beneath its heavy veil of atmosphere. Vast, low continents of inorganic ooze punctured by ranges of crystalline upland and surrounded by inert chemical oceans. The only signs of advanced life – of life of any kind, indeed – were a string of city-sized structures arranged in a chain along the equatorial region of the main continent. The nature and composition of these structures was virtually impossible to read from orbit. The heretics had concentrated their invasion efforts on the three largest structures, and Admiral Spatian was targeting these areas, judging that the enemy would not be wasting time invading unviable sites.

Losses were high. The approaches were thick with enemy interceptors, micro-mines and the fire of surface to air defences. All of this was human warfare. There was no sign or hint of any saruthi participation at all.

Behind the main landing force came the Inquisitorial squads, five specialised assault units designed to follow the military in through the opening they made and oversee the primary objectives: the capture or destruction of the heretic conspirators and the obliteration of any further Necroteuch material. I had control of one squad; the others were led by Endor, Schongard, Molitor and Lord Inquisitor Rorken himself. Voke was too ill to command a squad, and his emissary, Heldane, accompanied Endor's party.

My own force, designated Purge Two, was made up of twenty Gudrunite riflemen, Bequin, Midas and a Deathwatch

Space Marine called Guilar. A member of the Adeptus Astartes had been seconded to each inquisitor. Fischig had demanded to accompany me, but he was still weak from his injuries and surgery and I had turned him down with a heavy heart. He remained on the battleship with Aemos, who was, by any standards, a non-combatant.

Our transport, an Imperial Guard dropship, left the *Saint Scythus* directly behind the force designated Purge One, in Lord Rorken's lander. We rode out the vibrating, shuddering descent strapped into the g-chairs of the troop bay.

Jeruss's men sang as we dropped. Their standard-issue Gudrunite uniforms had been augmented with fresh body armour from the fleet stores, and they had sewn Inquisitorial emblems onto their sleeves next to the regimental badge of the 50th Gudrunite Rifles. They were in good humour, eager and determined, encouraged, I believe, by the faith I had shown in selecting them. Madorthene had confided to me that they had scored consistently above average in the adverse training program. They joked and boasted and rang out Imperial battle hymns like veterans. Their experiences since the founding at Dorsay had baptised them very quickly indeed.

Bequin had also been transmuted by experience in the months since I had first met her on Hubris. A hard, serious woman had replaced the scatty, selfish pleasure-girl from the Sun-dome, as if she had at last found a calling that suited her. She had certainly thrown herself into her new life with dedication and vigour. I considered the changes a distinct improvement. Many are called to the service of our beloved Emperor, and many are found wanting. Despite the ordeals, Alizebeth Bequin had proved herself. If there was a point at which her transformation could be identified, it was the plateau. The sight of Mandragore's corpse had exorcised her fears.

Dressed in a black, armoured bodyglove and a long black velvet coat, she sat in the seat next to me, scrupulously checking her las-carbine. The chastener had trained her well. Her gloved hands made swift, professional movements over the weapon. Only the trim of black feathers around her coat's collar betrayed a vestige of the painted, frocked and decorated girl of old.

Midas sat the other side of me, ill at ease. He made a lousy passenger and I knew he wanted to be up in the dropship's cockpit instead of the Navy pilot. He wore his cerise jacket, despite the objections of the dour Guilar, who considered its brash colour 'unsuitable for combat'. His needle pistols were holstered, and his long Glavian rifle rested across his knees.

I wore brown leather body armour and my button-sleeve coat for the assault, a trade off between protection and mobility. The symbols of my office were proudly displayed on my chest above my sash. Librarian Brytnoth, in a gesture that honoured me, had sent a bolt pistol for my personal use. It was a compact, hand-crafted model with a casing of matt-green steel. The rectangular-pattern magazines slid into the handgrip, and I had one locked in place and another eight in the loops of my belt.

After eight minutes of violent descent, we levelled out and the vibrations diminished. Guilar, seated next to the ramp-hatch, made the sign of the aquila in the air and locked his helmet into place.

'Twenty seconds!' the pilot announced over the cabin vox.

We soared down free of the clouds and into the fire and darkness of the near-surface warzone, moving at full burn towards one of the orbitally identified city structures. The site was ringed by a series of what seemed to be colossal lakes or reservoirs, and the liquid they contained was ablaze, with raging walls of fire reaching up thousands of metres. Night-black smoke fanned from the fires and blocked the immediate daylight, and the world below was amber-lit by the seething flames and the crossfire of weapons.

The dropship shook as the braking jets fired, and we lurched around in a drunken yaw before settling. Guilar thumped a wall-stud and the ramp-doors opened with a yowl of metal on metal. Cold air and smoke blew into the cabin.

We came out onto a wide, glistening flat of white mud that squelched wetly under our running, jumping boots. The mud-flats lay between two of the burning lakes, and we could feel the heat of the immense fires on our faces. The coiling flames reflected in dazzling patterns off the wet mud.

Burning debris from a crashed lander littered the white flats, as well as the charred bodies of several Mirepoix. Las-fire cut the air above us. A kilometre ahead there were the familiar shapes of raised, hoop-like arches, 'tetragates' as they had been dubbed by the fleet's tech-priests, some shattered and broken by the assault. Beyond them rose the pearl-white flanks of a great edifice, the target structure, curved and segmented like a gigantic sea-shell, spotted with a thousand tiny scorch marks and blast-scars.

We advanced behind Guilar. The air smelled of fuel-vapour and another rich scent, like liquorice, that I couldn't readily identify.

'Purge Two, deploying on surface at chart mark seven,' I reported over the vox.

'Understood, Purge Two. Purge One and Purge Four report safe landing and deployment.'

So Rorken and Molitor's groups were down. No word yet of Endor or Schongard.

As we pushed past the first of the shattered hoops, Guilar faltered, pausing to shake his helmeted head. I could feel the wrongness already, the insidious twisting of the saruthi environment. It seemed likely the effect was being accentuated by the broken tetragates. These silent devices projected and sustained the saruthi tetrascapes, and they were now faulty and incomplete.

The Gudrunites noticed it too, but seemed unfazed.

'Take point!' I told Jeruss, and Guilar looked at me sharply.

'You need time to get used to this, Brother Guilar. Don't argue.'

Jeruss and three Gudrunites moved into the vanguard. Even they were having trouble, shambling awkwardly as if intoxicated. The angles of space and time were truly bent and twisted here.

Behind us, thrusters retched and our dropship rose off the gleaming mud, its ramp and landing struts folding up into its belly. It was barely sixty metres up when a missile struck it amidships and blew out its mainframe. The burning cockpit section tumbled away from the airburst and fell into a lake of fire. Metal debris from the destroyed main section peppered the white mud below.

But for the grace of the God-Emperor, we could all have been aboard it.

Moving at an unsteady trot, we came to the saruthi edifice. Its great, luminous form was the size of an Imperial hive and its foundations ran down beneath the white mud. I tried to get a sense of the structure, but it was no good and I quickly gave up rather than risk disorientation. It was like an ammonite with its polished segments and perfect curves, but my human eyes could not read its true shape. The overlaps and edges did not meet as one would expect, and conjured distracting optical illusions when any attempt was made to follow them from one point to another.

We reached the foot of it. There were no doors or entrances, and those who had come before us had tried to blast their way through the lustrous surface, only to find it apparently solid within.

I moved my squad back from the barrier and we retraced our approach down the line of the tetragates. Those nearest to the structure were still intact.

As I had anticipated, we stepped through the last one and were immediately inside the edifice, as if we had passed through the pearly walls.

Inside, there was a low radiance shed by some source inside the walls. It was warm, and the smell of liquorice was more pungent and intense. The floor, translucent and pearly, was concave and flowed up into the curve of the walls.

We moved forward, weapons ready. The corridor – and I use that word in the loosest sense – seemed to describe a spiral, like the inner form of a great conch or the canals of a human ear, but at no time did we feel anything but upright.

Opening into a horn-like cone, the spiral gave out into a huge, almost spherical chamber. It was impossible to estimate its true size, or define its true shape. It seemed to be some kind of ornamental garden or even farm. Silver walkways, suspended invisibly by gravity or some other force, ran between curving tanks of liquid that formed beds for huge, multi-coloured cycads and other bulbous, primitive plants. The fleshy growths towered around us, dripping with moisture and swathed in creepers and climbing succulents. Ropes of vine and beards of flowering foliage hung from invisible fixtures in the air above the beds. There were insects in here, flitting between the swollen bell-shapes, crescents and columns of the gigantic vegetation. One landed on my sleeve and I swatted it, noticing with revulsion that it had five legs, three wings and no symmetry.

We followed the silver path. It passed through a tetragate, and at once we found ourselves in another garden chamber, similarly filled with glossy, abundant plant life thriving in sculptural tanks. The tallest growths in here – giant yellowish horsetails streaked with orange veins – rose eighty or ninety metres above the floating pathway.

Guilar called a word of alarm, and his storm bolter began to fire, raking across this second chamber from the silver path on which we walked. The shots burst gourd-like plants in fibrous bursts of sap and hacked shreds of leaf and tendril into the air.

Return fire came at us. Las-fire and the crack of autorifles. Through the sickly growths of this indoor jungle, the soldiers of the heretics moved against us.

TWENTY-FOUR

**Purge Two engages
A silent revolution
Dazzo's triumph**

They came through the plant growth, along the silver paths, blasting, men clad in the stained uniforms of the 50th Gudrunite Rifles and the black armour of the naval security detail. Two of the Gudrunites in my squad toppled and fell from the path, their corpses disappearing into the oily waters of the tanks below. But most of the enemy gunfire was going wild.

Purge Two countered, lasguns barking. I moved to the front of the group and began firing my bolt pistol. There was precious little room for manoeuvre on the silver walkway, and even less cover.

My first shot went wide, so wide I wondered if the bolter was misaligned. Then I remembered the devious nature of the saruthi tetrascape and compensated. Two shots, two satisfying hits. Bequin and Midas both had the trick of it too, and Jeruss's boys were learning.

Guilar made a lot of noise, ripping through the gardens with his storm bolter. But it seemed to me he was still discomforted by the environment.

It was a salutary moment. To see one of the god-like warriors I have regarded with great awe ever since the day, thirty years ago, when I watched the White Scars take Almanadae, become fallible. For all his power, courage, superhuman vigour and advanced weapons, he was achieving nothing , whereas Yeltun, the youngest of the Gudrun boys, had made three kills already.

Was it arrogance? Overconfidence in his own abilities?

'Guilar! Brother Guilar! Adjust your fire!'

I heard him curse something about insolence, and move ahead down the path, detonating plant bulks with his shots.

'Why doesn't the bastard listen?' Midas complained, sighting his Glavian rifle and decapitating a heretic trooper at one hundred metres.

'Close up!' I ordered. 'Jeruss! Frag them!'

Jeruss and three others began to lob frag grenades over the thickets. Explosive flashes blew water ooze and vegetable matter up from the tanks, and the air became foggy with plant fibre and sappy moisture.

There was an abrupt change in tone in the enemy fire. The boom of a bolter rang out over the crack and snipe of the laser weapons.

I looked down the silver path in time to see Guilar jerk backwards as multiple bolter rounds struck his chest plate. With a cry of rage rather than pain, he went over, off the path, into the bubbling water of the tank behind us and vanished.

Thrusting the heretic foot soldiers out of the way, his killer came down the pathway towards us.

'Oh no!' Bequin cried. 'Please-by-the-Golden-Throne-no!'

Another of the Emperor's Children, the brother if not the twin of foul Mandragore. His scintillating cloak blew out behind him, and his steel-shod hooves shook the path. He was bellowing like a bull auroch. His bolter spat and the Gudrunite beside me burst apart.

The Children of the Emperor, shadowy sponsors of this entire enterprise, were here to protect their investment. Had they come, unbidden, after Mandragore's death? Had Dazzo or Locke summoned them?

I fired the bolter at him, joining the fusillade of desperate weapons blasts that Purge Two levelled in a frantic attempt to slow him down. Fear made the men forget the best of their training, and many of the shots were wild. He didn't seem to feel those few that struck his armour.

'Purge Two! This is Purge Two! The Children of the Emperor are here!' I yelled into my vox. I knew I would be dead in an instant. It was imperative that Fleet Command knew of this dire development.

A black shape burst up from the dark water, cascading froth and ooze in all directions. Brother Guilar slammed into the Chaos Marine, wrenching him over, and they both fell thrashing into the adjacent tank. Something, probably the heretic's bolter, fired repeatedly underwater and the side of the tank below the floating path splintered out in a rush of liquid. The soupy water flooded out, draining away into the gullies between the garden structures. As the fluid level dropped, the titanic combatants emerged, blackened with mire, wrestling and trading inhuman blows among the tangled roots and feeder tubes of the tank's murky bottom.

Ceramite-cased fists pounded into armour plates. Chips of plasteel flew from the impacts. The Chaos Marine's vast paws clawed at Guilar, tearing at his visor and shoulder guards.

Guilar drove him backwards, his feet churning in the shallow, thick water. They slammed in the bole of a cycad. The enemy grappled, getting a better grip, stabbing a jagged gauntlet spike through the armpit seal of the Deathwatch's imperator armour. Guilar staggered, and as he fell back, a massive backhanded slap knocked him over and tore his helmet off.

The Chaos Marine landed on the sprawling Guilar, tearing at his throat, driving fists like boulders into his face.

There was a bang of weapon discharge and a flash. His face destroyed and his collapsed skull burning from the inside, the Chaos filth fell back into the swamp water.

Guilar rose, unsteady, his storm bolter in his hand, blood pouring from the wounds in his face and neck.

It was a formidable victory. Jeruss and his men cheered and whooped and then renewed their advance on the remaining heretics. The enemy, resolve lost, pulled back and vanished into the dense thickets of the gardens.

Dripping, Guilar climbed back onto the path and looked down at me.

'I'm glad you're still with us, Brother Guilar,' I said.

We traced the paths on through the gardens of the saruthi, unopposed. The enemy dead we passed – floating in the tanks or sprawled on the pathways – had signs of branding on their faces. Chaos marks, burned into the skin by evil rather than heat. Admiral Spatian had hoped that some of the heretic forces, especially the Gudrunite Imperial Guard, might yet be restored to the Imperial cause. Like Jeruss and his men, most had been unwilling pawns caught up in Estrum's treason, and the fleet tacticians had presented models of victory wherein Locke and Dazzo found the bulk of their ground forces turning against them.

Such a hope was dashed. The minds of these good men had been burned away and poisoned by Chaos. The heretics had enforced the loyalty of their stolen armies.

Via tetragates we advanced, passing through six more garden spheres, then on into wide, tiled courtyards and halls of asymmetrical pillars whose function we could not imagine. Twice, we had brief skirmishes with heretic forces, driving them back into the warped cavities of the edifice. More often, we could hear ferocious war, full-blown battles that seemed right at hand but of which there was no visual or physical trace.

Contact with fleet command was fragmentary. Purge One – Lord Rorken's party – was locked in combat somewhere, and nothing had been heard of Molitor's Purge Four. Schongard's group, Purge Five, was lost somewhere in the tetrascape. Plaintive calls for aid came from them at irregular intervals, piteous half-sane ramblings about 'impossible spaces' and 'spirals of madness'.

From Titus Endor we heard nothing.

The main surface war still raged. Mirepoix commanders reported gains along the fire lakes that edged the target edifices, one of which was reportedly beginning to implode as if great harm had been done to it internally.

In a vault of smooth, polished beige that seemed to us to have no ceiling, we found our first saruthi. They were dead, a dozen of them, their grey bulks split and mauled, silver stilts torn off. Through the next gate lay a spiral room littered with a hundred more. Moving among the grey dead, their pallid limbs dripping with ichor, were several of the white slave beasts that had carried the Necroteuch onto the plateau. They seemed to me to have broken free as many dragged their wire restraints. Some had taken up silver stilts and were stabbing them slowly and repeatedly into the corpses of their grey masters.

I wondered if the pitiful white things were a separate race enslaved by the saruthi, or a bastardised, mutant caste kept in servitude. The invasion, it seemed, had freed them to turn on their owners and butcher them. Such is the price of slavery, sooner or later.

The slave-things offered us no threat. They didn't even appear to notice the humans moving amongst them. With silent, methodical determination, they mutilated the bodies of the saruthi.

In another chamber, an oval dish with tessellated tiles and a strangely warm atmosphere, living saruthi milled aimlessly in their hundreds. Some had lost stilts and were limping, others lay in trembling masses, their skulls flopped back on their bodies. The smell of liquorice, or whatever it was, reeked here. As we watched, white slave-things lumbered into the chamber through another tetragate and began to twist apart and maul the saruthi, one by one, with the calm, methodical motions of insects. The saruthi offered no resistance.

This story was repeated in other chambers and curving halls. saruthi lay dead or meandering without purpose, freed slaves finding them by touch and dismembering them.

I wonder, even now, as to the meaning of these alien scenes. Had the saruthi given up, resigned to their doom, or had some other circumstance stolen their will to live and resist? Not even the tech-priests or the xenobiologists could provide an answer. There is, ultimately, only the fact of their alien nature; abstract, inscrutable and beyond the capacity of the human mind to fathom.

When we found the archpriest Dazzo, he was close to death.

A battle of titanic proportions had taken place in the

tetrascape where he lay. Thousands of dead lay on the tiled floor: Mirepoix infantry and heretic troops alike. Two Children of the Emperor and three Deathwatch were among the fallen. The tetrascape, by far the largest of any we had seen in the edifice, reached away beyond the curve of all human dimensions, and the jumbled corpses covered the endless floor into infinity.

Dazzo lay at the foot of an asymmetrical block that rose from the tiles like a standing stone. His body was torn by gunshot wounds. Heldane sat nearby, his back to the great block, guarding the archpriest with an autopistol. Heldane's torso was smirched in blood and his breathing was laboured.

He saw us approach through the tetragate and lowered the gun weakly.

'What happened here, Heldane?'

'A battle,' he said, wheezing. 'We came upon it as it was raging. When Inquisitor Endor saw this wretch, he drove us into the fight to reach him. It was a blur after that.'

'Where's Endor?' I asked, looking around, hoping I would not see his corpse among the dead.

'Gone... gone after Locke.'

'Which way?'

He pointed weakly to a tetragate on the far side of the sea of bodies.

'Does Locke have the Necroteuch? The saruthi Necroteuch, I mean?'

'No,' Heldane said. 'But he has the primer.'

'The what?'

'Dazzo got it out of this thing somehow,' he said, slapping the stone block that supported him. 'A language primer. A translation tool. Without it, the saruthi version of the text is unreadable to us.'

'How in the Emperor's name did he do that?' Guilar asked.

'With his mind,' Heldane said. 'Can't you feel that after-burn of the psychic effort?'

I found that I could. The mental taste of a mind almost burned out. The raised block was clearly another part of the saruthi's mysterious technology, perhaps the equivalent of an Imperial cogitator, perhaps something more sentient, even something alive. Dazzo, whose psychic abilities I already knew to be monstrous, had identified it and psychically assaulted it, forcing it to give up its secrets. An extraordinary feat of the mind, a triumph of will.

'A polyhedron,' Heldane added. 'Irregular, small, made of pearl, it seemed to me. It just came out of the block into his hands. Materialised. I saw it happening as I fought my way to them. But the effort destroyed his mind. Endor cut him down. He hadn't the strength to resist.'

'How do you know it was this... primer?' asked Bequin.

'I read it in his dying mind. Like I said, there is no resist-ance left there. See for yourself.'

I crossed over to Dazzo and knelt next to him. Ragged breathing sucked in and out of his bloody mouth. I drove my mind into his, pushing aside pathetic strands of denial, and confirmed Heldane's story. With inhuman willpower, Dazzo had wrenched the language primer from the saruthi technol-ogy, and with it the whereabouts of the xenos Necroteuch. Dying, he had passed both to Locke to finish the task.

'Gregor!' Midas hissed. I turned. Far away, across the curve of the tetrascape, heretic troops were advancing through the dead. They began firing at us.

Guilar and the Gudrunites fired back, taking what cover they could to resist.

'Brother Guilar, I need you to hold these bastards at bay.'

'Where are you going, inquisitor?' he asked, sliding a fresh clip into his storm bolter.

'After Locke and Endor, to do what I can.'

TWENTY-FIVE

Xenos Necroteuch
Endgame
The blank-eyed man

We left the firefight behind us and plunged through the tetragate. Bequin, Midas and I, racing as fast as we could through the disorienting spirals and imbricating segments of the dying saruthi edifice.

As we ran, I reported the situation to fleet command, but had no reply or way of knowing if they'd understood me. Then I tried Titus Endor, but the vox was dead.

Moving at speed, the place became even more of a four-dimensional maze, but I had in my mind now the engram I had taken from Dazzo, the memory trace of the route to the xenos Necroteuch he had ripped from the block.

By my estimation – and it could hardly be trusted – we were approaching the heart of the edifice. Perhaps not the physical or geographic heart, but that part of the dimensional construct buried most deeply in the interlocking lamina of warped space and time.

There were more saruthi here, skittering and clicking around on their silver limb-braces without purpose or response. The smell of liquorice filled the warm, glowing tunnels and tiled chambers.

We heard screaming ahead of us, and the thump of gunfire.

'Titus? Titus! It's Eisenhorn! Do you read?'

The vox coughed into life. 'Gregor! For the love of the Emperor! I need–'

It broke again. More shots.

We hurried through a tetragate and almost at once had to dive for cover as las-fire flurried around us. The chamber we had entered was by no means the largest we had found in the place, but it was singular. Dark, and gloomy, it lacked the radiance that shone from the walls and floors elsewhere. The lustrous material that composed the rest of the edifice was here grey and dissected, as if dead.

Another block, like the one Heldane had been propped up against but many times the size, rose from the ashy floor, streaked with oily, greenish matter that ran down its flanks and pooled at the base. An asymmetrical shelf jutted from it, just above the height of an average human, and a blue octahedron sat upon it, glowing internally.

The xenos Necroteuch. Dazzo's engram immediately confirmed it.

The chamber stank with its evil, the liquorice smell, so rich and cloying it made us gag. Behind and above the main pillar, warped sculptures of metal, bone and other organic materials grew from the walls and curving roof. Vicious hooks on filthy chains dangled from these outgrowths. This was not saruthi handiwork but a touch of pure Chaos, spawned by the Necroteuch, infecting the xenos fabric of its sanctum.

Smaller pillars, irregular and unmatched, dotted the floor

around the main block. In between them, a gunfight was raging. The three of us ran from the exposure of the lit tetragate and found shelter behind the nearest of the smaller blocks. Las-shots wove in and out of the stone shapes, ricocheting and rebounding.

'Titus!'

'Gregor!' He was twenty metres away, a third of the way into the chamber, huddled behind a block and firing his laspistol at figures closer to the Necroteuch's resting place.

I glimpsed Locke, and eight or nine heretic troopers.

I looked to either side of me at Bequin and Midas. 'Choose your targets,' I told them. We began to fire in support of Endor, dropping at least one of the heretics. As they reeled from the salvo, Endor leapt up and ran forward. A las-shot clipped him and blew him back against a stone upright.

I ran forward myself, firing my bolt pistol which I had braced in both hands. I blew chunks from the blocks ahead of me, and hit at least one of the enemy gunners. I reached Endor.

He was wounded in the chest. It would be fatal if we couldn't get him clear quickly. I pulled him into cover, and waited while Bequin ran up through the rows to my side.

'Pressure, here!' I said, showing her, my hands wet with my old friend's blood. She did as she was told.

I became aware of thunderous noises from beyond the chamber. The place shook. More thunder rolled and a section of the curved ceiling suddenly splintered and collapsed, cascading wreckage down, allowing cold exterior light to shaft in. A second later, three more holes ruptured and burst through the roof, and from outside I could hear the muffled hammering of bombardment.

'Midas!'

He was already moving up to my left, ditching his needle

rifle for the pistols in the tight confines. Lethal Glavian needles hissed through the air. The ground continued to shake.
A further section of roof came down.

Leaving Endor with Bequin, I ducked from pillar to pillar,
braving the deluge of shots. Midas and I switched to our earpiece links and Glossia.

'Thorn ushers Aegis, a tempest sinister.'

'Aegis attending, tempest in three.'

I counted the three beats and ran forward as Midas hurled
his frag grenade to my left before opening fire with both
pistols.

The flash and bang of the blast obscured the bombardment
outside for a moment. A heretic was flung upwards, limbs
flailing, and glanced brokenly off a pillar before hitting the
ground.

Midas's 'tempest' of covering confusion had allowed me
to get within ten metres of Locke. I could no longer see him,
however. Keeping my grip on my bolt pistol, I drew my power
sword in my left hand and came around the block.

Locke and one of his men had chosen the exact same
moment to plough forward into me. We broke from cover
and came face to face in the narrow gap between pillars. My
pistol's first shot missed the lunging Locke and tore the left
arm off his accomplice. Before the wailing man had even hit
the ground, Locke's laspistol had put a round through the
meat of my right arm. A long-bladed dagger flashed forward
in his other hand. We slammed into each other. I tried to
sweep my power sword around, but it struck something and
Locke side-stepped. The basket hilt of his dagger smashed
into my face and knocked me over onto my back. With a grin
that he knew I could never copy, he raised his laspistol to fire
down into my brain.

Two tonnes of xenos-quarried stone pillar, sliced through at hip-height by my power blade, crushed him into the flaking ground.

I rose.

Gorgone Locke was still alive. His belly and pelvis were smashed under the fallen pillar and his arms were pinned. He gazed up at me through blinking, bewildered eyes.

'Gorgone Locke, in the eyes of the Holy Inquisition, you are thrice damned by action, association and belief,' I said, beginning the catechism of abolition.

'N-no...' he whispered.

As I completed the exclamation, I cut the mark of heresy into the flesh of his brow with the tip of my sword. By the time I had finished, he was dead from his crush injuries.

The shattering chamber still shook. On their long chains, the hooks swung. Dust and fragments dribbled down from the tears in the roof, falling through the bars of cold light. I reached down and found the pearl polyhedron in Locke's blood-soaked coat. The primer. I slipped it into my pocket and turned to see Midas approaching.

'The last of his rats have fled,' he said, holstering his pistols. He looked down at the dead ship master. 'So perish all heretics, eh?'

I reached up with on hand to take the xenos Necroteuch from its shelf – and found myself unable to move. Some enormous psychic force froze me rigid.

'So perish all heretics indeed,' said a voice. 'Turn him so he can see me.'

Involuntarily, I swung round, my hand still raised in the act of reaching out. I saw Midas, also paralysed and rigid, his dark features locked in a rictus of dismay.

Konrad Molitor, my brother inquisitor, was standing before me, smiling. His three hooded servants were at his side.

'Such valour, Gregor. Such dedication. I thought you'd be the one to find the prize.'

I tried to answer, but my mouth refused to obey me. Spittle bubbled between my clenched teeth.

Molitor looked around at his cowled companions. 'Let him speak,' he said.

The psychic constraints on my voice slackened. Speech was still an effort. 'W-what are you d-doing, Molitor?'

'Recovering the priceless Necroteuch, of course. We really, really can't have you destroying another copy now, can we?'

'W-we?'

'There are many who believe mankind will benefit more from the study of this artefact than from its destruction. I have come to safeguard those interests.'

'R-rorken will n-never allow... y-you will b-burn for–'

'My estimable Lord Brother Rorken will never know. Feel how this place quakes. See how the roof splinters and collapses? Ten minutes ago, I signalled to the fleet that the primary objective was achieved. I gave the code for Sanction Extremis. They believe the Necroteuch had been found and safely disposed of. Our forces are withdrawing, with all haste. The batteries of the fleet have begun to level these xenos places. No one will know that the divine Necroteuch has been carried off safely. Not a shred of evidence will survive the bombardment. Not a shred of evidence... nor any voice of dissent.'

His yellow-pupilled eyes regarded me. 'How brave of you to give your life in the assault on 56-Izar. Your name will be remembered on the roll of honour. I assure you, I'll see to that myself.'

'B-b-b-bastard...' I fought with my mind to break free, but it was impossible. This was not Molitor's hold on me. One of his retainers, or all three in concert, supremely powerful.

'Fetch it for me,' Molitor said to one of his men, gesturing to the Necroteuch with a wave of his checked sleeve. 'We would be well to leave promptly.'

The hammering bombardment was now a perpetual shaking roar. The robed figure slid forward and took down the blue octahedron, cupping it in elegant, long-nailed fingers. He seemed to study it, and looked round at Molitor.

'It is useless,' he said.

'What?'

'Unreadable. Locked within an impenetrable xenos language code.'

Molitor stammered. 'No! Impossible! Break the code!'

'Would that I could. It is beyond even my ability.'

'There must be a means of translation!'

The hooded man holding the Necroteuch looked round at me.

'He has a primer. The only primer. He's trying not to think about it, but I can see it in his mind. Look in his coat pocket.'

The smile returned to Molitor's face. He came close to me, reaching out a hand towards my coat. 'Devious to the last, Gregor. You whoreson wretch.'

A las-round blew his hand off at the wrist.

Molitor screamed and stumbled back, clutching his smoking stump.

Bequin, her face pursed grimly, her las-carbine at her shoulder and aimed at his heart, appeared beside me.

'Kill them! Kill them!' Molitor screamed. I felt the immediate pressure of the psychic vice tightening to finish me. Then I reeled away, freed. The psychic blank of Bequin's untouchable nature shielded me now she was at my side. The servant holding the Necroteuch took a step backwards in surprise.

Molitor, frantic with pain and anger, saw that his powerful psychic was thwarted somehow and yelled 'Albaara! T'harth!'

Code words. Trigger words. The pair of servants who had remained by his side sprang forward, their robes shredding away.

Arco-flagellants. Heretics reprogrammed and rebuilt with augmetics and bionics to serve as murderous slaves. The trigger words woke them from their calming states of bliss and plunged them into maniacal rages.

Out of their robes, they were foul, hunched things, encrusted with crude surgical implants and sacred charms. Their hands were lashing clutches of electrowhips, their eyes dull, bulbous orbits under the rims of the tarnished pacifier helmets bolted to their skulls.

Midas, Bequin and I fired our weapons together, raking them with punishment as they charged forward. The damage they suffered was immense, but still they came on, their bodies pumped with intoxicating adrenal fluid, pain-blockers and frenzy-inducing chemical stimulants. They didn't feel what we were doing to them.

One was just an arm's length from me when my desperate rain of bolts finally defeated it. A shot exploded the armoured matrix of chemical dispensers on its shoulder, spraying fluid into the air. In a second, it fell convulsing to the ground at our feet as the damage robbed it of its drug-source and left nothing but agony behind.

The other barely felt the punctures of Midas's too subtle needles. Frantically, we split to either side, out of its path. Braying and thrashing its whip-limbs, it pounded after Midas, who ducked left and right between pillars, trying to evade it.

Only his Glavian-bred grace and speed kept him out of its inexorably advancing grip.

He knew he had seconds left. Bequin and I were moving, but there was precious little we could do.

Midas pulled off his pouch of grenades, priming one as he twisted and side-stepped between the pillars, scarcely avoiding a withering lash of flexible metal whips that scored gouges in the stone.

Midas feinted left and then threw himself directly at the beast, snagging the strap of his pouch around its neck as he vaulted over its shoulder head first.

The grenades detonated in one stunning flash and atomised the ravening man-beast. Caught in the shockwave, Midas was thrown into a pillar and dropped unconscious.

'Eisenhorn! Eisenhorn!' Molitor was wailing as he and his remaining servant hunted for me. His voice was cracking with pain and fury.

'Stay at my side,' I told Bequin as we ran deeper into the chamber. 'That psychic can't touch me while I'm close to you.'

Half the ceiling and a significant part of the wall blew in. For a second the air was solid with billowing orange fire.

Deafened, our skins scorched by the blast, Bequin and I were back on our feet in a moment. The chamber was open to the sky now, and cold white light poured in, heavy with smoke.

'Come on!'

Together we scrambled towards the blast-damaged wall, picking our way up the smouldering slope of broken stone and whatever material the saruthi used for construction. This material was fused and bubbling, like plastic or flesh.

We headed for the light.

* * *

We emerged high on the curving upper face of the saruthi edifice. It was cold, and the wind that came across the segmented ridges of the polished white roof was brisk and full of the odours of smoke, fyceline and promethium.

We were at a dizzying height. The pearly flanks of the vast structure arced away to a ground far below and the surface was hard and polished like ice. Bequin slipped, and I managed to grab her before she slid away down the curve.

From up here, high in the alien sky, we could see across the lakes of fire and the vast smoke banks that roiled away for hundreds of kilometres. We could see flocks of troopships soaring up and away through the smoke cover towards the parent ships in orbit. On the flats of white mud far beneath us, Imperial troops ran to waiting dropships, discarding packs and helmets and even weapons in their haste to leave. Tanks and armoured carriers wallowed and puffed through the wet mud and up onto the tongue-like ramps of heavy lifters. Shells and las-fire flickered across the lakes and mud as the remaining heretic forces fought on heedless.

Lances and forks of dazzling energy bit down from the clouds, murdering the landscape. Obeying Molitor's instructions to the letter, Admiral Spatian was levelling the area. All five of us inquisitors, along with Cynewolf and key Deathwatch and selected officers of the invasion force, had been given the code words to unleash this doom. Molitor had sealed our fate. Once given, Sanction Extremis could not be revoked, even if my vox had been working instead of crippled by the electromagnetic bursts that accompanied every orbital strike. As per the battle plans, Spatian was systematically wasting the invasion site as fast as possible, even at the cost of his own retreating ground forces.

Another saruthi edifice, twenty kilometres away, died.

Shaped in a form that suggested a nautilus shell, its opalescent curves were cracked and split by blue-hot heavy lasers. The die-straight beams came down through the clouds from ships so far up they were invisible, and tore through the edifice like testamental judgment. Waves of fighter-bombers swept in, sowing payloads of munitions that bloomed in rippling seas of explosions. Guided warheads, sleek like airborne sharks, whined overhead on the last stage of their first and final journey from starship to target.

The edifice ruptured and blew out. Light-shock lit the hemisphere. A towering column of white ash-smoke rose, folding into a fifteen-kilometre torus-shaped cloud.

The sight was stunning, shocking. Bequin and I gazed at it. A few heartbeats later it was repeated behind us, forty kilometres distant, as another saruthi edifice was annihilated.

The edifice on whose smoothly curving upper surfaces we now stood was undoubtedly going to go the same way soon. Even now, I knew, the co-ordinates were being loaded into the fleet's gunnery servitors.

We ran along the lip of another curved segment. Afterburners red against the black smoke, more dropships came in, heading towards cheering, gesticulating huddles of Mirepoix infantry out on the flats. I was astounded at the selfless courage of the dropship crews. Spatian's bombardment wasn't waiting for them to move in and pull out. They were risking everything to make the surface run and retrieve as many troopers as they could.

'Gregor!' Bequin shouted in my ear.

I turned. Down the shell-form span of the roof behind us, Molitor and his henchman had appeared out of the blast hole. Unsteady, they scrambled up after us.

A las-shot whined past me, kissing the pearly surface and leaving a burn-scar.

'The primer, you whoreson bastard! Give me the primer!' Molitor yelled.

I gave him a full clip of bolt rounds instead.

The first of the thundering tracer shots splintered chunks out of the edifice roof. Then I hit and exploded his left thigh, his belly and his throat.

Konrad Molitor bucked and twitched as the rounds tore through him, and then fell. His mauled body slid down the curve of the roof and disappeared, leaving a smear of blood behind it.

His henchman advanced, heedless of the shots, throwing off his hooded robe.

He was naked beneath it. Tall, well muscled, with a golden cast to his skin. His face was handsome and tiny residual horns sprouted from his skull.

His eyes were blank.

My prophetic dreams were made flesh.

Terror seized me, turned my heart inside out.

TWENTY-SIX

Cherubael
The brink
Exterminatus

The blank-eyed man – though in truth he was not a man, but a daemon in human form – strode up the shining curve towards me. The glowing octahedron of the saruthi's unholy text was clasped in one nimble hand.

'I would like the primer now please, Gregor.'

'What *are* you?'

'This is no place for introductions.' He gestured about himself. Lances of annihilation blasted down into the mud-flats nearby.

'Humour me...' I managed.

'Very well. My name is Cherubael. Now, that primer. Time is ticking away.'

'Time will always tick away,' I said. 'Who made you?'

'Made me?' The blank-eyed man smiled at me duplicitously.

'You're... a *daemonhost*. A conjured thing. Tell me who made you and who commanded you and Molitor to come after this prize... and I might give you the primer.'

He laughed and licked his thin lips with a glossy forked tongue.

'Let us both be abundantly clear about this, *Gregor*. You will give me the primer. Either you will hand me the primer now, or I will come over to you and take it. And break every bone in your body. And defile that girl at your side. And break every bone in her body too. And then drag your jiggling carcasses down into the chamber below and string you both up on the hooks, and burn out your agony centres as I wait for the bombardment to flatten this place.'

He paused.

'Your choice.'

'You've been in my dreams for a long while now. Why is that?' I pressed.

'You are gifted, Gregor. And time is not the arrow that humans like to think it is. A second in the warp would show you that. Why, a second in the four-dimensional habitats of the saruthi should have proved it too. Your dreams were just nightmares of something yet to happen.'

'Who made you?' My voice was insistent. His answer was the one I least expected, and it left me all but stunned.

'The Holy Inquisition made me, Gregor. A brother of yours made me. Now, for the last time, give me that–'

The daemonhost swung around suddenly as voices called out from lower down the roof. Brother-Captain Cynewolf was clambering up out of the blast hole, flanked by Midas and another Deathwatcher carrying the limp form of Titus Endor.

Cynewolf raised his storm bolter and fired at the blank-eyed man.

Cherubael reached out and caught the glowing shells, plucking them out of the air.

'Go home, Astartes bastard!' he yelled down the sloping roof at Cynewolf. 'This has nothing to do with you!'

The fiend came up the ridge until he was facing me. I could see the tiny arcs of power darting across his glowing skin. I could smell the stink of corruption.

Eye to eye now.

He held out his hand, palm up, fingernails long and polished like claws.

'Clever of you to find an untouchable to cancel me out.' He looked over at Bequin. 'How did you manage that?'

'Fate, like time, is not linear, Cherubael. Surely you know that. I found Bequin in the same way that the dreams of you found me.'

He nodded. 'I like you, Gregor Eisenhorn. So very challenging and stimulating – for a human. I wish we had leisure to discourse and break bread... But we haven't!' he snapped suddenly. 'Give me the primer!'

I took out the polyhedron. His smile broadened.

I dropped the artefact onto the silky roof and, before it could slide away, crushed it under the heel of my boot.

The daemonhost took a step backwards, gazing down at the crunched dust.

He looked up at me again with his blank eyes. 'You are a man of singular dedication, Gregor. I would have enjoyed killing you, when the day and hour came. But you're dead already. This edifice is two hundred and forty seconds away from destruction. Cherish this–'

He tossed me the xenos Necroteuch and I caught it in one gloved hand.

'You've won. Take that consolation to the afterlife.'

He started to run, towards the lip of the roof, and then threw himself out in a perfect dive, arms raised. For a moment, he hung in space, then he forked his body in, executed a precise roll and disappeared into the lake of fire below.

I pulled Bequin to me as Cynewolf, Midas and the other Deathwatch Marine approached. Endor, crumpled in the Astartes' arms, looked dead. I prayed he was, for in a moment this place would dissolve in fire.

'Rosethorn from Aegis, above and... well, above, for Emperor's sake! Damn this Glossia crap! *Move!*'

My gun-cutter swung in over the edifice roof, ramp-jaws open. I could see Fischig at the helm through the cockpit screens, yelling at me. Aemos was at his side.

I watched 56-Izar die from the bridge of the *Saint Scythus* as we left orbit. Petals of flame the size of continents spread out under its milky skin. Sanction Extremis. *Exterminatus.*

After the deluge of fire, the virus bombs. The seething storms of tailored plagues. The nuclear atrocity.

It was a cinder by the time we left. No contact with the saruthi race was ever made again.

And the tainted, glowing light of the Necroteuch was extinguished forever.

EPILOGUE

At Pamophrey

At Pamophrey, we rested.

Forty weeks of voyage through the immaterium had dulled our sense of victory. The fleet dispersed at Thracian Primaris and the last I saw of Sergeant Jeruss was a waving hand across a smoky, beery bar.

I rented a villa out by the Sound at Pamophrey. Midas slept most of the day, and whiled away the night in games of regicide with Aemos and Fischig. Bequin bathed in the sun, and swam in the breakers.

I sat out on the salt-whipped stoop and watched over the beach like a god who has forgotten his creations.

Great labours still awaited us. Reports to be made, interviews and debriefings to be attended. Lord Rorken had called for a tribunal of enquiry, and the High Lords of Terra were awaiting a full account of the matter. Months of paperwork, hearings and evidential audits lay ahead. The identity of the force behind Molitor and his daemonhost remained a mystery, and though Lord Rorken was as anxious as myself to find an answer, I doubted any would readily emerge. The question might fester and stagnate, unanswered, in the slow, unwieldy bureaucracy of the Inquisition for years.

I would not allow that. As soon as I was free to engage upon another case, I would dedicate myself to finding Cherubael's master. The beloved rule of man had come close to great calamity thanks to his scheming.

I would not forget the saruthi. They were an object lesson – if any were truly needed – of how an entire, advanced culture might be consumed by Chaos.

Seabirds looped in the gusting tide wind. The breakers crashed.

The blank-eyed man still haunted my dreams.

After-echoes or ripples of the future?

I would have to wait and see.

ABOUT THE AUTHOR

Dan Abnett has written over fifty novels, including *Anarch*, the latest instalment in the acclaimed Gaunt's Ghosts series. He has also written the Ravenor and Eisenhorn books, the most recent of which is *The Magos*. For the Horus Heresy, he is the author of *Horus Rising, Legion, The Unremembered Empire, Know No Fear* and *Prospero Burns*, the last two of which were both *New York Times* bestsellers. He also scripted *Macragge's Honour*, the first Horus Heresy graphic novel, as well as numerous audio dramas and short stories set in the Warhammer 40,000 and Warhammer universes. He lives and works in Maidstone, Kent.

MALLEUS
by Dan Abnett

Inquisitor Eisenhorn must track down and defeat the forces who would destroy him or face the wrath of the Ordo Malleus...

An extract from

Malleus

Book two in the Eisenhorn series by Dan Abnett

The ruins were festering with shadows and dank salt. Rot-beetles scurried over the flaking mosaic portraits of long-dead worthies that stared out of alcoves. Worms crawled everywhere. The steady chirrup of insects from the salt-licks was like someone shaking a rattle. As we probed deeper, we came upon inner yards and grave-squares where neglect had shaken free place-stones and revealed the smeared bones of the long interred in the loamy earth below. In places, rot-browned skulls had been dug out and piled in loose pyramids.

It saddened me to see this holy place so befouled and dreary. Kiodrus had been a great man, had stood and fought at the right hand of the sacred Beati Sabbat during her mighty crusade. But that had been a long time ago and far away, and his cult of worship had faded. It would take another crusade into the distant Sabbat Worlds to rekindle interest in him and his forgotten deeds.

Qus called a halt and pointed towards the steps of an undercroft that led away below ground. I waved him back, indicating the tiny strip of red ribbon placed under a stone on the top step. A marker, left by Ravenor, indicating this was not a suitable entry point. Peering into the staircase gloom, I saw what he had seen: the half buried cables of a tremor-detector and what looked like bundles of tube charges.

We found three more entrances like it, all marked by Ravenor. The Beldame had secured her fastness well.

'Through there, do you think, sir?' Qus whispered, pointing towards the columns of a roofless cloister.

I was about to agree when Arianrhod hissed 'Barbarisater thirsts...'

I looked at her. She was prowling to the left, towards an archway in the base of the main bell-tower. She moved silently, the sabre held upright in a two-handed grip, her tasselled cloak floating out behind her like angelic wings.

I gestured to Qus and the women and we formed in behind her. I drew my prized bolt pistol, given to me by Librarian Brytnoth of the Adeptus Astartes Deathwatch Chapter on the eve of the Purge of Izar, almost a century before. It had never failed me.

The Beldame's minions came out of the night. Eight of them, just shadows that disengaged themselves from the surrounding darkness. Qus began to fire, blasting back a shadow that pounced at him. I fired too, raking bolt rounds into the ghostly opposition.

Beldame Sadia was a heretic witch and consorted with xenos breeds. She had a particular fascination with the beliefs and necromancies of the dark eldar, and had made it her life-cause to tap that foul alien heritage for power and lore. She was one of the only humans I knew of who had struck collaborative pacts with their wretched kabals. Rumour had it she had been recently initiated into the cult of Kaela Mensha Khaine, in his aspect as the Murder-God beloved of the eldar renegades.

As befitted such a loyalty, she recruited only convicted murderers for her minions. The men who attacked us in that blighted yard were base killers, shrouded in shadow fields she had bought, borrowed or stolen from her inhuman allies.

One swung at me with a long-bladed halberd and I blew off his head.

Just. My body was tired and my reactions were damnably slow.

I saw Arianrhod. She was a balletic blur, her beaded hair streaming out above her flying cloak. Barbarisater purred in her hands.

She severed the neck of one shadow with a backward slash, then pirouetted around and chopped another in two from neck to pelvis. The sabre was moving so fast I could barely see it. She stamped hard and reversed her direction of movement, causing a third shadow to sprawl as he overshot her. His head flew off, and the sabre swept on to impale a fourth without breaking its fluid motion. Then Arianrhod swept around, the sword held horizontally over her right shoulder. The steel haft of the fifth shadow's polearm was cut in two and he staggered back. Barbarisater described a figure of eight in the air and another shadow fell, cut into several sections.

The last minion turned and fled. A shot from Bequin's laspistol brought him down.

A pulse was pounding in my temple and I realised I had to sit down before I passed out. Qus grabbed me by the arm and helped me down onto a block of fallen wall stone.

'Gregor?'

'I'm all right, Alizebeth... give me a moment...'

'You shouldn't have come, you old fool! You should have left this to your disciples!'

'Shut up, Alizebeth.'

'I will not, Gregor. It's high time you understood your own limits.'

I looked up at her. 'I have no limits,' I said.

Qus laughed involuntarily.

'I believe him, Mistress Bequin,' said Ravenor, stepping from the shadows.

Emperor damn his stealth, even Arianrhod had not seen him coming. She had to force her sabre down to stop it slicing at him.

Gideon Ravenor was a shade shorter than me, but strong and well-made. He was only thirty-four years old. His long black hair was tied back from his sculpted, high cheek-boned face. He wore a grey bodyglove and a long leather storm coat. The psycannon mounted on his left shoulder whirred and clicked around to aim at Arianrhod.

'Careful, swordswoman,' he said. 'My weapon has you squarely.'

'And it will still have me squarely when your head is lying in the dust,' she replied.

They both laughed. I knew they had been lovers for over a year, but still in public they sparred and sported with each other.

Ravenor snapped his fingers and his companion, the festering mutant Gonvax, shambled out of hiding, drool stringing from his thick, malformed lips. He carried a flamer, the fuel-tanks strapped to the hump of his twisted back.

I rose. 'What have you found?' I asked Ravenor.

'The Beldame – and a way in,' he said.

Beldame Sadia's lair was in the sacrarium beneath the main chapel of the ruin. Ravenor had scouted it carefully, and found an entry point in one of the ruptured crypts that perhaps even she didn't know about.

My respect for Ravenor was growing daily. I had never had a disciple like him. He excelled at almost every skill an inquisitor is meant to have. I looked forward to the day when I supported his petition to inquisitorial status. He deserved it. The Inquisition needed men like him.

Single-file, we entered the crypt behind Ravenor. He drew our attention carefully to every pitfall and loose flag. The stench of salt and old bones was intolerable, and I felt increasingly weak in the close, hot air.

We emerged into a stone gallery that overlooked a wide subterranean chamber. Pitch-lamps sputtered in the darkness and there was a strong smell of dried herbs and fouler unguents.

Beings were worshipping in the chamber. Worshipping is the only word I can use. Naked, daubed in blood, twenty depraved humans were conducting a dark eldar rite around a torture pit in which a battered man was chained and stretched.

The stink of blood and excrement wafted to me. I tried not to throw up, for I knew the effort would make me pass out.

'There, you see him?' Ravenor whispered into my ear as we crawled to the edge of the gallery.

I made out a pale-skinned ghoul in the distant shadows.

'A haemonculus, sent by the Kabal of the Fell Witch to witness the Beldame's practices.'

I tried to make out detail, but the figure was too deep in the shadows. I registered grinning teeth and some form of blade device around the right hand.

'Where's Pye?' asked Bequin, whispering too.

Ravenor shook his head. Then he seized my arm and squeezed. Even whispers were no longer possible. The Beldame herself had entered the chamber. She walked on eight, spider legs, a huge augmetic chassis of hooked arachnid limbs that skittered on the stones. Inquisitor Atelath, Emperor grant him rest, had destroyed her real legs one hundred and fifty years before my birth.

She was veiled in black gauze that looked like cobwebs. I could actually feel her evil like a fever-sweat. She paused at the edge of the torture pit, raised her veil with withered hands and spat at the victim below. It was venom, squirted from the glands built into her mouth behind her augmetic fangs. The viscous fluid hit the sacrificial victim full in the face and he gurgled in agony as the front of his skull was eaten away.

Sadia began to speak, her voice low and sibilant. She spoke in the language of the dark eldar and her naked brethren writhed and moaned.

'I've seen enough,' I whispered. 'She's mine. Ravenor, can you manage the haemonculus?'

He nodded.

On my signal, we launched our attack, leaping down from the gallery, weapons blazing. Several of the worshippers were punched apart by Qus's heavy fire.

Whooping the battlecry of Carthae, Arianrhod flew at the haemonculus, way ahead of Ravenor.

I realised I had pushed it too far. I was giddy as I landed, and stumbled.

Her metal spider legs striking sparks from the flagstones, Beldame Sadia reared up at me, ululating. She pulled back her veil to spit at me.

Abruptly, she reeled backwards, thunderstruck by the combined force of Bequin and Zu Zeng who flanked her.

I gathered myself and fired at her, blowing one of the augmetic limbs off her spider-frame. She spat anyway, but missed. The venom sizzled into the cold stone slabs at my feet.

'Imperial Inquisition!' I bellowed. 'In the name of the hallowed God Emperor, you and your kind are charged with treason and manifest disbelief!'

I raised my weapon. She flew at me. Her sheer bulk brought me down.

One spider limb stabbed entirely through the meat of my left thigh. Her steel fangs, like curved needles, snarled into my face. I saw her eyes, for an instant, black and without limit or sanity. She spat.

I wrenched my head around to avoid the corrosive spew, and fired my bolt pistol up into her. The impact threw her backwards, all four hundred kilos of wizened witch and bionic carriage.

I rolled over.

The haemonculus had met Arianrhod's attack face on, the glaive around his right hand screaming as the xenos-made blades whirled. He was stick-thin and clad in shiny black leather, his grin a perpetual consequence of the way the colourless skin of his face was pinned back around his skull. He wore metal jewellery fashioned from the weapons of the warriors he had slain.

I could hear Ravenor crying out Arianrhod's name.

Barbarisater sliced at the darting eldar monster, but he evaded, his physical speed unbelievable. She swung again, placing two perfect kill strokes that somehow missed him altogether. He sent her lurching away in a mist of blood. For the first time since I had known her, I heard Arianrhod yelp in pain.

Flames belched across the chamber. Gonvax shambled forward, forever loyal to his master... and his master's lover. He tried to squirt flames at the haemonculus, but it was suddenly somehow behind him. Gonvax shrieked as the glaive eviscerated him.

With a howl, Arianrhod threw herself at the dark eldar. I saw her, for a moment, frozen in mid-air, her sabre descending. Then the two bodies struck each other, and flew apart.

The sabre had taken off the eldar's left arm at the shoulder. But his glaive...

I knew she was dead. No one could survive that, not even a noble swordswoman from far Carthae.

Bequin was pulling me up. 'Gregor! Gregor!'

Beldame Sadia, her spider carriage limping, was fleeing towards the staircase.

Something exploded behind me. I could hear Ravenor bellowing in rage and pain.

I ran after the Beldame.

The upper chapel, above ground, was silent and cold. Darknight flares glimmered through the lines of stained glass windows.

'You can't escape, Sadia!' I shouted, but my voice was thin and hoarse.

I glimpsed her as she skittered between the columns to my left. A shadow in the shadows.

'Sadia! Sadia, old hag, you have killed me! But you will die by my hand!'

To my right now, another skuttling shadow, half-seen. I moved that way.

I was stabbed hard from behind, in between my shoulder blades. I turned as I fell, and saw the manic face of the Beldame's arch-poisoner, Pye. He cackled and giggled, prancing, a spent injector tube clutched in each hand.

'Dead! Dead, dead, dead, dead, dead!' he warbled.

He had injected me with the secondary part of the poison. I fell over, my muscles already cramping.

'How does it feel, inquisitor?' Pye chuckled, capering towards me.

'Emperor damn you,' I gasped and shot him through the face.

I blacked out.